TWO TWINS

RENE S PEREZ II

Relax. Read. Repeat.

TWO TWINS
By Rene S Perez II
Published by TouchPoint Press
Brookland, AR 72417
www.touchpointpress.com

PAPERBACK ISBN: 978-1-956851-27-4

Editor: Kayla Faulkner
Cover Design: ColbieMyles.com
Cover Images: Painting by Natalya Mylius; Author photo by
Ulyana Charikova

First Edition

Printed in the United States of America.

For Julia—
My faithful doctor, my sweet Grace

SECTION ONE—
INDIE DARLINGS

CHAPTER ONE—(DECEMBER 31, 2017)

The end started on New Year's Eve. In what Rob would deem to be pathetically typical fashion, it happened at a party, but they didn't engage in a drunken shouting match or sloppily fall all over themselves on someone's back lawn. They weren't kids. In a city made appealing to musicians, artists, entrepreneurs, students, and powerful corporations alike by the kind of fun and cool created by and for grown people trying to live young, Rob and Maria considered themselves proudly adult.

They got the jobs. They bought the house. They watered and manicured the lawn. They weren't running from responsibility—enrolling in grad program after grad program in order to live off grants and loans. They hadn't settled for a one-bedroom apartment with rent that was the same as or more than a sensible mortgage. They found their suburb. They paid their HOA fees. They were professionals. They did not get drunk and make scenes at parties—work functions, at that—at least Maria didn't.

The fire pit didn't give enough heat to warm the back patio, but that was fine. Rob had stepped out from the party "for air." When he did, Maria pointed out how cold it was, flashing eyes that both begged for Rob to be a good sport and threatened consequences if he didn't comply.

"Just like I like it," he'd said, knowing that even though she knew he was lying, she wasn't going to push the issue. She knew at times like this, when he was uncomfortable or even just bored, it didn't take much to set Rob up for a fight, to give him a reason to burn the night down for everyone around him.

She gave the nod she'd come to use instead of rolling her eyes. It was a nod accompanied by a "Huh" when the nod was all she could do to suppress her judgment of her husband. Sometimes, when she really was just baffled by his demeanor and strange reactions to normal human interactions, the nod was silent. She gave the silent kind then, letting him face the cold of the patio alone and uncoated.

The patio was really something, though. Bigger than Rob and Maria's living room at home, it was expensively floored with the same exotic stone that lined the pillars which held the ceiling overhead. One wall was lined with matching stainless-steel appliances. It had a grill, an oven, a fridge, and what looked like an oven just for pizzas. Atop the fridge was a full bar, like the two set up inside. For people throwing such a shitty party, Maria's corporate overlords were pretty good hosts. Rob downed his bourbon, poured another, downed that one, then poured another glass for carrying around.

There were three couches around the fire pit. If Rob cared about warming up, he would sit at one of the couches and hunker down near the fire, but that wasn't important. That wasn't why he'd gone outside. If he sat at the couch, someone might take his attempt at comfort to mean he was amenable to conversation. No. He could already feel an occasional eye on him from in at the party. He would remain disengaged at the edge of involvement with the night—filling up on Asian fusion finger food and getting nice and top-shelf drunk.

He leaned on the rail that separated the patio from the back yard. He would've stepped out onto the grass to get a better look at the stars, but the gate leading to the yard was a complicated one, and he was too far into his night to try and hop over. He resigned to just standing there, bare forearms burning from the cold iron of the rail as he leaned on it and tried to project an air of deep thought and shallow detachment from the evening. The yard, like the rest of the house, was beautiful. It was immaculately groomed with sculptures running the length of the tree-lined lawn., which itself ran back out to the edge of the house's floodlight, seemingly out to forever, but really off the edge of a pretty steep drop-off (hence the necessity for such a serious and complicated gate down from the patio). This is what it was like to live on top, almost literally, he thought.

Out above the eternity illusion of the lawn's push to the horizon, Austin shone like a monument to the kinds of people who could afford to live in a place like this. That's all any of it was anymore, a factory for wealth to be built up in and doled out on. It didn't look like this when Rob got to town. The Frost Tower hadn't been built yet, nor had any of the residential high-rises that are now popping up all along downtown. Rob could count seven construction cranes erected, ready to continue the growth up, up, up, killing off what had once made Austin special, driving the black and brown people just east of the interstate out, out, out—relegating them to lives over in Manor, or down in Buda, or up in Round Rock. Was this home? Was this *Weird*?

Rob knew his Austin was a different one than the one transplants like him had inherited a generation before he did, they of a generation that could recognize the Austin in *Slacker* and remember when SXSW was their own little secret. Rob knew that even their Austin was different than the one of actual locals, *unicorns* they're called. He knew that even their Austin was different than the Austin of people who grew up in town north of 183 and east of 35. Rob knew this, but goddamn if looking out on his grown-up city didn't make him wistful for a place that wasn't ever real, a place that in all its good and bads you could never reach back into the past and find yourself comfortably in—and isn't that all a home is?

And to be here, in a Rob-could-only-guess-how-many-million-dollar home, on New Year's Eve, a night on which a decade ago Rob would certainly have been on stage, shirtless and sweaty despite the cold, playing whatever gig he could get in a bar that most certainly no longer exists, it made him feel dirty. It was the worst kind of selling out: He hadn't sold out on a level that would allow him to live in this place; he'd just bought in to the extent that instead of being out and having fun on New Year's Eve, he was at the home of the kind of people who had killed his city so that his wife could do some quality, out-of-the-office ass kissing. He finished his drink.

The bourbon's heat rose up from the back of Rob's throat up into his sinuses and rested behind his eyes. It was a fleeting heat, and Rob realized he'd either have to go in or double (triple? quadruple?) down on the drinking. The moment reminded him of a story he'd read about a survivor of the crashing of the *Titanic*. A guy, knowing the ship was going down, proceeded to pound down copious amounts of booze. He ambled to the bow of the ship, climbed over the rail, and when it went down, was able to withstand the cold of the northern Atlantic because the booze had lowered his body temperature. Standing there at the rail, Rob knew what he was going to do. He was, just then, the king of the world.

When he turned away from the rail to make his way to the bar, his eyes met with those of a ridiculous-sweatered party goer on the other side of the patio door glass. Recognition flashed in the man's eyes; he seemed to be expecting something of Rob. Rob tried to ignore the half second's acknowledgement of someone else in the world and busied himself with getting ice from the tray in the waist-high bar refrigerator. The man opened the door and made his way outside. It was happening.

"A whole bar to yourself? Smart man."

"Yeah. If my wife drags me out to a party with a bunch of assholes I don't know on New Year's Eve, I allow myself too many drinks and antisocial detachment from the group. Give and take, keeps marriages strong." Rob walked back to his spot on the rail and his view of the city without looking at the man who'd joined him.

"Ha! Give and take. Exactly. That's why my wife let me put the bar out here. When we're not hosting parties, this patio is one of the parts of this house that is truly mine. I mean, just look at that view."

Rob looked over at his host. The guy didn't look too much older than him. He was the kind of bad-looking healthy that kept a body healthy but a face looking stretched at the corners from faking smiles and interest in interactions like the one he was about to have with Rob. He looked like the personification of cigarettes and cocktails after a second workout of the day.

"Ken. Ken Jackson. Nice to meet you." He held his hand out here. The guy wore rings on his right hand.

"Rob Vera. Thanks for sharing your clubhouse with me."

"You know? When I was a kid, my parents had a real nice tree house built for me. It was three, really, at separate trees in different ends of the back yard. Can you imagine that?"

Of course, standing on this patio, attached to this house, Rob could imagine Mr. and Mrs. Jackson building such a thing for little towheaded Kenny.

"Back then, all the kids in the neighborhood would play at my house. Kids would even ride their bikes from a few neighborhoods over to play war. Turns out, if you have a kick-ass treehouse as an adult, you make new friends."

"My neighbor made a treehouse for his kid," Rob held out his drink. Ken tapped his glass in a toast. "If the bar is as well-stocked in that treehouse as it is in this clubhouse here, I'll make friends with that kid too."

They laughed. Ken gave Rob the kind of slap on the back that Rob normally wouldn't abide, but he was a guest in the man's house. The laughter died into desperate chuckles. Ken, determined not to be the one to drop the ball, let out a final 'heh'. Then they were silent. Each standing at the rail, looking out at their city, it didn't matter who either of them was, what they were in that place where such things seemed to matter. It should have been easier for Ken to stand there in the silent remnants of 2017. He was a king in his castle at the top of the village. He didn't have to worry about who below him his slop would roll down on. He didn't have to wonder what it meant to be there just then. People who don't have to worry about the cost of their spending didn't have to think in terms of selling out. They'd already won. Between the two, Rob was the one ignoring the realities of making nice with this guy on this day. Ken should have respected that.

"So. Who are you here with?"

Why'd he have to do that?

"My wife."

"Yeah, Rob. You said that. Who's your wife?"

"Maria." It became worth it to Rob, just then, to deal with the party crowd so as to not have to be out on that patio with Ken Jackson.

"Maria Whatsername? In legal?"

Rob nodded and threw back the smoky ice from the bottom of his glass, having to tap back the last pieces back to chew on in a show that he was done with his drink.

"She's wonderful!" Ken said. He grabbed Rob's glass and walked back to the bar, shouting back over his shoulder. "She's just great. She's been with us for a long time. *Us*, listen to me. I haven't worked there in years, but my wife's still there. Maria Smithey. Good gal. I think we were invited to—I mean, it was Smithey, right? What's she go by now?"

The empty glass was to be Rob's exit ticket, but Ken was in his element. He most certainly asserted himself as president of whatever clubs were housed in his tree house(s) back home. Ken was back across the patio, placing the glass in Rob's hand before Rob could respond. He stood there, excited, waiting for Rob to answer. Rob finally got a full look at Ken's eyes. There was blow behind their bloodshot dilation. The fucker had another, even better clubhouse.

"Zarate," Rob managed to say

"That's right, Zarate! That's it, man! Great girl. We got her right out of UT. Man, almost 10 years ago. What'd you say your last name was again, Rob?"

"Vera."

"That's it, man! I've heard of you. You're a musician, right? Like, real indie rock star guy?" Ken walked away before Rob could answer. He was back at the bar, pouring himself another drink and downing it in one go. For all of his New Year's Eves on stages or in green rooms, this was turning into the most clichéd, rock 'n' roll one he'd ever had. Ken left his glass on the bar.

"I mean, I've been in bands. . . . Toured with some guys . . ."

"You're a studio ace, right? A hired gun? I've heard about you. Didn't you used to be in a big band in the 90s, a real deal *120 Minutes* band?"

"Yeah, I've done that stuff. I'm on the shelf now." Rob held up his cast-covered right hand. "This has slowed me down a bit, but I make do. I've been teaching lately."

"Goddamn. How'd you do that?" Ken didn't wait for an answer. "I guess since you're messed up, you can't; so, you teach, right?"

Ken's laughter filled the silence that the lack of Rob's would have inhabited if Ken were in any shape to notice.

"Rob Vera, like true? Like Veracruz? That a stage name?"

"Sort of. See—"

"It makes sense now. You're Vera. She went from Smithey to Zarate. The new name threw me. I didn't know if she remarried. That was recent, right? You finally get her to take your name? I never get it when they don't."

"It's more complicated than any of that," Rob said.

"Oh, I know. It always is with them, isn't it? Rob Vera! Guitarist extraordinaire. I was invited to your wedding, but I just missed it. Small world, huh?"

It wasn't, Rob thought. It really wasn't. Ken was one of Maria's bosses. Of course, he would be invited. He was married to the company's CEO. Maria still worked there. Of course, she was invited to this party. Of course, she'd drag her husband along. Of course, Ken would be at the New Year's Eve party in his own house, at the bar out on his clubhouse patio. Of course.

"Yeah," Rob said. He was done trying to steer the conversation in any way. His hostile guard was dropped. He was ready for a show, and Ken seemed ready to provide one.

"Guitars, Rob. You can appreciate a good guitar. This'll flip your lid, man."

Before the awkward intrusion of his personal space could register in Rob's mind, Ken's hands were on his shoulders, pushing him inside and through the party. The party blurred past, as everyone inside knew that Ken's ass, alongside his wife's, was number one priority for kissing. Small talk and fake chuckles and double finger gun clicks were coming at Ken, through Rob, from everyone there. When they got near where Maria was standing, she looked at Rob in a way that was both relieved that Rob was getting along with someone and alarmed that it was with Ken. She seemed to know how the guy partied. She tried to mouth something.

Was it, "Be good?" "Behave?"

Rob stumbled a bit at a half staircase that Ken had led him to. Ken caught him from falling. He stopped his push and led the way down to a room in the lower level of the house. He got to the bottom of the staircase and walked on ahead into the dark. Before Rob had managed the stairs, Ken had turned on a series of wall lights with an iPad.

"Check this shit out," Ken said.

He poked at the device and slid his hand up slowly. The lights on one wall went up, revealing four guitars hanging from mounts. The soft halogen glow that fell on the guitars gave them a glossy, filtered look, like he was looking at a magazine centerfold in real 3-D space. They were Fenders: two Teles, a Strat, and a Jazzmaster, all pre-CBS. Ken punched at another button. The adjacent wall lit up. Three guitars on this one: a TV-Yellow Les Paul Special, an Epiphone Elitist Casino, and a double-necked Les Paul. As Ken punched the button to light up the third of his guitar-holding walls, the lights that hung from the ceiling were set to shine just a little brighter. The second Rob saw the guitars the wall held, he knew why.

There were also three guitars on this wall. One was easily recognizable as a piece of rock 'n' roll history. The black symmetrical 'V' with it's angular, irregular polygon pickguard, the gold hardware, and the knobs and vibrato set on the wrong side—Rob knew whose guitar this used to be.

"This is my country club, man. This is where I spend my early retirement. I don't golf, anyway. I mean, I do, but I don't like it. This is my paradise." Rob didn't look at him, but he could hear the grin in Ken's voice. "Over here you'll see—"

"Fenders. Pre-CBS. Cool Jazzmaster." Rob was looking at the second guitar on the brightest wall. It was a gold top Les Paul. Rob could also tell right away whose guitar this was just by looking at it. The Bigsby vibrato system, the aftermarket pickups, the six volume and tone knobs—Ken might be a joke, but he had done very, very well for himself if he could drop loot on these guitars.

"See! I love this! Most people don't know this stuff. They're just, like, 'Guitars. . . . Cool.' But you really know!"

When Rob saw the third guitar on the feature wall, however, he was done with playing impressed by Ken's toybox. The pre-CBS Fenders, the double-necked Les, and the Hendrix and Zappa guitars were just Corvettes—Maseratis, really—6-string mid-life crises that this jagoff could strap on and hold out on his hip—literal, pathetic phallic replacements. This last guitar, though, this acoustic, beautiful but otherwise unassuming instrument, was a step too far.

It was an SJ-200, Gibson's super-jumbo flattop. This model was a '48, a piece of American history. Ken was a grave robber, a tomb raider. A familiar heat burned behind Rob's neck. Like a monster he didn't ever really fight too hard to keep hidden, Rob's sense of righteous indignation was about to take over. A full moon shone above the track lights that showcased Ken's ill-begotten trophies. Fangs and claws were sprouting. Rob was going to make a scene.

"And over here, on the second wall, a TV-Special and an Elitist. This is the same year Elitist Lennon played. And the Special, it was called TV Yellow because—"

"Because white guitars would glare under lights on black and white TV. So, they started making them yellow." Rob could spout this asinine trivia all night. He picked it all up as a kid. It was part of what eventually led him to dive into his study of music. But that's all it amounted to—trivial, kiddie shit.

"I'm not even surprised, man. You know your stuff." Rob clapped his hands.

Rob still hadn't taken his eyes off the SJ. He couldn't. The beautiful symmetry, the sunburst finish, the elegantly decorated pickguard like a Nudie suit on a guitar, the gentleman's mustache bridge—it looked as beautiful as Rob hoped it sounded.

"And over here, Jimmy Page actually played this double-neck. I have a certificate of—"

"Fucking ridiculous." Rob walked over to the SJ.

"I know. Rock 'n' roll excess. Fuckin 'Stairway,' man."

"That's not what I meant. If you're a soldier, own a machine gun. If not, you're an asshole. Don't buy a monster truck for dropping the kids off at school. Fucking ridiculous." Rob stood in front of the SJ. His rant reverberated back at him from the guitar's sound hole. The machine was perfect.

"I consider it a work of art. All of these really. I'm an appreciatèur of art, of craftsmanship." Ken stroked the body of his prized possession, ran his hands down the 6-string neck and up the 12-string. "I see you have your eye on the gold top. That belonged to Zappa. He recorded—"

"See? That's what I'm talking about. I bet you can list all the mods Zappa made to that guitar, but you can't hear how these pickups catch and project these strings' vibrations. If you could, you certainly couldn't plug this into a Marshall and open it up. Fucking ridiculous."

"You may be an 'appreciatèur' of the craft behind these guitars, but your appreciation amounts to buying a painting—let's say by some guy who was a small part of a big movement. You buy this guy's most beautiful but least important painting."

"Like a Sisley."

"Sure. I mean, I guess. I'm no 'appreciatèur'. That's all you, pal. But you owning these instruments, these musical instruments that were meticulously engineered to be played, it's like buying a Sisley, putting it in a trash bag, and putting it in your closet behind your hanging suits and next to the hamper, stinking it up with the smell of your squash shorts and silk boxers."

"Listen Rob, I've been nothing but—"

"But this beauty right here, this '48 SJ-200, it really is a work of art. It's a piece of history." Rob ran his hands across the guitar's strings. He felt the grain of the body's wood. He had to.

"Well, finally some appreciation. It really is special."

Rob still hadn't taken his eyes off the guitar. He could hear Ken shifting his weight angrily. It didn't matter. He pulled down the SJ from its wall mount.

"Take it for a spin. Show me what it can do." Ken crossed his arms here and leaned back on his right leg looking simultaneously like he was skeptical of Rob's skill and about to punch him in the face. "Show me what you can do."

Right hand broken, Rob could still finger pick a perfect "duh-nuh-nuh-nuh neh-nuh-nuh-nuh neh-nuh-nuh-nuh duh-nuh-nuh-nuh." Hearing the opening notes to his precious "Stairway," Ken let go of his previous animosity. He was either a true lover of music, or he was too fucked up on the booze and blow to hang on to any short-term emotional memory. An involuntary "Yeah, man" called itself forth from a younger Ken—perhaps one who had snuck some beer and a bong into his childhood treehouse with a boombox and a girl who, like all the kids who had previously played in the playhouse, was only there for the hardly imaginable fancy fun that could be had at that fancy place; she, like them, would have looked past how unpleasant Ken was, because he had been raised to let his toys (a treehouse, expensive drugs and sound systems, relics of rock 'n' roll history) make his friends for him.

Here, for the first time since coming down to Ken's man cave guitar jail, Rob looked Ken in the eyes. Ken nodded his nonverbal "Right on, man" and Rob stopped playing just as Ken was going to close his eyes and ride the groove. Ken looked at Rob, and Rob regarded him for a solid half-second, pulling him down from whatever plane the coke and the whisky and the music had put him on. Then, with every bit of earnest condescension that he could muster, Rob rolled his eyes and gave a hard, deliberate headshake in disapproval.

"Seriously, Rob. What the fuck?" Ken kept on, but Rob couldn't hear him. Didn't try.

The C Rob had left off on was still hanging in the air, still singing out from the guitar. It really was a perfect machine. A flat top like this, Rob thought, demanded that he run up some chicken picking. He let out the most country-fried riffing he could summon, and the SJ bore it down and sent it out, up. Ken let out a sincere, but no less inauthentic or condescending 'hoo-boy!' He didn't seem to know that this was no longer about or for him. He'd killed the mood of that run.

Rob stopped and toyed with the real ivory tuning pegs. He plucked the E's and lightly touched harmonics up the neck.

"You wanna see what this machine can do, Ken? What I can make it do?"

Rob let the sweaty silence that followed his rhetorical question gestate. It came to term, past that, even. Ken, his pupils black spotlights of anticipation, had to talk. When he opened his mouth to do so, Rob played. He let his mind access conservatory, all of his past between then and now. He let his mind access "Recuerdos de la Alhambra."

Calibrated as his own finely-tuned machine was, the individual mechanisms of Rob knew how to work together—his mind knew to compensate for his broken hand and slowed the pace by sixty percent. Ken couldn't hear the change. All he could hear was music played as well as he'd ever heard it. His jaw dropped a little, but Rob didn't notice. He wasn't playing for that jaw, just like in younger days when he wasn't playing for cross-armed neckbeards in leather jackets at shows. Back then, he could admit now, he was playing for the pussy, but that got old. That's why he went to San Francisco, why he pushed past playing music and got into the craft of it—because playing for the sake and art of the playing became more important than "rock" or "punk" or "metal" (he'd tried and excelled at them all), even more important than girls. Music was as pure a science as concrete math. Similarly, it was more elusive the closer one got to mastery of it.

As ill-equipped as Rob was to play the piece, both hurt and out of practice, and as ill-suited as it was to the piece, the SJ overcame and sang.

Rob played up and up, through and through. He felt the past and who he could have, should have, been through it. Ken tried to follow along. He tapped at his thigh along with the beat, and Rob felt his interloping presence. He kept going, playing to an emotional crescendo. Then he got to a chord, a b-minor, and let it sing as he tossed the guitar up, just high enough to float out of Ken's reach, but not high or hard enough to hit the ceiling. Still, in his state, Ken had to scramble and fall to his knees to catch it.

Rob walked calmly away from Ken, regarding him no more than he had when he stood in awe of the SJ, stewing in his disdain for Ken and all of what he meant as a retired titan (and now kept husband of a Titaness) of new industry and as a rich bastard on a house on a hill and as a thief and appropriator of rock 'n' roll authenticity. He was at the top of the stairs that led up and out of the music room when Ken caught up with him.

If Rob had put any thought into what consequences would likely result from his actions, he wouldn't have been so surprised by Ken rushing up the stairs and tackling him from behind, but he hadn't. That was always Rob's problem (one of them, at least): so myopic was he in issuing out his sanctimonious 'fuck yous' to the world that he could never look past the impact of his blows to see the counterpunch that was coming back at him.

They spilled out into the hallway, their bodies a single entangled mass trying to gather its bearings in the doorway that led to the den where the party was in full swing. The revelers all turned to face the commotion. Ken had caught Rob pretty squarely around the waist with his shoulder. Rob had thought first, instinctively, to protect his hand. He'd lifted it over his head, and his face hit the wall pretty hard. Ken, however, had wrapped Rob with both hands in his tackle, and his head rammed the corner of the door frame that they now lay hurting beneath.

People rushed to Ken first, of course, the kiss-asses. Maria rushed over to Rob, but she stood over him, as if standing before the rubble of what a storm had done to her home before she could even think to lift a bit of what had been meant to house and protect her future but now had to be sorted through for what could be salvaged. That moment, right there, was the moment they would both later look back on as the real beginning of their real end. They could both feel it in the moment, but Rob had felt her look at him like that before. He had become accustomed, in his life, to disappointing those who loved him most and, for the most part, being able to get away with it. He had been taught, early on, that he didn't have to bend to the reasonable expectations of the world around him. On a micro and macro level, Rob had learned that if he could be him—as special and unrelatable and truly *him* as he was—the world would look past him being a shitty son or husband or bandmate or teacher. The world had to. It's almost a law of nature. That's how assholes and geniuses win, by shirking norms and expectations, by pushing past healthy and appropriate boundaries to the end they want regardless of who is hurt or offended, because if you keep the world around you in a constant state of "did he just do that?", no one will ever keep up with you. They couldn't. It'd be too uncomfortable, too awkward, and assholes and geniuses don't have time to trifle with awkwardness or uncomfortability; they're too busy getting what they want. And, though by no means in equal measure, Rob was most certainly an asshole and a genius.

Rob looked past his wife looming before him. Ken had been brought to his feet and was bleeding pretty profusely from a gash that had opened just above his hairline. It served him right, the bastard. Without stopping to ask what had happened, Maria turned to her boss who had come to take in the sight of the aftermath of her own natural disaster.

"Joanie, I am so sorry," she said.

Joanie didn't even look at her. "No worries. Boys will be boys, and all." How she got those words out of her mouth with her teeth clenched so tightly, Rob didn't know. He wouldn't think about it much longer, because the already cocaine- and booze-addled brain in Ken's head had clearly been concussed. Any time Rob had seen something similar to the look in Ken's eyes back in his days touring or the summer he spent recording in LA, he learned that nothing good was going to come from the time it would take Ken to pass out. Rob was about to suggest he and Maria leave, but his plea of, "Babe," was drowned out by Ken's shouting.

"This motherfucker! This goddamn motherfucker!"

Joanie tried, for a couple beats to calm her husband. She grabbed him by the wrists and calmly pleaded, "Ken. You have to calm down. Ken, please. Ken . . ." but she seemed to have some experience with this because she stopped trying at all and turned to Maria to apologetically ask that she and Rob leave.

Maria turned to Rob, offered her hand, and pulled him up. She walked toward the coat room to grab their coats.

"This motherfucker disrespects me! Talk shit about me? About what I've earned? I'll fucking kill you."

Several of the party-goers were subduing Ken, trying to take him out back to cool off. Rob hurried to follow Maria out. He was dizzy. He dragged his hand across where his face and head were tender. He was glad to have the better part of a week until he had to go back to school. He'd had to explain bruises away to students before, and his colleagues might just have to wonder how many bicycle, skateboard, and Segway (he'd actually been on a Segway tour the weekend he'd gotten into that fight, so the story came pretty easy to him) accidents this fool would have.

He didn't bother telling his side of the story on the way out of the driveway. He sat in Maria's angry silence for most of the way home. When the sound of the blinker signaling the car's entrance onto the Highway 183 interchange broke the silence, Maria was at a boil.

"Why do you always do this? Why can't you ever interact with a group of people on anyone else's terms without the night ending in a fight?"

"He attacked me. From behind, no less." Rob rubbed the side of his face for effect, to show the damage the maniac had done, but it only served to remind him that he was still in pain. He opened up the lit mirror on the visor overhead. "That's gonna be ugly in the morning."

"Don't do that. Don't blame him."

"He was drunk. He drank more than I had all night in just the time he was with me. High, too, gacked out. Coke and whiskey. Cash warned us about that."

Maria looked over at Rob. He closed his eyes and was leaning back in his chair. He was sitting and pitying himself for an evening she knew he had intended to ruin but had hoped, stupidly, that he wouldn't.

"No. You can't hide behind 'trouble finds me.' Adults don't do that. That's fine when you're twenty, when you're out on the road and trying to get your band kicked off of bills because the crowd is vibing on the wrong grooves—"

"*Vibing on the wrong grooves*?"

"Fuck you. Like I could ever speak the language of your stupid snobbery. I've climbed all the walls I've needed to climb to be able to stand you for all these years, all the rest I've just chalked up to you're you and I love even what I can't understand. But all this drama can't be part of that. It just can't anymore."

"He owned the wrong guitars." Rob didn't open his eyes when he said this.

"What?"

"He owned the wrong guitars. He didn't deserve them. He . . ."

"He owned the wrong guitars? You decide he doesn't need them, and so you, what? You goad him into a fight?" Maria exited the freeway. They were off the freeway and a few turns and a couple miles from their boring house in their boring neighborhood. They were just that far away from the night being behind them.

"I didn't want to fight him. I didn't think he'd attack me."

"Oh, I know you didn't. I've seen you do this before. You didn't think of anything other than how stupid and wrong he was. I've seen this too many times." Maria rolled through the first of the flashing yellows that lit the way to the street that led into their subdivision.

"If you knew these guitars, you'd understand. It's stupid," Rob looked to Maria, "but if you knew, you'd understand."

"I wouldn't, Rob. I wouldn't ever understand how wrong something could be that you have to pick. To pick and to pick and to pick to the point that someone is attacking you."

"But you would if you did. I'm trying to tell you. You would."

They made the turns and the stops on the residential streets that led to home in silence. Either of them could probably do the drive blindfolded. Rob looked again at his face in the mirror. He had done this. He had done it again. They pulled into the driveway and sat in the idling car.

"Do you even hear yourself? If only I could understand? You're so right, so . . . irrefutably right that no one can understand you. Not even me. It's a dangerous thing to never be wrong. You can just walk through life judging the world around you, blowing up anything that doesn't meet your standards. Insulting and hurting and slighting anyone who doesn't agree."

"But he. . . . Those guitars. . . . That guitar . . ."

Rob wanted to cry right then. He wanted to because it would signal to her that he did have the capacity to recognize his faults, and because his tears and sobs could always serve to end an argument with Maria. She always knew that whenever their arguments led to his tears, she had finally won, or at least she had been heard. In the moment he knew it would be cheap and manipulative, but it didn't matter. No tears were coming.

"The guitars didn't make you do anything. And at my work event? You can flush your career down the toilet by starting fights at gigs. You can break your hand to the point that you can't play. But don't you go and fuck my career up."

Rob was quiet here. He knew that, for as much as he could try to logic game his way out of culpability for what his actions caused others to do to him, he couldn't deny their consequences. Maria let out an "Ugh" that signaled the current act of their fight was over. She took the keys from the ignition and grabbed her purse to head inside. These breaks in action could signal the start of a peaceful night. They almost always called an unannounced truce before bed. Each fooling themselves into thinking the other was okay enough to peacefully sleep beside until one or both of them woke up with the retort they'd put to bed the night before in the front of their minds and on the tips of their tongues. With the unclicking of Maria's seatbelt, Rob thought, the matter of their night's conflict could be shelved until the next day. They were almost out of the car and into their home with their shaky peace when Maria's purse began to buzz. She took her phone out of the bag, read the message she'd been sent, and dropped her head onto the steering wheel.

"The cops are there," Maria said. "Happy New Year."

She didn't look at Rob. She just got up and out of the car. Rob couldn't think of anything to do but wade into the house after her. He'd given up his only defense. He'd let on that he thought he could maybe, possibly, concede that he knew he was some kind of wrong. It was going to be a long night.

CHAPTER TWO—(1984-2004)

Maria had felt a disconnect from her parents even before they told her that she was adopted, that they loved her like all other parents love all other children, that God hadn't blessed her momma with the ability to make a baby in her tummy, and so he blessed them with Maria. They told her that she was made in a different land, in Mexico, that they had picked her—*they* had picked *her*—and not everyone gets to do that. They told Maria that she was special, that their love for her was special, because she was God's blessing just for them. She was six.

It wasn't just that she looked so different from them; she had already noticed that without really noticing it. Mommy had yellow hair; Daddy had red. Her black hair was just another color in a world full of them. At school, she had friends with black skin and all different shades of peach skin. She had one teacher with brown skin like hers. All of the lunch ladies had brown skin too.

In school, her teacher had brought a prism into the classroom and turned off the lights. She had opened the blinds and held the prism out, explaining that light holds all colors that can be seen. The special glass she was holding just separated the colors and made a rainbow. Maria watched as the teacher turned the prism and moved it around in the sunlight, and bands of color, all of the colors, as the teacher had said, danced across the floor. Maria, to that point, thought that the world was like that, infinity colors that she either couldn't see or hadn't seen yet. One day she might see a kid with eyes that folded differently at the corners, and she'd know, from then on, that eyes could be that way. One day a lunch lady would speak to her in a beautiful singsong voice with words she didn't understand, and Maria would come to realize that different kinds of people spoke different kinds of languages. The world was bathed in light, and every day Maria would look at it through a different kind of magic glass and see a new color.

So it wasn't that she so very obviously did not look like the birth daughter of Eunice and Thom Smithey that made Maria feel alien in her home and family. Maria would later come to new understandings of what it meant to be the Smitheys' adopted daughter, to have been given up by one family and chosen by another, but to have at no point in the process been given her own choice in the matter, but that would come later. In those first six years, there was just the feeling of being handled like so much radioactive material. Maria couldn't really say that the Smitheys weren't natural parents. She had no frame of reference for comparison. She just knew that the love and affection they had to give was always given with hesitation, and she knew that it wasn't that they didn't care, but that they cared too much.

When they'd hold her, they'd hold her wondering if, hoping that, they were doing it right. Thom became uneasy in the presence of his young daughter's nudity, beginning to dress her quickly when he had to and no longer letting her run around happy and naked after bath and before bed. Eunice never quite got over her befuddlement at the irrationality of a small child. Maria's toddler tantrums and preschool headstrong, illogical arguing always frustrated Eunice's desire for sensible order, and when Maria would step too far out of bounds—breaking something out of frustration in public, hitting or biting her father in playful, painful anger, blurting out a curse word she must have picked up at school—Eunice, having to draw a clear line between right and wrong, would spank Maria with seemingly random force, at times striking the girl with a laughably soft pat, and at others swinging her clinched-tight cupped hand with such force that it seemed she was making up for all of the other spankings that had failed to satisfy her, like she was keeping a running score of how effective her corporal punishment had been for her, not for how well it had or hadn't taught the lesson that ended up lost in anger and satisfaction, frustration and relief.

All of this Maria would later look back on as having been done out of love. All they had were the tools their parents had given them, those and their own respective vows to never use certain other tools that their respective parents had used on them. Maria would come to get to know the Smitheys and their stories. She would come to understand all that they were capable of and forgive all that they weren't. They were, in fact, her parents. But that understanding would come later. It would be earned through perspective. She would only be able to enunciate it when she had more words and experiences than any six-year-old could have. But that did nothing for her then, when she felt different in her own home, alone in her own family.

When they did tell Maria, something in her six-year-old core exploded, a light that had burned there was snuffed, and what was left was so dense and dark that nothing in or around her could ever escape it. It was a mystery, a cartilaginous scar of curiosity that would forever grow with Maria and with her perception and knowledge of the world. At six, it was wondering what and where Mexico was. She'd heard the word "Mexican" used in talk about people and food, but now she was of that place, that word. Later, it was wondering what she was because she certainly wasn't white but, despite the brown of her skin and the black of her hair and eyes, she wasn't Mexican either. Later still, she would wonder about the people who gave her up, about *her* family.

Did Mexico make them give her up? That country's poverty? Its Catholicism? Did its violence and water you couldn't drink make them give her up? Don't drink the water, they'd tell her when she went to Cancun after high school graduation. Did that apply to her? She was of that land, so, of course, it did. As much as she wore that land on her skin, the bacteria in her stomach were red, white, and blue, emphasis on the white.

All of this mystery exploded in Maria, and it seemed Thom and Eunice had expected it to because they had purchased a book for the occasion and presented it to Maria, whose mind was reeling and whose world had slipped off its axis. A picture book in the style of so many other break-the-news-gently or facilitate/have-the-conversation-I-don't-know-how-to-myself books of that era, *"Why Was I Adopted"* was the *Everybody Poops* or *Free to Be . . . You and Me* of breaking the news to kids that they were adopted and trying to answer the looming "Why" of the whole situation.

It was so very '70s a document, so very Baby Boomer and Me Generation. One could imagine the exact kind of shell-shocked father, repressed mother, and dropped-out older siblings that led to someone thinking their feelings mattered *so much* that they decided to baby proof the world so that no one's feelings would be hurt at all. One could then imagine their younger siblings or kids calling bullshit on that and falling in love with Regan, cocaine, and upward mobility. But, kitschy and antiquated as the book presently seems to be, it truly did help Maria to answer questions she had and some she didn't know she had.

No matter how much her parents loved her, gave her an easy life, taught her self-respect, gave her from the very beginning that quality with which too many kids—not just orphans—are not imbued; they gave her dignity. No matter how they believed and tried to convey that she was *their* daughter, she always felt and knew with near-certainty regardless of all evidence to the contrary and all of the irrational certainty of a phobia that they were not *her* parents. She *had* parents. She even had a brother (she later learned). They were *hers*. The fact that they didn't ever want her for *theirs* didn't change that.

When Thom Smithey died unexpectedly in his sleep, just short of Maria's thirteenth birthday, Maria mourned the loss of a father. He had always loved her. Any rules he made that felt too strict or likes and mannerisms that he had that were uncool and annoying, she realized, came from a fatherly place. How she felt during the whole ordeal wasn't necessarily a surprise to Maria, as much as how naturally it all seemed to come. Over the course of the previous year of her life, Maria grew angrier and angrier with her parents and with feeling as different from them as she did. Of course, it was normal pubescent rebellion, but to Maria it was made all the more intense and complicated, like everything else had been made to that point in her life, like the fact that she was so different from the Smitheys, that she was adopted. But when Eunice told Maria the news—she'd woken up to a dead husband but still woke Maria up, dressed her, and sent her off to school like normal—none of the petty animosities or deep-seated feelings of disconnection surfaced. It was all just sadness over the loss of yet another parent.

This all should have brought Maria and Eunice closer together. Yet, all it did was make Eunice double down on her possessive behavior regarding the only family she had left in the world. Whereas, before, Eunice had always been protective, now she was downright restrictive of Maria, shooting down almost any request of Maria's for venturing out into the world. No, she couldn't go to the mall to loiter with friends. No, she couldn't sleep over at friends' houses or go weekend parties, supervised or not, if Eunice herself couldn't be there. Fine. Okay. Maybe she could go to the movie with a friend if Eunice could come along and watch too. And, what? What's so bad about that? It's not like Eunice would sit *with* Maria and her friends. She'd be a few rows back. No one would even notice her.

Maria tried to reason with her mother, but that would only lead to arguing. She used to be able to socialize with friends if Eunice or Thom had vetted the kids' parents. When Maria brought this up, Eunice didn't reply because the before to which Maria was referring, the *used to*, was still too fresh. Eunice couldn't deal with there ever having been a then. She couldn't reckon with the present because then she would have to deal with the fulcrum that facilitated this fracture of time and continuity, of what was and what now has to be. But, of course, "because I said so" wasn't enough, and so Maria would point to friends who were allowed more freedom than she was.

"Their parents let them," Maria pleaded.

"They're not your mother," Eunice replied.

"You're not either."

The first time Maria said this, she saw how deeply it cut her mother, who was already bleeding all over the floor of her life over the loss of Thom, and she felt truly awful. After that, every other time she said it, having learned its potential for damage and destruction, it was out of malice born from the typical teenage frustrations of a girl whose mettle was being tested in atypical fires.

Eunice reacted to every one of Maria's subsequent stone-throwings with a stubborn composure, composure that she slung back like stones of her own, because nothing made teenage Maria madder than having her will—to be free, to be normal, to hurt—ignored. Eunice would just smile the smile of a woman saved, blessed by His hand, with the knowledge that her intention was pure and her soul clean, that she was on the right side of eternity; she smiled that smile and said these exact words every time (she meant them too. She did love her daughter):

"I most certainly am your mother, dear heart. God did not bless me with bearing you, but he did light a path for me to you. He let me find you, and he let me choose you."

That first time, Maria watched the self-satisfaction settle on Eunice. It wasn't always that she could say the exact right thing at the exact right time. Nevertheless, she seemed to be, and would later reveal herself to have truly been, memorizing the speech she'd just given.

These fights would surface now and again, with neither party actually winning. Maria would storm off to her room in the silence, punctuated with heavy breathing, that followed the final shout whichever of them had thrown. In coming down from the adrenaline of having won—because each of them truly believed they'd won after these exchanges (biology be damned, Maria *was* Eunice's daughter)—Maria would acquiesce from her anger and allow that, fine, Eunice may be wrong, but she was only fighting this hard because she cared. Eunice would center herself in her piety because it didn't matter how loudly Maria had shouted or how hurtful her words were—Eunice was the mother, the steward of this young life in this crazy world. She was doing what she had to; she was right.

The rest of Maria's adolescence was a series of these shouts and silences. While their definitions of the two were very different, Eunice had taught Maria a real sense of right and wrong. She taught Maria to speak up in the face of injustice on behalf of herself or anyone else. She had made her good.

On a drive back from visiting some of Thom's relatives up in Conroe, Eunice said she could really use a cup of coffee. It wasn't that late, and the drive was only forty minutes, but Maria knew that this was Eunice's way of extending an olive branch. This was during Maria's tenth-grade year and between AP classes and SAT prep after school. On weekends, Maria had acquired quite an appetite for fancy five-dollar drinks that Eunice couldn't pronounce, but Maria assured her they were just coffee. They made their order, a small decaf for Eunice and a low-fat venti cinnamon dolce latte, and stood waiting for their drinks, exchanging light gossip about the wild and trashy Smithey cousins they'd just visited in Conroe, a town not too far away from their home in Humble. That family and their lifestyle were a world away—it was a world Thom had fled in search of education, order, and religion. Thank goodness he did, Eunice would say, as when he found God, he found her.

Eunice saw it happening before Maria did. Her eyes drew Maria to the conversation that was happening behind them.

"What do you mean you're out?" one of the customers asked.

"I mean, we're out."

The cashier folded his arms across his chest, putting on a stern face. He was a teenager, older than Maria, but pock-marked and ridiculous in his stance of fake authority. Behind him, a boy closer to Maria's age was stifling giggles.

"All you sell is coffee. How can you be out? We just want two plain coffees," the customer pleaded.

This was the first time Maria had noticed that the customer was with someone else, another man. The younger worker put two drinks on the counter and called out, "Eugene!" Neither Maria nor Eunice took their eyes off of the argument unfolding at the cash register while grabbing their drinks.

"You gave them drinks," the second man said.

"They didn't ask for coffee."

The first man looked directly at Maria as if knowing that he'd have no ally in Eunice.

"What'd you get?" he asked her.

"A cinnamon latte."

"Fine." The man turned to the cashier. "We'll have two venti Americanos."

"Nope," was all the cashier could manage. He was losing ground.

"You made her an espresso!"

Maria saw only now how big the customer was. She looked over at his friend and saw that he was big too. Strong, the kind of strong that didn't have to put up with things like this, but when the customer said this, he had a slight whine to his voice, like he was facing something unfair, and he knew that he could do nothing about it.

"Machine's on the fritz," the cashier said.

The customer slammed his hand on the counter.

"Am I going to have to go back there and pour my own coffee? Because I know those pots aren't empty." The second man put his hand across the chest of the customer. He made every effort to catch his friend's eyes, which had gone feral, in an attempt to calm him. Nevertheless, the customer pushed ahead, and the cashier stumbled back, afraid; his younger co-worker suddenly thought of something that needed doing in the back and left.

"Now, now," Eunice said. "You can't seriously be telling me that you have no coffee to serve."

The three men looked over at Eunice. The customer's shoulders fell, and he breathed hard, trying to calm down. The cashier realized he had been saved by the lady stepping in. He bucked back up.

"Ma'am, I don't have to tell you anything, and I don't have to serve these gentlemen."

"Now, I know you're no manager here," Eunice said. "Where is he? On lunch? Did he call in sick?"

"How do you know I'm not the manager?"

"Son," Eunice said with a chuckle, "if you were the manager, you wouldn't be asking me how I know you're not; you'd be telling me that you are."

The cashier deflated.

"Now, I have a few things I can do: I can sit here and sip my coffee and wait for the actual manager to show up, but he still might not, and I don't have that much time; I can just call up to your corporate office and let them know that," she made a show of studying his name tag, "Wyatt in their Conroe store told me that he couldn't serve coffee because all of the store's stock and machinery went sideways, and I'd give them, in that scenario, a full description of the two men you denied service; or I can stand here and watch you pour these men coffee."

The cashier said nothing. He gave his back to the customers, grabbed two cups, and filled them with coffee. When he put them on the counter, he didn't look at the men he'd denied before.

"How much is it, Wyatt?" Eunice asked.

"It's on the house, ma'am," he said. Then he went back to the kitchen with his young colleague and didn't come back out until after the four customers had left.

On their way out, Eunice made no effort to stop and talk to the men on whose behalf she'd just argued and won. The first customer was overwhelmed with emotion, and he broke down crying. His friend, boyfriend, Maria only now realized, grabbed him and let him cry on his chest. All of this floored Maria.

"Ma'am, I just have to say—" the boyfriend started.

"Now, son. You just go on about your way and enjoy your evening. God bless you. God bless you both." Eunice flashed the briefest of smiles and climbed into the car.

"Your mother," the boyfriend said to Maria, "she just saved us, our hope. Hell, she saved that dick in there from an ass-beating."

Maria had nothing to say. She just smiled, and the boyfriend knew what the smile meant. She got in the car and put her drink in the holder. Eunice put the car in reverse. When she shifted to drive to pull out, the customer who had been crying on his boyfriend popped up and started shouting, "Thank you! Thank you so much!" He was waving and blowing kisses.

Eunice just waved back at him and gave a short nod. Maria waved and blew kisses back.

"Mom, that was amazing!" Maria's gleeful shouts came out as shrieks.

"Honey, I just did what anyone would have done."

"No, you didn't, Mom. Those guys, people aren't always kind to them. You didn't have to—"

"Yes, I had to." Eunice cut Maria short. "Let me be clear, those men, what they do, is an abomination unto the Lord. If they don't repent, they'll burn in hell. But that judgment isn't for me to make. It's certainly not for some kid on a power trip to make. It's blasphemous to presume judgment where judgment belongs to no one but God."

Maria could feel her excitement dissipate with every beat of her heart. The thrill of the moment was fading, and all that was left was silence and Eunice's bigotry. Is this what being good was, doing right despite your own judgment? Was it enough to do right when you thought wrong? Was Eunice good? Maria didn't know. She only knew that, at that moment, she had made of herself a hero and then taken that hero away, and that Maria hated her for that.

When Maria got to Brown, she knew she had work to do on herself. In the free therapy sessions she attended through Counseling and Psychological Services, Maria's counselor talked a lot about codependency. Her counselor said that Eunice had used Maria, the responsibility she had for her, to not face Thom's death, or at least to not have to move on from it. Maria supposed this was right and used this assessment in dealing with trips home or icy phone calls from Texas. It became a self-fulfilling prophecy.

When Eunice didn't want Maria to take a summer internship her freshman year or study abroad her sophomore year, it was just her leveraging the control her pain at the loss of her husband had over Maria. When she insisted on putting fifty dollars in Maria's bank account every week, despite being on a fixed income and the fact that Thom had left Maria an inheritance, this was her knowing that having a daughter 1,800 miles away and no longer under her roof meant a slipping away of power. By giving Maria money, she was creating a new power dynamic where all others had faded; she was martyring herself for the cause of a happy daughter and a hint of vestigial normalcy, living for her daughter so that she wouldn't have to live for herself. Maria, even at seventeen, could see this.

Later, Maria would know how wrong she was. By then, of course, it would be too late, but she'd know.

"So, it was a homecoming dance?" The counselor laughed at this.

This was the first time Maria had met Roger. He'd made her feel comfortable up to this point, and he asked how she was transitioning to life in New England, what with the unseasonably cold spring they were facing. They had talked about high school, early life, losing Thom, adoption, then they got to what was bringing her in that day. She said it was how she left. It was Eunice. It all culminated with that damn dance.

"I mean, I know it's immature . . . ," Maria sat up here, having allowed herself to be lulled into dipping down in the expensive armchair in the counselor's office.

"No. I'm so sorry. I'm not laughing at that. It's just that . . . homecoming, that's a dance celebrating football or something? Am I wrong? I'm so sorry. It just seems so . . . *Texan*. I really do apologize; it's just an inappropriate thought that popped into my head." Roger sat up too. He pulled his chair around from behind his desk and sat it in front of the armchair.

"Oh, well. Yeah. I guess it is. I mean, I never cared about football."

"Right. And I bet you a lot of teenagers in Texas don't. I'm sorry. It's been a long day. Do you ever just laugh at a dumb thought at an exact wrong time?"

Maria relaxed. She pulled her hair back behind her ears.

"Of course, I do." She laughed here, and the counselor knew she was laughing with him at the absurd situation. They laughed together. "But you're right. It's about the homecoming game, and then there's a dance."

"Okay," Roger said. The last of the laughter in him dissipated, as did the laughter in Maria. "And, somehow, everything came to a head with yours?"

"Like I said, it sounds immature. But it wasn't just the dance. Obviously. It's that for four years I've had to live under her thumb. I couldn't leave home for anything but school and school-related events."

"And this dance was a school-related event?"

"Yes. Of course."

The counselor began nodding his head and taking notes.

"I mean, I was on the student council. I helped to decorate the cafeteria and everything. And she knew how much it meant to me to go."

"But still, she wouldn't let you go?"

"Exactly. Well, not quite. Initially, she said I could, but then I told her I wanted to go with a group of friends. We'd all go out to dinner before and there would be a party after. I'd be home by one. That's all I asked."

"And that was too much?"

"Was it, though? To just be normal for one night? So, then, we had this huge, shouting, screaming fight. And it was just too much."

"The fight?"

"Not that specific one. It was the fact that we were having one yet again to begin with. The last four years have just been too much. I honestly got the thought in my head that I'd run away, that I'd wait for her to fall asleep and go to the dance and just not come back. But that's just stupid." Maria reached for the tissue box on the counselor's desk.

"Well, I'm glad you realized that."

"I resigned myself to another night of crying in my room and listening to music, just wishing I had any life but my own, to a whole year and a half more of that. That's when I realized, I didn't have to do that. The next Monday, I went to a school counselor and asked what I had to do to graduate early. There was no big change. I just had to change a couple of honors classes to double-up on English. It was easy, really. Then, when I was done there, I went to the college counselor and applied to a few schools. This was the best one I got into, and so here I am."

Maria was done crying. She stood up and shook her legs out as she'd involuntarily pulled her knees up to her chest in the telling of the story.

"And let me tell you this, I'm proud of you for realizing that you needed to get out and for going about it in the smartest way possible. But, I see here on your paperwork that you're seventeen. Didn't your mother have to give you permission to graduate early? To attend here?"

"Yeah." Maria sat back down.

"And how did that go?"

"It broke her heart. She didn't even fight it."

"And now you're here. How'd she take that?"

"It's the best school I got into. She knows what it means to be at an Ivy."

"If you don't mind my asking, where else did you apply?"

"USC, Stanford, Gonzaga, and Harvard. I was accepted to all, waitlisted at Harvard."

"Let me tell you something, being up here in the very tippy-top corner of the country, doing the job that I do for students, I get a lot of people in here who are here because it's the farthest away place in the country for most of the country."

Maria didn't say anything. She looked at the clock and noticed the time was almost up. She had a lot going on in her head already.

"All I'd like to say before you go is this:" Roger got up from his chair and went to fill out an appointment reminder on a card at his desk. "You're a very bright girl. You're resourceful, and you're strong. But you're still a very young lady. You took great measures to improve a situation that was less than healthy. Well done. But you're also still a girl who ran away from home. You fled that place in search of freedom, and you'll also seek out emotional fulfillment. In your freedom, you'll find that there are fulfillments of all kinds and in all kinds of places. They won't all be healthy, and they won't all work. So, just know that as you go out there, you don't know all the answers. You don't have to. Dirty your hands. Make mistakes, but be safe."

Maria had never been treated like this, not only as an adult, but as a human person, fallible and unmoored. It made her feel excited and scared at the same time. It made her want her mom—not necessarily to be back living at home with mom's rules, but to lay her head on mom's lap on the couch with the TV playing something they weren't paying attention to because Eunice was stroking Maria's hair and Maria was under the hypnosis of being happy, life being right, and her mom in that moment being a real mother and she herself a real daughter. Maria wanted her mom to whisper that she was good, that she was smart, that she'd always do right. Instead, all she had was a cold slog in a coat not yet broken in and a dorm with a roommate who was pleasant enough, but still *there*, always there.

"I will. I'll be safe." Maria didn't want to leave.

The counselor gave her the card. "Same time next week, then?"

"Same time next week."

Brown was a world farther away from Humble than even its geographical distance could span. Maria thought she knew what to expect with the weather until she felt the chill of autumn New England rain soak through her hoodie. She thought she had become acclimated until she felt the first real gusts of winter wind and saw the breathtaking beauty of Providence covered in snow. Maria had mistaken the erudite, cool liberal civility on campus for how things were in Providence and how they were up north. She realized her misapprehension when she traveled to the home of her roommate, Aline, in her second year. Aline was from Pawtucket, and while the drive up 95 from campus was typical New England beautiful, Pawtucket and Aline's home were so much more down-to-earth than Maria had expected. It was like Humble, maybe even Conroe.

Aline's father was a fisherman. He had worked on boats and saved up to buy his own. He owned two now and captained one while Aline's oldest brother captained the other. He was a funny man and cursed up a storm. When they all sat to dinner, he sat at the head of the table and held court.

"You know how much that lobster would cost if you bought it from a store?" he asked Maria.

"Roldao!" Aline's mother protested. She was a retired secretary.

"I'm not talking about how much I paid for it. I asked her how much it would cost in a store."

"Still."

"Dad," Aline pleaded. She was their youngest. It was just the four of them sitting for dinner.

"Okay! Okay. No problem." Roldao held his palms up in surrender. Before Aline could see what he was mouthing, he silently told Maria the cost.

"Dad, please."

"Okay. Fine. How do you like the food? You like the Jag?" He pointed to the rice and beans on Maria's plate.

"Yes, sir. It's very good. It's almost like Mexican food," Maria said.

"Well, yes. We Portuguese are the Mexicans of New England," Roldao didn't look up from the work of his lobster when he said this.

"Dad!"

"What? What have I said wrong now?"

"Maria here is of Mexican heritage," Aline said.

"Well, yeah. No offense, sweetheart," he looked up at Maria, "but, of course, I can see she is Mexican. And what's wrong with that? I am proud to be Portuguese. I am proud to do real work in this country. I am proud of my work and what it's brought my family. My valedictorian daughter at Brown, my two sons have jobs and families, and I made New England, even if New England ignores me. Like the Mexicans. Maria knows."

Maria nodded, but she didn't know. She didn't know.

Mr. Domingues's populist minority solidarity was inclusive. He had earned his pride. It was a kind of pride that could only be earned, and he had assumed that Maria and her parents had earned it too. He was breaking bread with this young lady, sharing the fruits of his labor. Maria had no idea how much a lobster of any size would cost at a market. She had not built this country.

At school, however, the contexts that were assumed for Maria, while revealed in much more refined manners, ranged from bleeding-hearted patronizing to blue-blooded (or blue-blood aspirational) condescending.

Lunchroom conversations about struggle were pontificated upon and debated before summarily being offered over to Maria, who could serve as moderator and arbiter of what struggle meant because, of course, she would know, right? One conversation about New England and its Catholic families was turned over to Maria because, I mean, how many siblings did she have? How many cousins, right?

In kindness and as a manner of sad flirtation, one of her classmates asked, "And where do you work?"

This was before a marketing class midterm.

"Excuse me?" Maria asked as she shuffled one last time through her notes.

"For work-study. . . . Where do you work?"

Maria ran through the conversation she'd not been paying attention to in her head. He'd talked to her about his job cleaning dishes at V-dub, but why did he assume Maria was also a financial aid student? She had sat down after a night of studying, put her three pencils and highlighter on the table to prepare herself for battle, and this kid, this orange-red-haired, freckle-faced kid, took a seat next to her and decided that he knew enough about her just by looking at her to make an educated guess about the kind of person she was and the kind of place she'd come from. Maria set down her pencils and her highlighter. She wasn't moving. She just didn't answer, and the silence she seethed in was thick enough to push the guy up out of his seat and away from Maria. She worried that she was so mad as to be rattled, but Maria aced the test in the end.

Over the course of Maria's first two years at Brown, she lost count of the number of people who spoke Spanish to her, assuming that she could speak the language because of her appearance. This had happened back home, too, but it was usually done by Spanish speakers lost in a world of English looking for someone to help. Maria would try to help with her surface level knowledge of the language she took classes for in middle and high school; however, whoever she was helping didn't care or judge, as she was trying. Or it would be by someone who assumed that Maria was one of them, that she was part of their tribe. Those people were trying to include Maria in their own contexts. At Brown, they excluded her by assuming her, by othering her.

There were international students—students from Mexico and Bolivia and Chile and Argentina (those wonderfully haughty Argentines!)—that would rattle off their different timbres and sways of Spanish at Maria. These students seemed to hope Maria would be able to converse with them in their home language, but when they learned she couldn't, they politely switched to English. There were other American students, students like Maria who should have understood the Hispanic diaspora and cut her slack, who would speak Spanish to her and could not hide their disgust at the fact that she couldn't speak it back. They assumed that she had abandoned her language, her culture, her roots. They didn't know that it had abandoned her.

There were white American students who would speak their Spanish at Maria. Some of them did this to seem worldly. Some of them actually were worldly. There was one guy who had lisped the internal S when he said, "Hola. ¿Cómo estás?" These people were trying their best to reach out an olive branch, to lend a helping hand. Although, almost all of them looked at Maria with their head slightly crooked, like they were talking to impoverished second graders they had volunteered to read to—not the fake Castilian lisp guy, though. He was definitely trying to get laid.

On one such occasion, Maria was having lunch with Aline out on the V-dub courtyard, and a kid not a day over twenty-one wearing an actual bowtie walked up to their table and said, "Hola, señoritas. ¿Qué tal?" This happened in December, and while there was snow on the courtyard, the middle of afternoon sun had warmed outside to a comfortable if not the only bearable temperature that was preferable to the stifling warmth inside. Every word of the kid's too-confident pick-up line fell limp and lame out of his mouth and onto his coat. The sleaze of his self-satisfaction fell, too, as he grinned wide and breathed hard, awaiting the girls' response.

Maria just rolled her eyes and didn't bother looking in his direction.

"She doesn't speak Spanish," Aline said, herself not looking at the guy.

"¿Y usted?" he asked.

"God, you try too hard. Portuguese." Aline pointed a thumb at herself.

"Como você está?" The guy was really pleased with himself after asking this.

"Ugh. Go straighten your tie."

He looked down at his tie to see that it was straight. He looked up, finally feeling shamed for his brazenness, and stormed off. He muttered something about them being "bitches" as he left.

"I'd rather be a bitch than a cartoon character, you fucking douche," Aline yelled as he retreated.

He held up a middle finger back at the girls without looking back. The girls laughed. A girl at a table nearby came over and joined in the laughter.

"Oh my God. What a total jerk." She placed a hand on Maria's shoulder. "I hate when they do that, assume you speak Spanish because of how you look."

Maria hadn't really registered that the girl who had come over looked Mexican too.

"I mean, I was adopted. I'm from Utah for crying out loud."

The girl turned to walk away, still laughing at what she had seen. "Wait," Maria called after the girl. "Where were you adopted from?"

"Mexico," the girl said.

Maria was so floored by meeting someone whose circumstances and history were so much like hers that she couldn't help but gush.

"Oh my god. Do you know where you were adopted?"

"Juarez."

"When was this?"

"'82."

"Was it legal, like above board?"

"Listen, I would really like to talk to you about all of this, but I have to get to class."

The girl stepped back a bit. When she did, Maria realized that she had a hand on the girl's arm, as if her own body needed to feel a connection to this person and to their shared context. Maria let go. The girl pulled her backpack around and fished out an index card and a marker from its side pocket.

"Here. Email me, and we can see about getting coffee or dinner."

"Are you free tonight?" Maria asked, taking the card from the girl. She held it by its corners like it was a picture she was trying not to smudge. "For dinner?"

"Yes. That sounds great. But I really have to go. Email me with the details. I'm free after seven."

"Okay," Maria looked down at the notecard, "Kaylee. I will."

Kaylee flashed a big smile, gave Maria a pat on the arm, and turned to walk away. Maria couldn't help herself. There was no amount of cool composure worth maintaining in such a huge moment in her life. She grabbed Kaylee hard around the arms, not even letting her hug back. Kaylee just laughed it off and awkwardly patted at Maria's hips through the bear hug.

"We'll talk tonight," she said and left.

Kaylee was from Provo. She had five brothers and four sisters who had all helped raise her. They were all biological children of Kaylee's parents, Ammon and Ivy Hyde. Kaylee was the only adopted child of the Hydes. All the love and affection of that many people seemed, to Maria, to have made Kaylee a woman who expected the world to be beautiful and easy and who therefore made it so for herself and the people around her. Her positivity and goodness are what Maria believed Eunice's piety should have gifted her; instead, Eunice looked at the world and expected it to be ugly and damned, and Maria had known that she had to get out before Eunice had made the world ugly and damned for her too.

"So, you were happy?" Maria asked as they ate Thai food in the common room of Kaylee's dorm.

"Yes. Very. You weren't?"

"It's not that. I shouldn't have asked like that. It's just . . . weren't you curious?"

"Of course, I was. My parents got me this book—"

"'*Why Was I Adopted*'?"

"Yes! And my brothers and sisters all sat around in the den while I sat on my mom's lap and my dad read it to us. Then it all made sense."

"But still, didn't you want to know? Your real parents? Why they gave you up?"

"No. I mean, my parents had a dossier with all of the papers from the adoption. I know my mother worked in Juarez. I know she was a prostitute. I know that I was the third child she gave up for adoption. On paper, the process was all legal, but I know that money changed hands. I've seen the paper where she signed me away. I studied and studied that paper. I even touched her signature because I knew she had touched it, too. It was messy. It just had an M, some scribbling, a J, some scribbling, a B, and some more scribbling.

I've looked at it so many times over the years. My parents let me have the dossier. I would look at it and look at it, trying to read her writing. I finally realized that she couldn't even write her own name. How could I be mad at that? She was illiterate, couldn't even spell her own name. Of course, she had to give me up. And I got to be Kaylee Hyde. I get to be here at Brown. How many people who have ever gone here do you think were raised by illiterate prostitutes?"

Kaylee closed the Styrofoam container of her half-eaten pad thai on the table in front of her. She picked up her napkin and delicately wiped each of her fingers clean. She put the napkin down and dropped her shoulders into a post-meal 'ahh' position. She smiled big at Maria.

"But did you ever feel like you didn't belong here? Like you were missing some connection to your family that should have been there?"

"Of course. My parents were the best. *The* best. My brothers and sisters? The best. Even my community, they were great to me. Did you know that Mormons consider Mexicans to be among God's chosen people?"

Maria shook her head at this.

"They do. And they're all so nice, to anyone. But with this great childhood, in this home filled with love and almost a dozen people all wanting to play with me, to read to me, or to just tell me that I was a good girl, that I was *their* good girl, I still always felt like something was missing. Like, a lot of times when two people get married, they might fall out of love—maybe because they just don't feel it anymore—they stay together because it's what they know. They need each other, but they don't love each other. It was kind of like that, except I just never fell in love with them to begin with, not fully in love."

Kaylee cried at the thought of this, at the sound of her having actually said it out loud. Maria took her hand.

"I've felt like that too," Maria said. "When the Spanish conquered Latin America and forced conversions to Catholicism, indigenous people, including Aztecs in Mexico, hid idols of their old gods at the new churches near Catholic statues so that when they would go to church, they could still pray to and worship them. They knew that they had to adapt; they had lost the war. But they still held on to their past, to the homes and lives they had before. I feel like I've been hiding this longing since I was six. Is my mother still out there? My father? Are they okay?"

"Exactly! My parents have given me all of the information they had, but when I tried to find my biological siblings, I knew it upset them. It was like they had been hiding the same feeling of disconnect from me, and my revealing that I wanted to find my siblings uncovered the fact that they didn't want me to want that. It made their love for me seem conditional."

Maria sat up here. She pushed the food away from in front of her.

"You tried to find them?"

"I found one of them," Kaylee said.

Maria felt faint. "You found one? How did you find one of your siblings?"

"I contacted the lady my parents used. A lot of Mormons used her. They knew she kept things legal, and they believed she was moral and wouldn't get babies she might think were kidnapped or anything like that. It turned out that I have a brother in Missouri. He's a year older than me."

Maria was stunned. Her mind was swimming in the possibilities. The mystery of her own family was rekindled.

"Did you meet him?" she asked.

"No. He's in prison. I've sent him letters, but he only wrote back once. He didn't get a good family like I did. He was in and out of trouble his whole life. He said it was only a drug charge, that he'd get out, but he didn't want to meet me. He said he was embarrassed, but from the letter, he sounded angry too." Kaylee raised her palms and shrugged. "I tried. And my biological sister wasn't adopted through the same agency."

"My mother never told me who she got me through. She would always change the subject," Maria confessed.

"Then, of course, the mystery has been killing you! There are forums online for people like us. I used to search them looking for any clue about my siblings before I asked my parents. Then, when I found my brother and realized he didn't want to meet me, I wrote the story there. It was very helpful." Kaylee pulled her laptop out from her book bag. After a few clicks, she had emailed Maria a couple of links to forums. They sat there and eased themselves into the silence left in the wake of the breakthroughs, each weighing the coincidence that had put them there together, each dealing with reawakening existential dilemmas.

The dusk outside had turned to darkness. Students were arriving home to the dorm from a day of classes, and the cold from outside had drafted in person by person, filling the common room with a cold that Maria didn't notice until she realized there were tears on her face. She looked over at Kaylee and could see that she had been crying too. They held each other for a while, crying on each other, then parted from their embrace with relieved smiles on their faces. They looked at each other and laughed at the states they were in. Maria knew that after their shared silent awe and contemplation, they would be best friends forever.

Years later, when law school and then work took Maria back to Texas, and family took Kaylee back to Utah, they would still count each other as best friends. They would make trips to visit each other. They would help each other through relationships and breakups, careers and doubts, a miscarriage, the death of one of Kaylee's brothers, and a divorce. And for most of their lives, as best friends, they would not talk about why they became friends, about the fact that they shared a homeland and a history of having been given away from that land, feeling rejected by it. Of course, the odd news report or made-for-TV movie would prompt one of them to pick up the phone and talk to the other about adoption, but mostly they just cared about each other. That night, though, they spoke more about their shared history in the teary silence of the cold common room than they ever would with anyone else ever again. That night, in cold, dark silence, they each found themselves not alone for the first time in their lives.

Aline wasn't home that night, a Thursday night, as she didn't have classes on Friday and was back on again with her on-and-off boyfriend up in Pawtucket. Maria knew that it was telling when she picked up her phone to share with someone—anyone—the news about her strange and wonderful meeting with Kaylee, about all of the old questions made new and the new potential avenues for answering those questions, she chose to call Roger instead of Eunice. She knew he would not be in the office, so she left a frantic message on his phone.

"Roger, this is Maria, Maria Smithey. I just. . . . I met someone, a girl. She's from Mexico like me. She was adopted like me. She's Mormon, and she has this big family who all love her, and she had this happy childhood, but still, she feels it, the longing . . . like she's incomplete. And she even found one of her siblings. Her parents had kept all her paperwork. They let her see it. She even sent me links to an online forum of people like us and . . . ," Maria began to cry here.

"It's just so big. I'm happy and excited. I feel like I'm thinking and feeling about this stuff that I wasn't allowed to for a long time. It's big. And I'm happy." Maria began crying harder. Between sobs, she spoke as best she could into the phone, "It's just . . . so much . . . I'm so happy. I just . . . If I can see you Monday or tomorrow, I'd really appreciate it."

Maria hung up the phone and got up to pace the excited energy and emotion out back and forth on the fifteen feet of floor space between her bed and Aline's. After a while, she stopped crying, but her shoulders and arms were still shaking. She sat on her bed and debated calling Aline. She looked up at the mirror above Aline's dresser, at the pictures of her and her father on a boat, her and her brothers as kids, her and Donnie, the local boy with whom she was spending the night. He was nice enough, if not brutish, but New England brutish was a wise-ass, fast-talking, and joking kind of brutish. Donnie seemed to be trying to talk and joke past being there in a dorm room at Brown when he visited, whereas, in Texas, Donnie would mock stoicism and hide his station behind rote politeness. Maria remembered Donnie's visit and how he'd offered to make a drink for Maria as he was mixing a couple for Aline and himself.

Maria pulled her desk chair up to Aline's closet. She stood on the chair and opened the cabinet door above Aline's closet. Not much could be stored in the cabinet, which seemed only to cover water pipes running the length of the dormitory's entire ceiling. Maria reached as far over to the wall as she could and felt the bottle she knew was hiding there. She pulled it down and looked at it. She'd seen a bottle like this before, one snuck in a bag on a debate trip to San Antonio. She'd drunk from it then, in high school, but only a little, and only to have told herself she did it. Having seen this liquor brand in high school, Maria was fairly certain it was cheap. She took the carton of orange juice from the fridge and mixed a too-strong drink.

She sat at her desk and took a big swig. The coughing fit that followed this actually helped calm Maria when it subsided. The heat that rushed to her head seemed to center in her gaze at the computer. She read story after story of people who were adopted away from Mexico. There were some success stories of people finding siblings. One person had even caught up with their parents. However, most of the stories she read were by people seeking siblings or information on agencies from certain regions of the U.S. who had gotten kids from certain cities in Mexico.

There were several posts with several replies in threads about illegal adoptions. There were articles about unscrupulous baby brokers and forged documents, women who were used by kidnapping rings to pose as mothers to children that had been taken from hospitals or even plucked from strollers out in broad daylight. These posts and threads, Maria could see, were made by people who were as in the dark as she was. They were "what-if" posts. They were complicated answers to questions that otherwise held no believable or satisfying ones.

If Maria really had to choose between her biological parents having given her up, not bothered to fill out any more paperwork than necessary, having been so easily given up for just some money—money which, fine, was scarce and could really have improved lives—and having had a price tag put on her, or having been stolen from parents who ached for her after, who probably still lit candles for her at church and had made an altar around the one or two pictures of her that they'd kept, she would pick the latter, of course.

She read and read and read all night until she had run out of orange juice and was now drinking the vodka with just ice. She didn't remember getting into bed when Roger's call woke her in the morning, but when she saw his name on her cell phone, she woke back into the mystery of the night before. He said he could see her that afternoon, and she was almost excited enough to start shaking again, except after she hung up the phone, all of the previous night's drinking had caught up with her. She barely made it across the hallway in time to vomit. She brushed her teeth when she was done and climbed back into bed.

Maria had never skipped a class in her life, but that Friday, she would skip two, but she needed sleep. She couldn't tell if her hangover had kept her awake or if she had only had the most boring dream ever. Even though she slept for four and a half hours more and felt refreshed when she woke, she felt as if she had spent every second of that time awake, forcing herself to close her eyes against her excitement for what lay on the other side of sleep. She used to do this as a girl on so many Christmas Eve mornings when she felt like she would burst from anticipating the joy she'd unwrap under the tree.

"I've noted over the last year and a half that you've seemed to not be at all curious about your biological family," Roger said. He didn't have any clients that day and would leave that night for vacation. He was supposed to be packing, but he knew that Maria needed him from the message she'd left. "I thought that maybe you'd closed that chapter of the book."

"That's the thing. I didn't close that chapter. I was never given access to it. Whenever I asked my mom about my adoption, she would tell me the story of how she went down to the border with the last of the money she needed to pay. She said they came, counted the money, and gave her the papers. Then, they handed me to her, left, and, bam, just like that, she was a mom. But she never talked about who facilitated the adoption process. She never told me what she might know about my biological parents. I mean, babies were stolen from strollers and cribs in hospitals. If she doesn't know the story, it can't be good."

Maria had opted for a hot chocolate from the coffee shop to sip and huddle around during her walk across campus to Roger's office, as she felt like drinking caffeine just might make her heart explode. Instead, the sugar from the chocolate was mixing with the adrenaline of working this out with Roger, making Maria shake in her seat.

"You have to prepare yourself for the possibility that she doesn't know because she doesn't want to, because she never wanted to know."

This hit Maria hard, slowing her nerves and bringing her back down from the high of possibility she'd been on. Of course, she had to factor Eunice in—her insecurities, her manipulative nature. It wasn't just that Maria had stopped asking her questions, it was that Eunice had never seemed willing or able to provide those answers, and if she really wasn't able to provide answers, how hard had she tried to ignore or forget the truths and details of Maria's adoption? How culpable was she in her own ignorance?

Or. If ever she'd known about Maria's parents and didn't tell, didn't that mean that she might *never* tell? Might she play dumb forever? If she'd gone to such great lengths to control Maria as she had for nineteen years, what else more was there to control? To what end would Eunice go to not cede that control?

"There's a reason you called me last night," Roger continued, "and, I'm assuming, why you still haven't told her about meeting this Kaylee girl, about this information you're finding. Why is that?"

"I just . . " Maria had to answer the question for herself before she could answer it for him. "I want to make sure I have the most compelling argument possible. I have to let her know that I've done research and that this isn't just some fluke of coincidence that has me asking these questions. I need to be able to knock down any objection or insecurity on her part. I need to be able to . . ."

"To control the conversation?" Roger offered up helpfully. There didn't seem to be an ounce of "ah-ha!" in his tone. But still, Maria felt exposed.

"Well, yeah. I mean, is that so wrong?" Maria crossed her arms tightly across her chest. She felt cold in her back and raw in her stomach. She wanted to go back to bed.

"No. Of course not. To some extent, that's all that we ever try to do with communication. We want a need or desire met, or we want to avoid or change something, so we talk. We converse, and we try to affect change. But why did that put you off? Why did that feel bad for me to ask, just then?" Roger put down the pen he'd been using to take notes.

"'Control' just feels like a bad word. It seems shameful and cruel to want to control."

"To control *someone*, of course. What we commonly do is something more like trying to manipulate people when we try to control conversations."

Maria sat up to speak, but Roger cut her off.

"See? That word throws you too. Maria, none of this has to be nefarious. There doesn't always have to be malice behind these things. If I yell at you that you're dumb, that hurts. If I yell anything in anger, it hurts. But if you're going to cross the street and I see a car coming that you don't, I have to yell for you to stop. It's a tool. If my son wants to spend the night at his friend's house when we have a lot to do the next day, and it'll be a real pain to get him, I have to control the conversation we have. I have to appeal to his burgeoning sense of reason and negotiate with him. Every day, I try to manipulate him—every day. There is a world of choices, and a lot of them are easy, but I want him to make the good one. I am trying to make him a good person.

I think you're going to learn some things when you go home next week, but it may be more about how you interact with your mom and what her motivations are for how she is with you than anything else. I know things are strained. I know who she is and how wrong a lot of her actions were with you, but you need to meet her. You need to try to see her, grown-up to grown-up, so that you can come to understand, if not why she did what she did, but what she was trying to do when she did it."

"I just want her to know that I am dying to know. I've always been dying to know, and that doesn't mean I love her any less or that she failed. I just want to be able to tell her what I'm thinking, how important it was for me to meet Kaylee, and about all of the things I've learned because if I can do that, then I can. . . . I can make her see . . ."

"You can control the conversation. You can cut her off from her old tools of manipulation and control. Sometimes that's all we can do when we interact with our parents, our spouses, even. Sometimes we need to learn their tools, crib their strategies, and use them to allow us to be heard instead of suppressed. It ain't pretty. But no interpersonal communication is. If it is, it's fake."

Maria sat quietly after Roger said this. There was so much to think about. Roger picked up his pen again and jotted down more notes. Maria sat there, thinking to herself while listening to the sound of Roger's pen diagnosing her scratch on the fancy notebook he wrote in. They ran well over normal time, but Roger wasn't really counseling Maria for most of the rest of the two hours she spent there.

When he told her he had to get going, Maria nodded.

"Any other questions before we part?" he asked as he wrapped his scarf around his neck.

Maria shook her head no. Roger put his hand on her shoulder seeing her out the door, and she waited as he locked up his office. They walked to the elevator together and rode it silently to the lobby. When they got to the main exit, Roger was going left and Maria was going right. As they parted, Roger spoke over his shoulder at her, "Good luck next week."

Maria nodded and began to walk away.

"Hey!" Roger spoke up at her retreat. Maria turned around to face him. "Wish me luck too. No one's family is easy."

"Good luck, Roger. Merry Christmas." This made Maria smile.

"Happy Chanukah, Maria. Stay strong." Roger spoke this in a singsong over his shoulder at Maria. He hummed a tune as he walked away, towards the beginning of his holiday vacation. Maria knew that he was right because she could never imagine going home, not as the adult she felt herself to be then, not as the lawyer she knew she'd become when she really grew up, and not even if she were like Roger, in possession of all the right answers, hip to the hows and whys of it all, without needing to steel herself in preparation for what it meant to be back there, where it transported her back to in her mundane, haunted past.

As steeled as Maria had thought she'd made herself for her return to Humble for Christmas, she wasn't as prepared to face the mundanity of home without letting her guard drop as she thought she would be. There was eggnog in the fridge that neither Eunice nor Maria had a taste for, but Thom had always loved over the holidays. He enjoyed drinking a small glass of it every morning over Christmas break and having a decent helping of it with enough bourbon for Eunice to suck her teeth at on Christmas Eve. There were three dozen tamales in the fridge from the same cleaning lady from Thom's work who sold them at the plant to all of the workers and whom the Smitheys always saved a Christmas card for back even when they would all pose for a family photo for them. There were the same movies—*Miracle on 34th Street*, both *Home Alone*s, *It's a Wonderful Life*, and *A Christmas Story*—all serving to lull Maria back into the rhythm of Christmastime, of home and her perfunctory role there.

More than just returning to the machinery of home, Maria found actual comfort in it. She and Eunice fell asleep sharing a blanket in front of the TV on Maria's second day back home. Maria woke in the middle of the night to the sound of the *Home Alone* DVD menu music playing over and over again. It reminded her of past nights when, either out in the living room or Eunice's room, the two of them would fall asleep together, either after watching TV or after long conversations about Thom and how each of them missed him. Maria remembered that night clearly, in front of Macaulay Culkin posing a scream with his hands on his face, those nights gone by when she would wake up in the middle of the night and Eunice would be sleeping deeply. Maria had a choice to make on those nights. She could very easily slip out of the bed or her uncomfortable fold on the couch and off to her room without waking Eunice—Eunice could sleep through a bombing raid and not wake up; the only force in the world powerful enough to pull her up out from under so many layers of sleep being Maria and even the meekest whisper of the word "mommy"—but like those past nights gone by, Maria opted instead to scoot in that much closer to Eunice, to put up with the literal pain in the neck that would result from her sleeping on the couch, because it was always nice to wake up next to her in the morning, and to watch the happy surprise in her eyes when she registered what the morning's light peaking in from the windows meant. She would wake, look around puzzled, see the light, and always say her sweet, innocent "Whoops." Always. Maria loved that. Also, for more than any other reason, Maria just loved the comfort and security of sleeping next to her mom.

Dinner was an adventure every night that Maria stayed in, and she had yet to go out because the number of friends she still had in Humble decreased exponentially every trip she took back home. Over the last year and a half with four trips home, Maria had lost touch with all but two high school friends, and neither of them were in town as both of their respective families were on vacation out of state.

Eunice had cooked all of Maria's favorite dishes, and they had gotten takeout from all of their favorite neighborhood places. So, two days before Christmas, Maria looked up the best Chinese restaurant in Houston, and they drove down into a sketchier part of the city than Eunice would ever have frequented to have dinner.

The waiter tried his best to explain the fixed menu and the courses of food that would come out. Maria and Eunice were their most Texan polite, and each of them nodded and said it all sounded great. When he brought out soups, rice, and spring rolls, Eunice was worried that they'd been ripped off. Maria assured her there was more. She'd been to restaurants like this in Providence. But really, she didn't know. By the time they opened their fortune cookies, they'd eaten the best meal they'd ever shared. It was amazing. Not just because of how wonderfully the food was cooked, but because Eunice looked down at each foreign-looking dish that was set before her, looked up at Maria skeptically, and then dove in anyways. She ate everything. She ate octopus. She ate a deceptively spicy chicken dish that made her drink all of her water and most of Maria's before the waiter came and refilled them. She ate noodles in squid ink.

Squid ink!

Maria laughed at her mother's reactions, at her shock at really enjoying the experience. Eunice opened her fortune cookie.

"'You are a wise and kind person.' That's not even a fortune. It's a compliment." When she looked up at Maria acting indignant and slightly annoyed, Maria saw in Eunice someone who she might choose as a friend if she hadn't chosen her as a daughter.

Maria laughed as much that night as she ever had with Aline or Kaylee. It felt nice to be happy at home, to have been made happy by this fun, vibrant Eunice. Having left home, struck out on her in pursuit of an education and a future career, to now coming back to spend time with Eunice, not out with friends or in her room studying, seemed to have made Maria more of an adult to Eunice. Eunice seemed to be accepting of these new facets of her daughter, in turn, revealing of her own human facets too. The spirit of this budding friendship made Maria bring up Kaylee in the car.

"So, Mom. I made a new friend at school. A really special friend," Maria said, not moving her head off of her headrest, just rolling it over to face Eunice.

"A really special friend, huh? What's his name?" Eunice took her right hand off the wheel to give Maria a playful poke on her side. "Is he cute?"

"No, Mom. It's not a boy. It's not like that. I met this girl from Utah. Her name is Kaylee."

"Kaylee? That name's not too out there, but it's definitely a Mormon name. She's Mormon, right?"

They were off the freeway and stopped at a flashing yellow intersection. Eunice was checking left and right, left and right, before making her left turn onto the road home.

"Yes. Well, she was raised Mormon. She doesn't know if the faith's for her."

"With all due respect, it's a weird one. They're very nice people, but they've got some kooky beliefs."

They passed the corner store and the McDonald's that served as the entrance markers for their neighborhood, the ones that Maria would see as a kid and know, *I'm almost home.*

"I know, Mom. But that's not what's special about her. She's from

Mexico, like me. Adopted, like me. Can you believe that? Meeting someone like that at Brown?"

They were stopped at the last stop sign before they arrived home. Eunice didn't look left or right. She just sat there behind the wheel, the sound of the blinker clicking filling the trench of silence that had opened between her and her daughter. She turned onto their street.

"That really is something, sweetheart." Eunice didn't look at Maria when she said this, and Maria heard the crackly dry patch in the back of Eunice's throat. That sound did not fill her with confidence, but she pushed on, still propelled by the mood of the evening.

"Mom, she spoke to her parents about the adoption agency that brokered her adoption. She reached out to them. She found out all about her mother, and she found out that she has siblings in the states. She even contacted one of them. Can you believe it?"

Eunice put the car in park and turned it off. She still didn't look at Maria and spoke to her on her way out of the car. "I almost can't, sweetheart."

Maria followed after her like a small dog chasing a treat. Eunice put her keys on the bar that separated the kitchen from the living room and stood there, not turning back to face Maria.

"She showed me websites and forums where people like me share stories about their adoptions. A lot of people have found a lot of information they didn't have before. I printed some of the stories. I can show you."

Maria went to her bedroom and grabbed the folder that had been burning a hole in her backpack since she got home. When she returned to the living room, Eunice was gone. Maria checked the dining room to see if she was waiting there to sit and talk over cups of cocoa, but she wasn't. She found her sitting at the foot of her still-made bed.

Maria lifted the folder to show her mother, "There are tons of stories in here of people who were kidnapped, just snatched from their strollers, some even taken from hospitals. Mom, people were stolen and sold for money to people in the states who, sure, wanted to love a kid and make life better for them, but who paid crooked brokers. It's all in here." Maria held the folder out for Eunice to grab, but she wouldn't.

"You think we would have gotten you illegally? You think we would have saved money by dealing with someone shady?" Eunice said looking at Maria, and Maria couldn't tell if she was slightly offended by what she thought Maria could be accusing her of or if there was something more to the cold contempt in her eyes.

"I don't know who you dealt with because you never told me. I asked you so many questions, and you never gave me any answers. Ever. How can you not have answers? How could you not have paperwork if it was above board? I'm not accusing you of anything." Maria sat on the bed next to her mother and put an arm around her. "I know you would have done anything to get me. I just want to know what that means now. There are all of these stories, and any of them could be mine. I could have been stolen. I could have been kidnapped. The system is corrupt, and people are desperate. I just want to know what my story is. All I've ever wanted to know is what my story is."

Eunice stayed seated upright, not easing an inch into her daughter's embrace. She was looking away again, straight ahead at the vanity mirror above the dresser on the wall opposite the bed. Maria looked toward the mirror and could see that Eunice wasn't looking at them. She was looking past them, and Maria didn't know what she could have been thinking. In that moment, Eunice was a stranger to her, and it scared her that this person who could feel so far away from and incompatible with her could ever have raised her. In that moment, no shared history, wiped tears, kissed skinned knees, or hushed away nightmares could change the fact that while Maria may have been Eunice's daughter, just then, in that moment of Eunice's stony silence, she wasn't Maria's mom.

"You weren't stolen," Eunice said, now looking at Maria's reflection.

"I know. Probably. I know how many people needed to give kids up. I get that. But if you could tell me who the broker was, what agency they worked for, or if there was paperwork, then I could know for sure. I could finally know my story."

Maria took her unwelcomed arm away from Eunice, and the distance that grew between them served to snap Eunice out of the trance she was in. She looked at Maria scooting away on the bed and grabbed her tight in a full, heavy hug. She squeezed onto her daughter as if she was afraid that Maria might have just realized that she could get up and go and never come back.

"Please, sweetheart. Please, just . . ." Eunice had nothing. All she could do was squeeze Maria tighter.

"How can I go on not knowing? Now that I know all there is to know, how can I still go on without knowing anything?"

Maria pulled away a bit from Eunice's embrace, but Eunice held her tighter. She gave one last big squeeze and kissed Maria on the forehead like she hadn't in years. She looked desperate, and it hurt Maria to have put her in such a state.

"Wait," Eunice said, afraid of Maria leaving the room. "Just wait."

She got up to face her and put her hands on her shoulders. She looked hard at her daughter as if she was trying to remember or to commit to memory the face she'd seen every day for nineteen years. She held Maria's face in her hands and smiled. She walked away, and Maria heard a hall closet door open. She heard Eunice move items around the closet and shuffle through papers. *Answers*, Maria thought. *Finally, answers!*

Then, there was silence. Sitting on the bed, Maria tried to sift through that silence for answers—it was like the last nineteen years of her life all over again. Had Eunice found what she was looking for? Had she not? *Could* she not? Maria sat there waiting. Why? Because Eunice had asked her to. That was the only reason why. She got up to investigate what was going on out in the hallway and almost walked into Eunice. Eunice gave a slight jump at having almost bumped into her daughter. Maria could see she was crying, hard.

"Hey," Maria said calmly.

She gave Eunice a deep hug, and Eunice melted into her, digging her face deep into Maria's chest. Maria stood there for a bit, feeling Eunice's chest heave, her warm tears wetting Maria's shirt. Eunice stepped back a bit and, unable to speak over her sobbing, held up a picture she'd dug out of the closet.

Maria took it from her. It was a fading polaroid print of a tired-looking Mexican lady on a hospital bed holding two babies, twins. She turned the picture over and saw a small sentence written in small, messy print.

"Perdoname, hija." There was a messy signature that started with an M and a Z. That was all.

"What's this?" Maria could feel herself hyperventilating.

Eunice just cried harder at this.

"Mom, what is this?"

Maria felt like she was going to pass out. She hardly made it back to the bed to sit down and try to even out her breathing. She looked hard at the picture. The tired woman was undeniably related to Maria, undeniably her mother. Eunice stepped into the room and slid down the wall by the doorway. She sat there crying, racing to find her composure.

"Ma . . . Mom, what's . . . ," Maria could hardly speak.

"They were pregnant with twins. They couldn't afford to keep you both. They couldn't even afford a safe place to deliver you. The agency told us about them. We paid all the fees. We paid the hospital bills. We didn't know if we were even going to get you. What if there were complications? What if only one came out and they didn't want to give you up? But we wanted you. So, we paid. We paid and waited in a hotel in the Valley. Finally, the agency people came, and we gave them the last of the money. You were wrapped in a blanket, and when they dropped you off, they took the blanket from you. I think they would have taken the cloth diaper pinned to you if you hadn't soiled it. They just handed you over, naked in a dirty diaper, and said the mother had wanted you to have this picture. That's you, your birth mother, and your brother."

Maria doubled over and rocked with her head between her knees, trying to not throw up. She was crying now, too. She was only able to manage one word:

"Brother?"

"They had two. One was a boy. We got you."

Eunice got up and sat next to Maria. Maria's emotional needs superseded Eunice's need to find her own composure just then. Maria was still her daughter, and she still had maternal instincts. She didn't touch Maria because she couldn't even guess the kind of pain the girl was going through, even though she'd spent nineteen years imagining, fearing what it would be like. Each year she kept the secret, Eunice knew the truth would become bigger and more devastating, but every year she didn't tell her there was more reason not to.

"But, Maria, we got you, thank God. And you got us. You got this life and all of our love. You go to Brown, for crying out loud." Eunice knew she was sounding desperate, so she stopped talking altogether.

"Nineteen years. You've known this for nineteen years and never told me? And Dad?" Maria was still talking from between her knees.

"We wanted to wait until you were old enough. It's a lot to deal with. We didn't want you to feel . . . rejected. So, we waited. We thought high school would be the right time, when you could understand the world, understand poverty, the choice they had to make. So, we waited. But then your father died. He died, and I didn't take it well. And you took it well enough, but you had still lost your father. You were thirteen, then fourteen, then fifteen, and then you were gone. I know why you left. I know I pushed you away by holding on too much. But every day I didn't tell you was another day you didn't have to know, didn't have to deal with it. And every day I didn't tell you made it another day worse. I just couldn't."

Maria sat up and looked at Eunice. Eunice had a frightened, pleading look on her face. Maria looked back at the picture. It was taken in Mexico, the land she was taken from. She had a brother, a *twin*. They occupied the same womb together. She wondered if they'd held hands, if they'd done anything in utero to comfort one another. She wondered what it might have felt like, having a twin, having someone who experienced the world with her, its ins and outs, down to the tiniest detail, who would have known where she hid her toys and the inexplicable-to-anyone-on-the-outside reasoning for why. She had always felt foreign and alone. Could it have been because she wasn't meant to be alone? She'd come into the world with a partner, someone who was supposed to be *hers*. She looked at the picture again and, if not for the color blankets wrapped around them, couldn't differentiate between her brother and herself. All that she saw of herself in the picture was her mother—her brows, her eyes, the coal-black of her hair.

They'd known and hadn't told her. Eunice had known and not told her. Maybe it was for the best, but it was another decision made for her under the pretenses of being for her well-being. But it wasn't. It was just another country she'd been given, another country that had been taken away from her. It was another abnegation of her own potential self-determination, of her nature. She had been rejected anew, forced into a life and a family and a context that very clearly wasn't hers, but now she was stolen from. She'd had a brother and decisions made for her that were supposedly all for the better yet had taken her from him.

She sat there and looked at the picture one more time, and a thought came to mind that settled everything for her, steeled her resolve in the plan she'd just made to leave. Had they told him about her? Did he know? Did he miss her, imagine her? Something about seeing this done to someone besides her made the situation clear to Maria. She had to go.

"Is there anything else?" Maria said, looking away from Eunice.

"No, honey." Eunice looked to be guesstimating the extent of the damage that had been done.

Maria got up and went straight to her room. She only had a suitcase and a duffle, but that wouldn't be enough. She went to the garage. It was at the end of the hall, which led to Eunice's room, and she could see her sitting there, watching. When she saw Maria walk out of the garage with Thom's old work suitcase, she began crying again, this time hysterically. Echoes of quickly fading filial devotion inside of Maria made her want to stop what she was doing and console Eunice, but she had lost too much in that moment; too much had been taken away.

Maria went to her childhood room and made quick work of packing her clothes, all of her clothes. She looked around the room full of trinkets and trite reminders of the life she'd been forced to lead. Nothing there mattered to her. All of it just tied her to that place, to that world. She grabbed all of the toiletries that she needed and left behind what she didn't. When she zipped open the side pocket of Thom's suitcase, Maria found two pictures. Thom had apparently kept them there to have with him on his travels. One was a thirty-five-millimeter picture of Eunice sitting outside with what appeared to be a two-year-old Maria deeply asleep on her shoulder. On it, Thom had written, "Audubon Park, '86." The other picture was a 5x7 school portrait in which Maria flashed a big smile despite missing two of her top teeth. The back of that one just said, "3rd Grade."

Maria stared at the pictures, and the anger inside of her made her throw them down on the bed. She continued to throw her toiletries in the side pocket of the suitcase. She took it and her own suitcase to the garage where her '97 Camry sat, a car that she only ever used to drive to school and around town to see friends. She put the suitcases in the trunk. She went back for her duffle and grabbed the picture of herself and her real family from the desk where she'd put it when she began packing.

She looked at her room for what she honestly believed might be the last time. What did home mean if you felt as empty as she did about leaving it? She knew it wasn't home, that she didn't know what that word even meant. She looked to the bed, at the pictures that she'd thrown on it. They were both facing down. All she could see was Thom's handwriting, and seeing that handwriting, remembering him, knowing he would only have kept the truth from her as long as he needed to, but in the end, she knew that he would have told her. He would have handled it right. She missed Thom at that moment. She knew that all of this would have been different if he hadn't died. Conceding that point in her mind laid the eventual framework to her forgiving Eunice, but only in time. On that night, nothing was going to be forgiven. Nothing was going to be forgiven for years.

Maria walked to the bed and grabbed the photos. She turned off the light but didn't bother to close the door to the room and didn't bother to look back.

Eunice stood in the garage in front of Maria's car. She wasn't blocking Maria's door or her path out of the driveway. She just stood there hugging herself. When Maria slammed the trunk down, it seemed to startle Eunice and bring her back from wherever her mind was wandering in the cold of the garage.

"Please don't leave, honey. Please. Where are you going to go?"

Maria didn't answer. She got into the car and adjusted her mirrors. She looked at her mother standing in front of the car.

"Maria, please. I'm sorry. Please don't go. Maria, it's Christmas—"

Maria slammed the door on her mother's plea. She turned on the car and hit the button to open the garage door on the visor. The sound of the garage door opening and the engine running further drowned out Eunice's pleas. Maria put the car in reverse and turned to back out of the garage. When she got to the bottom of the driveway, Maria looked up and saw Eunice crying, yelling, "I'm sorry! I'm sorry!"

She knew she was breaking her mother's heart. She was doing it on purpose, and she knew it. But sometimes, all you can do to make the hurt go away is to hurt someone else. Eunice was the only person Maria could hurt in this situation. She drove off, not really knowing exactly how she'd get back to Rhode Island. She drove all night and slept a few hours at a rest stop in Memphis. There, she plotted her course back to school on a map she bought, but then she remembered that campus was closed over the holidays. She hadn't thought of this.

Her phone was off. It had been the whole ride over. She could open it now and see how many times her mom had called. She could be daunted and tempted by that number to check her voicemail. She didn't want to do that, so she plotted a course instead for Pawtucket. When she got to the Domingues' house, she was bleary-eyed and freezing—she'd left her heavy coat at the dorm. Aline and her family were shocked but kind. They took her in, fed her, and asked minimal questions because clearly Maria had been through a lot.

After a nap, Maria came downstairs to find more Domingueses in the house than she had met in two years of knowing the family. Aline met her at the bottom of the stairs with a glass of eggnog.

"Merry Christmas, love. Here, drink. There's a lot of bourbon. What can I say? We're a family of sailors."

Maria drank deep from the glass, and it made her miss Thom. She missed Eunice. She thought she missed home, but then she realized she missed youth. She missed not knowing, being protected. She was alone now, an adult in the world. She looked around at these people. The room buzzed with the glow of their love for one another. Maria hadn't realized it was Christmas until Aline told her.

"Merry Christmas, Aline."

Maria sat at the table and quietly ate her food. She was polite, but no one was too familiar with her, and they all seemed to sense that she was not in a mood for talking. When dinner was over, the family all went to the den. They were watching *Miracle on 34th Street*. Maria went upstairs to get her phone. She still hadn't turned it on. She knew she needed to call her mother. She knew, but she couldn't.

She pulled Thom's pictures from her duffle and studied each of them. She looked at her mother and her brother. She looked at her missing-toothed smile. She looked at herself as a child, safe in the arms of one of only two people who had ever made her feel that way in a photo and snapped by the other. She looked at those photos and knew she wasn't going to call Eunice. Every person in those photos was gone. Not one of them was any closer to Maria than the ones a country and a world away. She didn't know her real family. She had been lied to by her adoptive one. And that girl, that happy, safe girl in the arms of her mother and smiling in the school picture, Maria was certain she'd never existed. She was an illusion created to comfort and placate her so that she could be what everyone else needed her to be—so she could be gone for her family in Mexico and there for her family in America. *For them.*

Maria put the photos and her phone back in her duffle. She went downstairs, drank more eggnog, and watched movies with a family that wasn't hers. She shared in their joy but didn't experience it. It wasn't as hard to do as one might think. Maria had been practicing for it all her life.

CHAPTER THREE—*(2010)*

Rob and Maria, the singular unit of symbiotic co-dependence they would become, started at a party. It was a silly affair, the party, strange by design. The friend of a friend who was throwing it had graduated from throwing fraternity luaus and toga parties to hosting *events* like the one where Rob and Maria met—a top-shelf BYOB party where mixologists were set up at stations at which party-goers could be set up with fancy cocktails of either their choosing or of the mixologists' artistic design. Guests were encouraged to tip, and enough of them had brought plates of food so that there was something of a buffet. Fancy cheeses and more kinds of hummus than one could count on both hands awaited hungry guests alongside spring rolls, egg rolls, and various homemade salsas with organic chips. Gluten-free and vegan offerings were labeled as such. Attire ranged from shorts and flip-flops to people in tweed jackets and all manner of necktie—cravats, single-Windsor's, debate-club skinnies, bows, and bolos—all worn with some level of irony and sincerity, some a mixture of the two. These were mostly recent graduates of UT or young transplants in town trying their hands at movies, music, tech, or bumming; they were, one and all, adults playing kids playing grown-up, all laughing at the levity of adulthood—let's dress up and eat fancy and mock sophisticated adult life so that when sophisticated adult life actually sneaks up on us, we can pretend like we've been laughing at it the whole time, like we were all in on the joke the whole time, like it was yet another thing we could scoff and 'whatever' at. This was Austin in 2010.

The guy throwing the party, some kid with a master's in marketing from Stanford's Graduate Business School, had seemingly crowd-funded a party. He had even put the word out that the event was a talent showcase with a stage and a PA system, securing a lineup of performers to entertain the crowd at no cost to himself. It was quite the grift, a modern-day Tom Sawyer convincing the neighborhood kids to whitewash the fence for him, except facilitated by social media.

Maria went to the party as a reaction to one of the first crests of what would become a flowing tide of panic when feeling like she was living too old a life at too young an age. She left home at seventeen, having worked her way to the top of the class and expended all of the patience she had for her mother's control. She left a group of kids with whom she'd grown up and all of Humble and the entire Houston metroplex, for that matter, behind her as she graduated a year early, skipping even the graduation ceremony that was held at her school to travel up to Providence and move into the dorm in time for the early summer school session.

She finished her double major (Philosophy and Poly-Sci) and got into UT Law, telling herself—and her mom during one of their sporadic sign-of-life, check-in phone calls—that it was because the school was one of the best. But truthfully, she wanted to be closer to home because her estrangement from her mother, as justified as and right as she was in her stance, left her worrying as the days turned into weeks and weeks turned into months and, as with the lie her mother had kept from Maria for so long, months turned to years, and no matter how righteous Maria was on her end of the radio silence, it still filled her with doubt and worry for the only mother she'd ever had, the only parent she really had left. At Brown, Maria had all but lived at the library, skipping out on all of the parties that Aline and Kaylee didn't physically drag her to and skipping out on the kind of college life that most undergrads wanted and were taught to expect by so many movies and TV shows.

And for what? The job she grabbed before even finishing up law school, where she spent weeks of billable time buried under stacks of paper and countless client calls where phrases and clauses of contracts were debated more than the contracts themselves were ever negotiated, at least by Maria. It certainly wasn't the courtroom "I object, your honor!" skirted power suit lawyering like she'd imagined when she decided on the profession as a child. She did most of her work from home in PJs. Was it all for that? Was it for the Far West apartment, the cat, and the fichus she always forgot to water on the sad apartment balcony?

She'd lived the life she was supposed to, and this was what it got her. So when she ran into an old high school friend at H-E-B and he told her she should go to the party, she knew she had a choice: She could fall asleep in front of the TV, the Amy's frozen pizza she'd heated gone cold and half-eaten on the coffee table, or she could fish a blouse and a skirt that weren't too obviously business casual from her closet, throw on some lipstick, grab a Red Bull from the Wag-a-Bag, and give herself up to the kind of Friday night a twenty-six year old was supposed to have.

The house she ended up at in a northeast neighborhood she'd never been to was small, a shotgun house that she walked through to a backyard replete with all the toppings of a hipster Shangri-La. There was a ping-pong table on cinder blocks, a stage at the back of the yard, vintage lawn furniture strewn about, and a plastic wading pool filled with sand, a bucket, plastic shovel, and a beach ball all unused atop of it.

The yard was big, and most people were grouped at the three cocktail stations set up at either of its sides. Maria went to the nearest makeshift bar and joined a group of party-goers who were being taught the proper way to make some cocktail whose name she hadn't heard before.

She had almost eased herself into the event. A string quartet—an actual string quartet—played on the stage, and their music hung over the self-satisfied 'oohs' and 'ahs' of guests admiring the cocktails being made. It almost lulled her into the same smug amusement with how wonderful the night was, how wonderful the party was, how wonderful all the people there were.

The sound of laughter in the distance pulled her out of the ambiance. Behind the mixologist on the other side of chain-link fences, a group of men were laughing. Tuning herself into the backyard's frequency two houses down, Maria could hear Norteño music playing. A grill was fired up, and the men—four of them, three old enough to be her father and one who could've been her brother's age—were drinking cans of beer. The men weren't necessarily laughing at the party, but Maria saw the men look over at the spectacle she'd volunteered to join. It must have been a funny sight, just like anything they saw the twenty-somethings who *chose* to live in the neighborhood where most residents *had* to live because it was cheap enough do.

These weren't a bunch of kids being kids. They were adults playing dress-up and celebrating their own immaturity. Worse than that, they took their leisure so seriously that it was scored by a fucking string quartet.

In another life, the one Maria imagined, she would be in that other yard, listening to the accordion music because it didn't speak to her as an obligation of personal anthropology. She felt just then, as she always did, like she was on the wrong side of a fence that separated her from her culture. So, she headed away from the bars and the gaze of the real people two doors down. She got as close to the stage as she could because if she had to swim in these waters, she figured she might as well dive down and drown herself in it.

She only heard the last part of one song. When the quartet rang out their last notes, everyone in the yard clapped, even the people who hadn't been paying attention. Right as the applause died down and the last claps echoed in the air, a shout sounded from one of the men two yards over, "¡Vete a la chingada, putos!"

Maria wanted to believe that she laughed before the rest of the party did, that she was in on the Mexican joke, that the Spanish the man had shouted meant more to her than to the rest of the partiers who were only laughing, at best, so as not to be alone in being laughed at or, at worst, laughing at the quaint, local color of this neighborhood where they were tourists—sampling lives they would never really have to live. She wanted to feel like her laughter was different from the crowd's roar at the party, but how could she or anyone else really ever tell?

The cellist was just getting off stage toting his instrument case on his back like a kindergartener wearing a too-big backpack when the next act went up. He had on faded jeans, an untucked polo shirt under a brown blazer, and a baseball cap worn on the back of his skull, brim pointing to the sky. His curly tufts of bangs falling on his forehead in a mixture of "Aww shucks" playfulness and faux-hip-hop cool. It was too much. He was too much. Maria cringed at the sight of him and hoped the men two doors down couldn't see him, or at least that they couldn't see her there and judge her for being involved with it all.

"Evening folks, I'm Danny Gustin J." The singer plugged in his guitar and fiddled with some knobs on the PA board. "I'm going to play a couple songs for you."

When he belted out his first word, "Baby!" all white-soul affect and scrunched-up-face singing, Maria was done. She turned around to leave, but a crowd had formed behind her. She had to scoot and excuse herself through groups of people. She was almost clear of the crowd, a clear path out ahead of her, when she felt a foot underneath her own and almost fell for having had it pulled away from under her step. She did a kind of side jump away from the foot she'd stepped on and held her hands up as a non-verbal apology. She was looking behind herself at the rolled-eye dismissal of the person whose foot she'd stepped on when she ran into someone. He caught her by her elbows and helped her catch her balance. She didn't even get a good look at him before he started talking.

"Can you believe this asshole? I bet he gave himself a kiss in the mirror before he left his apartment tonight." The man didn't look away from the stage when he said this. "I mean, I bet you he wore puka shells in his senior class photo."

Maria laughed at this, and laughing at anything or feeling good about anything in that moment was enough to ease her embarrassment at having tripped over one person and into another. She no longer felt so strong an urge to be anywhere but where she was at that moment. She looked up at the stage. Danny Gustin J. was through a couple of verses and his first singing of his song's chorus and was doing a James Brown foot shuffle thing while he played a few instrumental bars.

"He probably misquoted Bob Marley for his senior quote too," Maria said.

The man looked at her here. He let half a smile climb up the right side of his face. He pulled his head back a bit to get a good look at Maria as if evaluating if she were real.

"You're giving him too much credit. Dave Matthews. He definitely misquoted Dave Matthews." The man looked back at the stage.

"Everlast," Maria said with finality. "He misquoted Everlast."

The man let an easy laugh issue through his nose and looked down while shaking his head and closing his eyes. He looked at Maria, then up at the stage, then back at Maria.

"You know, I think you've got him figured out. I bet you have everyone figured out—even me. Just don't tell me what you see when you look at me. I don't think I can handle it. My name's Rob, by the way." He held his hand out, and Maria shook it.

"Maria."

"What brings you out to this party tonight, Maria?" Rob had turned his back to the stage and was facing Maria. He was tall, so he had to bend down to ask his question into Maria's ear.

"A friend. An old friend. Some guy I knew in high school, really. I ran into him at H-E-B, and he said I should come to this party, and I don't know . . ."

"You came out because you're young and free, and that's what you're supposed to do?"

"Something like that."

Rob nodded at this and turned back around to face the stage.

"And you?" Maria leaned up and asked at Rob's shoulder.

He leaned over and answered, "I know the guy running this thing. I've worked with him on a few things. He's kind of a douche, but these things always have good food, so I came."

Danny Gustin J. played the last note of his song, and the crowd gave sparse applause. He waved his thanks and even put his hands together in prayer and gave a bow to a group of really drunk girls who were woo-ing with really-drunk-girl fervor. Then, he changed the tuning on his guitar and stepped back up to the mic.

"Thanks again, guys," he said as if he were talking to a stadium full of people. "I've just got one more. See if you can spot it."

Maria didn't immediately recognize the song, but when he began singing, she recognized it as one that had been getting heavy rotation on the Top-40 station she listened to on her way to and from work every day. It was a cover of a Justin Bieber song. The drunk girls wooed even louder. Some people rolled their eyes, but mostly everyone just listened to or ignored it like they had been doing before.

"Ugh, this guy's the worst," Maria said.

"Come on. I mean, he's terrible, but he's just typical. He's just an asshole with a guitar." Rob looked down at Maria, and as far as she could tell, he wasn't joking. "This city is like Mecca for assholes with guitars. They're the kinds of assholes who one day decided that their playing and singing was good enough that it gave them license to stand up and sing into the silence of the crowd. To be fair, it's a pretty specific kind of asshole who thinks they have something to say worth asking people to listen to. Just think of the psychology of this moment. He's on a stage above the rest of us, expecting our attention, amplifying his voice, and playing above our conversations. And for what? A Justin Bieber cover song? He asks for silence, and he chooses to fill it with that?"

"Who's got someone figured out now?" Maria saw a real passion in Rob. He believed what he was saying. He wasn't just filling the silence.

"Oh, I don't have him figured out, I just know his type. This really is inexcusable. Can you do me a favor, Maria? I need to talk to this Danny guy. It's just too much to deal with to have this in the air. Will you wait for me? I'll just go up to the stage and have a word with him. Will you please not leave? I really want to talk to you."

Maria didn't know if Rob was joking. He seemed funny enough, but she didn't think he'd really go up there and talk to this goofy singer. She did know that she wanted to keep talking to him too, though.

"Okay," she told him.

"Okay?"

"Okay."

"Alright. I'll be right back."

Rob walked around the crowd. By the time he got to the stage, Danny Gustin J. was wrapping up. He finished the song and was bowing and waving to the crowd. Rob climbed up onto the stage and was met with a skeptical Danny. Maria couldn't believe he was actually doing it. She was trying her best to read the two men's body language on the stage until she realized that everyone in the crowd was looking over at the men two doors down. They were standing arm-in-arm, swaying and chanting soccer-style:

"PU-TO! PU-TO! PU-TO!"

This time, the crowd was split. Half of them were laughing, and half of them seemed scandalized by the chant. Maria heard a couple girls say something about "bullshit macho culture," but when they caught sight of Maria, they got very quiet and looked away, embarrassed. In her younger days, Maria would have asked the girls exactly what culture they were talking about and exactly what they knew about that culture, but she was tired, and she wanted to see what Rob was saying.

All she could see was Rob pointing to the back of the audience. Was he talking about her? He pointed to the guitar and to the PA. Danny Gustin J. looked at the back of the audience and seemed to be doing a weird kind of math in his head. Rob pointed to the PA and mic and threw his hands up as if to say, "Come on, man."

Danny Gustin J. shrugged his shoulders, took the guitar off, and handed it to Rob. Rob slung the guitar strap over his shoulder, turned off the volume, and tuned the guitar. Maria didn't understand what was going on, but she watched as Rob made quick work of playing with harmonics up and down the fretboard. He turned the guitar's volume back on and tapped at the microphone. He was live.

"Let's keep it going for Danny Gustin J.," Rob said. When people started their unenthusiastic clapping, Rob spoke over them. "PU-TO! PU-TO! PU-TO!"

The crowd laughed, and the men two yards over hooted and hollered. From where Maria was standing at the back of the crowd, she could see Danny Gustin J. seething at the side of the stage.

"My name's Rob. Just Rob. I just play the guitar."

The pockets of laughter that remained in the yard were dying down, and the silence that filled the backyard made Maria feel nervous and scared for Rob. The fact that she felt anything for him standing there on that stage after his little diatribe was strange. She felt played, but she couldn't not watch him up there, and she felt worried for Rob, although he didn't look to be worried for himself. He pulled a pick out of his pocket and bit down on it with his teeth. He hitched the strap on his shoulder so that the guitar was high on his chest.

"This first thing's by Tarrega, if any of you care," he muttered into the mic.

He wiped his hands on his pants, stretched his fingers out, and let out a calm breath. He played the first chords of the song and went from there. It was a slow waltz that consisted of a steady drone and deceptively many notes. His left hand moved elegantly up and down the fretboard, landing on the final notes of runs with a flourish, coming off the fretboard and down to his hip when open notes rang out. As he played, the silence became electric with the sound of feet shuffling, arms uncrossing, and the stifling of chuckles. In the years to come, Maria would become used to the sounds and sights of a group of people reckoning with and becoming disarmed by the presence of real, virtuosic beauty; tonight, though, she was busy standing there, being disarmed by it herself.

The song ended with Rob laying his hand across the fretboard and pulling it off, this time with no flourish to let the note that rang outdo all the work of wowing the crowd. They didn't know what had hit them by the time Rob had reached to his shoulder to let the strap back down, grabbed the pick from between his teeth, and picked up on a high note on the fretboard that carried harmonically from the one that still sounded from the previous song. He played a fast run of notes—more metal and bluesy than classical—speeding up to a galloping chug. He slid to the top of the fretboard and galloped out some power chords—*na-nuh-nuh-na-na na-nuh-nuh-na-na na-nuh-nuh-na-na*—then back down to solo some more, then back up to the power chords—*na-nuh-nuh-na-na na-nuh-nuh-na-na na-nuh-nuh-na-na*. Then he was done.

"That last bit was mine," he mumbled into the mic.

It was hard to hear what he had said because the crowd was clapping and whooping like mad. Maria noticed that even the men two yards down were whistling and shouting their approval in Spanish. At the side of the stage, Maria could see Danny Gustin J. gesture angrily at the crowd while Rob shrugged his anger away. Rob handed over the guitar and gave Danny Gustin J. a slap on the back, not turning around to look him in his red face.

Some people kept their backs turned to Rob as he walked away from the stage, some to not give him the satisfaction, and some not knowing what to say or do after someone could do what Rob had just done on the stage and then just step down back onto the ground and walk among them. Some people floated over as to just happen upon Rob and mention, "Hey, that was cool." Others still, mostly girls but a few guys too, rushed over to Rob. They were telling him how great that was, how great he was, asking if he wanted to grab a drink, and if he was in a band. Rob gave his practiced 'thank yous' and 'no, thank yous'. He was gracious and curt. As he got closer, Maria heard him say to a lady on the older end of the audience's age spectrum, "Sorry. I'd love to, but I have a friend waiting for me."

When he got to Maria at the back of the crowd, he gave a performative, "There you are! I thought I'd lost you. You ready?"

He looked, pleading into Maria's eyes. She nodded, unprepared to perform, herself. He smiled a small little smile that was just for her, grabbed her hand, and headed into the house and out of the party. As they left, they didn't look back at the people trying to talk to Rob or see Danny Gustin J. getting back onstage to try and win back some of the luster that had been knocked off of his ego. However, when they got through the house and to the front yard, they could only faintly hear the smooth hip-folk stylings, which sounded like the musical embodiment of a baseball cap worn on the back of a skull, brim pointing to the sky, curly tufts of bangs falling just so on the forehead, over the sounds of drunken Mexican men two doors down, and some drunken hipsters in the party they'd just left shouting a chant of, "PU-TO! PU-TO! PU-TO!"

Maria was still holding Rob's hand. They laughed at the sound of the chant and at the faint sound of Danny Gustin J. shouting, "Fuck it!" into the microphone. They were halfway up the street when Maria realized Rob was actually taking her somewhere. She stood firm and tried to let go of Rob's hand. When he didn't let go of hers, she felt the tug of him realizing she'd stopped.

"Where are you taking me?" she asked.

"I'm sorry. I just had to get out. My first instinct was to go to my van." Rob was panting, and Maria realized just then that she was too. The joy and excitement of the moment had taken over him, just as it had for her. "I mean, it looked like you were on your way out before. I didn't think you'd mind heading out. Besides, I didn't want you to be someone I only met at a party and had a cool conversation with and then lost. I didn't want you to be a story I'd end up drunkenly telling my roommates about later tonight."

Maria crossed her arms here and took half a step back.

"Whoa, I mean," Rob took his own half-step back and held his hands up at his sides, "if you didn't want to leave just then, I'm sorry. I thought you were enjoying our conversation."

"And what was that? All that stuff about assholes with guitars expecting silence, assuming they have something worth saying? Assuming their voices matter? What was that, you playing me?"

"Playing you? No. Of course not. I meant every word of what I said." Rob put his hands down along with his shoulders. "It's just that . . ."

"Just that you thought what you played was worth filling the silence?" Maria pointed back in the direction of the house.

Rob's arms closed across his chest. He sank down almost to Maria's own height.

"Or did you see me ready to leave, fed up with the party, and disliking the music and see an opening? Did you think you'd play your pretty little song and do your cool solo thing, and I'd just get in your car and go home with you because you're great at something? Is that your game? Going to open mics to do your guitar thing and take girls home? I bet you do that all the time."

"Yes, it was worth filling up the silence. I owed it to the silence to make up for what that asshole just played. And, let me tell you, I've done that before. Yeah, I've done it before, but not to get a girl. I don't mind bad playing. I don't even mind assholes with guitars. But when assholes get up there and do that shit, the preening, dancing cool shit, I have to get up, and I have to make it up to the silence. And if a girl or two who was going to hop on some Danny fuckin' J. or another decides to go home with me instead, and if my playing can prove him to be a hack and a phony, then that's just a bonus. But let me tell you this too, I've never, ever, stayed around after I do that, and I've never had a girl waiting for me at the back of the room whose hand I could grab and who could run away with me, because I always run away." Rob didn't realize he was pointing at Maria now.

She seemed to understand what he was saying, but Rob couldn't tell because no one ever understood what he was talking about when he talked about what was and wasn't worthy of covering up the silence. At least, from what he could tell, she didn't look mad. She looked away from him, thinking. He thought he could still save this.

"And, just for the sake of accuracy and honesty, I wasn't an asshole with a guitar. I was an asshole with a pick. I borrowed the guitar."

Maria laughed, and both she and Rob knew that the night had been saved, the *they* that they might become had been saved.

"So, where were you going to take me? You got us out here to your van. Where were you taking us?"

"I wasn't taking us anywhere, just getting away." Rob pulled his phone out of his pocket to check the time. "I mean, I'd love to take you back to my apartment. Something about you climbing on top of me comes to mind, but I have a gig to get to. I'd love it if you joined me."

Maria didn't want to feel the heat of blushing on her face, but she did. She could've fought against the draw of Rob now standing tall again in front of her, but what for?

"This late?" she asked.

"Late? It's eleven. We go on at midnight, and, knowing the band that's opening for us, we probably won't get on until twelve-thirty."

"So, you are in a band?" Maria asked.

"Not really. I have a couple of really cool rock bands I play with. One of them is playing tonight. But I also play live with a couple of country acts and a jazz ensemble. My schedule's crazy, but it works."

"So, you're some hotshot ringer who goes to parties like that to shame goofy assholes whiteboy-rapping and dancing on stage?"

"No, I'm a musician. I don't pass up on offers of free food or booze. And the guy who was throwing the party knows me. He always invites me to these things. I think he knows I can't help myself sometimes, so he invites me hoping I'll do what I do. He's using me for my outbursts, and I'm using him for his friends' fancy food and booze. The Austin music scene—we all chew the same gum, record in the same studios, and mooch off the same promoters."

Maria only nodded here. Rob seemed to be real and adult, both of those qualities that seemed so lacking in all of her contemporaries, even those at her work who were all lawyers or programmers with advanced degrees who still seemed to be reveling in the shock of being on their own schedules with more disposable income than they could think of ways to waste.

They were mostly people like Maria who had spent their college years in libraries and among study groups, but while she had dived into her books as a means of getting out of school free and clear of her past life under the indenture of her mother, they had mostly done so out of social awkwardness or at least as a result of parental pushing toward academics which had deprived them of normal interaction and, therefore, made them socially awkward. Maria didn't realize how similar she was to these people because no one realizes how socially awkward they are when they never socialize, and even if she could realize this, she would have just attributed to it like she did everything else to having been adopted away from where she was supposed to be, to having been lied to by the only person left in the world she was supposed to trust implicitly. What she did know, though, was that her coworkers were all sleeping with one another, all going out into the Austin nightlife, and cashing in years of hard work on fancy cars, expensive haircuts, and trendy wardrobes that made them the players on the scene for once. All of the men Maria worked with had hit on her within her first month of employment, and none of them were too hung up on her having rejected them—they were young, rich, and in the land of the young and temporarily broke. They were on top of the world. But they weren't real.

"So," Rob asked, "do you wanna come out to a show? I can get you in for free, get you drink tickets . . ."

"You know, Rob, I'd love to—"

"Don't." Rob held his hands up fists-out as if begging. "Don't say no when you can say yes. Please, don't. I just haven't met anyone like you or talked to anyone like this in—"

"Whoa, buddy," Maria said. She grabbed his wrists and put his hands down. She later would not be able to explain to herself why—she wouldn't necessarily be regretting it either—but she pulled Rob to her by the wrists and gave him a kiss on the side of his mouth. "Believe it or not, this is late for me, and I have to go in to work tomorrow."

Rob pulled his head back up to get another new look at Maria. She still held onto his wrists, so he lowered his head onto her shoulder.

"I bet you could call in . . . maybe get someone to cover for you?"

"Call in? I'm salaried. I don't need someone to cover my shift. I have a project due Monday." Maria let go of Rob's wrists and pushed him up by his shoulders. He hung down, making himself heavy in mock protest.

"Alright. I can't expect you to skip your work to come and hang out with me, but can we hang out? Please."

"Again with this begging stuff," Maria laughed. Rob pulled back from her grasp on his shoulders.

"Hey, now. I'm not begging. Don't get me wrong, I want this. I want to get to know you, but I'm not begging."

Maria pulled her phone out of her purse. "Just when I thought I had you figured out, you go and throw that curveball. We'll need to hang out again so I can make my final diagnosis. What's your number?"

Rob told her, and she sent him a text with her name and a winky-face emoji. Rob looked down at it and back up at Maria. He smiled but shook his head.

"No one talks anymore. And that's fine by me. But if I call you and ask you out, I'd be able to hear the disinterest or excitement in your voice. But you set a text precedent, so now I won't have tone on my side. Tone is very important in my line of work."

Maria smiled at this and typed again on her phone. She pressed the send button and looked up at Rob. His phone buzzed in his hand, and he read it. "Busy tomorrow. Brunch on Sunday." This time she added a tongue-out emoji.

"I have gigs all day tomorrow, so late brunch, okay?" Rob said into his phone.

Maria laughed and typed more. She hit send again and looked up at Rob.

"Late brunch is fine. Lunch, even. It's more about the company than the eggs." This one had an emoji with cool eyes and a wry smile.

Rob put his phone down into his pocket and looked at Maria. She put her phone back in her purse too.

"Okay," he said. "I'll text you tomorrow."

"Okay," Maria said.

"You know those smiley face things are a cheap imitation of real tone, right?" Rob put his arms around Maria's neck and leaned down to kiss her. She leaned back, away from his kiss but not out of his arms.

"Oh, are they? You'll have to tell me about that Sunday. Have a good gig . . . or show, or whatever."

Rob ran his hands through his hair. He looked down at Maria and saw her anew for a third time. That third look could have been considered the start of them for him, but remembering back to Rob and Maria's official start, it would be eclipsed by the Sunday that lay ahead of them. In this moment, right before their start, Rob saw only beauty and potential in this ever-changing Maria he'd met at some party he'd only attended for a free pre-show meal and cocktail or two.

"I will," he said. And he did.

They'd settled on meeting at a café off Barton Springs at twelve-thirty. Maria gave up on being mad at one-fifteen when she finished the food she'd ordered herself and took out her laptop to work on redlining an agreement for work. The day was pleasant enough in the shade of the patio where she sat. The café had bottomless coffee, so Maria was content to sit and work anywhere that wasn't her apartment or, worse, her empty office with its lakeside view of people wakeboarding and drinking in pontoon boats and party barges, having fun like Maria probably should have been having on a nice Sunday in Austin. It was nearly two when she saw Rob walk into the café's dining area and worriedly scan each of the customers at their tables, hoping he'd find her. When he didn't, he walked out to the patio. He saw her almost immediately and looked relieved, joyed even, to see her. He started over toward her, and Maria slammed her laptop shut, folded her arms across her chest, and put on her best bitch face. It seemed to work because Rob stopped dead in his tracks for a beat to steady his breathing and steel himself for the onslaught. It was almost worth the fact that Maria wasn't sure when she'd last saved her edits on the document she was knee-deep in.

"Thank God you're still here," Rob said when he got to the table. He moved to pull out the chair across from Maria to sit in, but her feet were on it, and she pushed down hard on it so that he couldn't.

"You have got to be fucking kidding me."

"I'm so sorry. I mean it. I'm never late. I hate being late. I'll show up an hour early and circle the block just so I won't be late. To anything. Not just dates."

Rob had given up on the chair and moved over to Maria's side. He was crouching down beside her, his hands on the arm of her chair. He spoke quietly. His tone and his familiar occupation of Maria's personal space forced her to break her angry pose if only initially to address his encroachment with hostility, but hearing his voice and seeing his face, sweaty and desperate, very clearly having just gone through an ordeal, calmed her. She took her feet off the chair and turned in her seat away from Rob. He knew an inch was being given to him, and he didn't expect a yard, so he stood up and seated himself across from her.

"My drummer, the drummer for the band I played with yesterday, needed my van. The singer had brought him, but she left with a girl. So, he was stuck and couldn't just get a ride from anyone. But then the drummer, the asshole, decides he needs to stay behind because this bartender chick was really into him but couldn't leave until three. I told him I had to get home. I told him I had a date—"

"That's a lot of girls," Maria said.

"Well, yeah . . . a little over half of the world's population are girls?" Rob's voice trailed because he seemed to know where this was going.

Maria laughed at this. "I mean hooking up, jackass. How often do you take girls home from shows?"

Rob sat back in his chair and shook his head. "Is that really a first date question?"

"First date? This isn't a date. You missed our date. You're just some guy I ran into while working at a café." Maria was already over-caffeinated, but she picked up the cold, near-empty mug that sat on the table in front of her and drank from it, in need of something to do with her hands.

"Alright, sometimes. No more than you would take a guy home from a night out dancing with the girls . . ."

A night out dancing with the girls? Maria was glad she didn't seem as lonely and awkward as she felt. "So, your drummer needed your van?"

"Yeah, he needed my van. I mean, we'd already loaded his drums into it. But I told him I needed to get home. I needed to get here today. So, the bartender gave me her car."

"She gave you her car?"

"Well, let me borrow it. They kept my van; I took their car." Rob seemed to think this was a completely normal thing to do. "I mean, my van's kind of a piece of shit, and I'm in two bands with this guy. We're pretty much in bed for a big chunk of each of our money. I knew he wouldn't fuck me over on this."

"So, what happened?" Without thinking, Maria opened her laptop back up. She couldn't help herself. She had to see if she'd saved her last changes to the document.

"He fucked me over." Rob looked down at her empty coffee cup, grabbed it, walked to the coffee urn inside, and came back out with cups of half and half and a variety of sweeteners. "I don't know how you take it."

Maria waved away the offer of coffee. "Wait, how'd he fuck you over?"

Rob took a drink of black coffee from the mug. "I get up, shower, get dressed, then I get ready to leave early, but the car won't start."

The tension in Maria's angry shoulders faded as her chest fell into a deep belly laugh.

"Yeah. Real funny. So, the car won't start, and I'm pissed. I have to call him and wake him up, but I realized I didn't have my phone, so I went in to get it, and it's not on the nightstand where I always keep it. That's when I realized my phone's in the van."

Maria laughed even harder and gave a sympathetic, "Oh, no . . ."

"So, fine. No problem. He only lives a little over a mile away. I'm pissed, but I can still make it. I mean it when I say I leave early to get places. But I get to his house, and he's not there. The van's not there either."

"They went to her place?"

"Yeah. Well, probably. I don't know. All I knew was that I needed to get here. I'm up in Hyde Park. I don't have my phone to call a cab. So, I walked, hoping I would find a cab. None. No cabs on the street except one that was in fare. I walked all the way from 45th Street and didn't get a cab until I got on Cesar Chavez. I got on and came here. I'm so sorry." Rob took another drink of the coffee and sat, awaiting his judgment.

"And you just thought I'd still be here? You thought I'd be waiting for you, like I didn't have anywhere better to go?" Maria knew her insecurities were surfacing, but she also knew Rob couldn't recognize them yet.

"No. I mean, I hoped. I hoped that you had run into a friend and stayed to talk. I hoped you had maybe shown up late yourself. I don't know what I thought, but I hoped you were here because I didn't want to miss out on this, on sitting here with you, even if you're mad. I didn't want to miss out on you."

Maria looked at her computer. All of her changes had been saved. She closed the document and opened her email to make sure no emergencies had arisen with the work she and her team were doing for the next day's presentation. She closed the browser and the Word doc and shut down her computer after seeing there were no new emails.

"Well, are you hungry?" she asked.

Rob let out an exhausted breath. By some miracle, not only was she still there when he arrived, she hadn't rejected him when he showed. His journey was complete, and only then did he feel its toll. "Holy hell, I am so hungry right now."

"Well, go order something, and we can start our first date," Maria told him.

Rob came back to the table with a metal number stand, one cup of water, and one soda. He looked at Maria sitting patient and understanding and felt even more stress wash away. He couldn't help but laugh. Maria seemed to understand, so she laughed too. Rob reached across the table and grabbed Maria's right hand in his left. He was holding it in the manner of someone offering to pray with you, but he just laughed and gave it a quick squeeze, which Maria returned. Rob picked up his cup of water and gulped it down in one go. He sat up and took a deep breath.

"So, what do you do that you work so much? Saturday, Sunday. . . . you have a big thing tomorrow. What do you do?"

Rob had an earnest comportment about him. It was refreshing and unnerving as if someone really wanting to hear answers to the questions they asked was some alien kind of custom. His interest and focus were intense, and that was really one of the first things about him that made Maria fall in love with him—it certainly had been one of the reasons she hadn't just blown him off after his upstaging act two nights before—but that pureness of attention would later reveal itself to be alienating and, at times, neglectful because as *there* as Rob was when he was interested, it was obvious when his attention or his interest was absent, and Rob was nothing if not purely and soberly earnest. He would not feign interest, nor would he be bothered with feigning anything—that would be a waste of his time and mental energy, mental energy he would never forfeit for anyone or anything—but all of that would come later. On that Sunday afternoon, Maria felt heard, listened to, because she was.

"I'm a lawyer."

"Oh, wow." A waitress brought Rob his sandwich. He thanked her and took a bite. "So, do you have, like, court tomorrow?" he asked, his hand covering his chewing mouth.

"No. I'm not that kind of lawyer . . . no 'Ladies and gentlemen of the jury' and all that stuff. I work for a tech company that does all kinds of work for other companies. I help write and rewrite our agreements with them. I make sure we hold our end of the bargain on deals and that they do too. Boring stuff, really. I'm a fine-tooth comb."

"But you're a lawyer?" Rob put down his sandwich, wiped his mouth with his napkin, and pushed his plate away a bit. "Sorry. I was really hungry."

Maria smiled at this. "Well, yeah. I have my law degree. I've passed the Texas Bar Exam, so I'm licensed and all that."

"That's pretty impressive."

"Yeah. I guess."

"I mean, your parents must be proud."

"Naturally." Maria reached across the table and picked a fry off of Rob's plate.

"And what do they do? Mr. and Mrs.?"

"Smithey."

Rob raised an eyebrow at this. "Smithey?"

"Yeah. I was adopted. I know I don't look like a Smithey. I've heard it all my life." Maria looked away. She grabbed her phone from her pocket to look at the time.

"Hey, I'm sorry. I didn't mean to make things awkward. I just wanted to get your last name to look you up because if I miss our next date and lose my phone, I want to be able to find you. I can't remember phone numbers anymore. I just wanted to get your last name."

"It's fine. I'm used to it." Maria put her phone down on the table.

"I mean it. I'm sorry. I'm sorry, Maria Smithey." Maria had looked down at Rob's plate, so he dipped his head down to meet her gaze. "Really."

"Apology accepted," Maria said.

"I really do want to know who you are. I want to know your story." Rob took another bite of his sandwich. "So, what do your folks do? What do the Smitheys do?"

"Well, my dad doesn't do anything. He's dead."

Rob coughed his sandwich up into his sinuses at this. It was all he could do to not spit it out. Maria had to laugh. Rob grabbed his soda and sipped it, trying to catch his breath.

"Come on! Really?"

Maria kept laughing, but again, she looked at him sympathetically. She tried to stifle her laughter and nodded that, yes, her father was in fact dead. Rob dropped his face into his hands and shook his head. The sight of this made Maria laugh harder.

"It's okay, Rob. How could you have known?" She reached across and put a hand on his shoulder.

"Well, with how this date's gone, I should have known. I should just stop talking right now. If you promise not to give up on me, I'll shut up right now. I promise I'm not always this bad at things like this—normal conversation, not even just dating."

Maria touched the side of Rob's face gently. "My mom's an accountant and the events coordinator at our church."

Rob looked up here. "So, you're religious?"

"Eh."

"But your mom is?"

"Oh yeah." Maria grabbed more of Rob's fries. "Definitely, and you?"

"Not religious at all." Rob passed the whole plate over to Maria. He was done with chewing for a while.

"I meant work. Are you just a musician?"

"Yup. Just a musician."

"I don't mean it like that. I don't mean *just*."

"I know." Rob's hands were finally back on the table, his arms no longer protecting his vital organs in the face of so much vulnerability. "I fully support myself as a musician. I have a degree in guitar performance. I was a couple of credits and a comprehensive recital away from a master's degree, but I didn't really need it, and a band I was in hit pretty big around that time. We toured all over and got nominated for big awards and stuff. After that fell apart, I ended up back here in Texas. And now I work as a musician because at a certain point, all you need to do is be able to play better than a bunch of self-taught guys to go out there, do gigs and sessions, and make a name for yourself."

"And that's why you're in Austin?"

"Yup. I mean, I like it here. But if you know the right people and know how to play, there's almost always work."

Maria reached into her laptop bag and pulled out a pair of sunglasses. She put them on. "Now that's a cool profession. Way cooler than just doing a lot of highlighting. You ready to go?"

"Yeah. Thing is, I need a ride." Rob finished the last of his soda and grabbed the trash and dishes from the table.

"Obviously."

The drive up to the drummer's house was short, as the streets were relatively empty on a lazy Sunday afternoon. Maria parked the car in front of the house Rob had directed her to, but he didn't get out. He looked at the driveway and up the street.

"No van," he said.

"Doesn't look like it."

"I'm sorry to use up your time like this, but could you please drive me to my house. The only thing I can figure is he'll take it there." Rob had the same pained look on his face as when he had tripped over his honest interest in Maria's parents, like something potentially precious was slipping from his hands. Maria found that charming.

"No worries. Just point the way."

Rob issued a tired "Thank God" before they even turned onto his street. He could see his van parked on the street in front of his house.

Maria parked behind the van and Rob got out and walked up to his van, looking inside to check the state it was left in. He tried the driver's side door and saw it was open. He flipped up the center armrest and pulled out his phone from the stowage. Maria joined him, standing by the van.

"What do you know? I missed a few calls." Rob flashed a guilty smile here. "And I have a few voicemails."

"Yeah. I'm honestly going to ask you not to listen to those. They don't paint me in the most flattering light." Maria went to grab the phone, but Rob pulled it back.

"Of course, I'll delete them. That's only fair."

Rob swiped through his phone.

"There are some texts there I'm not exactly proud of too," Maria said.

"Hey, we're even. Okay, Blake says the keys are in the visor." Rob pulled the visor down and caught the keys that fell out. "They're grabbing a beer over at Crown and Anchor to wait for me to show up with her keys. You want to go grab a beer?"

"No, It's Sunday. I have to look back over my work one last time for tomorrow, so I'd better not."

"Alright. I'll text him to let him know we're here." Rob typed and sent the message. "Will you please come in for a bit so our first date doesn't end with you running errands for me?"

Maria looked at Rob half-seated in his van. She looked the van over. It was old, maybe a little crappy, but it was clean. She looked at Rob's little house and wondered how he lived.

"Sure."

The apartment was sparse but orderly. There were only a couch and a wooden dining chair in the living room. Next to the chair was a small guitar amp and three separate electric guitar cases. A large acoustic guitar sat on a stand next to the amplifier. Maria sat on the couch and awaited the mineral water Rob was getting for her. When he handed her the cool bottle, Maria realized how hot she felt. She wiped at her brow with the back of her hand.

"Let me turn the air on," Rob said, having seen Maria acknowledge her sweat. He walked up the small hallway to the thermostat.

"So, these are the tools of your trade?" Maria called at him.

"Yeah," Rob said as he sat on the couch beside Maria, "some of them. I'm recording with a guy right now, so a couple of my guitars are at his studio, but this is me. This is what I do."

"Will you play something for me?" Maria asked.

"Oh, come on. I don't want to do that." Rob was blushing a bit.

"So you'll take some guy's guitar and play to a crowd of strangers, but you won't grab one of yours and play for me?"

"Well, yeah. That was to spite that guy. That was 100% a 'fuck him.' This would be some kind of clichéd attempt at wowing you. I don't want to do that." Rob, who had sat with his arm on the back of the couch, not necessarily around Maria, but open to her, closed himself down, resting his forearms on his knees.

"Then don't wow me. Don't try to play the best thing you can play. Don't be fancy. I just want to know you too. If playing the guitar is what you do, if it's what you are, I want to learn about it." Maria put her hand on the back of Rob's neck and rubbed her fingers behind his left ear. "My mother's an accountant. My father worked for Shell in Houston. I don't really know what he did, but he wore a suit to work, and he left me money when he died, so something important. I just want to get to know you too."

Rob nodded his head and looked over at Maria. He leaned over toward her and gave her a brief, deep kiss. He stood up, and Maria clapped happily at the fact that he was going to play for her. He walked up the hallway, past the guitars in the living room, and came back holding a smaller nylon string guitar. He sat on the chair with the guitar on his front thigh. He interlaced his fingers in front of him and cracked his knuckles, took a deep breath, and put his hands at the ready-to-play position. He hadn't struck a note when the door burst open, and Blake bounded in.

"Come on, man! We've been waiting all day for—" Blake started.

When he saw how Rob was sitting, just about to start playing, and Maria sitting on the couch, ready to listen, Blake seemed to realize he had stumbled upon a mating ritual in progress. He was a musician himself—a drummer, sure, but a musician, nonetheless. Of course, he knew the power of a concert played to an audience of one. He stopped in his tracks in the doorway, the woman who had come with him walking into his back.

"Hold on," he told her. "Say, Rob, can I get the keys?"

"Sure, they're—" Rob pointed in the direction of the kitchen.

"Don't get up, man. I'll get them. Hi, I'm Blake." Blake gave a sheepish wave at Maria, and before she could reply, he had stepped into the kitchen, grabbed the keys, and was almost out the door.

"Listen, Blake. The car wouldn't start this morning," Rob said. "It made a weird noise like—"

"Don't worry about it, man." Blake was half out the door.

"Hey, man, if you need a ride or some help or something . . ."

"Yeah. I'll let you know. See you tomorrow."

The door closed, and Rob and Maria were left seated as they had been before, but the feeling of the moment had changed. Blake had walked in on the kind of scene Rob had wanted to avoid playing out. The eggshells Blake was walking on were real. Something was happening. Even though Rob didn't like the idea of it being what it seemed like, it didn't change what it was. He laid his guitar on the floor next to him.

"I should see if he needs help." Rob stood up and gestured to the front door. Just as he did, the unmistakable sound of an old engine turning over and rumbling came from the driveway. Maria smiled at this. Rob ran his hand through his hair and gave a nervous laugh. "He's a mechanic. Like, a real one. He works at a shop with his brother."

Maria pursed her lips and gave an exaggerated nod. "Sure. I bet he does."

Rob sat on the couch beside Maria, farther away from her than he had before. He leaned back on the arm and crossed his legs on the cushion facing her. He smiled away any embarrassment he was feeling, happy to not be playing, happy to not have lost this moment having to drive Blake and the bartender anywhere.

"I'm serious. He's a car wiz."

"Sure. I bet." Maria turned back on her armrest and sat cross-legged, facing Rob.

"I can take you to his shop. We practice there. I have a key."

"Will you still play?" Maria sat up and crawled onto Rob. She kissed him on the cheek and rested her head on his shoulder. "Please?"

"I'd rather not."

Maria pouted her face and gave a playful whimper.

"Seriously." Rob leaned back and looked down into Maria's eyes. "You'll hear me play, I promise. You can come to my shows. I mean, I haven't practiced today. If you want to hang around, I can do that. It's mostly boring, scales and stuff, but we can do that. Right now, I want to look at you, and I want you to look at me and just be us for a minute. Ask me anything."

Maria kissed him again on the cheek before sitting up and crossing her legs, her knees touching his. "Okay, but don't be mad if I ask about the guitar thing because it fascinates me."

"What about it fascinates you?"

"I mean, you studied it, right?"

"Yes, ma'am. San Francisco Conservatory of Music. I was in grad school here at UT."

"That's just so . . . atypical. I mean, you are an artist. You make art, and art that anyone can make in a garage—"

"Well, not just anyone . . ."

Maria put her hands on Rob's knees. "Exactly! It's this thing that anyone can do, like riding a bike. But you're like a Tour de France guy. You're like Lance Armstrong."

"Are weed and whiskey performance enhancers?" Rob put his hands on Maria's.

"Technically, but testing is really lax. But I mean it. There was this thing you wanted to do, you realized you were good at it, then you went out to make yourself great at it, at this thing that, I mean, everyone dreams they could do."

"I wouldn't have gone to college if I had to study something real."

"But it is real. You made it real. And what's real anyway? Studying law?" Maria pulled her hands away from Rob, exiting his romantic space and signaling her real interest in her query.

"Well, yes. When did you know you wanted to be a lawyer?"

"When I was a little girl, my parents pushed me in that direction, too. All parents do. Didn't your parents want you to be a lawyer?"

"My parents wanted me to be whatever I wanted."

"That sounds nice."

"It can be."

"How would that not be nice?"

Rob shrugged at this and looked away. Maria decided not to push the issue.

"I just like the fact that you took this impractical passion, this impractical path, and you went about making it practical. That's it. I would never have dreamed of doing something like that, I couldn't even fathom it."

"Well, if you could go back and do it all over again, what would you do?"

"Knowing myself, being one hundred percent truthful, I'd probably be a lawyer. Not even an exciting courtroom performer. I'd go back, make all the logical decisions at every turn and end up here and now with my files and my highlighter." It was Maria's turn to shrug and look away.

"I don't know if that's sad or awesome."

"Neither do I."

They sat there quiet long enough for each of them to drift off into their own pasts, to their potential parallel-universe lives; their knees touching, anchoring each of them in the now and in themselves as a pair. Maria knew that no matter how badly she might have yearned for something else, some other thing that she couldn't even imagine because any other thing was too elusive, she would have always ended up as the person that she was destined to be. Rob wondered what a different life might have made of him. That thought took him to a thought he hadn't had in a long time; it took him to his brother. Sitting there like that, remembering the brother he hadn't really thought of in years, put the idea of him at the top of Rob's head, which is why he came up with the analogy he would use when their silent contemplation ended, and Maria asked him a question.

"So, you're good, right?"

"What, like as a person?"

"No." Maria put her hands back on Rob's knees. "At the guitar."

Rob laughed at this. "Yeah. I'm pretty good."

"No. Don't be modest. How good are you?"

Rob thought about how to put it, and the echoes of Maurice informed his answer. "You can't hear how good I play. You can't hear any of my flaws. Only a few handfuls of people in the world can. It's like a secret language, like what twins have."

The word awakened in Maria the story she hadn't told anew in so long that it made her realize how long it had been since she'd made a new friend she cared about enough to share it with. She smiled at the thought that she had found someone worth telling. The smile faded as the circumstances and truth of what she was about to tell him surfaced. Rob noticed and looked concerned.

"I'm a twin," was all she could say.

"Do you guys have a secret language?" Rob was tentative about this because of the look on Maria's face.

"No, it's not like that. My parents, my birth parents, put me up for adoption. It was Mexico. They could only afford one kid, if that. They kept the boy." Maria raised her hands at her sides as if to say *that's life* as if that really were what life was like for anyone but her.

Rob felt he'd been allowed to see behind a secret curtain. He was honored and wanted to reciprocate, which is why he told Maria the story he almost never told anyone—because what for?

"I'm a twin too."

Maria looked at him skeptically. "Really?"

"Yes. Well, kind of. My brother was stillborn."

"Oh, no."

"Yeah. They didn't know until the day I was born. They already had two of everything, a double stroller, all that."

Maria put her hands on Rob's face. She was crying, but he wasn't.

"I can't imagine," she said.

"Well, neither can I, really. I don't really remember anything about it specifically. Just about, you know, after . . ." Rob pulled back gently from Maria's hands. She sat back a bit, respecting Rob's moment. He went to get up, and Maria moved back on the couch to allow him space. "I'm going to have a beer. You want one?"

"No. I'm fine," Maria said.

She sat there feeling even more connected to Rob. A new world had formed in him for her. She wanted to fall into it, into him, but she felt alone. Sitting there on the couch, Rob taking longer than he should have to get a beer from the fridge, Maria felt a new kind of alone because the person she wanted next to her was away. The thin wall that separated them was a cruel one. It scared her to feel something like this, something she'd never felt for anyone outside of Kaylee, but this was thicker—it was more tactile, and it had mixed up with romantic and sexual attraction—and that scared her.

"So, we have that," Rob said when he returned. "We're both twins."

When he sat, he returned to his previous posture, back on the armrest, crossed legs facing Maria. That meant the world to her at that moment. He had left, but when he came back, he was still open to her. She was a little less scared then.

"Yeah. Small world," she said.

"Aren't you glad you didn't leave earlier? I am." Rob put the bottle of beer on the ground and grabbed Maria's hands. "Thank you so much for still being there. Thank you for letting me have a second first date."

"You owe me now. Forever indebted."

"I promise to keep trying to pay you back. I mean it."

The way Rob looked at Maria made her believe him. It was as true as everything Rob ever meant or did. Maria knew she would have to learn the parameters of Rob's devotion to his own truth. She knew she was communicating with a new kind of person.

"Elvis had a twin who was stillborn too. Did you know that?"

Rob nodded and took a drink of his beer. "Jesse Garon."

"Who's that?"

"Jesse Garon. That was going to be his name—Elvis Aaron and Jesse Garon."

"*Was* going to? It was his name. If you name something, it has a name. Did your brother have a name?"

Rob hesitated to answer the question. He had run from the answer, the name, his name for years. He hadn't had to answer that question in almost two decades.

"Maurice," he told her.

"Maurice. Rob and Maurice? Family name?"

It had definitely been over two decades, long enough for Rob to have nearly forgotten his own real name.

"No, not a family name." It was hard to say, but he knew he was going to tell her the truth when he first thought she might ask. "Maurice and Robin were the names of two of the Bee Gees."

"The Bee Gees?"

When Maria laughed, it didn't upset Rob. Every time he had said it before and someone laughed, he had lashed out—both verbally and violently—but when Maria laughed her compassionate laugh, Rob had to laugh too.

"They were twins too. It was the '70s."

"So, your name is Robin?"

"Well, no. . . . I changed it legally when I was eighteen." Rob had to look away here. In telling this story to someone like Maria was, for the first time, the fact that Rob had changed his name was the embarrassing part of the story. "I hated it. It bothered me, so I changed it."

"Wow."

"I know. It was petty, but it really ate at me."

"What did your parents say?"

"It broke my mom's heart, so it pissed my dad off."

Maria was crying again. Again, Rob wasn't.

"It really broke her heart," Rob said.

The sex they had that afternoon wasn't necessarily bad as much as it was labored. Maria wasn't used to having sex with someone she wanted to have sex with. She'd mostly only ever had sex drunkenly after parties or with partners of convenience. Aline's boyfriend's best friend in Pawtucket had been reliable to call on when she needed to blow off steam or just feel free enough to let her body and her *self*, who she was and where she was going in her life, not matter for one night or a lazy weekend in Pawtucket. She'd never felt this way about someone so quickly, and she'd certainly never gone to bed with someone after a first date.

Rob, for his part, was so preoccupied with the sex he was having, the experience he was trying to have with and give to Maria, that his attention had shifted from her to the act he was performing with her. Sex had become performative for Rob. He was there ready to spin plates and run off a checklist of angles and maneuvers because he was used to the connection he made with someone in bed being transactional. He'd give as good as he got because that's all that it was about, getting. Rob was selfish in his giving because it was important for him to know he'd been gotten. He would focus on a woman, making sure that, for his own sense of prowess, power, and self-worth, she would feel pleasure, that he would have given that pleasure.

Maria could feel Rob withdrawing from her, diving into the act of what they were doing, and so she also withdrew a bit from the act, tensing and pulling up away from Rob, who had slid down in the bed. He looked up at her from between her legs and seemed shocked to see her there, looking at him, looking for him, present in bed and expecting to share a whole experience with him, not just to share the pleasure in the moment. He moved back up beside her.

"Hi," she said.

"Hello, Maria."

"How's your Sunday going?" she asked.

"Well, it started off really bad, but it's looking up right now."

"Yeah. You seem like you're having fun."

"You're not?"

"Of course, I am. Let's just slow down. Let's enjoy this a bit, enjoy the me and you. You didn't want to play your guitar for me. You didn't want to try to wow me. Stop trying to wow me. Just be here with me."

Rob looked at Maria suspiciously for a second, and, in that second, the whole moment could have imploded in his insecurity at having been redirected, but then she kissed him. She kissed him, rubbed his chest, and looked at him with powerfully playful eyes that he wanted to see forever. He kissed her back and didn't for a second look away from those eyes.

Maria fell asleep listening to Rob's heavy breathing slow and calm. Their bodies adhered to one another through a layer of shared sticky, slick sweat. She felt safe with her face resting on his chest, feeling the slow rise and fall of it lull her into her own relaxation. They lay there, naked and spent, the fading light of dusk buzzing behind the sheets that covered Rob's windows, painting the room an obscure haze of orange, born anew in each other—two twins in a new world that had formed for them both within each other. They had fallen into it, into them. She didn't wake when he got up, so deeply she had fallen asleep.

It was the sound of his guitar that woke her. He was playing scales, as he had told her he did to practice. She woke to the sound and looked over to the clock on the dresser at the opposite wall of the room. It was almost ten. She had work to do, work at least to go over one more time before tomorrow. She knew she had to get up, get dressed, and leave, but she lay there a while listening.

There was a pretty, logical order to the scales. Each note built on the others to form something that made sonic sense. Rob played each scale several times at different speeds. It was impressive, listening to the kind of work that has to be done to make something special look like it takes no work to achieve. After the last note of the last scale, Maria heard Rob crack his knuckles and take a deep breath.

The song Rob played then was something Maria couldn't describe. She didn't have the language for it. Of course, she could say it sounded classical, Spanish even. She could say that it was beautiful or romantic, but she knew she could only look at it and see beauty and romance the way she would look at a painting and say that it was beautiful and captivating without knowing why or how it was. All Maria knew was that it moved her. It was a strange, sublime experience hearing that music being played that well and for it to be coming from only one room over. Maria got up and wrapped the bed's top sheet around herself. When she entered the living room, Rob was sitting shirtless and barefoot in a pair of jeans. He might have heard her enter; he might have smelled her or felt an atmospheric shift as she entered the room and just ignored her—she couldn't know. All she knew was that he didn't open his eyes when she walked into the room. He didn't open his eyes when she sat at the couch and watched him play, watched him at work in his art. He just played and played, making facial expressions at the notes like they were talking to him and he was agreeing with them, asking them for more. He just played and played, a clip-on light atop his music stand the only light in the room, serving as a kind of soft spotlight for him. When he finished, he opened his eyes and seemed genuinely surprised to see Maria there.

"Hi again," she said.

Rob smiled. "I told you I'd play for you."

"That was beautiful."

"Yes, it was."

"I can't believe you can play like that."

"I wasn't talking about the playing." Rob nodded back in the direction of his bedroom.

"Oh, shut up. I'm being serious. I can't believe you can play like that."

Rob shrugged. "It's what I do."

"I really have to go right now, but can you play a bit more? Please?"

Rob looked at Maria on the couch, her right leg was bare up to where the sheet was draped around her thigh. He didn't understand the full measure of the day's good fortune. It was all too much coincidence and perfect bad timing that had put this beautiful woman naked on his couch, asking him to play for her. He had even told her his name. He'd only known her for less than three days, and he'd told her his name. Sure, they'd just fucked, but he told her. *That* was intimacy. *That* made him just as naked there in the living room as Maria was, if not more so—she did have the sheet covering her.

"Maria, if it'll get you to stay, I'll never stop playing."

He'd wonder, later, and she would too at times, when he stopped playing for her—after it kept her there that first night and brought her back every other night after that—when did Rob stop playing for Maria? Neither of them would ever come to remember when or why he stopped, but they would always have that first night. They'd always have that music.

CHAPTER FOUR—*(1942-2011)*

Rob was raised with a ghost, and not just a ghost in the form of the porcelain urn he'd had to walk past every day he lived at home, which was far bigger than it needed to be to contain his never-born brother's ashes. He was an identical progression of what his brother would have grown up to be, an exact, age-progressed living portrait left behind to remind and hurt anew his parents every time they looked at his beautiful, miracle face. They had gotten their Robin, but they'd lost their Maurice. Rob was a carbon copy on this side of what the boy on the other side would have been, what he was becoming over there if people kept growing on that side, and so Rob was not only raised with a ghost, he was raised as a ghost too.

In the manner of a ghost, Rob was spoken *at* instead of spoken *to*. He was filled with his parents' hopes and expectations of their children, which is to say he was actually filled with the hopes and expectations they had for themselves, met or unmet, or in the funhouse-mirror-of-egotistical-self-perception manner of what we think we are, should be, aren't, and should have been. Isn't that all a ghost is: a bump in the night, or a shifting of air pressure causing a door to shake that we embody and imbue with our fears and insecurities? His mother wanted to fill him with enough love and light for two, as she had given and would continue to give all of her sadness and anger to his dead brother and his death. Meanwhile, his father wanted to take all of the lessons he'd learned about culture, strength, and power and give them to his son so that the boy could be a super-powered version of himself—that fantasy where we go back and put our current knowledge and wisdom into ourselves as a child and know for a certainty that, with all of that power, the world will be ours. It probably would have worked, too, if Rob hadn't grown a personality and voice of his own.

• • •

Venancio "Ben" Vera was born to lead. His uncle never let him forget it, and Venancio wanted Rob to know that he was too.

In 1948, when Venancio was only six years old, George Berham Parr stole an election by adding two hundred votes to a Jim Wells County ballot box a full six days after Election Day. The ballots were all clearly written by the same hand, and they were found neatly stacked in ballot box thirteen in alphabetical order. The votes were not counted until all others in Texas had been tallied, and Parr's preferred candidate was found to be trailing. When the very fishy circumstances were considered, an investigation was launched, but they didn't get Parr, not for that one, and not for a while.

The eventual winner of the election, a Democratic senate primary, would go on to win the general, and that esteemed senator from the great state of Texas would later be tapped as running mate for an Irish Catholic kid who looked good on TV, could give a hell of a speech, and was a war hero to boot, but who might need a redneck next to him on the national stage because, damn, he sure was pretty undeniably a New England Yankee. It can be said that if George Berham Parr hadn't made a ballot box appear out of nowhere in Alice, TX, Lyndon Baines Johnson would never have been Vice President and, therefore, would never have become president. Parr didn't need a ballot box to mysteriously appear from out of nowhere in Greenton, TX. He had Venancio Sr. and Venceslao Vera on the ground in Greenton, and so Parr knew that votes there would go his way.

"That was Tio Venceslao and your grandpa," Venancio would tell Rob after recounting the tale yet again during one of the interminable afternoons Rob spent in his father's office when his father tried to engage in a bit of character-building, kill some time between patients, and in the long minutes before Perla would finish whatever she was doing and come get their boy.

The Vera brothers would ride their horses the few miles to the meeting house Parr kept on the south tip of Duval County—a county his father, Archie, had taken and kept control of with his own fraudulent election, and a subsequent courthouse fire set to cover it up in 1914. They would mostly just drink, listen to music, and shoot guns. But sometimes, they would conspire to steal elections or scare off carpetbaggers from Austin looking to either prosecute or profit from (sometimes both) the Parrs' illegal activities down south.

The house was just north of Greenton on State Highway 16, and when in town, Venancio and his Tio Venceslao would force Rob to sit in the backseat next to an ice chest full of beers they'd drink on their drive up and down 'the Y' in town. The drive would always veer out toward Falfurrias and stop by the graves of Venancio Sr. and Sintia Vera, Rob's grandparents, at the Greenton Cemetery, and then continue north on 16 toward Freer, stopping at the spooky abandoned house. Some local kids had spray-painted the words 'texas chainsaw masacer [sic]'—because what better male bonding could there be for young Rob than drunken driving and reminiscences, which were often shared in a language he couldn't understand?

Parr, like his father, made the brilliant political move of learning to speak Spanish. Their constituents lived in Spanish-speaking enclaves on land their respective families had lived on since it was Mexico. The Vera brothers learned that this ability to influence in two languages was real power and insisted on speaking to Parr only in English. Venceslao told his nephew that the Parrs wouldn't forever be the whites in charge of the land then referred to as "Medio Mexico," that there would likely be many after them, and those who would come after the Parrs would likely use their own inability and unwillingness to speak Spanish as a different, more malignant power.

Growing up, Venceslao would chide and criticize his nephew when he slipped into Spanglish when he was supposed to be speaking proper Spanish, or when his pronunciation of English would swing this way or that in a musical, Tex-Mex inflection. When little Venancio would get visibly upset by this, his uncle would wave his feelings away.

"Ya. Basta. It's what your father would tell you."

Venancio took this conflicted South Texas-centric idea of communication to Austin when he went there for college. At first, it was his speaking that alienated Venancio because as intent as his uncle was on having Venancio speak clearly and properly in both English and Spanish, the standard by which he taught was his own speaking. Venceslao's brother, Venancio Sr., was the more educated of the two. He had finished through grade nine when he was called to work on the ranch that he and his brother were born on, the ranch where he would later die when a cow he was loading onto a trailer got spooked by a snake and trampled him to death, reuniting him in the afterlife with Sintia, the young bride he'd lost in the birth of his young son who would be left in the care of the surviving Vera brother. Venceslao regretted that his younger brother had to drop out of school to join him, but neither of them ever said it. They couldn't; there was work to do.

If Venancio's brown skin wasn't enough to set him apart from his classmates, his drawl certainly was. To a certain extent, he could wash away a bit of his Mexican-ness by adopting more prominently the diminutive, 'Ben,' in the place of his given name, but he couldn't wash the Rio Grande Plain off his tongue any more than he could the Mexico in his pigmentation. It's a particular, wholly South Texas Mexican accent that comes from the Rio Grande plain. It's not the same kind of Valley accent that people from, say, Brownsville or Edinburg have—theirs is more Mexican, almost more proper-Spanish sounding since both towns are so close to the border, its citizens living and working on both sides of it. It's closer to a Laredo accent, but there's something lost in transit from the ranches near Greenton and Falfurrias and Bruni and Freer that isn't found in Laredo with all of its cattle and oil that's raised on and pulled from the land on the plain.

In 1960, all Ben's white classmates heard was Mexican. His brown classmates, though, heard him speak and knew who and what he was to a T. He was 'rancho'—the cousin or cousins they'd run from in their hometowns, those stark reminders of an old country they'd never known or bothered to learn about. He was an interloper, misconceived by one-half of the people on campus as being from elsewhere and resented by the other for reminding them of a place they only knew in the abstract way.

There were politically active students too. A group of them lived in a house on the east side. Nick and Eli, the group's leaders, cousins who weren't enrolled at UT, never seemed to trust Venancio. He wasn't from Austin like all of the residents of the house were, so why would he care about local politics? From the day Ben walked into the house, the cousins postured up and looked at him like he might strike at any time.

It could have been that Ben had the air of a leader about him because, for all of his life, he had been a leader. Everyone in Greenton knew Venancio as he was still known there, and they knew his uncle and remembered his father. It made sense to them all that he would be class president, valedictorian, and captain of the football team. These cousins seemed to think he would want to take some of the power they'd gained— because that's all they were doing; they weren't affecting any real change in town, just building a network that only mattered to those in it. What they didn't realize was how petty and insignificant it all seemed to Ben. They couldn't steal an election; they certainly couldn't steal two, and when they did run someone for local office, they went to great lengths to mobilize voters, make up signage, and take out an ad in the newspaper only to find out on the day of the election that the candidate they'd chosen lived out of the district he was running to represent. Or, maybe, their problem with Ben was that he didn't try very hard to hide the fact of how small it all seemed to him.

All of these elements of Ben not belonging and the cousins not trusting him came to a head one Tuesday when he rode downtown with the cousins and some of his classmates to the Frito factory that employed a large number of Mexican Americans. They waited out behind the loading dock to talk the workers into registering to vote. Many of the workers said they couldn't part with the one dollar and fifty cents poll tax, and the only counter the cousins had was that voting meant real American freedom, and that was worth more than a buck and a half. Most of the workers strung them along, saying they'd do it later; some actually registered to vote, but others just laughed in the faces of the kids in their school clothes who were asking them to pay, to vote, or to care.

Nick caught Ben rolling his eyes and shaking his head at his fourth rejection in a row. He walked away from the worker he had been talking to and walked straight over to Ben.

"Do you have somewhere to be? Something else to do?"

He pushed the registration cards he was holding into Ben's chest. Ben looked down at the cards and up at Nick. Behind Nick stood Eli, arms crossed, looking angry. The other students, three of them, cut short the conversations they were having with the workers.

"No. This all just seems so . . . inefficient." Ben waved at the factory.

"Inefficient? There are over four hundred Mexican American workers here. Do you expect them to come to us?"

"No, of course not. It's just, back home, my uncle had everyone in our county and all of our neighbors registered. Everyone."

"He got everyone to register and pay the poll tax? Your uncle some kind of rancho brujo? He do magic? Either that, or you're full of shit." Eli laughed behind him, but Nick didn't break eye contact with Ben.

"Everyone. As soon as they turned eighteen. They were registered and ready to vote our way."

"And what way was that?"

"Democrat. We would tell them the names, and they'd pick. This here, it's just unorganized."

Nick didn't like that.

"What's this 'we?' You would go with them? Your uncles ran for office? They paid the poll taxes? Whose wallet were they in?"

"My dad, my uncle . . ." Ben's posture shifted, betraying the fact that he was going to conveniently leave the Parrs out of the conversation. Nick saw this and jumped on it.

"Whose dirty work were they doing? That's what it was. They were stooges for some rich white man who let them milk his cows and eat the crust off his bread as long as they manipulated their Mexican brothers and sisters? Were they his slaves? Did your uncle milk his cows? Did you fetch his water? Clean his boots? Did your mom leave the back door open when your dad went out to do your white boss's dirty work so he could—"

It ended there. The last word that Ben heard was 'dad.' Nick had managed to say the rest, but the words evaporated into nothing when Ben's shoulder hit his stomach. His head hit the truck behind him, not necessarily knocking him out, but disorienting him to the point that Ben got a few quick, satisfying punches in before his own lights were put out by a kick to the head from Eli (Ben never mentioned the actual insult in the telling Rob this story, that wasn't the point of the story). When he came to, some of the factory workers had sat him up under a tree and brought water to him to clean the cuts on his face where the beating had continued.

It was a four-to-one fight, the workers told him. They had had to intervene to get the beating to stop. One of the men called them cowards in English. 'Pinches cobardes,' Ben agreed in Spanish. One of the workers who was coming off a shift gave Ben a ride back to campus. He had been inside when the fight happened and missed it. He asked Ben what he had done to upset his friends like that.

Ben couldn't explain it, not all of it, so he spoke the only truth he'd gained that day, a truth he would try to convey to his son in the retelling: "They're not my friends."

Ben took eighteen hours of classes every semester in order to graduate early. He kept his head down for the rest of his time in Austin, not wanting to be seen, not wanting to regard what he was seen as in the eyes of his peers. All of this, though—all of the parties he didn't attend, all of the football games he skipped, all of the six-hour bus trips he took home as frequently as he could—was not done in shame. Ben did not feel less than. He felt superior. He felt superior in the worst and most frustrating way: he knew they were all wrong, but they were wrong in ways so big, they would never understand it.

Ben took something else from the beating that day behind the Frito factory, or, really, he left something else there. Teeth. He left two teeth on Nueces Street in the aftermath of his fight. It took him three days to get the money together to fix them. He had to keep his mouth shut, consuming only liquid as opening his mouth exposed the nerve endings at the roots of the stumps of his cracked teeth to air, which caused pain so excruciating that he did not even try to eat. He went to class on these days. Of course he did but having to remain closed of mouth and grimacing in pain made him seem angrier than he actually was. Carrying himself thus, he could see what was expected of him, and when he fulfilled those expectations, he received a kind of begrudged respect because, sure, he may have seemed like an angry Mexican—all swarthiness and Spanish passion and noble indigenous Mesoamerican stoicism—but at least that was a Mexican they could understand. They'd never met a Mexican valedictorian. They'd never seen one wearing a crown and sash and watched him slow dance with the head cheerleader at homecoming. They'd never been to Greenton, to *Medio Mexico*.

The shut-mouthed grimace on his face wasn't all his two lost teeth had brought him. When he could finally make his appointment, he looked in the Yellow Pages and picked the only Spanish name he found.

The dentist did not enter the room until it was time for the procedure. When he greeted Ben, Ben gave pause at the sound of his thickly accented voice. The dentist, Dr. Rayón, noticed this and smiled, then patted Ben on the shoulder.

"They make doctors in Mexico too . . ." he looked down at the chart in front of him and pulled up the readers that hung from a string around his neck, "Venancio." He laughed big and comfortably, pointing to the framed diploma on the wall. He was the first person in Austin, of all the others at school who also read it off of official papers, who pronounced the name correctly. "Padre Hidalgo studied there. Many leaders of the independence movement did."

As the gas from the uncomfortable mask Dr. Rayón had put on him caused the edges of his vision to dull and blur, Venancio focused on the diploma. *Universidad Michoacana de San Nicolás de Hidalgo.*

Mexico.

Something clicked. Ben had already felt such dissatisfaction in Austin and outside of Greenton. Being Mexican was a hindrance there—well, being Mexican and a winner, being Mexican and named Venancio Vera, raised by an uncle to lead like his father led. He wasn't built for Austin, and Austin wasn't ready for him. Mexico. That could be it. Mexico could be the answer.

Mexico was not the answer.

This was not part of the story he would tell Rob, though. Instead, it was Perla who would explain what Mexico did to Ben, initially by way of justification and apology for why Rob's father was the way he was, then, later, as contextual framework for her own story. 'See what I married? How cut off and angry he is?' she would say to a son not yet compassionate enough to hear the questions in the telling. It was three more years as an outcast. At first, his labored, unpolished Spanish, marked as it was by slow Texican phrasing and foreign slang, gave Venancio, as, of course, he was called in Mexico, away as an American. Different, newer kinds of resentment toward him, however, would come to arise in his classmates.

He was older than most of them because, and he did not know this until he had arrived at school, in Mexico, students didn't need an undergraduate degree in order to study dentistry. They only needed to have completed a science-intense course of study and to have passed entrance exams. To the students who were from wealthy families, Venancio carried himself like a peasant; to the students who were not, Venancio was regarded with great suspicion that he might be a literal spy.

As Dr. Rayón had said three years earlier, UMSNH had been an incubator for the thinkers and activists who would lead the Mexican Independence movement. Similarly revolutionary students made up a large portion of the student body when Venancio attended. These students loved Castro and communism, and they were not afraid to say so. When local bus fares were going to be raised, the students took to the streets. Venancio happened upon the protests but ignored them as he had already learned what the Marxists thought of him. It wasn't until the next day that he would learn that one of the protestors had died, killed by soldiers who were now on his campus, wielding rifles and questioning students. This was in 1966, Venancio's last year in Morelia, Michoacán—the last time he would ever enter Mexico again.

Venceslao picked his nephew up at the Greenton Filling Station, the town's official bus stop, even though Venancio could have very easily walked the half-mile to his home, but his uncle wouldn't hear of it after the twelve-hour bus ride. It all seemed to have shrunk in his absence—the home, the town, the uncle. It felt old-shoe comfortable, but it also felt three sizes too small.

Venancio had lunch and a couple of beers with his uncle, visited the graves of his mother and father at the Greenton Cemetery, and drove up and down 'the Y' three times before running into some old friends with whom he had a couple more beers. Finally, Venancio drove by the high school to see if it would arouse in him any of the old feelings of confidence and self-assuredness that he only then realized he had lost in his six years away in places that didn't want him.

It did not.

It only made him realize what had been taken away from him. A dull bitterness filled Venancio that day. He had been given a gift in having been born and raised where he was, and he'd squandered it out in a world that didn't care about it. Austin taught him he was too Mexican; Mexico taught him he was too American ("Wouldn't that make you mad too?" Perla would tell Rob every time she told the story). The whole experience taught him that he was wrong. He was not enough. Greenton was culpable in all of this too. It had given itself to him on a silver platter. It hadn't taught him how to go out and to get. Venancio had to learn the hard way how his charmed early life had left him ill-equipped to fight for success.

He knew he had to go out and be on his own. He didn't need to smile, charm, and win anyone or anything.

• • •

Venancio had settled on Corpus Christi like many Greentonites do with their own personal 'big city' dreams as the place where he could build his empire. He took the lessons he'd learned from his uncle and Parr, and set up shop on the west side of the city, creating a loyal customer base among the town's Mexican Americans, using his Spanish with his older customers and his English with their kids and grandchildren who refused to learn, or who they themselves had refused to teach, having been beaten in their childhoods by nuns and priests who struck with all of their might to force out the Spanish and to force in the America, the God too, but mostly the America.

He took what he'd learned in Austin and worked to mobilize voters to get to the polls to advance the Mexican American cause in Corpus and, more specifically, helped his patients and their neighbors find resources at either LULAC or La Raza. This aimed to help advocate for their fair pay and fight for withheld or stolen wages from bosses who threatened, oftentimes wrong-headedly as these were mostly American citizens, to call immigration if anyone complained. He would play both sides of the activist political spectrum—both the "we're good little Americans" center and the militant "still pissed at the theft of Aztlan" far left—in order to help the Mexicans of Corpus, not because he felt any real affinity or allegiance to them, but because they were his customers, and paying customers can't pay unless they're paid.

Venancio tried to expose his son to the art of building and maintaining an empire when he was old enough to tag along without being too antsy or distracting. Venancio wanted Rob to watch and learn, but he didn't want to actually have to teach him. He'd bring him into the office or to the barbershops or taquerias where deals and pacts were made. More could be done for the Mexicans of Corpus over steaming bowls of caldo at the Hi-ho than in smoky rooms with leather chairs, oak tables, and snifters of brandy up in Austin. By the time Rob was old enough to come along, Venancio had learned he had already been softened and spoiled by his mother. There wasn't much he could do to her, however, as she had poured herself into a career in real estate that she'd toyed with before Robin was born as a means of distraction after Maurice wasn't. By the time Robin was five, she'd secured enough deals, often with him on her shoulder or hip, to have her own flourishing business, to have added enough on her own to the Vera empire to make it beyond reproach from Venancio, who was as responsible as she was for not making their son stronger, as he'd been emotionally and mentally absent from the boy's raising.

Perla thought Venancio's distance from Robin was his own way of dealing with the loss of Maurice, but it wasn't. He just didn't know how to be a father to a boy. He certainly didn't know what it was like to be fathered. He just knew how to be taught the way his uncle had taught him, and so he waited until his son was old enough to receive that teaching. He also truly believed that his absence was irrelevant, as he was giving his son the biggest piece of a young life he himself had never gotten as a child—he was giving him a mother, and, as far as he could tell, he was giving him a great one in Perla.

One day, a man came into the office and asked if he could speak to Dr. Vera. Rob watched his dad put down the newspaper he had lazily been reading, sit up, and lean his head in the direction of the wall that separated his office from reception. He rolled over in his high-backed chair to the small closet at the end of the wall adjacent to his desk and opened its door. The closet held two black and white monitors, each of whose screens were split four ways displaying live feeds from each of the exam rooms, the operating room, the waiting room, and reception. He lifted his reading glasses over his eyes and squinted, studying the screen. When he recognized the young man standing at the counter, asking for his time, he smiled and nodded.

Rob couldn't make out what his father saw on the screen, and before he could focus his eyes on the small screens in the distance, the door closed, and his father had scooted his chair back to his desk. He grabbed the desktop and slid his legs underneath, folding his hands over one another in front of him as a knock came at the door.

"Dr. Vera?" the receptionist asked from the other side of the door.

"Come in," he said, affecting great concentration and business.

The receptionist poked her head in the door. Before she could speak, Dr. Vera cut her off.

"Young Mr. Arriaga?" he asked without looking at her.

"Yes, sir. He says it's a personal call."

"I know it is. He had work done very recently. He still owes me money for it, in fact. Tell him I'm busy right now, but I may be able to see him between patients."

"Yes, sir."

When she was gone, Venancio looked down at Rob who was reading a book at the chair in front of his desk.

"Do you know why young Mr. Arriaga is here, Robin?"

"No, sir."

"Take a guess."

"To pay you the money he owes you?"

"No, mijo. He owes me more than he can pay at once. As I recall, he's a few days late in making his last payment. That's something he'd put in the drop box."

"To bring you the payment and apologize for it being late? I've seen people do that."

"No. Wrong again. You've seen people do that, but they only ever do that when bringing in their last payment. When they owe me money, they never show their faces around here, especially if they're late like him."

Venancio looked at Rob and was pleased to see the boy sit and consider what the answer could be. He looked like he was doing complex math in his head. He looked up at his dad with a shrug. Venancio couldn't help but laugh.

"Unless he broke a tooth opening a bottle, he's here to ask for more money."

Robin nodded. This made sense. He sat up in his chair, waiting for Mr. Arriaga to come in and prove his father right, but his father just slumped back down in his chair and went back to reading his newspaper. He reached ahead on the desk to where his coffee mug was. Rob could hear the slow sip and gulp of his father savoring his drink.

"Get me another," Venancio told his son from behind the newspaper.

Rob went back into the lounge and refilled his father's mug with coffee and two splashes of whole milk, making it without much effort into the exact right shade of brown his father liked. When he came back into the office, he placed the mug where the mug was supposed to go. His father, not putting down his newspaper, seemed to wait for Rob to sit down before reaching out for the mug, grabbing it, taking a sip, and letting out a slightly satisfied "ahh" that was the only indication he ever gave that Rob had done well.

Rob squirmed in his seat at the excitement of being involved in a new game with his father. He couldn't wait for Mr. Arriaga to come in and either ask for more money or not. He believed his father was right because he was always right. Even his wildest and weirdest estimations of what people were doing and why were almost always right. But he usually only pronounced them aloud to himself, rambling about someone's motivations or the causal chain of their machinations, ending his thoughts with his final assessment of a given situation. His two most common diagnoses of these situations were ". . . trying to use me" or ". . . trying to fuck me."

Rob was excited to see which of these would be the situation, but his excitement waned as he realized that his father wasn't just settling into his new cup of coffee or finishing an article in the paper before calling Mr. Arriaga in. He was wasting time. He was making the man wait. Initially, his satisfaction at seeing how this situation would play out was delayed, upset Rob. Venancio sat there just taking his time sipping and reading. Every time he would sit back to manipulate the newspaper, opening it up and folding it back or down to get to the continuations of stories and shuffle the pages to get to whole new sections of the paper, Rob would sit up thinking that surely this was it.

It wasn't until Venancio pressed the button on the intercom box on his desk to tell the receptionist, "I have few minutes for Mr. Arriaga now," that

Robin realized what was really upsetting about the situation. When Arriaga came in, he looked pained to even be there. He was thrown off by the fact that there was a young boy in the room.

"I have my son with me today," Venancio mentioned, waving away any concern Arriaga may have had at the boy being there, disregarding any of the shame or stress being added to the situation by having to make his case in front of the kid.

Even though he was drifting into and out of Spanish, Rob understood most of what the man was saying because he was using Spanish in a way that aided his conveyance of his truth, unlike Rob's parents, who used the language to hide the truth from him. Arriaga talked about being laid off. He talked sadly about past due bills and having to move his family in with his mom. He apologized for falling behind on the payments. Then he got optimistic. He talked about a new opportunity. He said he just needed money for clothes and a haircut. He said he could be done digging ditches. He said he could actually get a job inside, at a desk.

When Arriaga was done talking, Venancio just nodded. He made a show of getting up slowly from his desk, and after reaching back for his wallet, he rolled his shoulder in its socket and winced like the act of reaching back for his personal money had aggravated an old money-lending wound. He pulled out two limp bills and held them out over the desk for Arriaga to take. Before Arriaga reached them, Venancio pulled them back and restated the terms of the first loan. He put the bills down on his end of the desk, sat down, and pulled a ledger book out from one of the desk's drawers. Arriaga stood there, still reaching for the bills that weren't there anymore for a moment. Then he awkwardly put his hands into his pocket.

Venancio showed him figures in the book, wrote down new numbers, and held the bills out again. Rob couldn't see Arriaga's face, but from where he was sitting, it looked like Arriaga was hesitant to reach out and try to grab the bills again. Venancio nodded at him, and Arriaga grabbed the bills. Before he let go of his grip on the bills, Venancio gave a warm smile and said, "Good luck, mijo. I know you can do it."

When Arriaga left, Venancio didn't pick the newspaper back up. Instead, he looked right at Rob and asked, "What did I tell you? More money. That's the only reason he would show up back here. More money."

Rob nodded, no longer caring to be included in this game.

"Why did I give him the money?" Venancio asked.

Rob looked down at the bottom of his father's desk. The front of it led down to about three inches off the ground. Rob could see that the cleaning lady's vacuum couldn't reach under the ledge, and the way the fluorescent lights overhead fell on the desk; Rob could see that the carpet under the desk was markedly different than could be seen on the ground in front of it.

"To help him," Rob offered, knowing he was wrong but not caring to be perfunctorily right.

"He owes me $237. Why would I let him borrow two hundred dollars more if he's already delinquent in his payments?" Venancio was smiling big, unable to hide his excitement at an opportunity to teach his son a lesson.

"Because he has a job interview. He can get ready for his job interview and get his family out of his mom's house. So he doesn't have to dig ditches anymore."

Rob had not yet developed his own personal set of values. He had not yet had to wrestle with ethics, to compromise his values or pervert those ethics through twisted junky logic so he could justify lying to this girl (or on an occasion or two, this guy) for a warm bed, a midnight snack, and a breakfast in the morning or stealing from this friend, acquaintance, or stranger for money to chase a fix. That would come later. This was 1985. Rob was just shy of eight years old, and all that he knew of right and wrong was what his father had laid out as being the right (usually weak) thing to do and why it only made sense to do it sometimes. All that Rob knew of the moment he was in was that he didn't like what his father had done to Arriaga—not the money lending or even the self-serving reasons for lending it—by making him wait and toying with him in the office.

"No, son," Venancio was using the voice he used when he repeated something to Rob, thinking Rob hadn't understood something but really not understanding that what was happening was that Rob just didn't agree with him. "It's nice that I can help him. Helping people is good, but what I did there was make an investment. An investment is money you put into a project hoping that it yields returns. The interest he'll pay me on the money I loaned him is nice, but he's the investment. He'll get this job. He'll get insurance. He'll move out of his house and be able to come in for checkups, bring his kids in too, instead of just coming in when a toothache is about to turn septic and kill him like the last time he came in."

"So, he's an investment," Rob said.

"Yes. Exactly."

"And you give him money so he can give you yeel?"

"Yield. Yes."

"And you only invest in what you know will yield?" Rob was looking directly at his father, but his father had already lost interest in the conversation. He had taken out his planner and was marking off what he had already done and what he still needed to do that day.

"Of course," Venancio didn't look up. "That's called smart investing."

"What if he needed help and you didn't think he could pay you back?"

Venancio had returned to his newspaper and didn't bother to put it down as he said, "Then that wouldn't be a smart investment, would it? But the Arriaga boy, he's a good, smart kid, and a hard worker. He's a sure thing."

"And if he wasn't, you wouldn't help him because he wouldn't yield for you. You don't help to help. You help so that it will yield."

Venancio put his paper down and looked at Rob like he always looked at him, like he was condescending to address a bother on any terms other than his own. "Well, I'm not in the business of giving money away, am I?"

"I thought your business was fixing teeth."

Venancio looked annoyed now. This was new for Rob. He had been looked at in only a handful of ways by his father, and none of those ways held Rob in focus. Venancio had never looked at Rob in any way that attempted to reckon with the boy who stood before him, the person he'd made. Rob had, at that point, only been a set of implications about Venancio, about the man he was and the kind of man he wanted to raise, about what it meant to have a son and what that meant about him not having had a father. But the annoyed look Venancio flashed at Rob, tinged as it was with the danger of an as-yet unprecedented reprisal, transformed Rob in the eyes of his father in a manner in which he had only recently been transformed in his mother's. He had transcended by arguing with his father as he had by displaying a natural talent to his mother. He became more than a reflection of his father's ego, more than just an opportunity to right the perceived wrongs done unto him by a world that seemed to have it in for him, just like he became more than just a corporeal reminder of a spirit that died when the rest of her world died upon his birth. Rob, for the first time in his life, had been seen, and he decided then that he would never not be seen again.

"Of course, fixing teeth is my business. I don't do that for free, do I? I have very generous payment plans. I make my services available to anyone who needs them, but I don't work for free." Venancio squinted his eyes at the challenge in front of him, but he didn't seem to recognize the shape of what was coming. How could he? The boy had never talked to him like this.

"You don't work for free unless Channel 3 is here to cover it, right? Because if you do that for free, everyone seeing it on the news and thinking you're nice enough to do it for free is a yield, right? That's why you did something nice, so people could think you did something nice."

"Those kids needed that work!" Venancio wasn't used to having to raise his voice, not in his dealings with his employees or his customers, not in trying to build or peddle influence. He looked more puzzled at the agitator in front of him than angry at the agitation.

There had been two kids, brothers—one eight and one ten. They'd been kidnapped by their father from his estranged wife. They'd been missing for four years, found on a ranch east of Bishop, TX. Their father, crazy and paranoid, hid them in a barn, feeding them only junk food. It was all over the news when a state trooper ended up in a shootout after a high-speed chase that had followed what would be a routine broken tail light stop. The boys were reunited with their mother. Hope prevailed. Venancio offered his services, just as others had theirs, to help the boys. Sure, there were cameras, but the boys, their mouths full of all that decay. Venancio could have bought a Corvette if he'd billed out all the work he did.

"So, you'll do that for any kid? Anyone who needs it? For free?"

Venancio was done with being shocked at his son's challenge. He stared hard at the boy, boiling in his contempt. Rob maintained the same inquisitive look on his face, playing precocious and curious when he and Venancio both knew he was actually being something else entirely. At least the boy was giving that much. At least he was playing innocent, hiding his disrespect behind that. At least he had enough respect to hide his disrespect.

"I need to get ready for a procedure," Venancio told Rob. "Take your book and wait in the break room."

Rob took his book and went into the break room, which was one door over across the hall. He sat at the round table with his back to the door, listening to hear his father walk down the hallway to the exam rooms or operating rooms that were down the hall beyond the break room. Rob didn't hear him go back to any of the rooms, at least not in the twenty minutes he spent sitting there pretending to read before his mother came into the break room to pick him up unexpectedly.

Rob always loved it when his mother would pick him up from the office before the end of the day. Even if she was taking him for a haircut or dragging him on a shopping trip, anything was better than the boredom of the office where he wasn't allowed to bring his guitar. Driving home, Perla looked at Rob quizzically, seeming to try to formulate a question about what had happened, but she couldn't figure out what to ask. It was almost as if she didn't really know the person she'd be asking. Rob liked this, as being his own person was new, and it was better than being a ghost.

• • •

It was easier with Perla. In fact, it had been effortless. Perla had always loved music. She loved the ranchera music she heard at home and spilling from the window-perched radios in her neighborhood as a child. She loved the honky-tonk her father and grandfather would listen to when playing dominoes with their friends. On good nights, nights when he'd been paid or when he'd won money betting on games or playing cards, her dad would sit her on his knee and ask her to sing a song. She'd play shy and act like she didn't want to, and he'd laugh and beg her please, then she would sit tall and belt out the only lines of the song she knew:

"I've got a feeling called the blu-ooh-hoos, since my baby said goodbye. Lord, I don't know what I'll do-ooh-hoo. All I do is sit and sigh."

She knew the next couple of lines but could never get them out for her father and his friends laughing and him squeezing her, kissing her, and telling her what a good girl she was. She enjoyed that little bit of spotlight the music afforded her, sure, but it was the feeling of making her father something close to proud that made Perla get up any time they asked her to sing and dance and be cute. It was that feeling that made her listen to the radio as closely as possible in order to pick up new scraps of songs to use in her little performances.

But that music was his. Perla interacted with it, used it to connect with her father and his friends. This was because even at that early an age, she could sense in her parents, her father in particular, feelings of disappointment that she'd been born female, that she'd been born as her. Her father's eyes lit when they gazed upon her male cousins, even the neighborhood boys, the sons of his friends already excelling in school or sport, or already having dropped out of school to work and help bring home money to the family. Her father looked at them as if assessing prospects for future sons-in-law, for the son he always wanted and would eventually get through his daughter when the time came.

Perla's tributes to her father, to the kind of love and respect she wanted from him, were the Hank Williams blue notes and Javier Solis booms and belts she would employ while sitting on her father's lap, or the shuffling atop a barroom table when her mother would send her in to bring him out where she would have to negotiate his departure from the bar by getting up and singing one for the room. But something happened to Perla, to all of her friends and all the youth of America when she was seven that would transform music for Perla from a tenuous link to a father whose attention and affection were adrift not only for her, she would later realize, but for his entire domestic life, into a portal out of the west side of Corpus Christi, TX and to a whole world of art and expression. And when she saw those mop-headed boys, all smiles and shy yet cool, on TV, she understood why the girls in the crowd were screaming, crying, and fainting because for once music, commerce, was being made for her. Those British boys looked down the barrel of the camera and into Perla's eyes and heart, and it didn't matter that her parents scoffed it off and didn't understand it. They didn't need to understand it. It wasn't for them. It was for her.

Rob didn't have any memory of his childhood home that wasn't set to a soundtrack dictated by his mother's tastes and record collection. Before Robin and Maurice would even have developed ears in utero, much less the ability to hear—Venancio let her know about his—Perla was spinning her *Bee Gees* album on the hi-fi, clutching at her still pre-bump belly and swaying to the tunes. As her pregnancy progressed, Perla took to opening the headphones, stretching out the headband to fit on her belly and play directly to her growing boys.

A month before she was due, the "How Deep Is Your Love" single was released. Over that last month of her pregnancy, Perla had abandoned most of her record collection in favor of playing the song over and over. She'd blare it through the headphones, keeping one held down to her belly and the other held up and playing at her.

"How Deep is Your Love" became one of Perla's own greatest hits as anytime it, the Bee Gees, disco or the '70s, pregnancy, Robin's actual name, or musicianship came up, she would tell the story of the last of her pregnancy and include the single, the Bee Gees, and the names. It was one of a handful of stories Perla would use in the personal mythologizing she did when recounting her life.

There were stories of a loving but fatally flawed father, of his deep affection for and disappointment in Perla—because that story, just like all the others, served to paint a picture of a childhood that was simultaneously ideal and traumatic. In telling those stories, Perla could frame herself as being simultaneously the victim and hero in an epic, which provided her with the only character currency she thought mattered: virtue and misery.

Depending on the given situation, Perla might tell the story of her love of music—her father, the bar, the drunks all cheering and giving her nickels to put in the candy machine that was only ever stocked with Boston baked beans. "To this day, if I eat or even see those little red candies," she'd always culminate the story by saying, "I think of the smell of cheap beer and whiskey . . ." Or she'd tell the story of her father teaching her to drive—how patient and kind he was, how he didn't even get mad at her grinding the gears—but she'd always make sure to end her telling of that story or any other by anchoring it to one of her life's tragedies.

"He taught me when I was ten. I was tall enough to reach the pedals, and times were different then. It was so I could drive him home when he was too drunk," she'd say, setting up the crown jewel of that particular story and her teen years and young adulthood, when she'd learned her misery could be worn like a badge of honor:

"And he wouldn't always let me drive home, even if he was too drunk, and I wouldn't argue with him because if she taught me nothing else, my mom taught me not to argue with a drunk. Well, what do you know? One night, when my father went out to the bar, he decided not to take me. My cousins were over, and he decided not to pull me away from them. He hit a truck head-on on his way home that night. He died and took a young couple with him. I truly don't know if it was a blessing that I didn't go or if I could have saved his life that night. I could have saved that young couple too. But who knows? I might have gone, and he still might have insisted on driving. He might have taken me too . . ."

She would always end her telling of these stories with a pause. Sometimes, tears would come to her eyes. Every time, however, she would pause for effect. She would tease out and relish in the oncoming, "Oh, I'm so sorry" or "How terrible that must have been," that her audience would give her. To Rob's trained eye, she was pausing for just these utterances of sympathy or consolation. As he saw it, she didn't only tell the stories again and again for those responses, but for her to be reminded of the gravity and weight of what had happened to her, as if she needed to have the impact it all had on her life justified anew with every new telling. He would realize, later, that she wasn't trying to project virtue and misery-tempered strength; she was trying to convince herself she had them.

While Rob never felt or acted like a "mama's boy" like he sometimes heard his father accuse his mother of trying to make him, he had become initially inured to his mother's stories and the desperate way in which she told them. That similarity, however, between both Perla and her memories, eventually led Rob to resent her as much as he did her stories. At least that's what he thought at the time, what he thought he felt, but he couldn't really understand at all.

He would look back later at himself and his mother, each taking refuge in the other. It was never the stories that bothered him, with their expectant beats and tones; it was the desperation underneath them. Why did she need so badly to be validated, to be heard and seen? So absent was his father in his own day-to-day emotional life that it didn't seem remarkable to Rob growing up that he was absent from Perla's too. He couldn't see the loneliness of Perla being emotionally neglected, only the cloying need that it created in her.

Of course, he couldn't see it. He wouldn't be able to until it was too late, and his own story of misery would begin to form in the regret of realizing it too late. He wouldn't share the story like his mother would have, not for currency or for anything else. He'd save it, pack it away in his subconscious to bring out in his own lonely times when he knew he would otherwise have been able to call and talk to his mother, to listen to her retell one of her old greatest hits. He would always have the story and every memory of his mother to take out and torture himself with. He didn't realize he was doing it, but while he wasn't using the misery to self-mythologize, he was definitely using it to self-flagellate because when it's too late to make use of real love, when you can't use it to make you good, you can always use it for self-torture. While Rob was too flawed to be truly virtuous, he could wallow in his flaws and find virtue in knowing—in hating himself for knowing—that he was no good. So, as his mother had shared her stories to reconcile the suffering of her past with the eventual comfortable success she'd find and, thereby, validate her deserving the life she got, Rob kept his under his hat. In his life, he'd always come by love with ease—whether it was because of his privileged upbringing or his musical gifts. Finding the kind of disgust he felt for himself in the world around him was more elusive, but he didn't have to look for it because he kept it there, under his hat with the memory of and longing for a sad mom and the handful of stories she would share over and over in the hope that they would be heard and eventually matter because they had to matter. Her pain had to matter. It just had to. Even if her son stopped listening and came to resent her telling them, her stories would make her pain matter.

Most of the memories of his own obliviousness to his mother's pain and the bounds of her need for him, for anyone, really, but for her son to love her like maybe a son shouldn't have to love his mom but like Rob certainly wasn't cut out for, were right at the surface, ready for Rob to use to hurt and hate himself over.

Perla's favorite story to share was Maurice, and in telling it, she was only ever really telling the story of Robin. Rob's own story started, like so many of his mother's stories started with her own, with a father who was always out of reach, stuck in his head and trying to outrun (or outdrink) a past that had only failed to break him. Like Perla wasn't for her father, Rob wasn't enough for his. In Perla's case, it was a few flukes of biology—an X chromosome where a Y would have been preferred along with a genetic makeup that predisposed her father to needing another drink and another and another in an attempt to quench a thirst that would never die—that made any attempt on her part to connect to her father fall short. For Rob, it was the ripples that were casted out after the first time he pissed his father off, that feeling of being seen, heard, and felt on his own terms. Well, that and the guitar.

After the death of Maurice, Perla fell into a state wherein she simultaneously was in active denial of reality while also wallowing in the pain of it. She poured herself into loving and caring for Robin. She hardly ever let Ben, as only she was allowed to call him, and never in public as he no longer even offered up the diminutive to white customers or community members in acquiescence of their unwillingness to try to pronounce a new name, hold him, which was fine. Ben had no real desire to hold the pudgy, unformed pre-body, or even to learn how to do so.

All of Robin's early milestones filled Perla with a deep sense of loss. When he cooed his first intentional coo—not just gas passing up past his vocal cords—at a month old, Perla was instantly filled with hopeful anticipation of a time when he could say "Mama" or "I love you." But she also felt a new sense of loss, as she would never hear Maurice tell her the same or, worse, that Robin wouldn't have him to talk to, that he'd lost the best friend he'd ever have. Did he miss his brother like she did? Did he feel the same loss when Maurice died? Did something die in him like it did in her?

Every time Rob cried and kept crying even when his obvious needs were met—when he was fed, freshly diapered, and covered appropriately for temperature—Perla was certain that it was for Maurice that Robin was crying out. He'd had him in the womb. They'd had each other. When Robin was born into this world, he would have to have been awaiting his brother's arrival just behind him; he would have to have expected Maurice to join him, to have him at his side, there to face the big, scary world with him. He couldn't have known, just as the doctors didn't, that back in the womb he'd just vacated, his little brother was choking on the umbilical cord they'd shared as they'd shared all of their existence. Any time Robin would cry, Perla knew that if his brother was there—even if it only would have ever resulted in both of them crying—it would have been better because he wouldn't be alone. He wasn't meant to be alone.

Of course, he was crying.

Of course, he was angry and crying all the time.

Of course, he drunkenly attacked his father after being caught sneaking back into his bedroom in the middle of the night in the ninth grade.

Of course, his clothes reeked of marijuana when she pulled them from the hamper.

Of course, he hurt her, was careless with her feelings, and, at times, outright malicious in the things he'd say to her.

Of course, he dropped out of school at sixteen.

Of course, they'd had to put him in therapy, threaten rehab, and then put him in rehab only to threaten to call the police and then bail him out and threaten to not pay for a lawyer or use his father's connections to get him off the hook.

Of course, they got him off the hook.

Of course.

He wasn't supposed to be alone. Maurice was supposed to be there.

However, it was when he started crawling, scooting, really, that Perla was hit so hard as to not know if she could take it. She saw him turn his head and try to swing his shoulders up and over. He'd already been rolling over, and she'd already gotten way too excited about that. Then he managed to get up on his elbows, something he'd been doing for over a month during tummy time and inched his knees forward and his little butt into the air. Perla watched her little Robin as intently as she ever did, and when he started his ambulating, she jumped up and clapped her hands, cheering him on.

"Go baby. Go baby. You can do it," she said while clapping and stifling giggles to not startle him, but then he took off. He inched forward, then did it again, and again and, sure enough, he was scooting across the carpet in the living room. Perla jumped up in elation. It was a small jump, just a couple inches up, but when her feet hit the ground, she didn't feel like her 132 pounds hit the earth, but that the weight of the world came up to meet her with all of its cruel, indifferent force.

At that moment, Perla's mind was immediately bewildered at having to wonder what had happened. It felt like when she landed, she snapped or sprained something, but not an ankle or foot; Perla felt like her whole body, her whole self, had snapped on impact. She was lost in this brief moment's confusion when she realized she couldn't breathe. She pulled her hands to her chest and realized they were numb. She didn't feel the pain of her chest tightening until she looked down at Robin, still happy on the floor, scooting and scooting and babbling his happiness over his newfound freedom.

There he was, free but alone, inching away from her, happy but ignorant of the dangers he was wandering toward. The living room was big. He had plenty of room to roam, but the 180 degrees directly in front of him were floor-length blinds, a standup lamp, and a brick fireplace with iron fireplace tools hanging from a stand that could very easily be pulled down on a baby, unaware of its dangers.

Perla felt dizzy, the corners of her vision blurring. She knew, if nothing else, if she were dying, as she truly felt like she was, she had to get help for Robin. She allowed herself to fall back down on the couch behind her. She tried to calm her breathing, but she couldn't stop her wheezing hyperventilating. Crying for help wasn't an option. She tried and could force no sound. Besides, it was only straining her, and she knew she couldn't pass out. She knew she had to will herself past the devil she felt was sitting on her chest. She tried again to calm herself, but at that point, Robin picked up too much speed in his scooting and thrust his little body too far forward a little too fast and fell face-first into the carpet in front of him.

When his face hit the floor, the pain and panic that had filled Perla were dulled to the point of not existing. Robin lay there for a beat, contemplating what it meant to fall on his face for the first—but certainly not last—time in his life, then erupted into real cries of pain. He lay like that, his face in the carpet and his screams hardly muffled and seemed to realize something was off because he rolled onto his side in search of his mother. When he found her in his eye line, he looked at her confused and scared because the lady who had rushed to comfort him any other time he'd ever cried was there, right in front of him, not moving.

Perla knew she had to act. It hurt her more than the pain of not breathing that Robin was there on the floor, pleading with his screams and his eyes for her to grab him and hold him to make it all better. Ben was just a few doors down the big hallway, but he had accustomed himself to tuning out the cries of the boy to the extent that, by then, when Robin cried in the night in the crib across the floor at the foot of their bed, Ben was no longer just pretending to sleep through it; his deep-sleep breathing remaining steady and undisturbed. Maybe he'd come eventually, but 'maybe' and 'eventually' weren't enough. She allowed herself to sink toward the corner of the couch and swung her dead hand at the lamp on the end table that flanked it. When the lamp hit the wall and fell to the floor, its base didn't break, but its glass shade and bulb within it did.

Robin cried harder now, further confused by and more scared of his mother's behavior. Perla couldn't even consider his new state of fear and pain because almost as soon as the lampshade shattered against the wall and the lamp base hit the floor, Ben cried out from his office, "What the hell was that?"

He had a doctor's air of calm upon entering the room, and his presence relieved some of the weight sitting on Perla's chest. Some air was finally actually entering her lungs. She pulled in deep gasps in painful heaves for only the smallest wisps of air to hit their mark. It hurt, and it couldn't have been pretty, but it was getting better. Ben was there. It was already better.

He immediately went into triage mode, and the relief Perla had initially felt was replaced by an annoyance that bordered on rage at the fact that Ben was trying to talk to her, asking her medical questions she didn't yet have the answer to, all while Robin lay on the floor crying onto the carpet. Ben checked her pulse. He reeled back a bit when his fingers hit her radial artery. He moved up to her carotid as if hoping he'd gotten false data from her wrist. After verifying his first findings, Ben wordlessly left the room.

Perla couldn't hear him walk over to his office. She couldn't hear him grab his leather physician's bag. All she could hear was Robin crying. She focused on his eyes, which were pleading with her, screaming at her in a language that was louder and more real than the words, "Why won't you pick me up?" Her breath was coming back to her. She focused on Robin on the floor in front of her. She could squeeze her hands into fists again, still not able to feel them. She could feel nothing but the heat of her body and the cold of tears running down her face regrouping after having fielded an attack from itself. She pulled her hands up to clumsily wipe them away. The darkness on the periphery of her vision had dissipated, as had the stars sparkling around it. Perla wasn't dying.

Ben re-entered the room with his bag in one hand and his stethoscope in the other. He placed the bag beside Perla and quickly got to the work of getting more diagnostic data on the faulty wife who sat in front of him. Still, he did not pick up Robin. He pulled a tongue depressor out of his bag and, without prompting Perla to open her mouth, checked her airway. He pulled a penlight out from the bag and inspected her eyes, first looking into them, then moving the pen across the front of her face to see how they would react. Finally, he put the penlight down and looked at her. He looked past the distance between the distressed body in front of him and looked the woman he'd fallen in love with upon moving to Corpus Christi to build his empire, the one who had stood by his side as he went from practice to practice, saving money, always scrimping and saving so he could own his own practice, who had lived with him on pot after pot of fideo and beans, the woman who was raising his son, the heir to it all. He wrapped his arms around her and squeezed her gently. He wiped the sweat from her forehead and the tears that had newly fallen on her cheeks and kissed her gently on the lips.

"Robin," she said louder than she thought she could.

Ben looked back at the baby and moved in his direction. When he finally realized the boy was crying, he stopped. He reached into the bag and pulled out a syringe and vial. He drew the contents of the vial into the syringe.

"I'll get him. I'll get him, but you need to rest," Ben said.

Before he could inject her, Perla held her hands up and shook her head hard.

"No. Not yet. Please, give me Robin. Let me hold him. Let me feed him. Before you inject me, let me feed him."

Ben looked back at the baby, then at Perla. He put the syringe on the end table. He picked Robin up tenderly, standing there on the carpet in his own world of love and caring, and attempted comfort for the boy, kissing him and rubbing his back and "Shh-shh-shh-ing" him. He brought Robin to the couch but did not hand him over to Perla.

"Are you sure you can hold him?"

Perla opened and closed her hands, more in an attempt to reassure herself that she could than to satisfy Ben's concern.

"Hold your hands out, palms-up," Ben instructed her. "Now rotate your hands down. Now bend your arms at the elbow."

When Perla did all of these motions, Ben sat down beside her and helped her hold Robin as he fed off her breast. The feel of Robin suckling, the sound of him gulping and gulping and his breath calming brought Perla's body to as close to normal as it would get before Ben injected her with the sedative, and she slept the whole rest of the day.

This is not the story.

It's not a story Perla would tell even though it contained major hallmarks of one of her greatest hits: her being hurt and scared, made acutely aware of her mortality. She was the hero, overcoming physiology and psychology to allow herself to act as boldly as she needed to in destroying a costly lamp. It showed how badly Robin needed his mother, how in the face of the world and the laws of gravity and nature betraying him, all the boy needed was his mother's love and her life essence. It could even be one of the few stories she could share of Ben's love for her and their son—but it was not one Perla ever shared. It hurt too much.

Causally, however, it was the first, or maybe second, act in the story of Robin and his music. Sure, she included the part about Maurice, about the Bee Gees, about "How Deep Is Your Love"—any of her stories after she lost him had to include him, and any story she told about Robin had to include music—but not the second act, the breakdown. She wouldn't tell anyone the story about feeling like she was dying, about Robin scooting and falling and crying, and her desperate swing at the lamp.

She wouldn't tell about Ben's concern, about the fact that he told her she'd had a panic attack and really needed to get help. She wouldn't tell about the psychologist and the Klonopin she was afraid to take but may have saved her life once or twice. She wouldn't tell about how many she found herself taking or how she switched Robin to formula at a time she felt was too early because she knew he shouldn't be getting Benzodiazepines in her milk, but she also knew she couldn't stop taking them. She wouldn't tell about having to white-knuckle getting off of them.

The eventually abused prescription wasn't the only thing that Perla got out of her time in therapy directly after the panic attack. While bedside manner was clearly not one of the man's strong suits, the good doctor, in his inability to have any real substantive conversation with Perla about what she was going through, asked if there might be something she could devote her time to, any kind of distraction from the sad reality of being reminded of the loss of a son while watching another grow and prosper.

"Could you join a club? Maybe get a small job to make some spending money? Have you ever heard of Tupperware?" He hardly looked her in the eyes as he suggested this. He was seeing her as a favor to her husband. He'd already written the prescription.

At this point, Perla wasn't listening to him any more than he was her. She would never have gone back to see him had she not, three months later, taken one of the pills he'd given her when, after putting Robin down for a nap, she felt her chest tighten again. After that, and after she took all the pills and exhausted the refills prescribed to her, she went back, but by that point, she'd already taken the absent-minded advice the doctor had given her. She'd gone back to the last agency she'd worked for as a realtor—she'd sold three houses over a couple of years without much effort, so they were glad to have her back.

She wouldn't tell that part of the story, even though it was integral to the actual happening of it. Instead, she'd pick up the telling of it a couple years later, when she'd opened her own business, but before she'd moved into her own offices. She did everything: writing up contracts, contacting owners and lenders, even working a couple of times to convince Ben to lend some money for their down payments before she could do so herself out of her own money.

She did stagings of homes herself. She had various props for the families coming in—toy playsets to put in living rooms or dens if a family looking to buy had kids, dummy kitchen appliances she'd bought from an old theater that was going out of business in San Antonio. She'd even brought the hi-fi unit she'd listened to the Bee Gees on when she was pregnant, which, by then, had become obsolete but was still fancy, and a guitar she would keep on a stand next to it in a family room that may be too stuffy for a young customer looking for a bachelor or party pad.

Now and then, Robin would pluck away at the strings when she had to work in her home office and would let him join her—it was off-limits to him at all other times on account of an incident with some orange juice-stained paperwork that he never fessed up to. She thought it was sweet, her already seemingly perceptive boy plinking and plucking the strings, sliding his little hand up and down the neck like it was a standup bass.

One day, Perla had to fit the preparations for the next day's open house between taking a young couple to view homes for sale and getting to a different open house—all while lugging a bag of enough toys and snacks to keep Robin mostly sated and distracted while she did her work. Robin was always very well-behaved. He had a calm enough nature in those days before he realized how fun and satisfying trouble could be, so it wasn't too big a burden on Perla to have him around. His presence even managed to be an asset on more than one occasion, when buyers' poker faces were softened by his presence. She turned the TV on in their living room for Robin and gave him a cookie as a reward for having been so well-behaved while they drove the buyers around town.

The room was in utter chaos, or at least as much chaos as Perla ever allowed in her home. Objects from two separate stagings were in different corners of the room. Perla had left them out, as she was about to use one, and she had recently come to the decision that moving into an office space and hiring help were necessary, as her business was certainly booming. She had to run to her office to file her notes and put in the offer from the buyers she'd just left on her schedule, then to the kitchen to grab from the fridge the trays of cookie dough she would put in the oven at the house she and Robin would head to. She took care of all of that and got the cookie trays and Robin's travel bag in the car. All she needed to do was to put Robin in the car and head over to the open house.

When she walked into the living room, she heard the familiar sound of Robin plucking away at the strings of the guitar. She paid no particular attention to the sound because she did not expect it to be music. It wasn't even the sound of the music that made her realize what was happening—it was the intense focus on Robin's face, how he seemed to be communing with the guitar in a way that he never had with her, and she had never seen anyone else be with a musical instrument like that. She stopped in her tracks and did a double-take at the sight of him. Then she caught on to what he was playing.

It was a rudimentary, one-string slide, "duh nu-nu-nu nuh, duh nu-nu-nu nuh, duh nu-nu-nu nuh, duh nu-nu-nu, duh nu-nu-nu," but it was unmistakably "25 or 6 to 4" by Chicago. When Perla realized what she was hearing, what Robin was doing, she jumped back a bit. The simple riff was all Robin had, but he kept at it, even going so far as to try it on a different string, which produced a strange discordance, as the guitar was nowhere near in tune.

More than proud, Perla was impressed. That couldn't be normal. Everyone thinks their kids are special, but this actually was. So previously convinced had Perla been of Robin's specialness, she didn't really think too deeply about how monumental it was that he, four months shy of his third birthday, could play like that by ear. She was proud, of course, but she didn't know yet what that moment foretold. She didn't know what it meant about Robin's connection to music, his preternatural ability at it. Right there, in the same room where Perla had her first panic attack, on the same floor he had fallen down onto, Robin revealed to his mother something too big for her to see. The moment was special, sure; he was special, though that had never been in doubt; but Robin had revealed to Perla what his destiny was meant to be.

It was music. Of course, it was. She'd named him and his brother after musicians, twins who were part of a family that created sweet beauty in a bitterly dark world—a world of fools, breaking them down. She'd played the music right into her belly. No day went by when she didn't play music— Bee Gees, Frampton, the Beatles, Freddie Fender, Chicago—of course, it was music. Robin had a gift, and Perla had given it to him. The Beatles gave her the world in 1963, and she had turned around and given it to her son. There in the living room, at the foot of the fireplace, Robin was showing her on that untuned guitar that he'd received it.

"I came into the living room," Perla said, "and Robin was playing—"

"Mom." Rob's tone was harsher than most people were used to hearing when directed from a son to a mother, and sometimes he forgot to soften it around outsiders.

Heidi, the girl Rob had brought home to take back to his room one afternoon when he thought his mother would be in the office, shot Robin a look that said that no matter how punk he wanted her to be, no matter how hardcore she was in dress or spirit, some lines shouldn't be crossed like he'd crossed with his mother. If she'd only known.

"Fine. Fine, ROB. Rob was playing the guitar. It was a song by Chicago, do you know Chicago?" When Heidi shook her head, Perla continued, "They were one of my favorite bands. I played them all the time. It was a song by Chicago, '25 or 6 to 4,' a real rock and roller."

Rob wanted to die just then. He'd told his mom he was going to play some songs for Heidi, which he might have at some point, but that really wasn't the plan. Perla seemed to take his mention of music as a cue to make the moment about herself. She didn't mention the couple they'd taken to tour homes before or the open house they were late to after. She just said, "Back when I was starting my business, I had all kinds of stuff here at the house because I hadn't bought my offices yet. For young customers, I had a hi-fi and an old guitar I'd put in homes," and off she went.

"And I was just floored when I came in and Robin, ROB, Rob was playing the song. He was two. Two! Can you believe that?"

Heidi looked at Rob with real affection in her eyes. If he had let her, his mother would have sealed the deal for him that afternoon like he had for her so many times over the course of business when he was in tow. All that Rob could feel in that moment was heat behind his neck and ears, anticipating that his mother was about to go into the story of his name.

"I can't, Mrs. Vera. It's pretty impressive," Heidi told her.

"I know he doesn't like that old music now. I mean, he's so good at guitar I can't even believe he ever started with that song. But that's what he had around him, those oldies—Chicago, The Beatles, the Bee Gees. Did you know that's how Robin got his name? I bet he didn't tell you that."

Again, Heidi looked over at Rob. It was still affectionate, but now it was playful too. Rob, however, did not feel playful. He felt exposed and judged and pushed to the edge because even then, at sixteen, it wasn't often that Rob wasn't in control of almost any situation he was in. Having heard the story, again and again, Rob waited for his cue.

"Well, like I said, all of those old bands, they just meant so much to me. I would listen to records any free chance I got when I was young. I used to sing songs for my dad and his friends. He would sit me on his knee or even stand me on a table, and I would just sing big and loud for anyone who cared to listen. My dad didn't make much money, but he went to Montgomery Ward one day and bought me a suitcase record player that I just adored. He bought me a couple of children's records and a Hank Williams record. It may have been the happiest day of my life, except when Rob was born, of course." She lied there. Of course, she did. The story sounded better that way.

"I still have that record player. But by the time I was pregnant with

Rob, it was all busted up, and the arm had fallen off a couple times, so when it broke off again, Dr. Vera, Rob's dad, said he would get it fixed. When he came home that night, he said he wasn't able to get it fixed. He said they no longer had the part. I was crushed. I actually cried. But right behind him was a delivery truck. We were always scrimping and saving up so he could open his own office, but he went out and bought me a beautiful hi-fi record player. I fell in love with all of my music all over again, listening and listening to them over and over on the new, fancy system.

"When I went to my three-month checkup, the doctor heard two heartbeats. It was twins. I remembered an article I'd read in *Rolling Stone* about the Bee Gees, who I had liked well enough, but this was right before *Saturday Night Fever* when they blew up huge. I remembered it, and when their next single came out, I bought it and couldn't stop listening to it, over and over. I loved it. I looked at the liner notes. The twins were Robin and Maurice. So, the names. . . . It just felt right.

"I just loved the song so much, so I bought all their old records, even ordered a couple from the store that hadn't been released in America. I became obsessed, and I just listened to that song over and over. I would listen to it on the nice speakers, but so that my boys could love it too, I plugged in the headphones and put them right on my belly and played "How Deep Is Your Love" over and over for my Robin and Maurice."

"Maybe that's why Maurice killed himself in there." Robin looked hard into his mother's eyes and pointed to her belly. "Maybe he heard that piece of shit dickless disco ballad one time too many and decided to hang himself with the umbilical cord."

This was supposed to be the part of the story where Perla would have mentioned Maurice, mentioned the tragedy of losing him briefly, and emphasized how lucky they were to have Robin, 'Rob,' she would have remembered to call him this time. She would have likely gone off to the office or to a home or to meet prospective buyers, but she just stood there gut-punched, her eyes pouring like faucets that were turned on at the exact moment Rob finished his attack.

Robin walked out of the kitchen where they had all been standing around the island counter for his room where his guitar, drugs, and bed were. Shocked, Heidi had no choice but to follow him. She seemed to shake off the stupor of having just seen a boy crush his mostly pleasant mother in two sentences. She grabbed Rob by the shoulder and spun him around.

"What the fuck was that?" she demanded.

Rob just pointed in the direction of the room they'd just left, unable to talk for his fury at her having made him do what he just did. If he'd been crying like he was minutes away from being, maybe Heidi might have spared him. She certainly wasn't going to fuck him, not anymore, but perhaps she wouldn't have done what she ended up doing. But he wasn't crying. He had an angry fire in his eyes when he pointed with all of his impotent fury at the wall that separated them from the kitchen and stammered an angry, "Fuck. Her!"

Clearly, at that moment, Rob's words failed him. His emotions had just failed him, so had his ego. If he could see past the anger he didn't understand, past the sadness that undergirded it like it did with everything else he did, he could explain why what she was doing led to what he said, why her robbery of his own ability to write his own story, to be his own person, pissed him off and made him so weak that he felt the need to hurt. If only. He didn't really have that in him. He just had failure upon failure at being someone he wanted to be, someone he wouldn't look back on later and hate. He had that, and a failure to see Heidi's overhand right coming at him and knocking him down and, for a moment, out.

From the ground, Rob could hear Heidi storming out. She stopped at the kitchen for a beat, and, for all Rob could tell, she could have hugged his mother or stood and waited for words that wouldn't come, but he'd never know. He'd never see Heidi again. She was a singer in a punk band, a high school dropout who lived and breathed her music and the lifestyle that surrounded it, who had the words 'FUCK' and 'YOU' tattooed across her fists with a needle and some Indian ink and had inserted safety pins into the cartilage around her right ear by hand, and she was still disgusted by how Rob had treated his mother.

Rob pulled himself up and slammed the door to his bedroom behind him. He looked at himself in the mirror above his dresser and saw a thin stream of blood tracing the left side of his face. It wasn't the blood. It wasn't the pain of being hit or the realization that he'd made a complete childish fool of himself in front of Heidi that made him cry. He knew how badly he had hurt his mother, and he knew that it wasn't because of any story about his name or how he learned to play the guitar.

What made him act that way? What pain or emptiness was there in him that made him lash out? He'd heard his mother's excuses for him before. He knew she chalked it all up to that first loss. But that loss was hers. Maurice was her dead son more than he was ever Rob's dead brother. He was just another story that Rob had gotten tired of hearing. But could that have been it? Could he have been set up to need to burn the world down around him from birth? Rob didn't know. He wasn't really trying to figure out who he was; he was already too wrapped up in hating himself to try to figure out why.

When he brought Maria home for the first time, Perla shared the story, of course. They all sat in the living room, having coffee after a big dinner. The guitar was there, and Rob didn't realize how unarmed he had been made—either by Maria or by time having passed or by both, plus the fact that he was feeling light in the place where he used to feel so much darkness. He walked over to the guitar that hung from the stand in Perla's Rob Shrine Corner—there were three separate framed letters and the envelopes that had once contained them naming Rob among many other songwriters and producers as a nominee for Grammys (each for hip-hop songs that had sampled his playing and had obligatorily named him as a co-writer). There were also clippings from the *Corpus Christi Caller-Times* weekender sections which mentioned Rob as being a native of the city when he visited, and one feature done in the *Caller-Times* about Rob and the band he'd quit conservatory in San Francisco he got to tour with. He picked up the guitar, and got to quick, easy work, tuning it by ear. He strummed a few simple chords.

"My god, this is a shitty guitar," he said, not looking up from his noodling.

"Oh, hush," Perla said. "It was only ever meant to be a prop."

Rob chuckled here. He stopped his playing, fluid and intricate as it ever was on any guitar and plunked out the opening riff to "25 or 6 to 4." Here, he looked up at his mother. The warmth of how loved he made her feel in that moment was a kind of warmth he hoped he could keep kindled and stoked forever in the hope that some amount of it might retroactively erase how unnecessarily cold he had been to her in the past.

Perla gasped sharp and short and pulled her open palms to her chest like she was trying to squeeze the memory. Her eyes watered, and happy chuckles bounced her shoulders up and down. She caught Maria sitting in the spot, albeit on a new couch several living room furniture iterations later, where she'd collapsed three decades earlier and fought against brain and body in rebellion to gather the strength needed to smash a lamp.

"Do you know that song?" Perla asked her.

"I've heard it before, I think. On the radio, maybe."

"When Rob was only two years old, I came in here and heard him playing that song. It's a song I used to listen to a lot—Chicago, the band, they're one of my favorites. And I guess he just picked it up. That's when I knew he was special."

Rob kept playing, not turning to look at his mother or the woman he knew he loved, but whose future with him remained a scary, exciting mystery. "It's about doing so much coke you don't know what time of night it is," he said over his shoulder.

"Robin!" Perla said in play admonition. She held her hands over her mouth like a child might at accidentally cursing in front of her parents. Maria ignored this.

"What?" Rob laughed. "It was the seventies."

Perla looked relieved. "He's right. It was from the seventies. I had the biggest record collection. The biggest. I'd collected since I was a kid. I still have all of them. Most are in storage. I keep some here even though I haven't had a turntable in the house in years. Music meant so much to me. I would listen to records every day and night. I knew I was playing it for him, but I didn't know he would pick it up like that. He was two!"

"Well, that's how you got his name, right? From a band? The Bee Gees?" Maria wasn't trying to endear herself to Perla; she wasn't trying to do the hard work of making Perla love her son any more than she did—and she loved him with all of her heart—or to make Rob feel at all worthy of that love. She was just continuing the conversation with all of her cards on the table and with her heart open to the possibility of love happening, not because she necessarily needed to be loved, but because she'd lived a life that made her constantly hunger for evidence of love, true and uncomplicated, existing in the world.

Perla was stunned. She turned to Rob, and the silence of her anticipating his gaze made him turn to face her. He gave her a look and half a shrug that said, "Sure, I told her" and "It's not a big deal" and "Of course, I told her. I love her." Maria would always remember Perla as having been kind and warm, but it was that moment, after Rob gave her that shrug, that she would recall as having been when Perla stopped treating her like a welcome guest, another girl, not unlike the weird-looking ones with crude tattoos and too many holes in their faces he would bring back when he lived in town, and started treating Maria like a daughter.

"He was a twin. I didn't know he told you that. When I found out I was having twins, I already liked the Bee Gees enough, but I found out that two of them were twins. How silly is that? Naming your kids after band people? And the Bee Gees! But I was young, and it felt right.

"But it wasn't just that they were twins and two of the Bee Gees were. When I was more than halfway done with the pregnancy—it was summer, I was carrying around twins, I was miserable!—I was really trying to do anything I could to keep peace of mind. So, I would go to the record store and get new singles and albums of bands I liked. There was a song, 'How Deep Is Your Love.'"

"I know that one!" Maria was hanging on every of Perla's words. "My mom loved the movie."

"Yes! The movie. This was before it even came out. I just loved the song so much. It sounded to me like a song for me and my boys. Like they were this blessing that was going to come, and they were going to save me, and I was going to love them, and even if the whole world was against us, I'd love them forever."

Perla was invigorated by the prospect of being asked to tell the story, by having an audience request a golden oldie. Maria sank a bit into her seat and couldn't hide her tears for the brother and mother she never had, for a woman who needed her as a blessing and a savior, who would have fought the world for her. Rob stopped playing. He couldn't hide behind his music or even hold the guitar up to cover his heart. He'd never heard this part of it.

"I truly fell in love with the song. I was obsessed with it, and it clicked— the twins: mine, theirs. So, I named them Robin and Maurice. And I wore that single out. And even when the soundtrack came out, I just played that song over and over. I would put it on the hi-fi and plug in the headphones."

Rob had to turn away here.

"I would put the headphones on my belly—I probably ruined them, but who cares—and I would play the song over and over and over again for my Robin and Maurice."

Rob, of course, didn't make the same joke. Dick or not, he never really wanted to make his mother cry. He just stared at the wall in front of him. But again, she waited for him to look back at her so that she could show him that she forgave him, that she loved him. Rob didn't feel worthy of such love and forgiveness, but Perla gave it because she had learned that she could look back on all the pain of life and crumble under the weight of its psychic burden, or she could repackage it, dust it off and salvage it from bitter anger and salvage herself from it.

She'd lived the pain of the moments, so now she could look at hindsight's scars and use them to show the world it hadn't beaten her. She'd borne life's slings and arrows, and she'd turned them into strength and love. She chose grace because unanswered "whys" are maddening. Grace was losing and losing and choosing to ignore the score and keep on playing. Grace was telling that story in that living room, and remembering the pain of its last telling, seeing Robin shrink at remembering how he'd hurt her and sinking further when he recognized the memory in is mother's eye, and waiting there like all those nights when he'd go out and come home at all hours, in various states of inebriation, so that she could see him and hold him and forgive him again and again and again, like she did that evening in the soft glow of the living room with his future wife.

"I lost my Maurice, but I got to keep my Robin. My sweet, beautiful Robin." The tears that fell couldn't dampen the smile she beamed at her son.

Rob was frozen in his tracks, the guitar, ridiculous and inadequate, in his hand. He could have scored the moment, but he didn't know how to rise to the occasion. Maria got up and sat right next to Perla on the couch. She put an arm around her, and the woman fell right into her embrace.

"I had a twin too," Maria confessed.

"You did?" Perla asked. "Did?"

"Maybe I do. I don't know. I was born in Mexico. My parents couldn't afford us both . . ."

"Oh, Mija." The Spanish just came to Perla's lips, Spanish she no longer used on a daily basis, as there were now whole days that went by when Ben and she wouldn't talk. "That's just so terrible."

No one ever really understood what to make of the truth of Maria when she revealed it to them. Mostly, they scanned her eyes to gauge how much the truth hurt her so they could give an appropriate amount of pity. Perla sitting there in her own tears, hurting over her own loss, did not hesitate to declare the situation to be as terrible as it was. Maria appreciated this.

"You didn't know them? You don't have your story. I'm so sorry." Perla made a strange swim move where she effortlessly shifted from being sunken in Maria's embrace to where she was the one holding her, stroking her hair, even in one quick motion.

"I'm so, so sorry," she said onto the top of Maria's head. "But let me tell you, I'm more sorry for your mom than I am for you. Look at you— you're a lawyer. You're a strong woman, smart. You went to an Ivy League school, and she doesn't get to see that. It makes me so sad. It breaks my heart because I can guarantee you that she dreams about you. I can guarantee she misses you like a part of her got chopped off, and she dreams about you, imagining what you'd look like and the woman you would be. I'm sorry you went through what you went through. I really am, but my heart just breaks for your mom."

The evening fell apart here. Rob looked over at his mother and the love of his life, the mushy mess they'd made of each other. There was nothing he could say or do for either of them that they hadn't already taken care of themselves. Maria was there, loved and seen like she hadn't been maybe ever, and his mother was there, happy as any woman to use her wisdom and pain to heal someone young and innocent that was in pain.

There was nothing for Rob to do but to take a seat at the end of the couch, opposite the two most important people in his life, put the guitar back in tune, and make the cheap piece of shit sing more beautifully than it had any right to.

SECTION TWO—
SXSW

CHAPTER FIVE—*(2018)*

It had been longer than Rob could immediately recall since he'd been downtown or headed to a show that he wasn't playing in. Despite it making up a large part of his professional life, the main lifeblood of where his money was made, really, Rob hated downtown. He particularly hated it during *South by Southwest*. It was more congested by assholes wearing lanyards and laminates, the colors of which designated in gauche Day-Glo importance whose ass was to be kissed because they were press or industry or just rich assholes in town (they'd been doing it since back in [insert the year when they thought it was still hip and indie but which was well past when the festival had been bought out and co-opted by the same assholes whose ignoring it used to make it special] they'd have you know), more congested even than 6th ever was on a weekend night. 6th had its drunken college kids and "young" professionals/layabouts who were either unaware or in denial of the fact that they were probably too old to be over on 4th or, if they were hipster enough, down on Rainey or up in North Loop. Rob had a clicker in the glovebox of his car that opened the private garage to a studio just off Lavaca and MLK and was lucky enough to have found a spot there. It wasn't too hot out, so he didn't mind walking the mile through the streets that even he had to admit were just a little more alive than normal for a Thursday night.

It was just past early. The sun hung around out beyond the beautiful, blessed part of Austin. It had been hot earlier, but the air forgot that, and the wind that blew up Rob's shirt cooled his sweat-slicked back and let him know the night might just end up being a good one. That was enough, a spring night out on the town, no matter what time of year or what part of town, because Rob needed the night to be good. It had been too long since he'd had a good night. He was going to be damned if Maria was going to be out with her work cronies—which, even if they had been talking and sleeping in the same bed over the last few months, would have meant he wasn't invited (not that he'd go without protest) after the New Year's debacle at her boss's house—while he sat at home.

So, there he was, downtown after having driven through the more-infuriating-than-normal *South-by* traffic, making his way over to Stubb's because he figured there were always enough local artists or producers there or that he could spot a manager or security guy he knew well enough who'd let him in badgeless and unaffiliated. Crossing in front of the state Capitol building on 11th, to Rob's right, downtown bustled with the business of a normal weeknight and the added influx of music, movie, and tech industry people—if Rob needed any reassurance of the fact that *South-by* had died, the Elon Musks and Al Gores and Rand Pauls and Astro Tellers and their hordes of sycophantic disciples were it, like the seat at the table that had always been left open by the artists for thinkers and been overtaken by politicians and influencers there to push their brands, themselves, to anyone willing to have them, and everyone was because that's what the festival had programmed. Rob was too occupied in his phone, scanning his Facebook and Twitter feeds to see if anyone he knew was at Stubb's. He scrolled past plenty of pictures of the week's festivities, but he couldn't find anyone who was there—it was all just white noise of hip and fun and people laying claim to those as what their lives were, what they were.

Rob was scrolling through the contacts in his phone, running down the schedules of friends who were on tour, on vacation, who in his phone might be at the venue, and who might be called upon, texted, for a favor that Rob was willing to indebt himself to ask of them. By the time he got to the venue and looked up from his phone, it was all for naught. Standing outside a door marked "Not an Entrance," smoking a cigarette, was Danny

El, a local producer/engineer/cellist Rob had worked with on more tracks than he could count. He was talking on his phone, busy but not seeming too concerned with the outcome of his conversation. His eyes lit up at the sight of Rob like finally, a real compatriot had shown up to cling to in this sea of wannabes and, worse, real deals who wanted his time and his opinion and his handshake to work on something later.

He reached his right hand out to shake Rob's and, with his left, rotated his phone ninety degrees so that the microphone was up and out of his face. "How's the hand, bud?"

The cast had been removed from Rob's hand, but he still wore a soft brace mostly to inform the world around him that it was hurt so no one would expect too much of it or treat it too roughly. Rob held out his left hand, and Danny grabbed it like they were going to jump off a cliff together and gave it a quick up and down. "Good. I've been practicing. It's sore, but good."

Danny nodded and got back to his phone call. When Rob hung around, Danny pointed a thumb back to the venue, asking if Rob was going in. Rob nodded yes. Danny raised an eyebrow. Rob held his palms up expectantly, showing he needed to talk. Danny lifted the phone up again.

"It's me plus six. I'm showing some kids what it's like to be at shows, what *South-by*'s like."

This amused Danny. He looked at Rob incredulously.

"I'm serious," Rob assured him.

"No problem."

And there it was, a night of fun for a handful of kids and a colleague from Rob's temporary day job, all made in the time Danny finished a smoke and a phone call with an overeager manager. The cool air would have been enough for Rob, but this was now big enough to throw in Maria's face. All of this fun and otherwise kind mentorship could be as good and positive as it was, but that didn't change the fact that Rob was doing it out of spite so he could tell himself he hadn't lost the night.

The Sunday before, in their empty discussion of what the week to come had in store, Maria, tired from having driven over to Humble the day before and back in just over twenty-four hours to be ready for the week, had told Rob that she would be out on Thursday for a "work thing." She hadn't told him specifically what the outing would be—a golf-related outing—just that she'd be out for drinks with people from work. When Rob instinctively told her that he'd be going out too, Maria suspected that Rob was as full of shit as he actually was. She asked where he was going, and he told her a *South-by* show, and Maria knew, she just knew she was right.

"I have a kid at school I want to take," he was quick to say.

"You're taking a kid to a show? Like, alone in your car?"

Rob knew how bad it sounded, so he backtracked and refined his story. "Well, I have one who I really want to show around. He's got real potential, real drive." This was true enough. "I talked to Galindo, and he said it'd be a good little trip for a few kids, not just our guitar guys, but some of his choir kids too. He's going too. I sure as hell ain't driving any kids."

Rob couldn't tell if Maria actually believed him or if she was just done caring. All he knew was that he was not going to be home alone on Thursday night. He would go to work the next day and suggest to Galindo that they take the kids to a show that Thursday, saying that he could pull some strings and get into a showcase somewhere. He would say it was for Benji because he was so into the music. It would all happen as he planned in the few seconds it took him to come up with the lie. He would do all of this so that he could stay entrenched on his side of the fight he was in with Maria.

She was mad at him? She was being cold to him? Fine. That was the name of the game: being fine—fine with splitting the couch, fine with the cold shoulder, fine with feeling alone in her presence. Rob was dedicated to winning. Rob was going to out-fine her.

CHAPTER SIX

U ptown and several worlds away from Stubb's and *SXSW*, Maria had entered a facility and been accosted by the fake, eager enthusiasm of young salespeople in solid grey polos and khaki shorts and skirts. They'd asked if she'd shown up to Topgolf for a party, if she was meeting a group or a date, and if she had a membership because anyone could get a membership for just five dollars, and any group could get a tee box on just one membership. It was too much to deal with, and Maria just took a left away from the entrance to the building and toward the bar. She heard two of the salespeople, both of them likely not able to legally drink yet, scoff, and she could feel their eyes roll behind her.

Maria sat at a fancy cushioned stool at the corner of the bar. She put her arms down on the granite top in front of her and was met with the dampness of it having just been wiped over and the stickiness of the job having been done poorly. All of its fancy tile and wood grain and all of its ten big-screen TVs over the bar playing various sports clips above backlit bottles of fancy liquor, the stink of stale beer in the place and the clientele it served couldn't hide the fact that she was sitting in a dolled up West Campus frat bar—a *Cain and Able's* with golf. It had a full menu of deep-fried food served on oversized, square ceramic plates as if that privileged class of collar-turned-up-on-pastel-Lacoste-polo douchebag had grabbed his diploma and graduated from plastic-jug vodka and flip cup to top-shelf bottle service and respectful silence in their friends' backswings. The bubbly bartender put a coaster down in front of Maria and didn't hide her contempt when Maria asked if she could just get a water.

Maria knew she should look for her work party—they'd agreed to meet there at eight, and it was almost nine—but she sat for a minute drinking from her water and staring mindlessly up at a putting tutorial on the screen directly above her. Her mind was swimming from the work she'd done that week. After any given workday, Maria could close her eyes and see highlighted legalese behind her eyelids. She had dreams wherein stacks of green and maroon paper classification folders would move by some leap-of-dream-logic force that she watched herself 'do' from the right side of her desk to the left, the stack on the left getting bigger and bigger while the stack on her right never diminished. That was all well and good. She had long come to accept and even embrace the Sisyphean nature of her work— it would always be there on her desk and in her inbox, a wave pool she would dive into and swim through but never across. There was a kind of Zen to be found in a constant state of overwhelmedness.

The workweek usually weighed heavy on her shoulders by Thursday. Her neck and collarbone usually ached, and her brain was almost always mush by that point in the week. Sitting stupefied at the bar, the water sitting in front of her sweating a hole into the cocktail napkin underneath it, her co-workers somewhere in the building blowing off steam and drinking away the end of the week, ensuring productivity would be slow to nonexistent the next day, Maria wasn't beaten down by work—work could kick her around over and over without beating her down like this. Sure, there was the situation with Rob. She'd always had him to distract her and draw her out of herself. Life with him was the exact opposite of life at work, and that had previously served to provide her with a sense of balance. After the disaster at New Year's, Maria was left without the stabilizing force of his instability as it contrasted the other half of her life, and it occurred to her that, while her life was previously balanced and whole, she still wasn't.

That was enough to deal with, but after her last visit to Humble, a second visit on consecutive weekends, and after seeing for herself and talking to doctors about just how bad Eunice had gotten, everything was upside down. Rob had dropped his guard for a bit when she said she was concerned enough to drive back over again. When first she announced that she felt like she had to drive to see her mom because something seemed off, he ignored it, but that second weekend, he knew her, as well as her relationship with her mother, well enough to be concerned. The ceasefire was brief, but it was full enough that Rob offered to accompany her on the drive if she needed. She declined his offer. His concern, the yearning affection he conveyed in how he held her exactly how she needed when she was lost in rowing for some scrap of control against squalls of existence's indifference, could have reignited something in her, in them. But she didn't have capacity for appreciating what she should have been able to count on anyway. She was trying to plot potentialities and contingencies—how bad it could be, what kind of help different prognoses would necessitate—to crunch the numbers of cost, both financial and energy-related—how much money was there, if any, of what Thom would have left his wife, all the drives over to Humble and how that would hurt her work and her well-being. But there was no plan, no checklist, no spreadsheet, or color-coded binder that could guard Maria from the simple facts of the matter: her mom was sick, and there was nothing Maria could do short of turning back time and changing her genetics, or turning back time and asking her mom to invest better or differently, or turning back time and undoing all the waste they'd made of it, all the silence, all the anger, all the passive and active aggressions they'd played out in their respective mirror-image self-righteousness. It was too much, and Rob saw that, so he grabbed her and held her like he hadn't in months.

There'd been the nights, the moments of weakness when either of them would make the eyes or sneak a touch or even just slide into their marriage bed on a night that wasn't theirs and abandon all semblance of stillness, somehow holding power on their side of the freeze-out. And this was fine because they accepted the other, they conceded their side those nights, and because they each hungered for the other and all the ways they could express and quench that need. They let their needs burn themselves out in concert before one would leave the bedroom for the couch where he or she would get the first full night of sleep they'd had since the last time.

But this wasn't that. Rob held her in the same tender embrace he'd used when she told him about her adoption, about Eunice lying and Thom dying, about how alone it all made her feel in the world. It was exactly what she needed at that moment. It could have been the guitar, the confidence that his ability and skill instilled in him, and the determined focus his practice and training showed her he was capable of that made her fall in love with Rob, but it was how much he could mean an embrace when she needed it, and how much it could make it all better that made her truly love him—it was what made her look past how his preoccupation with the music could make him withdraw mentally and emotionally, how always dazzling the world around him with virtuosity had enabled Rob to skip some important steps in his communication skills development. But no matter how right it was just then, no matter how deeply she loved him, how stubbornly loveable he was to anyone who had put in as much work as she had, it wasn't enough. It wasn't enough to counteract his flame-out act, the mid-life crisis she didn't even have the energy to name, because he wouldn't have the capacity to step outside of his own perspective to see she was right. It wasn't enough to fix how that had affected her professional life, maybe even her career.

Maybe it wasn't fair to begrudge Rob's love for not being enough, particularly when it wasn't just him that it wasn't enough to fix. It was also her mother's age and neurology and all that about what her impending end meant about Maria and how she had failed as a daughter and what that meant about how Eunice had failed her initially. It wasn't fair, but this wasn't a lawsuit. There was no agreed-upon logic to Rob and his angers and offenses, no law to govern their marriage. She was tired of fair and sensible. Playing fair gave Rob the upper hand.

So, she withdrew from his embrace and told him she would drive over alone. There was still kind love in his eyes when she stepped back. Did he mean that love? Had this crisis put an organic crack in the wall that separated them, or was Rob capitalizing on Maria in her weakened state? It didn't matter. She didn't feel like being the bigger person. She was tired of that.

"Can I get the bed tonight? I'll drive tomorrow. You can have it that night and the one after. I just want good sleep because tomorrow's going to be a long day." In the silence of Rob either re-orienting himself to his wartime posture or trying to search for the exact right words he could say in surrender or negotiation, Maria gave him one more quick shove over to the bad side of the brink. "Or not. Whatever. I just need to get some sleep.

See you in the morning." She walked away from him to the closet in the hallway to grab her pillow and blanket, not turning back to offer Rob the opportunity to give up the bed or his side of the war.

"If you're going to sit at the bar and skirt the party, you might as well be drinking." Joanie took the stool next to Maria, startling but not surprising her. "Two Grey Goose martinis," she told the bartender.

"Make mine gin," Maria told the girl. When an amused look came over Joanie, she explained, "I had a really bad night with vodka, once. After that, I just can't."

Joanie nodded and gave a chuckle. "After a vacation in Puerto Rico, I still can't drink rum. God. That was over thirty years ago."

Maria allowed Joanie her momentary reverie. What else could she do? They sat there in the din of drunken young professionals, the amused smile leaving Joanie's face as she stared out the window at the company party at a tee box, Ken holding court and all the kiss-asses around him falling over themselves to laugh at his dumb jokes just a little louder than all the other kiss-asses around them. When the drinks were placed in front of them, Joanie took a long, measured drink from hers before turning to Maria and speaking.

"He brought his own clubs."

Maria wasn't sure what Joanie was talking about.

"Ken. My better half out there. He brought his own clubs. Can you believe that? That's like someone taking their own fucking microphone to karaoke." She pointed out to the party, to Ken swinging back and striking the ball with a practiced red-faced skill that truly showed the payoff of drunken hour after drunken hour at the golf course.

"I met Rob at a party that had an open mic. He borrowed some guy's guitar and went up and played for 'oohs' and 'ahs.' He used to do it all the time to impress people and show people up. That's how I met him, in fact."

"Well, he's a professional, right? Ken sure as hell isn't a professional golfer." Joanie shook her head at the sight of Ken bounding around to give everyone high-fives after hitting his last shot.

"What's worse? Someone bringing their own microphone to karaoke or a professional singer showing up to blow everyone away and show how much better he is than them?" Maria stared down at the olive at the bottom of her glass and thought of Rob downtown at someone's show, either getting onstage to play or getting his face smashed in after telling someone exactly why and how they sucked.

"What exactly are we doing here, Zarate?" Joanie said the word like she'd never heard it spoken aloud, only read it, rhyming it with karate. "Are we really competing over whose husband is a bigger asshole? You're a talented young attorney, and I'm the CEO of a fucking powerful company. I'm a *millionaire*, for fuck's sake." She whispered the word 'millionaire' like it was a dirty secret. "Surely we've got a couple of personalities to rub together outside of our beloved fuckups."

There was plenty Maria could think to say, but half of them had to do with apologizing for Rob, and the other half had to do with work, hardly cocktail conversation. It wasn't that Maria was necessarily on eggshells around Joanie, it was just that she didn't have much more to talk about than work and Rob, those two halves of what she'd become. Well, there was where she'd come from and what she'd driven to Humble to confront the previous weekend, but that wasn't any kind of conversation to open with. She shrugged at Joanie and had a drink.

"Well, aren't we a fucking pair?" Joanie said. "Do you golf? Would you rather be out there?"

"God, no," Maria said, and the urgency with which she said it pleased Joanie.

"Good. You don't golf, and you don't do vodka. That's a start. I think you might be the only person in legal who doesn't golf, or at least the only person not out there pretending to like golf." Joanie cocked her head in the direction of the party. "That's the real problem—their ass-kissing. It's just dumb that Ken brought his clubs. But Appleman, Melancon, and Campbell out there all brought their clubs too. He's creating a culture of smug douchebaggery, and I'm too tired to try to fight it."

"So, you're saying Ken's an asshole?" Maria asked.

"Ha fucking ha, Zarate. Fine, I'm done. You say something. Why don't you drink vodka?"

Maria thought about the question for a second, then told a story about being a sophomore at Brown, about having a roommate from Pawtucket whose boyfriend would come over to party, about a bottle of vodka she knew was hidden in a cabinet above a closet. She told Joanie about never having drunk before, she'd even diverged to tell the story about the townie boyfriend's pal she used to fuck. She mentioned the three-day hangover that followed her little binge, but not about meeting Kaylee, about their bond and the rabbit-hole she'd fallen down that set her off that first time. They laughed and unwound and ordered another round, content to sit in the stale-beer stink of the bar that they'd both already grown accustomed to, drinking and laughing and playing nice and collegial like one wasn't the other's boss and the other's husband hadn't gotten the cops called to the one's New Year's party.

CHAPTER SEVEN

Galindo stopped in the middle of Red River Street, the traffic of locals fed up with the bullshit extra chore of getting home in *South-by* traffic and taxi and rideshare drivers trying their best to get their fares dropped off as quickly as possible to return back to the feeding frenzy that came alive in its anger at the asshole who stopped, turned on his hazards (the Austin version of the "Texas wave" that allowed you forgiveness for almost any driving transgression as long as you showed that you knew you were wrong), and was shouting out his driver's side window at a man outside Stubb's who looked just as disgusted as they were by the brazen act of self-involvement.

"Where do I park?" Galindo shouted out the window.

Rob couldn't fight his body's instincts to raise his hands at his side in a shrug of surrender. He shook his head spasmodically.

"Have you never been downtown?" he was finally able to shout.

"Well, yeah, but there's so much more traffic. I thought you might know somewhere good, like a VIP or something."

Galindo was so earnest in his presumption that Rob would have some kind of magic insider secret parking tip that Rob drowned out the sounds of cars behind Galindo and drivers pulling around him shouting curses as they passed. Galindo became like a freshman holding his seventy-five-dollar student guitar for the first time. Rob had never had the patience for students when he was paid big money to give lessons to established guitarists—usually self-taught bashers and shredders or, worse, assholes who had been taking lessons since puberty and thought that meant their bad habits and techniques meant something more than extra work for Rob that they would ultimately ignore—but these high school kids were something else. They were blank slates and, outside of their normal teenage bad attitudes about a world that didn't take them seriously enough, had good attitudes about learning, playing, and creating. That was Galindo at that moment, a baby giraffe on wobbly legs in a brand-new world. Rob took a deep breath.

"Just pay to park it under 35. You have cash?" he shouted, taking the time now that he was back in the moment to flip off a car that had parked right next to Galindo for a beat to stand on the horn and shout at the guy who had four teenagers in the car with him.

"Yeah," Galindo shouted back.

"Go. I'll be here."

Rob was leaning against the wall by the exit door of Stubb's, rapt in his phone, checking Maria's Facebook wall, and scrolling around the other dumb corners of the internet he always wandered to, but checking back to her page again and again. She didn't post very often, but her statuses and even the presented-without-comment pictures she uploaded were small glimpses into her day, and that was all Rob needed. He could see a picture of some small scrap of ignorable nothing that caught Maria's eye and know exactly what part of it made her chuckle, spit-take, or roll her eyes. So versed was he in her that they didn't need words to finish each other's sentences because they just needed half a shared point of view to finish each other's snark. The world was a joke, and only Rob and Maria knew all the same punchlines.

She was out, but she hadn't posted anything. This meant she was as bored or uncomfortable as he was then, probably even more so, because at least his night took him out to a world he knew. Hers took her out to a new one she knew she'd hate. Under any other circumstance, Rob wouldn't have been so happy to know she was likely miserable uptown, but after the past three months, he was adrift even though he wouldn't have admitted it to himself, and to have her be any way other than nearly as miserable as he was would have just hurt and soured him even more than his baseline factory settings.

"Hey, Rob." The voice calling came as a surprise to Rob, who was lost in a trip down the memory lane of Maria's Facebook photos. She hadn't posted much since New Year's, but the pictures before then told a story too. She never smiled really. He knew that, but when did he stop making her smile? Rob was expecting Galindo and the kids to come up 8th Street from where he'd sent them to park. The voice that called him came from up Red River. "Am I late?"

"Benji, you're right on time." Apart from the fact that he really liked the kid, Rob was happy to see him because while the story he'd told Maria was that Benji—this great kid who was really good at guitar and really serious about music, all of which were true—was the reason for the night, it was really so that he could run from Maria being gone, from his having pushed her as he had. "You are exactly right on time."

Benji was effortlessly cool. He hadn't put on any airs or costumes for the occasion. He was just the same plain him, soccer t-shirt and jeans with plain shoes. Rob would have liked to look at the kid and say he saw himself as a teen in there, but Benji was self-taught, ferocious in his raw playing, and smart enough to know what he wanted even though he knew he had no real means for getting it. Before Rob heard him play a single note, he appreciated how removed Benji seemed from the trappings of being a teenager when and where he was. Unlike Rob had when he was younger, Benji didn't try for anything that seemed cool and didn't try as hard as he could've, wearing the uniforms of rebellion, buying the leather, ripping, scuffing, and drawing on the expensive clothes his parents bought him so that he could exist as a well-manicured middle finger on an uncalloused, powder-soft hand. Benji was real, and that seemed even cooler in the middle of *South-by* when so many people from all over the world were strutting around like they mattered so goddamn much and so many musicians scoffing at the whole thing like none of it mattered at all.

"It's real cool that you can get us into stuff like this. I've never been to a show downtown." Benji didn't look Rob in the eye for the sensory overload of all the people, many of them beautiful, most of them white, some of whom lived in town, but none of whom were his neighbors.

He looked small at that moment, more teenaged and childlike than

Rob had ever seen him. The center of the city reflected in Benji's overwhelmed eyes took Rob back two decades before in downtown San Francisco, a cheap dorm right on the edge of the Tenderloin, to nights when he would practice or drink until he would blackout from the drink or the exhaustion or both because if he would slow down on either, the reality that he was alone, just sixteen years old, half a country from home, might catch up to him, and the fear that he kept denying might bring about the tears that he couldn't always.

"It's no big deal." Rob wanted to put a hand on the kid's shoulder, to give him some warmth, to let him know without saying that he'd been there before too, that it would all be okay, but he couldn't—not just because he wasn't there yet, wasn't at a place where he could feel like anything other than a fraud or even a creep touching this kid in even the most mentor-like of ways, but because he didn't really know if it would all be okay, and he wasn't a teacher enough yet to know that it was the compassionate thing, the responsible thing most times, to lie and say that it all would.

"I mean, it kind of is. I've never been to a show, much less backstage. Hey, will you take a picture of me by the marquee and, like, email it to me?"

"Sure. Do you want me to take it with your phone?"

"I don't have one. Well, my brother is using it." This was the first time Benji looked away from the world around him and at Rob. He gave a that's-just-how-it-is shrug.

"No problem." Rob took his phone out of his pocket, walked over to the marquee with Benji, and snapped a few shots. He flipped through the shots for Benji, who nodded his approval and gave his email address. "So, you've never been to a show?"

"Not unless you count getting dragged out to *Plaza de Toros* to wade through horse shit to listen to Mexicans in electric blue suits and cowboy hats sing about how beautiful Sinaloa is to a bunch of drunks, but I don't count that. Thanks for the pics."

Rob had stopped assuming what it meant to live in and be from Austin when he had made small talk with a class of beginning guitar students the previous December. Of the twelve of them, only one had been to the annual *Trail of Lights* down at Zilker Park, which was only about eleven miles away but didn't belong to them like it did the rest of town. More than half of them had never heard of or, they didn't think, been to Zilker Park. Only half had been to Barton Springs. Two of them didn't like it. "It's too cold, sir—" Rob hadn't yet broken them of calling him 'sir.' "I swim at my cousin's apartment," one had said.

"Well, Benji, that's no good. That's just no goddamn good."

Benji raised an eyebrow and smiled sideways at this, now knowing Rob enough to know that he wasn't being judged and to see through his pretty cheap ingratiation tool of casual cursing.

"This show. . . . It's the wrong show. It's all wrong for a first show." Rob pulled his phone out and scanned his own Facebook newsfeed to see if anyone posted about any exciting shows to catch that night.

"Nah. It's good. It's exciting. Backstage at a show downtown and all that, I'd never get to do that."

"You're right, you wouldn't. It's going to be fun. Take in the experience. Eat as much barbecue as you can stuff in your gut. But these bands are garbage pop acts trying to act cooler than they are by holding guitars and singing about drugs and fucking. This just won't do." Rob couldn't find anything, but he knew Danny had his ear to the ground and could point him in the right direction for something good.

"I didn't bring much money," Benji said, looking concerned as if all he was listening for were warnings of turns in the night that might reveal him as not belonging.

"Good." Rob put his phone away. "If you spend one red cent at these gigs, you're a sucker. You shouldn't pay to get in anywhere. If the show's not free, you don't need to be there. And these showcases are all about burning money on cheap hype. When we get inside, look at everything that's being eaten and drunk in there—either a label or a management team or both paid for all of it just so the press will come and cover the next big thing, and other labels and management teams will look at the spread they laid out and try to top it at their show up at the Speakeasy or something like that. It's all a big-spending war pissing contest. We're just getting caught in the crossfire. Go in there and eat their barbecue and ice cream. Drink their sodas and branded bottled water. It's not there for you or me, but we get to mop up some perks. It's called swag, and it was called that before rappers started using the word."

Benji seemed to stand taller after Rob told him this. "Is it good barbecue?"

"You know, it's really fucking good barbecue."

Benji lit up at this. He clapped his hand together loudly and rubbed them excitedly. "I would have settled for just kinda fucking good barbecue."

The voices of excited teens shouting for Benji rang out from up the street. It was Galindo and the kids. The eager happiness from Benji's face disappeared, not faking upset or stern like Rob would have at that age but raising his shields like he always expected the world around him to attack, always ready for fight or flight. Rob wished he'd put his dumb hand on the kid's shoulder when it was emotionally appropriate to do so because from where he stood, the kid could stand to be touched by a hand that was obviously not trying to hurt him. The kids did their little slap hands, the kinds that Rob had seen and been taught by kids at his father's office, kids his father mentored and guided, many of whom were now dentists, periodontists, or techs both at his father's three offices around Corpus and out in the world on their own, but most of them were now just statistics.

"Rob said the food and drinks are free," Benji told his friends.

"No way!" one said excitedly.

"Like, *free* free?" another asked.

"That's what he said," Benji pointed to Rob.

Rob nodded. The kids whooped and took their phones out to let their folks know via text or let the world know via social media. Galindo stood by Rob and gave him a short nod. He was a short, fat man with hips that extended past the point of being laughable and were just pitiable. A band geek and music education major, he was a man living the only life he'd ever wanted. His passion was for music, marching and concert, and teaching kids how transformative love for something as seemingly niche and insignificant as a trumpet can change a life. He used to be a working musician. As a kid, he played and sang in his father's group, touring all of the southwest and Mexico. His picture—young, chubby-faced, already cursed by those hips—hung in the Texas Conjunto Music Hall of Fame. He brought mariachi music to and even taught accordion lessons at the school he and Rob taught at, a novel idea: reaching the kids where they were, where they came from. He reached out to a friend of his from grad school, one who Rob studied with at conservatory, to try and hire a local musician who was successful and had practical music industry experience part-time. Rob got the gig. He should have been grateful, and he was, but he couldn't get over his hang-ups regarding someone as earnest, eager, and as vulnerable as Galindo. He was a good man and a great teacher, but damn, was he just a grown-up band geek.

"This is really something, Rob. I can't believe we get to share this with the kids. Thanks so much for the opportunity."

"No problem, Mr. G. I'm just glad to put my experience and connections to use. It's no big deal."

"It is to them, Rob." Galindo put a gentle hand on Rob's shoulder, and, for all of his sincerity, Rob was glad he hadn't just made himself for Benji the same kind of asshole Galindo was making of himself in that moment. Rob just walked away, and Galindo seemed to get it because for the rest of the night, he kept as much distance as possible between them.

CHAPTER EIGHT

"Alright," Joanie said, the smile on her face sloppier from her enthusiasm for the conversation and company than from the drink. She had just as much practice at boozy high-powered work conversation as her husband had at drunken golf, if not far more so. "I have to level with you."

Maria had switched to Diet Pepsi, but she still felt the warm lightness of the night. It was the gin, sure, but it was the fun too. This was more fun than she'd had in a long time, carefree and innocent fun she couldn't have with Aline or Kaylee anymore—they were all too tied into their own lives to have any such fun without it being weighed down by the realities of the dramas and traumas big and small they all shared and helped each other with. "Okay."

"I was really pissed at you after New Year," Joanie said.

Maria laughed hard at this. Their asshole husbands. They said they weren't going to talk about them.

"So pissed I wanted to fire you."

There was no way to have the laughter stolen from the bottom of your slightly buzzed belly gracefully. Maria stammered, but Joanie pushed past.

"I'm not proud of it. It was petty, but I was mad, and if you can't fire someone who pisses you off, what's the point of owning a business?"

Maria couldn't control the look of bewilderment on her face. "Listen, Joanie—" she tried to say, but again, Joanie spoke over her shock.

"I'm not going to fire you. I never was. I knew I never was. But it still felt good to think about it. I was letting myself be petty, but I wasn't going to be dumb. I knew I couldn't fire you after my husband attacked yours in front of a whole house of witnesses without taking a wrongful termination suit right in the ass. So, I looked into you. I got on legal's Sharepoint, just to see what you did, to look into how you spent your time.

"Now, I'm being more honest than I should be, for a lot of reasons. And this might be the dumbest thing I've done in a long time, but I'm okay with that because I like you. I opened Sharepoint knowing that it was wrong, anything I would do to you, and if I was honest with myself, I'd be doing it to lash out at Ken too, for being a baby and a drunk and a sometimes blow hound. But I looked into legal, into your work there, and I have to say, you're kind of a rock star."

Maria still didn't know which way was up, but she was able to grasp on to that one bit of positivity. She laughed a nervous laugh. "Can I get another one of those Beefeater martinis," she said loudly as a kind of joke, but the bartender heard and busied herself with actually making it.

"Here's the real dumb part of what I'm going to tell you—you work laps around everyone in legal. It's not even close. Even if I wanted to fire you, I looked at that, and then the dust-up a couple of weeks ago happened, and you took charge and made sure we didn't take a hit, I just knew that I had to. . . . I don't know, shake your hand or pat your back or something like that."

"Or listen to my dumb, ginny college dating and drinking stories?"

Joanie laughed. "Yeah. I guess that's the thing to do."

Maria let out a small, excited squeal of joy that surprised even her. The sound of it and the sight of Maria's hands rushing to cover her mouth in shame at having lost control took the laughter from Joanie's throat and put a different kind of smile on her face.

"Oh, no. You're a lightweight. I'll get us some chicken wings or whatever." She grabbed the menu and spoke while scanning it for something heavy and appetizing enough to share in order to put some food in the young attorney's belly. "You really have to up your tolerance if you're going to sit down to do business over drinks, especially when it's with the boys, which it almost always is. Half of them are actual goddamn drunks, but the other half will try to get you nice and drunk so you're pliant to whatever they're pretending like they're not angling for at work."

"But this, we're not doing business. We're bullshitting. We're *gabbing*." Maria laughed at the sound of that word, at the thought of the two of them as a couple of old hens having a coffee chat. "And I don't do work over drinks. I'm prudent. I'm measured. I'm the most boring lawyer in the world."

"Jesus Christ. You're lucky I like you. You're lucky our husbands got into a fight and made me want to fire you because if I hadn't looked into you and had this conversation, I'd give up on you here and now."

Joanie flagged the waitress down and ordered more food than they could possibly eat together, as well as a soda refill for Maria. When the waitress left for her computer and punched in their order, Joanie pushed the menu away from their stretch of the bar and looked over to see Maria looking hurt, reeling at the swing from playful banter to work talk.

"And knock that shit off too," Joanie said. "If I'm going to make you my high-powered attorney and close confidant, you're going to have to learn how to deal with me. And I'm being nice right now, for crying out loud!"

"Am I going to be, like, your protégé now?" Maria pulled the newly refreshed soda to her and took a sip after saying this.

"*Protégé*?" Joanie said. "You're *really* lucky I like you." The first plate of their order arrived, and Joanie bit into a piece of deep-fried whatever. "Oh god. That's so terrible it's great. Eat up before I get you to sign away your salary or something."

Maria grabbed a piece of the food and took a bite. It was piping hot, and she had to take another deep drink of her soda. She coughed, and some of the food came out. It was mac and cheese in some kind of fried roll. There was bacon in it. And like the night and the year Maria had been having, it was terrible and great. She finished the roll in one bite and grabbed another.

"Attagirl," Joanie said. "Lesson number one: never be afraid to eat. I hate it when women don't eat, especially if they're drinking. If you're at a wing place, get wings. Get that sticky shit on your face and fingers. If it grosses the guys out, good. Fuck 'em. You're not there to look good."

Maria nodded. She had never been golfing, but if there could always be martinis and fried food without any actual golfing whatsoever, she thought it could suit her.

CHAPTER NINE

Inside the venue, the kids took their pictures of the stage and lights and took selfies with all manner of uninteresting object they thought looked cool. Benji walked behind them all a step. He was taking it all in on his own terms, laughing and forcing smiles whenever his friends looked to him to validate their jokes or silliness. He finally looked over to Rob, who motioned him over. They went over to where Danny was standing, typing slowly on his phone.

"You know, I miss writing real notes. I used to buy pocket-sized marble notebooks and fill them with notes about bands, how to improve songs, how to mic certain things in certain studios. These fucking phones won't be satisfied until they can have all of our thoughts and attention." He hadn't looked up to see that Rob was with someone, only having seen his him approach peripherally.

"Alright, grandpa." Rob shook his head and pointed a dismissive thumb at Danny, telling Benji nonverbally to look at this silly old bastard.

"Fuck you, man." All the playfulness left Danny's voice when he looked over and saw Benji with Rob. "C'mon, Rob. You didn't tell me you were with a kid. Well," he gave Benji a closer once-over, "you're, what, sixteen?"

Benji shook his head.

"Seventeen?"

He nodded.

"Well, then, fuck you, Rob. I ain't a grandpa yet, not that I know of."

Benji laughed. He didn't seem nervous about hanging out with Danny. He didn't know that anyone would be.

"Benji, this is Danny. Danny, this is Benji." Rob stepped half a step back so the two could shake hands. "Benji is a student of mine. He's real good. Danny and I go way back. We've gigged together for so many acts, but he's a producer now, and now and then when he needs the exact right kind of player, he calls me."

"'Exact right kind of player,' shit. I call him when I got no one else." Danny winked at Benji. "What kind of good is he?" he asked Rob.

"Raw. Self-taught. A dirty kind of touch and style you can't teach." During no part of this did Rob look at Benji. He was giving an honest assessment, not trying to bolster the kid's self-esteem.

"Raw, dirty, and self-taught." Danny nodded at this. He looked over at Benji. "People like your teacher here spend their entire lives studying and taking lessons and go to fancy conservatories and grad schools, and it's little shits like you that change the world."

Rob didn't want to see the smile on Benji's face behind him. He wanted to allow him to save face if he was blushing like Rob would have been if he'd been told that by a fancy grown-up producer when he was sixteen, his fuck-the-world defense mechanisms wouldn't have been able to stand up to such cool kindness, and he didn't want to rob Benji of his own if they had faltered just then. "I dropped out of grad school. Shit, I dropped out of high school."

"When'd you start taking lessons?" Danny asked.

Rob waved away Danny's joke and line of reasoning. "Yeah, yeah, yeah . . ."

"That's what I thought." Danny pointed his thumb at Rob and gave his own check-this-asshole-out nod.

"You dropped out of high school?" Benji asked Rob.

Danny laughed at this, laughed hard. He stomped his leather-booted foot on the ground and slapped his thigh.

"Say, Benj, what do you say you go grab some food before the music starts?" Rob turned to see Benji confused and intrigued. Benji didn't move. He looked questioningly at Rob.

"Yeah. Go attack that barbecue." Danny seemed as practiced at redirecting kids as the best teachers Rob had the opportunity to work with. "Put some of that spicy sauce on it. It's all free. Go eat these asshole label people into first-quarter losses."

When Benji left, Rob gave Danny a mock-severe look. Danny raised his palms in the air and shrugged his shoulders up high near his ears. "I was just busting your balls, man. I didn't tell you to brag about dropping out of high school."

The two of them laughed. The house lights went down, and the band came out. They were just a bunch of skinny blond kids, dressed in a kind of millennial-hipster-rockstar-chic attire that might have looked appropriate on the skeleton of Ron Wood in an '80s Stones video or on Scott Weiland in the late '90s. These assholes didn't have those kinds of millionaire detachment from cool, sincere, or ironic aspirational personas. They knew their lame gold jackets, patterned silk blouses, and corduroy overalls (the singer was wearing corduroy overalls with one strap undone over a mesh tank top!) were all a finely-tuned, calculated hip. They were NSYNC before they dropped the promoter who made them, but with playing live instruments and an inability to hit their harmonies.

"Would you look at these assholes?" Rob couldn't look away from the stage.

"In their defense, they're from Sweden. So . . ." Danny had already pulled his phone out and was typing as fast as he could get his thumbs to go.

"Alright. Being from Sweden, I can forgive the Eurotrash blouses, but look at that singer. Look at that jacket on the bass player. Fuck these guys." Rob walked over to the table just behind where they were standing in the very back of the audience and grabbed a bottle of water, then walked back. "This shit's terrible."

"Come on. It's no more terrible than any of the synth-pop shit that's out right now."

"You're not defending this, are you?"

Danny put his phone back in his pocket. He had heard all he needed to hear to know what working with this band would be like, what he needed of them, and what they'd need of him. "It is what it is. The pendulum is swinging this way now. It can be done well. Have you heard Jaffe's new album? It's alright. It's just where we are. At least they're not tuning their guitars down and trying to rap poorly about hating everything or dressing like nineteenth century Irish dandies, banging on a single kick drum, and turning everything into a wax-mustache singalong. This is it now. This too shall pass."

"You're saying all of this because you're actually going to produce this shit, aren't you?"

"Hey, man. Well, yes and no. A gig's a gig. I've got a girl in college and two mortgages to pay. This is the life," he said, pointing to the kids on stage, all fluffy hair and eyeliner and abs and pecs peeking out just so. "Shit like this is the clock I have to punch. It beats playing weddings or teaching lessons to tech bros trying to relive a youth where they weren't stuffed into lockers and could actually get laid.

"So, yeah, I'll take this gig. I'll throw this shit in Pro Tools and smooth out the edges. I'll babysit these YouTube stars and cash the label check. The lights'll stay on at the studio. I'll record actually good bands. Speaking of, Britt's in town next week to record a Spoon cover with some new band."

"Nice," Rob said, nodding in appreciation of the good.

"Yeah. There's always good stuff to work on. I can turn up the faders and turn down my headphones for shit like this. It's no skin off my back. The real problem, the thing that gets me about even being at this fucking thing right now, is I never thought when I joined bands and got serious about recording, paying attention in the studio and all that, I never thought I'd end up being the grownup in the room. Try to remember back to the first time you were in a studio. Try to remember the engineer. That guy in the Hendrix T-shirt was probably ten years younger than you are now. And he was fucking ancient!"

Rob nodded at this. "Mine wore a Rush T-shirt and wouldn't shut the fuck up about getting a 'vibrant, Alex Lifeson tone.' Weird old studio guys . . ."

"And now we're that guy. We're the fucking dinosaur telling kids about how *Sgt. Pepper* was recorded on 4-tracks or playing "Be My Baby" and begging them, just begging them to listen to the castanet."

"Speak for yourself, Danny. I'm—"

"You're what? You're here with fuckin' kids, man." Danny pointed to the front of the crowd, where most of the kids were dancing to the music.

"That's not the same thing. I'm—"

"Just doing it between gigs? Until your Rush cover band really takes off?"

Rob walked back to the drink table and pulled the first beer he could grab out of an ice tub. When he walked back over to Danny, he still hadn't looked at it, hadn't noticed it was a Corona. He was lost in thought, mindlessly trying to twist off the top of the pop-top bottle, when Danny grabbed the bottle out of his hands, popped off the top with his belt buckle, and handed it back to him. Rob snapped out of it.

"I hear what you're saying, but it's different. I think this is different. I think I could do this teaching thing, maybe as something I like, something apart from music. They're different worlds." Rob took a drink from the bottle. He didn't like Corona, but he needed to be drawn out of himself and the moment in any sensory way he could find.

"Fine. Let's say teacher-you and musician-you are two different people—do you think that guitar makes you younger? Does that guitar change the fact that the sound guy at the studio is ten years younger than you now?"

"Goddamn, Danny. Are you trying to bum me out right now?" Rob finished the beer in two more successive gulps, walked back to the drink table, and grabbed another, this time grabbing the bar blade from the table to pop off its top. "Seriously. I was having a good night."

Danny couldn't help but laugh at this. "I'm sorry, man. Fuckin' *Southby*, right? So much glitter and bullshit, industry parties and showcases and all that—it brings on some dark thoughts."

"That, we can agree on." Rob held his drink up as a kind of salute. For want of his own drink to tap to Rob's, Danny gave a slow, groovy, closed-eyed nod.

"It's not even all that stuff that gets me. Not really. Industry shit is supposed to be fake. I mean, I can't even tell you which label is paying for these drinks or that barbecue. It's the real ones, the pure ones. Remember when this was everything? Your first big showcase? The first fucking food spread you didn't realize you were paying for out of tour expenses? Remember not being so jaded that free barbecue and beer didn't piss you off? Before you could see the strings?" Here, Danny walked back to the bar and came back with two plastic cups. He drank one of the drinks quick, put the second cup into the now empty one, and watched the band on stage with new, old eyes. He wasn't a producer just then. He was an old man, and their ball had rolled into his yard.

"Goddamn, Dan. You have to knock that off. Now you're bumming yourself out as much as you're bumming me out." Rob took his phone out. Maria hadn't posted anything.

"I guess I am, Mr. Vera. Also, you sure you're allowed to drink in front of these kids?" Danny made eyes at the beer in Rob's hand.

"Fuck it." Rob couldn't really affect not caring because it hadn't crossed his mind that he wasn't supposed to drink or what it meant to be there as a teacher, the grown-up in these kids' room. "I'm not their real teacher, just an asshole with a guitar. They bring me around to make 'em feel cool."

"Rock star exchange program?" Danny finally cracked a smile again.

"There you go." Rob held his drink up again. Danny tapped his plastic cup to it, and Rob made a small show of drinking it slowly and with intentional savor. He belched loudly when he put it down. Rob caught Galindo looking over at him, not really like an authority figure, but gauging the situation he'd have to handle if Rob was intent on making one. Rob nodded at Galindo, who, emotionally-needy band geek or not, didn't nod back, but looked back to the band playing. Rob had played cool and irreverent. He didn't know if he'd done it for Danny or Galindo, or even if he did it for Benji and what he reminded Rob of, but for the rest of the night, Rob didn't touch another drink.

CHAPTER TEN

Maria had consolidated four partially-finished plates of food and half a flatbread pizza from a tray that sat on a stand on the bar in front of Joanie. More than impressing a boss or successfully skirting a party she didn't really want to be at, she no longer felt intoxicated from the gin she'd had, but the light spirit of the night held her aloft on the buzz of having made a friend. Coming back from the ladies' room for the fourth time, she was slowed momentarily at the far end of the bar when she looked up and saw someone sitting in her seat, picking food from the plate, and talking to Joanie without even looking at her. As she got closer, she could see that it was Ken. The sight of him stopped Maria in her tracks.

The thought of leaving altogether briefly entered her mind, and she stumbled forward a bit at the force of her upper body not stopping as quickly as her feet. She saw Joanie see her. Joanie cut off whatever Ken was saying and gave him a curt directive from the corner of her mouth. Maria headed over. Ken got up from Maria's stool and gave her a 'what's up' that tried too hard to be cool. That was fine by her. She didn't need or want him to be any more open with her because she certainly didn't want to open up to him.

"I was telling Joanie here that those savages out there ate all the food. I was glad to see you guys had ordered some goodies." He stood on the other side of Joanie, not bothering to pull out the stool there to sit, opting instead to just reach over and speak across his wife. "I had to come in and fuel up. They're trying to rob me blind on prop bets, but I've got 'em right where I want 'em."

"Please don't hustle my employees out of too much money," Joanie said.

"They've got it coming," Ken said, wiping his hands on his pants.

"Ken, I'm serious." Joanie looked over into his eyes, and he seemed to sober up momentarily like there had always been a rational adult just below the surface of his overgrown-teenager behavior.

"Oh, Joan, I know. If I end the night on top, I'll tell them to keep their money until they can win it back next time. If I lose, I'll pay. I'm just having fun fucking with these guys. I know I'm still the boss's husband. And you're not going to tell them any of them that, right?" Ken leaned back to address Maria behind his wife's back.

Maria mimed zipping her lips. A wry smile came over Ken. He leaned back in playful appraisal of Maria and of her being there at the bar the whole night with Joanie. He squinted his eyes and nodded his approval, like he could see the hustle that was happening inside. Maria could only counter his gesture with an awkward thumbs up.

"Alright, I'm off to school these bitches on the longball." He dunked a chicken tender in a cup of marinara that was on the plate and stuffed it in his mouth. He kissed Joanie tenderly on the cheek. She turned to meet his lips, and they kissed in a manner that was just a bit lustier than they likely would have if either of them had been slightly less drunk. "Maria," he said when he pulled away from his wife, "have a great night. And when you get home, you tell that husband of yours to fuck himself, would you?"

Joanie swung a hard slap at Ken's back. He ducked it easily and left, laughing. Maria laughed too. Joanie gave her a playful shove that was harder, pushed by the leftover impulse to smack that had been left unsatisfied by hitting Ken.

"Don't encourage him," she said to Maria.

"Oh, he's fine. And, I mean, he's right. Rob can go fuck himself." Completely full of food and tired of soda, Maria crossed her arms around her chest and rested her elbows on the bar.

"Are you guys fighting or something?" Joanie shook the olive around the bottom of her empty glass before fishing it out. When Maria didn't speak, Joanie looked over at her and saw that she was hiding something in her silence. "It's not still about New Year's, is it?"

Maria offered a meek shrug.

"You have to be kidding me! The cops were called to my house. Warnings were issued. Several people decided that pretty big quantities of pretty expensive stuff had to be flushed like we were teenagers getting busted throwing a goddamn kegger at someone's mom's house. We're not still fighting over that."

Hearing this made Maria feel better about the aftermath of Rob's dickhead rock 'n' roll evangelist act. If that was all it was about, it would all have been over. Ceasefire. Armistice. V-T(op) G(olf) Day. But she knew that wasn't the case. The state they were in was a long time coming. There were other incidents. There was an anger inside of Rob that she'd tried to calm, then tried to understand, then tried her best to accept. It never came out at home, but he lost work, got into fights, and burned bridges because of it.

There were periods of coldness too. Maria did her best to ride the waves of Rob's temperament, to love so hard her missives could reach past the vacuous chasm of his periods of emotional withdrawal. That's what wives were supposed to do. That's what marriage was supposed to be— riding out and loving past the hard times to get to the good, and there was good; there was deep, passionate, fulfilling good.

Maria reminded herself in the low periods that Rob was an artist. This is what that does to someone. He was an artist, he was angry, and he would get lost in all of that music and anger in his mind. She knew this, and she accepted this because he was not just brilliant, impressive, and passionate. He was her husband.

He was *hers*.

After a life of being abandoned and adopted, cast out and lied to, Maria had only ever been everyone else's. She was one family's burden and another's blessing. She was the daughter unwanted by one family and embraced by the other. She was *theirs*, but they weren't hers. Her biological parents were never her mom and dad, her *amá* and *apá*. The Smitheys weren't either. They were, in a manner. They were, but they weren't. Their love came with conditions. They were her parents on their terms. They shaped the reality of their relationship to her, hid truths and, thereby, and didn't allow her to have an informed decision.

Rob hid nothing. Her love for and relationship with him wasn't based on any lies. Rob wore his ugly truths like a crown. He always had. They were only now starting to really affect Maria. That one night was the stone on top of a stack she'd carried dutifully, proudly, that finally broke a part of her.

"No. Not really. It started with that. I mean, it didn't start with that, but that just hit too hard. It opened my eyes to some things. He's a button-pusher. I know he's an asshole, but he's my asshole. It just made me realize how exhausting it is to put up with that. And that's what I have to do because he's not going to change." Maria looked at the empty stretch of bar in front of her, then at the cold and unappetizing food that remained on the plate between Joanie and her. For want of something to hold and hide behind, she grabbed the drink sitting in front of Joanie and took a big gulp. The vodka slid down cold and felt as if it landed broad and hard on her back. She cringed and shivered at the taste.

"Easy, now," Joanie said and gave Maria a soft pat on the shoulder. "You want me to get you another drink?"

Maria, face still puckered up in disgust, shook her hard at the proposition of another drink. "God. Even good vodka tastes like what you think witch hazel would."

"Well, I guess this means you have a decision to make, doesn't it?" Joanie caught the bartender's eye, pointed to her martini glass, and held up a single index finger.

"No, I'm done for the night. Thanks."

"With your husband. If you're three months out from the thing you're supposed to be fighting about, but you say that's not why you're fighting, you have a decision to make. Get her a water too, please," Joanie told the bartender upon being given her drink. "You know, Ken wasn't always like this. Not just the whole rich doofus thing. It's not just about bringing his own clubs to Topgolf. He was a very serious man when we first met. It's what I fell in love with. He was this wildly creative computer guy. I mean, he was creative about boring business stuff—analytics, accounting, computing—but still, he was impressive. Sundry Services wouldn't be what it is today without his first programs.

"But he was driving himself crazy with work, just going and going and going and going. He couldn't stop thinking of ways to cut corners, shave time off of deliveries of services, streamline and improve, and make us more efficient by minuscule, imperceptible degrees. That was the drive that I fell in love with, and it was driving him crazy—driving me crazy with him, and I had to be in the boardroom, having to interface with clients and make deals. So, I told him enough was enough. We were big enough. We had exposed a need in business system computations and filled it. Our nearest competitors couldn't reach us by a long shot, and if they could, there are enough companies who need these services. He built the machine. He could rest. It took a lot of convincing, but he listened."

"I almost can't imagine him like that," Maria confessed.

"He wasn't always this sunbaked office mascot or the boss's husband that makes every meeting he attends a party."

"Joanie, I didn't mean—" Maria started.

"Hey. You know yours, and I know mine. Anyway, he took that leap for me. He did it for me. And you know what? Now I have a child on my hands. I asked for it, and so I have to deal with it. And, let's be honest, he's fun. Annoying, sure, but fun." Joanie took the plastic sword that ran through the olive out of her glass and drained her drink. "Goddamn, thank God for Uber."

"Well, so he changed for you. Rob hasn't changed a bit since I've met him," Maria said.

"That's not the choice you have to make, asking him to change or not. You have to choose whether it's all worth putting up with. You have to decide if you can live with it." Joanie pointed down to her glass again, giving the bartender a moment of pause. "I'm not driving, for fuck's sake." She took her phone out of her pocket, peeled its sleek plastic mesh from its back, and pulled out a fifty that she kept there, maybe specifically for moments of petty bribery such as this. She put it in the tip vase on the bar with a flourish. The bartender looked around to see if she was being watched, seemed to decide she wasn't, and got to shaking up another martini.

"I don't know anymore." Maria buried her face in her hands. "I love him."

"Fuck that. That's all pheromones and shared history. All your chips on the table, is it worth it? Do you stick with it and put up with drunken fistfights like I do?"

"Of course. He's my husband."

"What does that matter? He could just as easily not be. You can shake hands and say 'good game' and pack it up and go your separate ways. He's your husband . . . because there's a paper that says so? Because you swore to God?"

Just then, after more drinks than even a relatively sober Maria could count, Joanie's tolerance was flagging. Either that or the booze and false familiarity of a new friendship had told her she could lower her guard. Her right eye sagged lazily such that it was nearly closed.

"It's more than that," Maria said.

"Well, good. Is that, whatever it is, enough to keep putting up with him?"

Maria stammered at this, but Joanie didn't notice. She could have unburdened her whole soul at that moment, and Joanie wouldn't have stopped speaking. "You know why I'm still with Ken? Because we can't have kids. He has his reasons why he can't, and I have my reasons why I can't, so we don't. I know he wanted them, but work got to where we were too tired even to adopt. Then he went off the deep end with the fun, and so it's just us. I can watch him fall apart. I can watch him buy another guitar he can't really play. I can put up with the small humiliations being with him puts me through because he's only putting me through them. I realized after New Year's that if there were kids, I would have to leave. And I couldn't even give an ultimatum because he did this for me. That's the dumb, fucked up math you have to do when you love someone and you build a life and a goddamn fortune with that someone, and it's still not right. So, that's what you have to do. You have to sit down and do some dumb, fucked up math." She pulled the fresh glass to her, pulled out the olive sword, and slid the olive into her mouth. She pushed the otherwise full drink across the bar and motioned for the check. "Now, let's go outside." Here, Joanie seemed to call on some deep-down reserve of composure, because she stepped down from her stool, looked up in the convex overhead mirror to check the state of her hair and straighten the creased-from-leaning-into-conversation lapel of her blouse, and shook off the drunkenness that was spilling over the top of business-casual seriousness. She was really practiced at this. "I have to show my face to the employees and watch my husband make an ass out of himself."

CHAPTER ELEVEN

After watching the Swedish singer dance around plucking his guitar in a way that was meant to imitate the right hand of a hip-hop producer on a toy synthesizer finger-pecking out a melody, Rob couldn't take it anymore. "This is too much, Danny. They suck. You know of any actual good shit being played anywhere tonight?"

"Listen, man. I didn't invite you out tonight. You found me." Danny had taken his phone out and was taking another note.

"I know, and I'm grateful. I really am, but this is Benji's first show, and it would be cool to show him something real, something with teeth." Rob knew what this truth would do to Danny because it was doing the same to him. It was making him stick his neck out a little further than he normally would, making him show he cared.

"His first show?!" Danny looked hard at Rob, abandoning the note he was taking, searching his friend to determine if he was telling the truth long enough that the glow of his phone died as the device slipped into sleep mode. "And he's really good, that's no bullshit?"

"I mean, he doesn't necessarily have conservatory chops, but he's got fire."

Danny seemed to find the truth in Rob's face—that the kid was real, that Rob cared, that this could really mean something to the kid, and that

Rob wasn't just being a snob—and punched in the code to his phone and fired off a text. "There's a band playing at the Palm Door. They may have already started, but they're worth catching. A post-hardcore band from Mexico, fucking brutal but tight. They don't sing in English. They don't give a fuck."

"So, all their songs are in Spanish?" Rob asked. When Danny nodded, mid text, Rob knew what they had to do. Before leaving to announce the change in plans, he announced to himself more than Danny, "That's pretty badass."

When Rob announced to the group that a better band was playing just around the block on 6th, the kids hesitated. They didn't want to be rude, but they were clearly enjoying themselves at the show. They were into the band, which Rob looked past because that's what the band was: a shrill drone of nonsense and bullshit to ears older than twenty, but pure gold for teenagers.

"You're coming with me," he told Benji. "You have to hear this other band. They're legit. Danny's on the phone right now getting us in. He's hitting up contacts, calling in favors, all because I told him you're legit."

Pride beamed in Benji's eyes. "Can I?" he asked Galindo.

Rob snorted at this deference to Galindo. Of course, Benji could come. He looked over at Galindo and was surprised to find him considering the situation, hesitant to let the kid go.

"Your parents expect you to be with me," Galindo said.

"I just told them I was at a club downtown. They didn't even drop me off, my cousin did."

"He'll be with a—" Rob realized that however awkward it would be to announce himself as a teacher just then, because he'd never called himself that, it would be an outright insult to Galindo to do so. "He'll be with an adult."

Galindo thought about it. He looked over at Rob and could see he wasn't impaired. "Are they planning on picking you up here, or is your cousin?"

"I'm cabbing back," Benji said, sounding believable to anyone not as seasoned a liar as Rob.

Galindo looked Rob hard in the eyes. They'd only ever talked about music, about theory. Galindo had given some helpful tips about managing a class, but he had done so, Rob could see now, as an afterthought. The stakes for Rob at the school were so low as to be nonexistent. Sure, he only had half a foot in the door. Sure, he hadn't wanted the gig to matter, to matter to Galindo or the school or the kids, but he hadn't realized how much *he* really didn't until he made himself matter.

"He'll be your responsibility," Galindo told him. "You'll be the adult, not just another guy in the room."

"Don't worry," Rob said. "I take full responsibility. One hundred percent. Consider your ass covered and mine on the line." Rob made to give Galindo a collegial slap on the back, one like he'd done many times over the last several months, but Galindo pulled away to address Rob on a different level.

"I don't care about my ass. I don't care about your ass. I'm not afraid of getting in trouble. I need to know that boy is looked after." Galindo pointed to Benji, who, for his part, looked away like he was watching a pal of his get lectured by a parent. "We're out in the world. There are no principals with walkies, security guards, or SROs. You're his protector."

Rob had only ever called him 'Galindo' or 'Mr. G,' he was a lifelong minimizer of people by way of nicknames and diminutives—he'd taken to calling his father 'Ben' like only his mother was allowed to at thirteen to piss him off and hadn't, to that day, stopped—and Rob wasn't trying to play any kind of card in the moment, but when he said, "Joseph, he'll be fine. I promise," it sounded more real than anything he'd ever said outside of 'I do,' and Rob didn't know if that was because he meant it enough to use Galindo's first name, or because he meant it so much that he believed it too.

Galindo nodded at Rob and told Benji to listen to him. Benji clapped his hands in excitement and thanked Galindo profusely. He gave goodbyes to all of his friends and thanked Galindo one more time before heading out. As they approached the exit of the venue, Benji seemed surprised that Danny was joining them, but he rolled with it because he was a fast learner and, no matter how far north of 183 his home was, no matter the fact that he essentially lived in an ethnic enclave that was in large part divorced from the culture of Austin, one which only still existed because there were large swaths of it too urban, too brown and too black and too ghetto to be gentrified by rich hipster assholes looking for cheap real estate and authentic foreign cuisine or smug social justice assholes looking to save the natives from the blight of urban decay and from the rich hipster assholes and from themselves, he was still an Austinite, and in those moments that can only happen in that city—when Vince Young or Matthew McConaughey or Kevin Durant show up to your school bearing shoes or sports gear, followed by film crews to document their largesse—there was only one thing to do, and that thing seemed second nature in town, like there's something in its riverbed sediments that seeps into the taps that are fed by Colorado River water that flows into Lake Austin, and that something, that local flavor informed everyone that the way to be was to act like it was no big deal—like the weird was normal and that original slogan actually meant anything more to the town than a hook for selling tacky tie-dyed shirts.

Benji stopped just before the exit and looked back at his friends, who were dancing with just a bit more abandon in his absence, and at the band on stage. When Rob asked if he was ready to go, Benji told him, "I don't know, man. The barbecue was pretty good."

"I'm sure there will be food at the next place," Rob said back over his shoulder. He and Danny were already outside.

"But, like, it was really, really good," Benji said again.

When Rob turned around to look at him, he could see that Benji was joking. "Oh, fuck you, kid. Let's go."

Benji laughed full and real. It wasn't loud or prolonged, but it was as much real emotion as Rob had seen the kid betray the whole time he'd known him. Danny laughed at Rob's mock-annoyance.

"I like this kid, Rob. I really like this kid." He put Benji in a headlock here, and a pang went through Rob like Danny might hurt him. Rob knew, of course, that Danny wouldn't, but he thought it was a good sign that he'd worried, that he was now tuned to a different kind of frequency where the kid's well-being was to be considered, monitored, and maintained.

"Well, you can keep him. Let's get over there. I think you're really going to like this show."

They only walked a block down and half a block over, but the feeling of being on an adventure, of being out in search of fun instead of some new iteration of some old thing to gripe over and grumble at, made the walk over electric, and Rob could tell Danny felt it too. They were out showing a kid the ropes that only they knew, and maybe that was enough to make being the old guys in the room sufferable, if not altogether enjoyable.

CHAPTER TWELVE

Maria made herself stay and socialize, really just pretending to laugh at the men's increasingly vulgar jokes and poor golfing, for at least forty-five minutes. She figured that that would be enough time to establish that she was a team player and would give her the excuse that it was getting late and she'd better be heading home. When everybody whooped and hollered over her leaving, Joanie stepped up and gave everyone her most matronly, "Oh, you guys, hush." When a red-faced Melancon couldn't stop himself from saying, "Come on, Zarate," he'd pronounced it the karate way too, "you didn't even play. You just sat inside and gossiped the whole time with—" Joanie was quick to dispense with her happy-fun party self and shot him down more with her tone than her words.

"Melancon, you can shut the fuck up, or you can leave."

Silence followed as all of the air was taken not only from their party but from the two tee boxes on either side of them. All eyes turned to look at Melancon, who went pale and sicker than the drinks and fried food in his belly were capable of making him.

"It sure sounds to me like you're going to shut the fuck up, but why don't you sit there and practice while I walk Maria to her car?" Joanie looked hard at Melancon and, seeming to have deemed him put appropriately in check, put the playful lilt back in her voice. "You're up,

Appleman. Head down, ass up, and maybe you'll stop shanking the goddamn thing. If he gets that shot out straight, the next round's on me. I don't even care how far."

Back in the main entrance, a new team of four bright-eyed, khaki-shorted upsellers had been stationed in the lobby, and each asked if Maria and Joanie had memberships to the establishment. Maria walked past without looking at them, and Joanie gave a curt non-answer that Maria couldn't fully hear.

"Damn, that place is so much to deal with," Maria said when they got out.

"It's a real pain in the ass. I'll give you that. The funny thing is, I am a member. Both Ken and I have membership cards in case either of us need to entertain for something like this. Or, you know, something like this for Ken. You find a company that's featured in *Fortune* and *Business Insider*, and you sell, fight, and go to war to hang on to your market to make a global name for yourself, and you'll still have to have a membership card to a strip-mall driving range in your wallet between the Black Card and the corporate AmEx." Joanie rolled her eyes and shook her head.

Maria offered up the sincerest shrug she could because what did she really know of such problems? "At least you can use it for team building with young lawyers on your staff or, you know, as an opportunity to berate Melancon in front of half of north Austin."

"Fuck him. He's a pain. And he does roughly a third of the work you do but is still paid about forty percent more than you. Remember those numbers at your next review but forget who told them to you." Joanie tipped her forehead down and stared stern eyes at Maria. "There's a lot from tonight you should probably keep under your hat. I like you, but I don't really know if I can fully trust you."

"I said a lot too. It was nice. I haven't had this feeling, like I just made a new friend, in a while." Maria couldn't hide her excited smile. For once in a business-related setting, she wasn't hiding her emotions, and, for once, she didn't feel like she had to deflect the gaze and attention of everyone around her.

"But you need to understand that I was halfway to firing you when your husband and mine got into a schoolyard game of grab-ass. What do you think I'll do if you fuck me over with any of this?" Here, Joanie stood taller than normal; here, she was a force that could barnstorm any boardroom and stare down any hostility that might approach her or all that she had worked to build. Maria stuttered her bewilderment at the idea of ever betraying the friendly confidentiality of their conversation, the confidence of her new friend. "Good. I believe 'struck retarded' was the right reaction just then."

Maria forced a beleaguered smile and held her palms up in a show of polite, compliant resignation. The sight of this gesture, coupled with enough self-awareness on her part letting her know just how exhausting she could be, delighted Joanie. She pulled Maria in for a hug, for which Maria was wholly unprepared. The confused ragdoll way Maria allowed herself to be reeled in made Joanie laugh, but the way she placed her head on Joanie's shoulder sparked feelings of sororal empathy in Joanie.

"Are you sure you're good to drive?" she asked into the back of Maria's head.

"Yes." Maria didn't pull up from her sunken cling onto her new friend.

Joanie gave one last squeeze, then pushed Maria back to address her seriously. "I rolled a car once. This was years ago. God, it was sixteen years ago. We were already contracting work, but spinning plates taking orders, because he and I were our only workforce. We were saving capital, keeping overhead low, probably approaching breach on some of the way too many jobs we were doing. We had just made enough to put down for the office. We'd sold our house and were living there.

"One night, I was coming home from a meeting downtown. There were drinks. There was a big dinner bill I footed because of appearance, appearance, appearance. And there was a big Mercedes E-Class we were leasing. I was driving down the really winding stretch of 2222, just east of 360. I drove it every day, and I guess I got too comfortable or was too drunk. I don't know. I didn't realize what had happened until I heard people shouting at me, asking if I was okay. We'd already been married for several years, but the way Ken reacted—the calm, caring way he reacted, a way I know I wouldn't be capable of—it told me I had been right. Marriage is a gamble, and I had won. I knew then that if he ever cheated on me or went crazy or became wildly successful and turned into a fucking teenager perpetually on summer vacation, I'd always stand by him."

Maria could only nod blankly at this. Her mind had already gone where Joanie was taking her.

"Ask yourself if you've had that moment. Ask yourself what it was, and if it was enough to push you through this." Joanie could see she'd lost Maria to thought. "Call me if you need to talk."

"I will," Maria said. "Thanks for tonight."

CHAPTER THIRTEEN

Palm Door on 6th is decidedly un-punk rock. Upon entering, the sight of the venue's interior reminded Rob of a wedding he'd been to the previous spring. All of these ridiculously expensive venues downtown blended in his mind with all the times he'd been hired to play country or jazz with an expensive established act that someone or other just *had* to have play at their wedding and for whom Daddy was, of course, ready to shell out big money to get. The venues all had parquet floors and at least one exposed brick wall, and maybe even a wall of original windows—typically not since not too many buildings' original windows had survived this long and those that did were not energy efficient or at all sound-dampening. Walking in, it all came back to Rob—how stupid he thought it was to have a fancy wedding right in the heart of "Dirty 6th," how generically gaudy the interior of the building was, like they'd gone for 'Austin Chic', but in the typical manner of the arms race of every third Austinite between the ages of twenty-two and forty being covered in tatt-sleeves that mean so much but, you know, ironically, the room had all the accoutrements but none of the soul.

The crowd was all lanyards and out-on-the-town business casual. Were he on his own, Rob would have walked out as quickly as he had walked in. He was a step behind Danny and Benji, and Danny had spotted someone he knew and was walking Benji over to introduce. Rob's suspicion of the room and the event subsided when he heard the music spilling over into the room from the band playing at the stage set up on the patio. The music seemed to reach Danny at the same time—his ears trained in drowning out bullshit and putting it on mute if something actually worth listening to presented itself, no matter how faint or far away. They each perked up simultaneously, and Danny wheeled around to find Rob's eyes, which were looking for him too. They nodded, and Rob headed toward the patio without looking again at Danny, who was tearing Benji from the conversation he was making with Danny's old friend. They had to go outside. The rock was beckoning them.

Out on the patio, underneath an event tent and with large fans circulating air through the crowd, the audience directly in front of the stage was alive and electric, actually engaged and sweaty like they were at a punk show in a garage on the ass-end of nowhere. They were restless and hungry for art and the kind of release you can get from communing with a band instead of being where they were, in the middle of drunk frat boy territory during the middle of the biggest sellout and poser-drawing festival on the calendar. A small handful of young brown co-eds knew all of the words to all of the shouted Spanish songs. It was a needed inspiration, and it was fucking good.

The song wound down a final shouted refrain that, at this point, even the audience members who weren't dedicated fans and couldn't even understand the Spanish they were shouting out syllabically, joined in. The musical breakdown that followed was intense. It raised the hairs on the back of Rob's neck in a manner that nothing quite like three guitars in synchronized chaos holding on for dear life to a rhythm section that couldn't be stopped could replicate.

"This is good, right?" Benji shouted at Rob.

Rob nodded without breaking his focus on the band, the members' individual techniques, and the way the whole thing coalesced—it was a perfect post-punk expression in a style Rob himself had played and *believed in* a couple of decades back, and that was really the highest kind of compliment Rob could give a band or musician, that they aspired to and embodied (or at least aspired to embody) an ethos that he had once embodied so purely himself, had bled for.

"But, like, *good* good," Benji continued.

Rob raised an eyebrow at this. He looked over to Benji and was made aware of, scared by, in fact, the kind of influence he'd had on this kid. He had taught to analyze, critique, and bitch about music so much that the kid couldn't just enjoy something so powerfully good and raw. Rob put an arm around Benji's shoulder and pulled him in close so as to not have to shout over the music.

"Kid," he said with as much earnest warmth as he could muster, "if I'm not bitching about a band after this long, it's good. Also, who cares what I think? I'm a grumpy old bastard. If you think it's good, it's good. Even if you're wrong."

Rob pulled back and gave an "I mean it. I really, really mean it" nod, giving Benji permission, really pleading with him, to enjoy the show. Benji smiled in a way that made him look every bit the kid he was, and it made Rob wonder how small and comically vulnerable he looked bucking up to bums and gutter punks in the Tenderloin and telling them to fuck off when they sized him up as potential prey in those first days and months alone in the city that was always colder than he thought California would be. The song ended, and Benji cupped his hands around his mouth to project his "woo!" to the stage. He didn't look up at Rob again. Instead, he looked around at the audience, taking in the world he'd entered as a participant in his own right as opposed to someone being given a tour of it. Rob cupped his own hands and let out an unpracticed "woo!" of his own.

"OTRA VEZ!" the singer shouted, "No quieres preguntar . . ."

"Motherfucker," Benji sighed to himself. His mind and his world were on fire.

The singer continued in Spanish too fast, too loud, and too effortless for Rob's ears to catch. The crowd began to sway in a way Rob was too old and too cool in some way or other that he couldn't put his finger on to join in on. Out on this patio with this young true believer next to him and these genuine real deals up on the stage, he felt like he was carrying a torch he hadn't known he'd passed on so many years back when he found himself taking more jazz brunch and chicken-picking country gigs at upscale faux honky-tonks and more theater shows than he could count for old folks in their Sunday best cowboy hats and four-hundred-dollar, going-out Tony Lamas. Rob suddenly felt tired and thirsty, like it was far later into the night and he'd been up on stage playing his ass off instead of out in audiences clinging to the only thing he was left with when there wasn't a guitar strapped on his shoulders and slung out on his hip: his narrow opinions on the authenticity and worth in the modes of expression of people younger and more vital, in and of themselves and to their respective music scenes and the music community at large.

"I'm going to the bar to get some water," he told Benji.

Benji didn't look over at Rob. In fact, he hardly broke his whole upper-body headbang sway to nod and say, "Cool."

Back at the bar, regardless of being two blocks down and one over from Galindo's judgement, Rob couldn't think of ordering a proper drink. There was a dryness in his throat that only water could come close to quenching. He picked up a plastic bottle and was already grabbing for another before he could completely drain the first. As he was used to, Danny had found what functioned as the velvet rope and made his way to the VIP section of the venue. He was again talking to the person Rob had pulled him from. Rob was glad that Danny didn't spot him in the back of the audience because as much as he didn't want to be out on the floor in an attempt to plug into the sway and thump of that mass, he also didn't want to be behind any velvet ropes, hobnobbing with industry suits or talking levels and effects with the weird old studio guys.

This was the point at which he normally would have just up and left. He would imagine or exaggerate some offense unto himself or of his sensibilities and decide his only courses of action were to leave or to lash out at someone, something, anything, everything. But the kid was there, and as willing as he'd become to disappoint Maria and to pull her away from a good time or even good friends or, on more than one occasion, her family, he couldn't rightly do that to Benji. He was stuck, and he knew it. He tried to drown out the audience, swiveled his barstool away from them, and closed his eyes and let his ears try to pull him to something true and undeniable, but the crowd was too alive, and the ears that otherwise could have picked out a mis-fingered microtone in the middle of an over-driven power chord, and more so the mind that needed to be clear to use them, were too disturbed to focus. The cool wind outside had gone cold, Texas cold at least, the temperature having dipped down into the upper sixties, and the sheer pleasantness of the night only served to slap Rob across the face with the undeniable fact of his not being able to enjoy it.

He finished his water more for something to do than to try to combat the dryness of his throat he'd already conceded wouldn't be relieved. He opened another bottle, but the taste of anything other than a poison, strong and comfortable, just made him all the angrier at being there on that patio, in the middle of something real that he wasn't part of making, serving as a chaperone under the auspices of the boring day job that was part of an always creeping-forward boring life on the wrong side of the stage and the mixing board and the classroom. He took one sip, and the cool comfort of the water was as small an offense as he could allow himself to lash out at. He pulled the bottle away from his lips and slammed it on the ground at the side of his stool. If it splashed on anyone around him and they wanted to say anything about it, Rob was ready to fight. Fuck the job. Fuck Danny's good graces and the work that could come from it. Fuck teaching, and fuck Galindo. Fuck Benji and all he stood for, what he reminded Rob about what he'd lost. If anyone had anything to say, Rob was ready to swing.

"What now, Venancio?" a voice that, under layers of screaming, whisky, and cigarette rasp, was immediately recognizable called from behind him.

Or was it familiar? Was it the voice of a younger, innocent girl that he could hear trapped in the older, tired one, or was it how she'd said his father's name—not even the fact of her having called him the name, but how she pronounced it as *Vuh-nancy-oh*—that unclenched the fists at Rob's sides? It was that play-insult that pulled him out of that night as he was inhabiting it, as a spectator, as an artist who could only ever regard any other's accomplishment—any award or contract or gig or applause— as one that should rightly have been his. Any association with that voice, just like it did twenty years prior, put him on the right side of cool. It took him back to lazy afternoons at Dolores Park, laughing at the naked hippies and keeping an eye out for anything easy enough to steal—he could practically taste the PBRs and the giant four-dollar burritos and cheap heroin in the back of his sinus cavity.

"Penelope?" he said before swiveling around to face Penny, picking up the ball of their old inside-joke that she'd tossed him like the game hadn't been on pause for over two decades, asking what the hell she was doing there and then rather than if it were really her.

But he knew why she was there. The world was small and its random chaos lazy enough. Their lives—no matter how harsh the break that tore them apart, left him broke and strung out in Corpus, trying an outpatient rehab while staying with his parents but eventually opting for an in-patient one when he realized sobriety would be easy enough after he detoxed and got some work scheduled, but life would've been impossible in his parents' house and her in an institution somewhere in Washington state that he hadn't stuck around or cared about enough to know the whereabouts of after he pulled her bleeding and almost dead from the gone-cold bath she'd almost died in after their second album got shelved and one or both of them (they argued over, and couldn't really remember anyway, the specifics of the meltdown) got catdragbird kicked off of the tour that was supposed to keep them paid, fed, and high and invincible—were on such similar paths that they'd have to run into each other sooner or later.

And there she was, Penny Pain, every minute of her forty-nine years on her face compounded by two decades of nonstop recording and touring outside of a few stints being either incarcerated or institutionalized. There was a quality about her that seemed mystical, like a witch or an angel sent to save him, but maybe that's just all his mind could make of a woman who embodied so much of what he needed in a moment like that but who he didn't, just then, want to fuck.

"At this moment, I don't know if it's actually you or if just knowing you live in Austin has made me hallucinate you here. I mean, you look like a goddamn middle-aged cartoon of yourself, sitting here choosing to be pissed off instead of letting yourself feel something good." Penny poked a finger at his chest, verifying that he was real. "But no one's called me Penelope since the last time you did. So, I guess I must not be too crazy yet."

"I don't think I've ever needed you to just show up out of nowhere more than I did just now. You want a drink?" Rob leaned back to do get a full view of the woman his Penny had grown into, or at least the woman Penny became after she stopped being his.

"That would sound real nice if it wasn't said by someone I lived with for years. And no thanks. I've got to go easy on the free booze because of my medications and on the food. If I get any fatter than the fucking

Seroquel is making me, I'll have to drink, and that'll cause me to nod off or run naked down the highway or something. You're looking good, Rob. Real good. Settling into the hippie life has done you good."

"Fuck you, 'hippie life.'" Rob grabbed an unopened water bottle and handed it to Penny, who nodded in obligation.

"Whatever, then. The 'Keep Austin Weird' life, whatever bumper sticker lifestyle you're espousing, is treating you well. I'm trying to compliment you here."

The band finished a song here, and when the applause died down, the singer spoke up, "Thank you, Austin. We are No Somos Marineros. We're from Mexico City. Our set is short, so we just wanted to come out and thank you all for ignoring the news that said it was going to storm today. Not a drop of rain, and it's been beautiful. I think we get why everyone always says 'you have to go to Austin,' and it's not just to do sets on fancy roofs."

The crowd shouted their approval at being pandered to. When that roar died down, someone in the front of the audience shouted, "Te Amo, Carlos!"

Before the rest of the audience could hear and register the empty expression of love, Penny shouted even louder from the back, "Fuck her, Carlos. *I* love you."

On stage, the band laughed, and the audience followed suit. The singer used his hand to shade his eyes from the glare of the overhead stage lights. Then, when he saw who had shouted it, he lit up. "Ladies and gentlemen, Miss Penny Pain! If you don't know her, you need to get to work. She's a fucking rock goddess, our bruja güera, and if you don't know what that means, ask one of these motherfuckers up front singing along to all the words. Thank you!"

Then they were off, blazing into their last three songs. Penny laughed and blushed, burying her face in Rob's chest, hiding from the gazes of the people she'd just impressed like it was 1995 again. In the crowd, Benji was still looking back at Rob, only now realizing that he was only a foot or two away from someone actually cool, not just someone who everyone swears was the real deal way back before he was born.

What was it about Penny there on his chest, taking refuge in him, using him as a prop to tease an audience and using the audience to tease him—

because that's all the audiences ever were, the set-ups to a joke whose punchline was that they, catdragbird and Penny and Rob, were getting away with something—that made Rob feel okay with being himself? He was forty-one years old, would be for a couple more weeks, still young compared to many of his contemporaries in the studio and on the stages he played on, but when he stood in front of a class or watched the fresh, hip brand-new band he could play with if he had the charts or was given a couple listens of their songs but with whom he shared no common language outside of notes and key and effects rigs and amp configurations—and he hadn't gotten where he'd gotten in theory, hadn't set out on the course he'd blazed for the music itself; he'd done it for how the music made him feel and for his adroitness at him made the world look at him—he felt cheated by time for never its having been charmed or awed enough to, just like the rest of the world had, change expectations for Rob and just let a thing or two slide. She certainly didn't make him feel younger. When she pulled back and looked up at Rob, the old woman Penny had become served to emphasize his own age. But she made it all seem okay. He'd allowed himself to become domesticated by the comfort of steady work and the city that made that work possible, the city that kept you intoxicated on its fun and its magic and its fine food and fine beer and fine living on the "cheap," and by, of course, Maria, his rock and his home who had enabled his growing soft through no fault of her own. Penny, standing there in front of him, worse for wear and still wild and incendiary behind the dull the antipsychotics barely held up between her crazy and the world that couldn't handle it.

"So, who the hell are you, Rob Vera? You look enough like you used to that I want to cry, but not enough that I want to kill you." Penny laid a soft hand on Rob's face.

Rob could think of an answer or two that would sound perfectly nonchalant and disaffected and cool like it was 1993 again, those narcotic days when ironic didn't mean you were trying to be funny by not trying to be funny and prolix English/Italian coffee orders weren't made by soccer moms, but he had no ego to protect with Penny—she'd seen him at his worst back then, and he was seeing her in a pretty bad way right now; besides, he was tired already. So, he went with the purest truth he could come up with that would encapsulate the last two decades of his life, and most of the two decades before it:

"You know, same old same old. I'm just an asshole with a guitar."

CHAPTER FOURTEEN

As soon as Maria got into her car, she checked her phone. She gave herself the night—it was business, she'd reasoned, work—to put the thing on Do Not Disturb. She could give herself, her job, really, a few hours' escape from her world collapsing around her. When she looked at the display, she saw a missed call from "Mom" and one from a number that wasn't saved into her phone, but one she had come to recognize and dread on sight. She pressed the voicemail button on her phone and placed the phone in the cupholder on the center console. Through the car's speakers, a weary voice spoke.

"Miss Smithey," Maria had corrected her twice, but clearly she had bigger things to worry about than getting the name of Eunice's daughter right, "Danielle here. She didn't recognize me again today, but she wasn't scared like yesterday. The message you recorded worked like a charm. It seems she went out for groceries this morning, and that's fine, but we really have to talk about her living situation. Every day is lost more and more. Tomorrow could be the day she forgets to turn off the stove or how to drive or that she needs to bathe. With your permission, I can take her car keys from her, but that still would leave her without transportation, should the need arise. And we don't know if she'd know to call 911. As you can tell, it's a domino effect of troubling situations.

"I know this is happening fast, but we need to make accommodations for what's coming—either a care facility or some kind of custodial care. It's past time. I can get you in contact with my company's social worker. She can walk you through everything. Call me."

It wasn't as bad as Maria had feared. The call from the day before, a patient yet bothered Danielle trying to calmly get a hysterical and fearful Eunice to just listen to Maria on the phone, had crushed her. She knew what was happening. She was fully aware of the situation, but that call had shown her even more evidence of the fact that this was happening, and it was happening at a rate that Maria and Eunice's doctors could neither control nor anticipate.

Maria had meant to bring up Eunice to Joanie, to let her know that she might need to take some time off in the immediate future, but their conversation got so personal so quickly that, at first, Maria couldn't interrupt the natural flow of back-and-forth and, eventually, she couldn't bring it up without it feeling opportunistic since Joanie had already let loose with a bargaining chip Maria wouldn't otherwise have gotten if they hadn't become friends just then. That was fine. The Fridays after happy hour Thursdays were always sparsely attended, and Maria never called in sick for one of them. Her workload was light enough, and she'd built up enough goodwill, her dishing session with Joanie notwithstanding.

When the next message played, the first four words took a sledgehammer to whatever composure she had maintained in not being as crushed by today's check-in from Danielle as she was by yesterday's. They were four simple words, spoken in as routine and ignorable a manner as any other four words ever spoken by a mother to her daughter. It was just that— the easy manner in which they were disregarded, because who doesn't disregard the greetings or disregard whole messages that follow them, of their parents—that made the whole situation happen. If only Eunice had ever changed up her words, changed her tone or her cadence, Maria might have listened to more of the messages. As it was, those four words, spoken as they always were, each time identical to each other, let Maria know without listening to full messages, that her mother was fine, just calling to check in, just playing her part as she was supposed to like Maria did when she replied to every third or fourth message.

"Maria, it's your mom." They all started exactly like this. Each of the messages she left had the same tone and inflection, with the "Maria" swinging up and the "it's your mom" falling back down as if Eunice expected Maria to perk up at hearing her name and then deflate at the realization of who was addressing her.

She had been doing just this, listening to voicemails while she drove home two weeks prior. There was an issue with a clause on a contract one of her co-workers must have fallen asleep on and whoever had her job at the company they were dealing with was as good as her, or at least maybe. They caught it and were trying to exploit the loophole, threatening a lawsuit if Sundry didn't thread the needle of the almost impossible delivery date and specifications. Maria's mind spun trying to work through the problem. There were lawyers on one side calling her to try to cook up a renegotiation and software engineers on the other trying to meet the impossible task set for them by a fluke of an errant clause.

She was driving up a long, boring stretch of FM 620 that, on good days, could be counted on to move quickly enough to allow her to drive home with mindless ease, but this wasn't a good day. Today, one person was fired for fucking up and another for not catching the fuck up. Today, two separate teams of people were rushing to Maria, not because she was their supervisor, but because they knew she could be counted on to get work done, counted on to return messages left on her personal phone after hours. Today, there was a wreck at 620 and Anderson Mill, and police presence sufficient enough at the scene that no one could illegally U-turn away from the delay up ahead. It was all so much she might have screamed, but the situation lightened to the point that she might just laugh until she passed out instead.

An avalanche of messages had been left on Maria's phone in the thirty-seven minutes it took for her to leave her office to give a situation update to an understandably pissed-off Joanie, who was still a degree or two colder to Maria than she needed to be in the wake of the blowup on New Year's. Maria walked out of her brief face-to-face with the boss she was always too intimidated to talk to even before the incident, shaken and exhausted, even though it was clear that she was the only person who had come before Joanie and offered anything more than excuses and finger-pointing.

There were ten missed calls and seven voicemails waiting for Maria when she got to her car. By the time she was within sight of the accident on Anderson Mill, she had listened to two sides of an echo chamber of panic. The sixth message was just a flustered software engineer saying, "I mean, okay . . . if we . . . okay . . . but then . . . Fuck!" He typed frantically for twenty seconds before seeming to realize the call he was still on. "Hello? Is this still . . . Sorry!"

Maria was still laughing at the sixth message when the seventh sounded in her car's speakers.

"Maria, it's your mom."

On any other day, Maria would have pressed the button on her steering wheel that showed a handset being placed on a receiver and just not listened to the message. She would have done this not out of anger or disrespect or any active disregard for her mother and the calls she always made. She would have done it mindlessly, putting it off for later just like she would have been doing if she'd actually had her phone in her hands when she heard those words and, in such a situation, pressed "Delete" after hearing those four words, because what could the fifth or sixth or twentieth word of any message like that have mattered if she knew that she'd call back eventually, probably on the weekend, or maybe on one of her easier drives home from work? But on this day, Maria was still laughing at the chaos unfolding at work and playing out on her voicemail, and a police officer who had pulled up to the scene of the accident had begun trying to direct three lanes of traffic into a single shoulder lane to get some kind of flow going past the accident.

"Just calling to see how things are over there, how you're doing." This was also remarkably similar to most messages Maria listened to. "I know you're always busy, always working. Try to remember to leave some time to have some fun. Not too much fun, though. Anyway, I'm just calling because I was just thinking the other day about how much you used to love dance and how we put you in the dance classes through church." Maria actually smiled at this memory. She hadn't thought of it in years. It was one of the first times she and Eunice fought. She wanted to continue taking classes, but they would be outside of the church, which meant Maria would have to travel for competition. Eunice said no. "Why did we ever stop that? You were so beautiful, so graceful. Why didn't we keep doing that? I asked your father, and he can't seem to remember either. Anyway, call me. Just so I can hear your voice. Stay warm, dear heart."

Maria's foot stuttered on the brake, causing her to lurch forward twice before stopping hard, causing her head to jump forward. The officer directing traffic onto the shoulder gave a hard 'stop' palm to the middle lane of traffic, letting everyone in the right continue on ahead as he walked over to the far-left lane where Maria was stopped. He gave the 'roll the window down' crank pantomime. Maria rolled her window down. He walked as close to the window as he could get and took a deep whiff as if trying to smell booze or crazy on her.

"Ma'am, are you alright to drive?" he asked.

Maria jabbed at the buttons on her steering wheel to stop her phone from playing saved messages aloud. "Yes, officer. I just . . . it's been a long day, and I . . . my mind wandered a little there. Sorry."

He pulled his glasses down on his nose and narrowed his gaze. Maria flashed the most compliant smile she could manage with her mind swimming in the waters of a large part her life beginning to fall apart. She had learned in Providence, in Pawtucket, really, that no matter how much she belonged, she would never look like she did, and so she would always be suspect. She discovered this when she got back to Humble and would venture out into the town and down into Houston by herself too.

"Glasses down," the officer said.

Maria didn't understand what she was being told. She stammered.

"Your sunglasses. Put them down."

She did, and the officer looked at the clarity of her eyes and the state of her pupil dilation. He pulled back. "A lot of people are having long days. Two of them just got into an accident. Pull over and get some coffee or some food or to rest if you need to." He walked away without awaiting a response. He held his right palm out to tell the middle lane to keep waiting, then his left toward the right lane, then he gave Maria the 'roll on through' sign.

It wasn't because of what he said, but Maria did pull into the parking lot of the H-E-B at the southeast corner of the intersection. She picked up her phone and scrolled through her voicemails for any messages left by her mother that she didn't take the time to listen to. There were nine that she could find. The oldest was a birthday greeting from three years prior. Each of them started the same. Most of the messages were recent, and in the last four she hadn't deleted, Eunice talks about the dance class. In one before those, she mentions missing Thom but says, "We'll have to have some eggnog in his honor when you get here next week." This was from January. A week after Maria had last visited Humble.

She sat there in the parking lot, unable to stop the tears from welling up in her eyes but not crying. She was too busy to cry. She opened up her work email and typed a message that she saved as a draft before calling back the head software engineer with her best bit of reassurance that the matter could likely be cleared up by legal, but if not, his work was imperative and crucial. She said without actually knowing if she ever would or could that she would personally let Joanie know how he'd stepped up. Then she called Appleman, who was her colleague but had a few months seniority on her, and gave him her best suggestions for how to amend the contract and negotiation strategies for dealing with the particular client with whom he now had to interface in place of the fired lawyer. She loaded him up with ideas, arguments, and carrots to dangle. Then she told him she would be out the next day and to please only contact her if absolutely necessary. The next day, on her first drive over to Humble, Appleman called her four times. She answered twice, but she let the rest go to voicemail.

She hadn't told Rob what was wrong that first weekend. He wouldn't have cared. Well, he would have if she'd shared more of the situation with him than she did. The second weekend, when she said she had to go back, he was ready to show up, but she pushed him back. That was what he had to offer. That was what made him worth fighting for, or at least worth stopping fighting for. He was her teammate, her family. For all of their fighting, all of their struggling for power and for claim to being right, she knew she could count on him. She hadn't had to in a long time. Neither of them had. So comfortable had they made their lives, relative to how each of them grew up—Maria in terms of their money, Rob in terms of a love that was willing to both love him back and call him on his bullshit and keep him on his toes—that they had only really become sparring partners. There was no force that they'd had to face as a team, no adversity to unite them, other than each other's grand successes and minor ambitions.

It was in his capacity to show up when she needed him as well as to lay bare the child in him who was coddled by half the world and only acknowledged as existing when he was fighting the other and asking for help that made Maria really love him when push came to shove and playing it cool gave way to a seriously committed relationship that itself gave way to "what are we doing here?" in their relationship. When Maria put her car in park in the driveway of their home, she knew she would have to again leave for Humble. She would let him know that night, and she would let him know that she needed him to be the man she fell in love with, the man who was worth putting up with fistfights and tantrums and artist-lost-in-his-mind freeze-outs. That night she would surrender because this situation with her mom was too big to face alone; this situation was just the kind of fight they could face together, and maybe just get back to them.

CHAPTER FIFTEEN

By the end of the night, Benji had stopped gushing over the band. They were great kids, wickedly smart, the kind of smart and determined that could make something bigger than any of them could make individually. Their English was great, but with Benji speaking his machine gun Spanish at them, they seemed to be seeing something new. No Somos Marineros were a young band, they only had an LP and some singles to their name, but they had already developed a following of Mexican fans in the states. But Benji, he of a Mexican enclave with direct ties only to the traditional music of Mexico, was a new kind of fan. He didn't know about them, didn't have anyone to point him to them who wouldn't just point him to the guys in sharp blue suits and crisp cowboy hats, but Benji didn't want to dance, and he didn't like his music driven by a tuba. Benji had been given a T-shirt and two CDs, and he'd given his email in exchange, offering to street team for them when they come back to Austin.

It was unseasonably cool out, and no one but Penny was in more than a T-shirt. She was in a ratty old leather jacket, a red one that was more Brit Pop than greaser. But there they stood, Rob and Penny leaning against a wall, the rest of them a huddle, slowly burning off adrenaline. Two of the band guys were looking up where to go next, where the next important show and prospects for free drinks were the best. The other three were smoking cigarettes—the whole reason for the excursion outside, as smoking was outlawed indoors.

"That's insane," one of the guitar players said of the ban. "But kind of cool, I guess."

They'd already picked Rob's brain the same way Benji had picked theirs. Rob knew that catdragbird was big in Mexico back then, but they were big everywhere in that 'next big thing' bubble way. He honestly didn't know anyone still knew or cared outside of record shop neckbeards and fans of Penny who had followed her from back then or had picked up on her recently and gone back into her catalog. All of the talk of the thing he'd helped create, the band he was in, the scene, it was refreshing. Nowadays, all anyone could talk to him about was a lick he put on this or the tone he got on that, and the only people who knew to listen for it were either talking shop or only bringing it up because they were aspirational guitar nerds.

"I still can't believe you're here, you and Penny. That's crazy," the other guitarist said. He took a drag from his cigarette and instinctively moved to hand it over to Benji.

Benji grabbed it but couldn't pull it to his mouth to take a drag before Rob grabbed his wrist with his left hand and took the cigarette out with his right. "Yeah right, dude," he said before taking a drag off the cigarette and handing it back to the young guitarist. Penny watched this exchange and smiled.

"You weren't much older than him when we met," she said.

"Please do me a favor and don't list all of the ways that I'm a hypocrite for doing that just then."

"No. That's not what I was going to do. You're, like, an actual grown-up now, aren't you?" She was smoking her own cigarette, a ridiculous-looking thing, a 120 slim that made her seem like she should have held it with velvet-gloved fingers. "I never in a million years would have imagined you capable of being responsible for anyone else, for yourself for that matter."

"To be completely honest, I'm just trying this grown-up thing for size. Benji here's the beater they let me take off the lot for a test drive."

"But teaching? I love the idea of that. In another life, one where I have a couple less felonies and one or two less misdemeanors of moral turpitude, I might like to be a teacher. I don't want to play barroom rock star into my 60s. I mean, I will, but records don't sell anymore, so I'm married to the road from now until I drop."

"Come on, you did theaters in Mexico," Carlos, the singer, was the only person outside of Benji and Rob, that one drag of a cigarette aside, not smoking in the group. "It's not that bad."

"Not bad." Penny cocked up her eyebrows and snorted out smoke in weary affirmation here. "It's not bad. It just feels final."

"But you're out there playing your music. You're still making great records. Your last two were great. I mean, really great," Rob said. "They were raw and honest but still sparse and poetic. I can't do that shit. I can't put my name on a marquee and expect twenty-somethings from Mexico City to give a shit. I have to play mindless and boring country and jazz shows to pay the bills. It's all look-at-me jackoff playing. You're still a goddamn artist."

"And why can't you? Record some songs. I remember how good of a singer you were. Why not write a couple of songs? Hell, record some covers. Just put something on wax or on ones and zeros or whatever the fuck it is now. You can get sets opening for just about anyone who comes into town. You get to cut to the front of the line with that." She gave Rob a light shove with her forearm, ash falling from the cigarette that was in her hand onto Rob's shirt. She flicked it off, then licked her finger like she was his aunt or something and brushed away the gray dust that remained.

"You know that's not my thing. You know I can't do that," Rob said.

"Yes, you can. You just won't. You're saying you're stuck to gigging as a hired hand on stage and in the studio. I can't do that shit. You think anyone'll pay me to play my shitty downstroke rhythm guitar or sing cigarette-wrecked harmonies on backup? For someone who thinks he has the goddamn world figured out, you'd think there might be a song or two in you. I know there is."

"I can just never. . . . There's never been anything worth . . ." Rob hadn't considered recording anything but instrumental tracks in years.

Sensing the conversation was getting serious with Rob and Penny, Carlos cocked his head over in the direction of the bar next door. Benji and the rest of the band followed. Rob didn't ask him to stay close and didn't follow him with his eyes to keep an account of him. He trusted Benji, and he trusted the band.

"Rob, who the fuck are you? Who's Rob? You can't tell me you still don't have any ideas. Please tell me you've grown a personality that doesn't just define itself by everything it hates. Even the goddamn Clash loved reggae. The Ramones loved the doo-wop, Spector stuff." The look of bemusement left Penny, and she seemed concerned and saddened by who she saw in front of her.

Rob felt judged, but he didn't have any fight in him. Besides, she wasn't saying anything that wasn't true. "Why would I speak up if what I'd say isn't worth hearing? Why would I ask anyone to listen to that?"

"I don't know, chickenshit. Why did the first people draw on caves? You have a self that's worth sharing. Get a little punk in you, you fucking band geek. It doesn't have to be perfect. Let it be dirty."

"That's a lot to think about," Rob said.

"No, it's not. Your thinking is great. Your thinking on my rage is what strapped us on a rocket so big we couldn't hold on. But maybe it's time to stop thinking. Carlos!" she shouted loud enough to summon the whole band, Benji right there in the middle of the pack, sharing laughter with these men from a country away but who already had so much more in common with him than Rob or his own countrymen did.

"¿Que pasa, bruja?" Carlos said with the last breath of a laugh.

"I swear, I love the way it sounds when you speak Spanish. When this asshole speaks it, it sounds like a lawnmower engine trying to pull a mini-van." She pointed a thumb at Rob.

"You speak Spanish?" Benji asked.

"Not if given the option. But when your van breaks down in Mexicali, sometimes you have to step up and use the Spanish you refused to learn to piss off your dad." Rob shrugged. "I do understand it, though. Mostly."

"You guys fly out tomorrow?" Penny asked.

"Yeah. Brutally early flight. So, we're going to just stay up. I think we know where we want to go next." Carlos looked over at his bass player, who nodded that they did indeed know where they were going in order to not let the night, the whole experience of this big show in this quaint little city that had already charmed them with fun, end a minute before it had to.

"Too bad Rob and Benji over there have school tomorrow," Penny said. "We could get really crazy if they didn't."

"Rob, I can totally stay out. I swear. No one will care." Benji's look of pleading was both endearing and frustrating. Rob didn't want to have to be the grown-up anymore.

"Kid, I'm fucking around. I'm going back to my hotel to draw the blinds and sleep for about fifteen hours." Penny tussled Benji's hair, and like any other of the men in the reformed circle of people, he would never have allowed it from almost anyone else in the world, but it being from Penny, Benji just smiled and all but kicked the ground in an awe-shucks way for how he pivoted around like the bad news had hit him across the face.

"Alright, then. Home. School. Yay." Benji waved his hands in mock celebration.

"That's right, 'yay,'" Penny said. "This is your homework, your real rock 'n' roll schooling. You're supposed to be bored. It's supposed to suck. That's where the real shit comes from. What are you doing Sunday?"

Rob raised an eyebrow at this. Penny put an arm around Rob. "I'm getting paid a ridiculous amount of money to play an acoustic living room set at some guy's house, and I was planning on asking old Rob here to bring out a guitar and accompany me."

"Oh my god. Yes." Benji clapped his hands and then gave Penny a big hug.

"Whoa," Rob said. "Sunday? I don't think I can—"

"Don't think. Just come out. We'll play some old catdrag songs, and you can just noodle around on my new stuff. You said you've heard it."

"I have, but—"

"But what? I can cut you in. It'll be a gig. Cancel your Bob Wills cover band gig or whatever. Come out and make some of our noise with me." Penny smiled like she was running a con, and she knew she'd hooked her mark.

"You know what? Fine." Rob held his hand out for Penny to shake. Instead, she pushed past it, squeezing him hard and planting a kiss on his cheek.

"Alright! It'll be fun. The people hosting are supposedly big fans who lived in the Bay Area when we started. They'll go nuts."

After exchanging hugs, handshakes, numbers, and business cards (Rob had one and was embarrassed to produce it, but the band was so good on stage, that Rob felt like offering his name and his connections in Austin was the right thing to do), the band went one way, Penny went another, and Rob and Benji were left to wrap the night up.

"Not bad for your first show, huh?" Rob said, only now hearing the ringing in his ears from the music of the night.

"Incredible. I can't believe how amazing the entire night was. They were awesome, and, like, I got to meet them. And Penny. You're a big deal. This is all so crazy." Benji shook his head at all of this.

The grin on his face made any of the night's annoyances worth it—the grin and the gig Rob had lined up for a Sunday show in some parallel universe where he'd stuck with catdragbird, Penny, drugs, and ugly action art instead of the fine art aesthetic.

"Yeah, well, you get through school. Grow up a little. Maybe enroll at UT. All of this is just another Thursday if you're plugged into the world. Mostly. There's not always free food. So, are they going to pick you up back over at Stubb's?" Rob had taken his phone out and was scrolling through the few of Penny's solo albums he had in his music. He would buy the other big ones and listen to them over the next couple of days just to be ready.

"About that . . ." Benji waited until Rob looked up from his phone, dragged away by the long pause, "can you give me a ride?"

"Are you kidding?" Rob slid his phone into his pocket.

"I figured someone would be going back up by school. As it stands, I had to pay my cousin to drive me down . . ." Benji looked away. He felt bad about putting Rob out, but he was too proud to be ashamed to ask for help. That's what teachers were for, particularly ones at their own school.

Rob was thinking. He would get Benji home, but the last thing he needed was to get into some kind of trouble, pulled over or in a fender bender and then fired or sued. "We'll figure something out."

Just then, a solution presented itself. The bright tingle of a bike bell ringing pulled Rob out of his thoughts. The woman powering the pedicab was shouting, "Who needs a ride? I can get you where you need to go." Rob looked at Benji and nodded that, oh yes, this was going to happen.

"She can't drive us all the way up to my neighborhood, can she?" Benji said, worried.

"Of course not. She'll take us up to my car. I'll get you a ride from there. 16th and Guadalupe," Rob told the cabbie.

He pulled his phone out of his pocket and was hailing an Uber for pickup at the studio. He asked Benji for an exact address to input. He'd noticed the woman's gaze linger on him as he got in the blue velvet seat behind her bike, but he didn't bother to look up because he was busy trying to solve the final problem of the night. Once he put in the fare, the app showed that due to surge pricing, the ride from the studio up to Benji's house would run $137.25. Rob's neck tightened. He had vowed to himself and to Maria that there was no cab fare too expensive to pay to avoid a DWI. That had been his M.O. on nights when he was playing keep-up with country ramblers and rock stars in town, putting back bottles of booze in single sittings just to maintain. This was, of course, a similar situation, but it was still a pain in the neck, literally. He hit the button to agree to the fare. The driver would be arriving there just after the pedicab did. He didn't want to take the situation out on Benji—he clearly would have done anything in his power to not inconvenience Rob, and he was clearly powerless. Rob closed his eyes and let the cool air blowing in his face calm him.

"You're Rob, right? Rob Vera?" The cabbie was looking at Rob through a makeshift rear-view mirror that stuck up from the middle of her handlebars.

"You're Ms. Hayden, right?" Benji said.

Rob was confused. He squinted hard at the mirror in front of the cyclist, trying to make out her face. She turned back to him and smiled. She did look familiar, like someone with whom he'd had sat through a bullshit meeting or two he didn't need or want to be at.

"Dude, she teaches at school," Benji said.

He seemed to be leering, but he was trying to read/follow an intricate tattoo that ran the length of Hayden's back. Rob still gave him a sharp elbow and flashed widened eyes at him, asking him to be cool. Benji sat up taller in his seat and stared out at the cars they were passing.

"Yeah. Ms. Hayden. I do pedicab driving on the side. It's good money, especially this week." She held her left hand out, signaling a turn, then churned her legs hard to speed through a left turn through the busy intersection.

"We came out to a couple showcases with some other guitar students. Galindo was with us too." The rhythmic whine of the bicycle gear turning its chain up and overcame to a dead stop when they arrived at the studio, making Rob push his awkward explanation of a night on the town with a student past the erstwhile noise sound even more forced and desperate than it needed to be. "Do you know Galindo?"

Ms. Hayden turned to face Rob, laughed at the moment, and wiped the sweat from her brow. "Yeah, I know the band director at our school."

Rob pulled his wallet out, fished out a twenty, and handed it over to the teacher, who he could now recognize as being Cypress Hill-tour bus high. She had pulled a wad of cash out of her fanny pack and was thumbing through bills to hand back to Rob. She caught him studying her, the state she was in, and she made a face like she had been caught.

"It's cool," Rob said. "We're cool."

This threw Hayden for a loop. She didn't know what to make of Rob and his seeming to insist on playing nonchalant in a moment where she was there ass-in-the-air exposed as something less than a composed, in-control adult. As in the classroom, Rob had learned that night, all the kids wanted, needed really, of adults was for them to stand as bedrocks of people in control in a world and society that didn't let them, the students, and teenagers, who a couple centuries ago would have been running farms and taking up arms to fend of invaders should they arrive, have any control themselves. It was a good thing that she was so high because she didn't stammer or backtrack or make the scene any more pronounced than it needed to be, and, on account of having been called out on his ogling, Benji could hardly bring himself to look Hayden in the eye.

"The change. We're cool." When this kicked Hayden out of her foggy panic feedback loop, Rob widened his eyes and gave the quickest of 'be cool' nods at her. She nodded back at him, and he looked up at the car idling directly in front of them. "Silver Avalon. That's your ride, Benji."

Benji looked up at the car and over at Rob, confused.

"I hailed an Uber. I don't know the rules about field trips or if this is even considered that, but I don't want to mess around and do something that will get Galindo in trouble. He'll take you right to your house."

Rob held his hand out for Benji to shake. Benji was reluctant to grab it, but Rob let him know the soft cast was just there so no one would hit it. He undid the Velcro binding and opened and closed his hand in its new freedom. Benji still grabbed it like he might a baby bird.

"Come on, kid. It's not broken. Shake it like you got a pair." Rob knew he was performing here, but he didn't know for whom. Sure, he had a new audience, but that line was one he'd picked up from his father, one from his lessons in masculinity and machismo that Rob always hated but which, like many of the others, Rob was learning over time had actual value to it, however antiquated and backward it may have been on paper.

Benji tightened his grip and gave Rob a firm shake. Rob nodded his approval at this and told him to email when he got home safe. As his car pulled off, Benji stared out the back windshield at Rob and Hayden and her pedicab in all of its crushed velvet hipster fashion and seemed awakened to the existence of a brand-new world inside of the one he'd always inhabited. He seemed already wistful for the young adulthood he had not only not yet lived past, but which still lay ahead of him, filling him not with promise but with angst at the years between where he was and where he wanted to be.

Rob could see in the kid's eyes, as the car pulled him away to the enclave that he and his family would no longer be able to afford in a decade—the Subarus, little neighborhood libraries, and the innovative investors buying up lots, tearing down single homes to replace with two to three chic micro-homes. He'd seen the passion in Benji's eyes when he met him, but he knew now that the kid would chase that passion. He couldn't remember the last time he was that hungry for life, at least not specifically. It would have to have been in catdragbird, writing the songs that he would play in a few days in someone's living room to a crowd of their friends and other fans who would be interested. Penny still seemed that hungry, but it could have just been the crazy in her brain or the drugs she had to take to calm it.

Rob wished Maria was waiting for him at home. She could always be counted on to help him come down after a show or a recording session while the fuel in his rockets burned out after having carried him up and up and up out of the atmosphere and halfway to the kind of contentment that can only be reached through perfect execution of the right kind of music for the right audience of people, which is to say, a kind of contentment that would never be reached. She would always listen to Rob when he would give her a run-down of what he'd done, what he'd made with his skill. She'd always try her best to understand his excitement, his passion. She would then just as faithfully give him time in the days thereafter to wallow in the silence that followed. She could always look at him and just know who he was in that moment, what he was capable of, what he needed.

Even if she were home when he got home, she wouldn't be there for him. She wouldn't even be there to spite him. He needed her, and she wouldn't be there, and so at that moment, he hated her.

"Jesus Christ." Hayden had taken her water bottle from the holder affixed to the crossbar underneath her seat, and she took a deep drink. "Do you think he knew?"

"Knew what, Snoop?" Rob got out of the carriage and moved a few steps from Hayden on his way to his car. Danny, the bands, both Mexican and Swedish, Benji's passion, the shell of herself Penny had become and what it said about him had put Rob in a mood, and knowing that he wasn't going to have Maria to talk him off the ledge the night had put his ego on already had Rob stewing and ready to fight.

"Fuck, fuck, fuck, fuck, fuck. Fuck!"

Rob had to turn to face Hayden because the last thing he was expecting at the moment was for her to fall apart sobbing as she seemed to be doing at that moment.

"Come on, now. He didn't know, I swear. But, I mean, even if he did, the kid's cool. He won't say anything. I promise." Rob knew it wasn't possible for Benji to be home already, but he took his phone out, opened his mail app, and swiped down to refresh the mailbox to put the device between himself and this person, who was dumping too much emotion and panic on him just then.

"But you could tell?" she asked.

"Well, I'm not going to lie. You look high off your ass—"

"Fuck!"

"But I'm certain he didn't notice." Rob slid his phone back in his pocket and held his palms up.

Hayden looked at him through teary eyes, trying to read on his face if he was lying. She looked over at his hand, at the cast on it. "What happened to that?"

"I broke it punching someone," Rob said, taking off the brace and rubbing his sweaty hand. "It's fine now, but I keep the brace so people can see it and think twice before hitting it or something."

"You're a musician, right? Like, big time?" She wiped the tears from her face and took another drink from her bottle.

"Yeah, something like that. But at school, I'm just a teacher. Well, sort of. I'm half a teacher."

"I'm Catie, by the way." She held her hand out, and Rob gave it a disinterested shake. "Come on, teach. Shake it like you got a pair."

Rob rolled his eyes and turned heel. He was done for the night. "Alright, Snoop. You have yourself a nice night," he said over his shoulder.

"Wait!" Hayden called to him in a panic. Now he was ready to roll up his sleeves and say something mean. He was ready to punish this lady for his night. "Please. Just, let me be honest with you."

"More honest than crying over a kid seeing you high bicycling downtown in a getup like you're on your way to a burlesque show?" Rob said. Again, it was fortuitous that Hayden was as gone as she was because what she said next came out before really registering what he said.

"I'm a fan of yours. Well, of Penny Pain. I have all your catdragbird stuff." She chuckled nervously.

This threw Rob off his back foot. He was no longer prepared to strike. He might have blushed then in a way he probably hadn't in years. He was glad for the dark of night because no matter how long he'd been performing, no matter how big the venues or the crowds he'd experienced, there still wasn't much he could do to minimize the ricochet of a pretty girl telling him she was a fan of his. He was just now allowing himself to see— he hadn't initially because he'd felt the need to cover his ass, being caught out on the town with a student by a teacher who didn't have the whole story, and then he didn't because of her need to cover her own ass at being as gone as she clearly was on a drug that, while widely used and accepted, was still illegal and taboo enough among the kids to cause problems in her classes—how pretty she was.

"catdragbird?" Rob asked. "How old are you?"

"Twenty-four, but my sister loved it. I have both albums and the EP. It, like, meant a lot to me as a kid. She's why I started writing. Shit, she's why I teach English. And you're why I play." Hayden seemed to realize that she now held the power between them and seemed to sense, maybe even see in Rob's eyes, how he was seeing her then. "And, for the record, I used to do burlesque in college."

"You just said a lot of things that made me feel both good about myself and old as fuck," Rob said.

"Oh, shut up. You're still playing, and you look good." She took half a cigarette out of her fanny pack and, upon lighting it, Rob realized it wasn't a cigarette she'd started earlier and had to snuff. Instead, it was a ceramic cigarette-shaped one-hitter. From the smell of the smoke that she let fall on her and ended up pushing out at him with her chuckles, Rob could tell it was good weed. She held out the one-hitter to Rob, and he shook his head no.

"Well, you had a panic attack at the kid maybe seeing you high and a little confession about being a fan. You want me to complete the roller coaster of emotions for you?"

"Yeah," the smoke distorted her vocal cords. She issued a couple of coughs, tapped the cashed weed from the pipe, and put it back in her pack.

"What are you doing Sunday?" Rob said.

"Nothing," she said fast and forcefully. "Well, I mean, I was going to do the pedicab for the last night of the festival. It'll be slow but still ridiculous money. But I'm up for anything. Roller coaster me."

"I'm going to be the special surprise guest on a living room show Penny's doing here in town." Rob knew how unfair it was to drop this knowledge in that moment, like fishing with dynamite, but he wasn't fully in the game. Not really. At that moment, he really wasn't trying to do anything more than make a fan's day—the fact of how she looked, of the tattoo peaking up from the sports bra under the cut-up T-shirt she was wearing and his natural curiosity at what it could be of, what it would look like on that body, didn't come into play at that moment.

"Get the fuck out!" Hayden shouted, and Rob won all the power back. There, the casual flirtatious bemusement that Hayden had put between the two of them was abandoned. Her eyes were wide with excitement at the idea of seeing Penny perform, at seeing him perform with her, that Rob knew from that moment on, if he wanted her, she would be his.

It had been a while since he'd sought out that kind of attention and feeling it at that moment put him on the right side of his age. Sure, he wasn't in No Somos Marineros, hadn't felt their kind of fire in longer than he could remember, or even at least up on stage at Stubb's with the Swedish jerk-offs who, despite the kind of art they were making, were made alive by it. But neither was he with Penny, sweet Penny in all of her actual pain and made older than she had to be by the substances she'd always turned to in an attempt to numb it.

If nothing else, that's what Penny had taught Rob when they were strung out and jonesing and ready to cut each other's throats for the last ten dollars of smack they could buy in the wake of a drug bust over in Hayward that took 1,200 pounds of it off the street and turned their friends, their fellow thieves and vagabonds into animals with murder in their eyes. He saw it in her eyes and knew it wasn't in his eyes or his heart or his veins. He learned that day that, while he had his own pains and demons, he was mostly just bored. He was a clichéd Gen-X asshole chasing a fix. She was scarred and seeking relief. He let her have the smack, went down to the corner bodega where he was technically banned but could still shop if Penny wasn't with him, got two bottles of Thunderbird, and drank himself to sleep. A week later, he called home and told Perla he needed help. The plane tickets arrived at his P.O. box two days later. When he told Penny that his mother had bought a ticket for her too, she said she would sell it. He said fine, but he was going. He had to. She cut her wrists. He still had blood on his shoes when he got on the plane for Texas.

That was so long ago. They'd both made it out, but she was worse for wear, and he'd made a decent life for himself. So, he wasn't a kid on fire, but he wasn't *just* an old guy in the room either. He was tied to a legendary artist, he'd done legendary work, but he wasn't out on a Legends Tour. He could take a group of kids out to a show, stand in as a teacher and grown-up, and that was fine because the very same name he'd made for himself that could get them in to shows had this girl, this ridiculously fit, functionally half-naked woman who had probably had to shake off flirtations and propositions and all manner of harassment in her night job wrapped around his finger and hanging on his every word. It made him feel ten feet tall, and it made him angry at Maria.

"Really. It's going to be interesting for me. We'll play as much catdragbird as she can remember, and I'll join her on acoustic for as many of her songs as I can without fucking them up." Rob took out his phone here.

"That's so amazing I might cry." Hayden's eyes literally were watering.

"Let me get your number," Rob said. When he tapped the number into his phone, he sent a text that just read 'Rob'. "I don't even know the exact address of where the show will be, but it should be a cool, intimate atmosphere."

She texted back a heart emoji. That was it. It could have meant anything and would have meant nothing if he wanted it not to. But then she asked a question that lit a path that branched off to other paths that branched off to more possibilities than Rob cared to count: "Listen, I'm a musician too. Can I send you a link to my SoundCloud so you can give my songs a listen and tell me what you think?"

"I'll be honest with you, maybe brutally," Rob said, probably lying.

"That's exactly what I want."

"I don't think I'll listen to it before Sunday," Rob said. "I don't want that to be hanging over Sunday. I have to play, and I don't want to be wondering if you're wondering, and it'd make it weird for you too."

"Of course! Of course. It's so cool of you to do this," Hayden said, "to listen to my music, to take kids to shows, even to be teaching at our school."

Rob knew what he was doing and why. He knew why he'd brought Galindo and the kids out, just like he knew why he had taken the part-time gig at the school to begin with. He certainly knew why he was willing to listen to whatever music he would find at the link he'd just been sent. Sure, he'd gotten away from Maria that night, from contending with her not needing him, but more than that, he had the crushing weight of his dissatisfaction with what all of his ability and talent had gotten him, all that any of it could ever get anyone.

You start a band, or you write a song. You light a fire. You work hard to make something. Some magic enters the equation, and you end up with something special, maybe even something perfect. But, even if it is perfect, this thing you've created—that band or that song or that solo or that tone— all you've made is that one thing. So, you delete the recording. You break up the band. You get into fights with dipshit bass players or show promoters. You stay on the safe side of nothing mattering or being good enough. Guitars are perfect for smashing, just like the world is perfect for burning down because even when either of them is put to their best uses, all they can give you is what you get, and all you ever get is bitter disappointment.

But there's good money in being a dissatisfied but accomplished musician. It keeps you paid and within range of free drinks and drugs. It keeps you inside the velvet rope, and it gets you laid. And before it does any of that, it puts a shocked look of pride and confusion at the level of your prodigal talent on the face of your mother. It makes her look at you, finally, and not see the brother that didn't make it. And on nights like this, nights when you feel old and alone and disgusted by your life and abandoned by your wife who was supposed to know better than to expect you to be anything better than you were, it makes women look at you like Hayden was looking at Rob.

He held his hand out for a shake, and she pushed past it and into a tight embrace of Rob, who didn't hold her back but just kept his hand held out like he was still waiting for the shake.

"For sure you'll text me about Sunday?" Hayden asked.

"I promise. But, for now, I have to get onto listening to Penny's new stuff. She puts out two albums a year, and it's been quite a few years. And you have money to make out there on the drunk and the lazy."

Hayden nodded, and he walked away because if he didn't, she wouldn't have ridden off. When he got to his car, he took his phone out and put on the most recent of Penny's albums he had. Before he could put the car in gear to leave, his phone buzzed.

"Seriously. I already rented my bike out to another rider for Sunday. Don't forget to txt me." Rob's eyes skipped past the series of different smiley face emoji that followed Hayden's words.

He didn't think too much about his response. "Sure thing, Snoop."

It took longer than it should to drive to Mopac, but that was fine. He had the music to listen to. He had homework. Listening to Penny's second-to-last record, the one before her most recent critical acclaim, Rob was impressed by and somewhat shocked at how much she still had it. The validation of Hayden's interest in his music, her obvious attraction to him, burned away as quickly as any of it ever did. Likewise, Rob's satisfaction with the night burned away as quickly as any satisfaction ever did. He'd only undertaken any of this to escape an empty house, and all he had ahead of him in the immediate future was an empty house to return to.

The songs were good—rudimentary and moody little criers in minor keys that he could very easily add depth and shading to. He'd listen to the intro of a song, let the verse turn into the chorus, and move on to the next. This wasn't any judgment of Penny or her music. This was what Rob did to acclimate himself to a new artist's work when he'd been hired on to either punch it up between demo and album cut or, easier, mimic onstage what someone else had done in the studio. He'd made it through both of Penny's two most recent albums and was truly proud of his old friend, his old lover, and his old everything. She'd stayed pure. Maybe it was because there was nothing anyone could remain true to quite like a person so afflicted had to stay true to their mental illness. Rob had high school freshmen in Beginners Guitar who could play better than her, sure, but she burned hot and bright as a person. She was a virtuoso of self, exactly the opposite of what Rob was because unstrapped of his guitar, what self did Rob have, really?

Exiting 183 for the road home, Rob scrolled through his phone to find catdragbird. Poor analog-to-digital transfer kept more crackle and hiss than Rob was used to hearing in the beginning of the first song. He'd missed that crackle and hiss. It always set sonic expectations low, and it always provided a soft cushion for a listener falling back down from the heights to which the music had lifted them. That tape hiss was the first and last sounds you heard; it was the pocket watch swinging in front of your eyes before you fell deep under the hypnosis at the declaration of "at the end of this tape, you will be brought back to the surface." That silence before and after the album made whatever music you were going to listen to part of a larger work, part of *the* album, part of everything. It made the album you'd just made with your girlfriend and two people from school as real and connected to the entire body of recorded music, which itself wore its own connections to all music ever played in history.

As much as Rob had missed the sound of analog ugly, and as nostalgic as he was for the tools he'd learned to build with as an apprentice, he wasn't prepared to hear with his old pro's ears the sounds he and Penny made on his 4-track in a studio he'd been able to check out at the conservatory. It was as adventurous and playful as it could be while still being as almost sophisticated as it was. If Rob were a more romantic guy, he might shed a tear at all the distance that separated who he'd become from who he was when he recorded those songs. But if Rob were a more romantic guy, he'd be as broke and as broken as Penny, still making the same music, but still on the same drugs too, or maybe even already dead from using them. No. What Rob felt was anger at having lost that. He admired the pureness of his younger self, back when he didn't have to pick nits off the hide of aesthetic and cool and legitimate in order to find fault enough in the world around him to gripe at. Back then, Rob was pure fuck-the-world anger. Back then, his music didn't have to be perfect, and the aim of his anger didn't have to be either. It was such a simple time, and he couldn't stand how complicated it all had gotten.

On tour in support of that first album, Rob had slept on pool tables, on countless couches or floors of young punks out on the scene more dedicated to keeping it going than actual fans of catdragbird. He'd stolen gasoline from stations all around the country and even siphoned it off of a couple of cars when things got rough. He'd pissed in Big Gulp cups and shit into plastic bags, squatting out over the side of the front row of back seats in the van they'd had to abandon on the side of the road outside of Barstow. He'd slept with women, Penny with men, for places for the band to stay, and they'd each crept out of the beds of their one night stands to steal whatever bills could be taken from wallets or purses, whatever food or booze could easily be taken under an arm under the cover of night. Penny had been caught once. The guy hit her. Rob had been caught a couple of times. Once, he'd had to shove a woman down to the ground who'd started hitting him—he wasn't proud of it, but it was what he'd had to do. It was an ugly life at times, but it was one he'd had to be awake to live through.

When pulling into his driveway, Rob's headlights held a spotlight on an existence that was crushing him in a state of perpetual sleep paralysis. He knew he was awake. He knew he could get up and move if only the spell he was under could be broken. He could hear and even see life around him happening. But this life, that house—the wife and the fact of her not just letting it go these last three months, not just giving up her end of the fight and conceded with the fact that she'd married an asshole and just accepted him as he was, the way all of the rest of the world had always accepted him—they were sitting on his chest and crushing him.

Rob knew himself well enough to know that it was what had happened this night—the Swedish and Mexican kids, the actual kids from his school, Penny and Snoop, all of *South-by*—that had him on edge and spiraling out. Still, seeing Maria's car in the driveway filled Rob with some small measure of relief because upon seeing it, he had somewhere to focus all of the negative energy that was coursing through him. It was after midnight, but he hit the button for the garage door opener. He'd done this in the past when he got home late as a way to both let Maria know by the sound of the noisy machine that he was home, he was safe, and, more recently, to do the same in a much less considerate way on nights when she had the bed and he had the couch, and he hoped with every bit of petty spite in him that the noise would disturb her rest.

But that wasn't the case on that night. On that night, the bed was his. She might not even necessarily hear him from the living room. To Rob's credit, he went straight to bed. He contented himself with seething at her from a distance, with resigning himself to sleep and a better day tomorrow. He didn't go looking for a fight.

CHAPTER SIXTEEN

The night had taken more out of Rob than he'd realized. When Maria crept into the bedroom, slipped into bed and nearly onto his back, and wrapped him in a hungry embrace, he looked at the clock and realized that, he was already fast asleep even though he'd only been in bed for less than ten minutes. Those ten minutes were enough for him to have been startled by the feel of her hand on his chest, but not enough to put to bed the anger the night had awoken in him. At the feel of Maria's tender kisses on the side of his neck and up to his hairline behind his ear, Rob felt a deep disgust at his own arousal and the state of his life and marriage that had him on fire at that moment for the crumbs of affection he'd been rationing and learning to live without in those recent months.

Maria didn't realize anything was different when Rob turned around and didn't kiss her. Instead, she returned every bit of anger and pent-up passion that Rob dealt out. Was it cold? Perhaps, but recently, their every bit of contact had been. Was it rough and removed? Of course, they'd been competing at hate-fucking each other just the same as they'd been competing at being right over the course of the year as it unfolded, and this seemed no different than that. He pulled back when she grabbed at his back and hips, she just grabbed and clawed at him harder. As they rolled over, and she tried to kiss at his lips and face as he turned his face away hard, she just bit at his ear and neck. When they finished, he got up without a word, without any kind of embrace or even a glance at Maria, just it as it had been those months.

It could be overcome. It was time. There was a monster for them to fight together. There was cause for them to team up and face, for them to make each other stronger and better like they always did. Lain there in bed, more vulnerable than for her naked body atop their soiled and sweaty sheets, Maria was ready to rip open her heart and pour it out for Rob. She was ready to be the bigger person or, at least, to admit she wasn't big enough to keep fighting and face what was happening to her mom in Humble. She was ready to surrender.

Rob eyed her suspiciously when he entered the room. She thought it was just mischief or, at worst, him standing his ground at the battle she was about to end. She expected this. This was all just more of the same that was about to end.

"You're still here?" he said, getting in bed and facing away from her. "You can't just come in here and fuck me and think that'll mean you don't have to go back to the couch. It's my night."

"I know it's your night. I just wanted to—" she was on her back, looking up at and talking to the moonlight-blue ceiling. "I need to talk to you. All of this time, all of this anger and pettiness, it's too much. It's been too much. If we can do this, if we can be husband and wife enough to still fuck in our bed at night, why can't we just be grown-up enough to sleep together, to stay together? Why can't we just get over it? I'm going to have to go back to Humble tomorrow. I'm going to have to be going back and forth for a bit here in the future, and I . . . I just can't do this anymore."

"What's happening in Humble?" Rob still didn't turn to face Maria.

"It's my mom. She's forgetting things. The doctor said it's pretty bad Alzheimer's, or, really, I guess they can't technically call it that. I have a home health nurse going every day, but it's not enough. She's not safe. I didn't know how bad it was. I didn't know because I'm so used to ignoring her, not answering her calls, not listening to her voicemails, being too busy rolling my eyes when I do talk to her to actually listen to her. She's been losing her mind, and I haven't been able to notice it because I've been too angry at the past to listen. Rob, I fucked up." Here she stopped talking to the ceiling and slid back over onto Rob's back.

The tears she cried on his back made Rob feel for her. They made him want to turn around and comfort her. Those tears almost ended it all. Had she said any of this before that night, before he saw Penny and before *South-by* made him feel old and Hayden made him feel still young enough to do something about it, had those tears fallen on him that first night she told him she was going home to Humble, it would have been over. But they hadn't.

"So, your world starts to fall apart, and I'm supposed to fix it? I'm supposed to turn around right now and hold you and let you cry to me? Is that it? Is that what's supposed to happen here? Why? Why should I be that kind right now when you haven't?"

The cruelty in Rob's words made Maria pull away. If she weren't on top of the covers, she would have hidden beneath them. As it was, all she could do to cover herself from attack, from shame and weakness, was to sit up in a small ball of herself and pull a pillow over her naked body.

"Because you're my husband, and I need you. I need you, Rob." Maria was crying hard now.

Rob turned around to face her now. The sight of her in tears aroused nothing that could stop the momentum of his anger. "You told me that night, you said that it's a dangerous thing to never be wrong. Well, you know what? It's a fucking pathetic thing to ever think that anyone should ever have to feel something just because you're feeling it. If you're going to use the bathroom to wash up before you hit the couch, don't leave the light on. I fucking hate it when you do that."

And with that, Rob rolled back over onto his side, facing away from the wife he'd broken. She got up and went straight to the living room. She didn't make any effort to stifle the sounds of her sobbing as she cried herself to sleep, and Rob did nothing to comfort her.

Rob hardly slept that night, or at least he felt that he hardly had, as he was tossed around by thoughts of the night and where his life had put him, where he felt Maria had put him. How could he live on this end of the relatively short drive from home to downtown and the whole of the music world hanging out down there? How had he gone from couch surfing in the East Bay to living out of vans to a pre-fab, subdivided life? Despite these old panic-inducing regrets popping up, he'd had a good night and was letting it calm and invigorate him. He turned over on his pillow, and the waking thought of how good a gig he would have with Penny came to mind. Then he worked a divot into his pillow that needed pounding out, and the thought of the sight of Snoop's tattoos came to mind, and the vibrant electricity of romantic power came to mind. When he'd just almost fallen asleep, the sweet thought of having won the night came to mind and put an effortless smile on his face. However much he did or didn't sleep, he was out, under a doze so peaceful and full that Maria had to repeat herself twice before he woke.

"Rob," she said, "you need to leave."

Maybe it was that his sleep had been restless and his mind running, or maybe it was that he was so dedicated to keeping the upper hand that he had slept with one rhetorical eye open, but Rob didn't so much as wipe the sleep from his eyes or even lift his head from the pillow before answering. "Why?"

"We can't keep doing this. We just can't. I can't. It's not healthy. It hasn't been for a long time. We're only hurting each other now. We always have, at least a little, I guess, but now it's all we're doing, hurting each other." She sounded patient, too exhausted to be otherwise.

Rob imagined she'd spent the night crying, that she'd cried herself to bed, woke up, and got right back to it. It was the most he'd made her feel something, outside of the physical, in the last three months. "No. Why should I have to leave? This house is as much mine as it is yours. You leave."

Maria wasn't ready for this. Rob wasn't either. At the sound of her frustrated stammering, Rob opened his eyes and propped himself up on a self-satisfied elbow. When he looked at her, he was momentarily shocked to see that she didn't have a night of crying puffing up her face. She didn't look broken. She looked tired. Rob convinced himself at that moment that her exhaustion was related to him, to their fight. If he'd allowed himself to think of her, her context, her pain at everything going on in her life that didn't include him, he might have had to apologize, to see what he was doing to her, or at least to see the state she was in while he was doing it to her. If Rob could take a step back from his victory march, he would have seen the woman he fell in love with standing in front of him in a world of pain he'd been in once before, one she'd helped bring him out of back in some of his darkest days since getting clean. If he could have seen that, he might have saved his marriage. But Rob wasn't one to save things, one to see beyond himself or his winning. Rob tore things down. Rob was blind to any part of the world that didn't echo his superiority, at least when he was right like he knew he was just then.

She just closed her eyes and shook her head. Rob waited for a retort, but she turned heel and walked into their shared closet. She walked out with arms full of clothes. She didn't slow down on her way out the door when she spoke tired words over her shoulder, "I have to go to Humble. I don't know how long I'll be."

Rob stayed on the bed, still propped up on his elbow, and let the disgust he felt wash over himself. He could get up. He could run after Maria and apologize, but for what? There was too much, and Rob didn't have time—and it didn't seem like she did, either—to apologize for being himself. He felt tired from a night out, felt old for being so tired after so tame a night. He slipped down onto his pillow, closing his eyes, his brain now racing with reasons why he was pathetic. He wasn't as real or raw as No Somos Marineros. Hell, the terrible Swedish band was more relevant than he'd been in over a decade. He had to settle for being trotted out as a special guest star in a goddamn nostalgia-act show-and-tell with a broken old punk who herself hadn't mattered in even longer than he had. And Snoop? Hayden? Had he really let two minutes of attention from a pretty girl set him on fire? Had he let it keep him awake at night like he was some kind of goddamn virgin, and she had promised him the world by sharing a Soundcloud link with him, which she'd clearly only done because she thought she might be able to use him?

He heard the sound of Maria's car door closing, its engine turning over, and her driving off. He didn't know why he always had to break his world, why he had to push and push and push so that he could feel comfortable in a state of conflict, but he'd done it again, and now he didn't know if he could undo it. He didn't realize it when he finally fell asleep, but he woke up sweaty and sore. He got out of bed and went into the soundproofed room upstairs where he practiced and recorded. He didn't know what to do but to play, and so he did. He started with scales, warming up and getting ready to dive hard into Penny's new music. He got into it, ending up playing until it was dark out. He had taken some notes for questions to ask Penny as an attempt to perfect his approach to her songs, even gone about rearranging several of their old originals for acoustic. By the time he got downstairs to check the kitchen for something to eat or drink that would make him feel anything other than numb, he had almost forgotten how badly he'd messed up with Maria that morning. Of course, he hadn't really forgotten, but the day he'd had—the fight, the realization of how big of a piece of shit he was, drowning out the sounds of his own shouting at himself in his mind with music—had put him in a place he was familiar with, it put him in a mood he was used to. It left him feeling alone, unplugged from anything outside of music, which was fine, because the studio he'd made in his mind, soundproofed as it was to keep the sounds of the world out more than to keep the chaos within contained, still had some of his decisions, the consequences of his actions, bleeding in, and that wouldn't do. He just couldn't handle it.

SECTION THREE—
REUNION TOUR

CHAPTER SEVENTEEN—*(2012)*

W hen they were less than a year into their marriage, Maria got all the proof she didn't know she needed that what she had with Rob was as real and nearly perfect as any relationship she could ever hope to have. It was only then, after a short courtship and quick marriage, that everyone involved—his parents, Eunice, Aline, Kaylee, even she and Rob if they were honest with themselves—was suspicious of as a being a mistake, had barely gotten off the ground that Maria was proven right in her choice to marry Rob.

On her way back from having met a client for an early-morning tour of a house out on the bluff, Perla Vera's car was struck head-on by a car traveling the wrong way on the JFK Causeway, the highway headed down and out of Corpus Christi to Flour Bluff and North Padre Island beyond it. It was nine-forty-five in the morning. The drunken man driving the other car also died on impact. He had been at a bar after working the third shift at the Army Depot fixing helicopter blades.

Rob had heard the dumb coincidence—and that's all he would allow himself to see it as, that's all he ever would have seen it as; the fact of his mom dying, the sentimentality for how she would have seen it, didn't change that—when he got the call from one of his father's receptionists.

"May I speak to Rob Vera?"

He could already hear tears and sniffles on the other end of the line. "Yes . . ."

Rob was always suspicious of any calls from the 3-6-1 area code, particularly those coming from one of his father's offices, like this one was. It was a dumb power-play thing he used to do, have someone call and direct Rob to, "Please hold for Dr. Venancio Vera."

"Rob," her voice broke here, "this is Irma at your father's office. Are you . . . um . . . you're not driving or anything right now, are you?"

"No."

"Rob, there's been an accident—" Rob never really thought it was a good thing that he was getting a call that his father had died, but at that moment, he felt an excited curiosity that died with Irma's next words. "Your mother was in a car accident. She didn't make it."

The weight of his first thought didn't land until it was followed by the feeling that it was wrong and unfair for the call to have been about Perla instead of Venancio. These were the immediate, passive thoughts that came, quickly subsumed and eclipsed by the only active concern Rob now had down in Corpus.

"And my dad? Is he okay?"

Upon hearing Rob ask this from the office (the second bedroom in their apartment, one Rob didn't mind letting her have as long as he could keep his guitars in the living room and practice out there on his acoustic), Maria stepped out to see if everything was okay. She approached Rob, holding his phone up to his right ear and his left hand over his left ear, staring up at the ceiling like he was listening back to a track trying to figure out how to make a guitar part work. She could tell he needed his space, so she sat down on the sofa next to where he stood.

"Of course," Irma seemed happy to be able to relay any kind of good news she had. "He wasn't in the car with her."

Rob knew his father wouldn't have been in that car with her any more than she would have been in a golf cart with him on the back nine at Lozano. "No. I mean, is he doing okay?"

"Oh, well . . ."

Rob could read the silence here. He understood that his father had probably disappeared, made himself scarce to insulate himself, keeping his pain and anger in and keeping the eyes and pity of outsiders out of sight and out of reach. He did this when his uncle died. He just left, handing off as many appointments as he could to other doctors or just rescheduling and canceling as needed. He didn't even tell Perla where he was going. He just left, headed, Perla assumed, for Greenton. She was right, almost. He rented a cabin at a ranch just outside of town where he did the quick work of signing off on the funeral arrangements. He had the undertaker call home to Perla to let her know of the scheduling.

"He's gone," Rob said in a way that let Irma off the hook for answering the question.

"Yes," she said. "We didn't—"

"Thank you, Irma. I'll be down there in a few hours."

Rob slipped the phone into his pocket, still looking up at the ceiling. Maria put a hand on his hip to remind him that she was there, and he was not alone.

"What is it?" she asked him.

Rob was reeling, more lost in trying to think out and plan the next several days than feeling what the truth he'd just heard. He looked down at her, through her, his eyes darting around, trying to keep up with his thoughts.

"Rob?" Maria stood up to face him. She grabbed his face in her hands as softly as she could.

"I need dress shoes. I ruined my old ones at a show."

"Rob, are you okay?"

"It was at a festival at a goddamn fairground. I had to walk through mud and horse shit. They were so wrecked I trashed them."

"Rob, please. Is your dad okay?"

Rob finally looked square at Maria, the sound of her misapprehension of what was happening having drawn him out of his head.

"My dad? He's fine. He left to take a breather. It's my mom. There was an accident. I need dress shoes. I need to get someone to cover for a couple gigs I have lined up. I'll have to do that and pack, and I need some new dress shoes."

Maria had immediately pulled her hands over her mouth when Rob said there was an accident. She decided right then that she needed to step up for Rob. Sure, she was losing a parent too, one who was as much as any other parent she had, one who she was a better child to than Rob was, but she'd already lost a parent (well, she'd lost three, but one who had chosen to parent her), and she knew how much it hurt. She knew that Rob didn't deal well with hurt or with his father, for that matter. She would step up for him. She would make it all okay.

She walked away from Rob, leaving him standing there in the living room. His head was spinning. He just needed a minute. Before he realized what had happened, he found himself sitting on the couch. When he finally realized that Maria was still there, it was because all of the commotion of her moving around frantically from room to room that snapped him out of his moment of shock. He'd lost himself trying to remember the last time he'd called his mother instead of just waiting for her to call him, the last time he'd told her he loved her instead of just 'you too'-ing her.

"Do you want to shower before we go?" Maria asked, standing in front of Rob, a bit of sweat present on her forehead, her voice calm but assertive.

"I . . . what?"

Rob looked past Maria at the packed bags in the hallway, the garment bag hanging from the knob on the front door.

"We have to go. We need to get down to Corpus. We need to help with arrangements. You need to be with your father."

"I need—" Rob started.

"We can buy shoes there. You can call whoever leads the bands you're supposed to gig with from the car. They can figure it out. They'll understand, or they can go to hell." Maria crouched down in front of Rob sitting on the couch. She put her hands on his thighs and stared action at his eyes. "Do you want to shower before we leave? It'll make for a more comfortable ride, and it might clear your mind."

Rob looked at Maria in front of him, then over again at the bags packed and ready to go. There was no degree to which a shower would take Rob out of the ride he was strapped to, no way it could slow, or even distract Rob from, its momentum.

"Let's just get on the road," he said.

So, they left.

The house Rob grew up in had become many different kinds of cold over the course of his lifetime. There was the haunted house chill of a young family mourning their dead baby, the frostbite numbness of a pilled-out mom and absent dad, and the sub-zero burn of a father's unbridled animosity toward the son he'd built an empire for and who wasn't even trying to live up to it. There had been blizzards of resentment blown out in stinging winds of disgust in the glances his mother flashed at his father upon his late-hour returns home from "the office" or early hour stumbles in when he'd had "business" to do over drinks with this local leader or an important group or another. The house had been a big, silent library cold when Rob was a kid, and he didn't know why his mother walked on eggshells around a house that had to be kept silent for his sleeping or otherwise occupied father. It had been an antiseptic, hospital cold when Rob sweated through heroin withdrawals, his mother standing by his bed along with his loyal nurse and his father, with the bedside manner of a man for whom the majority of the patients he saw were either locally numb or completely under, periodically checking Rob's vitals and, only once, begrudgingly giving him a shot to take some of the edge off of the hell he was going through.

And now here he was, wife in tow to remind him that he'd made it out, that he was past the place and all of its traumas, standing in the mausoleum cold of the foyer, calling out for his father like he might never have before, but who was he going to call out for now? She was gone. A new body was ready for the family tomb, Rob thought, looking up at the urn that was certainly too big to hold a baby.

"Dad?" Rob called out.

Maria stood behind him, taking in the sight of the house she'd visited so many times, but now was new to her too. When they heard a tired "huh?" coming loud and groggy from the hallway that led back to the bedrooms, she stepped forward and grabbed Rob's hand. Standing here in the antechamber to the place that he'd run from so young, the place he was still running from in his adulthood, she had never seen Rob look so small, and she couldn't blame him for ever leaving a place that could make that of him.

"I guess they called you?" Venancio's voice was nearing down the hall. "You should have called to let me know you were on your way."

"Did you think I wouldn't come?" Rob shouted out, louder than he needed to. Just as he shouted the last word, his father entered the room.

He was wearing an A-shirt, a pair of boxers, and ankle socks. "Still," he said before seeing Maria. "Goddamnit, Robin, you should have told me she was here."

"Once again, *Ben*," Rob said, wanting to match his father barb-for-barb in response to being called his birth name, but the name that only his mother was left using in his father's comfortable and successful old age resounded in that house like an echoing boom in her absence, "did you think I wouldn't bring my wife?"

"Yeah, well . . ." Venancio replied. He was courteous enough to turn his back to his guest but not so much so that he didn't do a deep yawn, loud and indulgent like he always yawned, startling Maria like it always startled her, and reach down for a full session of vigorously scratching at and under his testicles. "I'm not moving at full speed. Sue me. I'll rinse off real quick and dress. Make us some coffee, *Rob*."

"Alright, Dad."

In the kitchen, Maria tried her best to ignore the sadness of Perla's absence. This was not happening to her, not now. Right now, she had to be strong for Rob. There were Styrofoam takeout containers all over the island counter, and a bottle and a half of scotch stood empty on the counter near the sink. Rob busied himself making the coffee—throwing out old grounds from the basket, cleaning out the filter, preparing the water, and grinding the beans—in such a way that he seemed to have fallen back into an old rhythm in the kitchen.

As the coffee brewed, Rob finally turned to face the mess his father had made of his previous night's dinner. He opened up one of the containers to see what was inside and rolled his eyes at what he saw, at all of it. He grabbed a wastebasket from in the pantry, pulled off its swing-top cover, and shoved all of the garbage from the countertop down into it. He grabbed the empty bottle of scotch by the sink and threw it into the wastebasket before replacing its cover and putting it back in the pantry and stood reading the label of the still half-full bottle while he waited for the coffee.

"Well, I guess you can fall apart emotionally with some class if you have to," he said aloud, not to himself, but not to Maria either. When the coffee machine wheezed its last push of heat and its three sharp beeps sounded, Rob handed the bottle to Maria for her to inspect. She didn't really know what to say, what she was looking at or for. It wasn't until she heard Rob sniffling and fighting back sobs that she stopped faking interest or knowledge in Scotch quality.

It only then occurred to Maria that she had never seen Rob cry before. They'd only been married less than a year, and their courtship lasted all of nine months. There was still much for each of them to learn about each other; that was one way in which their marriage remained fresh and new and not the least bit scary. He didn't turn to face her when she approached, so she wrapped him in a tight embrace from behind. He reached up to take hold of her forearms.

Rob just held her like that for a moment, his tears falling on her arms, his sobs heaving in her embrace. He let go and reached up to grab a mug from the cupboard that stood open in front of it. He held it in his palms like a precious artifact. Maria had to tiptoe up to be able to see down over his shoulder at what had caught him off guard. It was just a plain navy-blue mug, but emblazoned on it was a different time, an old hope Rob had abandoned, but his mother never did. It said, "SFCM est. 1917."

"This might have been the last time I did something to make her happy, to make her proud," Rob said.

"She was always very proud of you."

"I know she was. And I know I made her happy too. But none of it was for her. None of it. She was dying of thirst in this fucking desert, and all I could give her were drops of whatever I did that might make her happy. She gave and gave and gave. School was her idea, dropping out to get my GED so I could study music seriously. Even then, I ran off to California. He was never here. I was all she had, and I left."

"You did what you had to for yourself." Maria moved to Rob's side in order to look him in the eyes. "Taking care of her wasn't your job."

"I know that. Taking care of her was never anyone's job. But I graduated for her. I delayed a tour between the albums to finish. She knew I didn't need it. But she asked me when we came through town on tour for the first record. We played the Ritz downtown, and she bragged and even brought friends, which had to be a trip. And before I left, she asked if I would graduate for her. She didn't beg or guilt me. She didn't mention her dead dad or my shitty one. She just said I was so close, and it would mean the world to her. She was so earnest. I didn't know how to be selfish enough to say no."

Rob put the mug back and was grabbing three others when his father walked in. Venancio stopped in his tracks at the sight of Rob crying. Sure, it had been years since he'd seen his son cry, but even back when he was a baby and small child, Venancio never knew what to do to comfort the boy. He never even tried. He didn't have to. That's what Perla was for. He looked up and saw the mug and seemed to realize the moment Rob was having, so he didn't address it. For his part, Rob didn't try to play off his crying, but he didn't address it either. He just gave his face one rub of his sleeve and turned red-eyed to face his father.

"Car crash?" Rob asked, filling up a cup with coffee and mixing milk to his father's liking like he was in the break room back at the dental office again. He handed over the mug to his father and poured one black for himself.

"Yes. Car crash." Venancio said. He took a sip from his coffee and gave his same old "Ah" of approval. "Drunk driver coming off a morning of drinking after the third shift at the base."

"Drunk driver?" Rob said incredulously.

"Yes," Venancio said.

"Coming from the base?" Rob said in the same tone.

"Yes," Venancio said.

Maria knew about Perla's father, about how he died and had potentially saved her life by not having her drive him to the bar that night. She didn't know, however, that he also worked at the Corpus Christi Army Depot repairing helicopter blades. She saw Rob and his father share a look in solemn acknowledgment of the eerie coincidence for a moment, then break their shared look and not return to it because, as much as they both knew she would have loved her story to end in so poetic and tragic a manner, it wasn't a poetic story to them or, at least, it wasn't their story—they still had to live through the rest of it.

"So, what's the plan?" Rob asked into his coffee cup.

"Well, we'll have the rosary in two days. Then we'll have the funeral on Monday." Venancio took a sip of his coffee, then walked over to a cupboard adjacent to the one Rob had just gotten the coffee cups from. He pulled down two lowball glasses, opened up the freezer, and pulled out two ice cubes. He dropped one cube in each glass and poured them nearly full of scotch from the bottle Maria had put down on the island counter when Rob started crying. "That will give us time to make the arrangements."

"Doesn't the funeral home figure that stuff out?" Rob picked up his glass and took a sip.

"Yes. And they're helping. There are just some things that will take some extra working to get right." Venancio downed his drink, grabbed the bottle, and pulled a stool up to the island. He filled his glass again and put his palms down on the counter on either side of it. "So, we'll have the rosary at Christ the King, but after that, they'll take the body over to Greenton, and we'll meet at the funeral home in the morning."

Rob put down the coffee he had switched back to drinking. "Greenton?"

"She and I had talked about this. Whoever died first, the other would pick where we get buried. I lived. I choose Greenton." He kept his left palm on the counter and very calmly grabbed his lowball glass and downed its contents. He cocked his chin over to Rob and only looked at him from the side of his eyes.

"No fucking way. No way. No!"

Rob stepped hard at his father. Venancio held a hard index finger out, and Rob stopped just short of his personal space. Then, Venancio turned to look him face-to-face. He didn't get up from his chair, but he slowly squared his shoulders over to face his son, his finger not moving from in front of Rob, pointing out the fact that while he may have worked his whole life to be able to give his son a soft life, he hadn't fully softened from the one he'd lived.

"She didn't want to be buried in Greenton. She always said she didn't want to be. She didn't want rattlesnakes and scorpions all over her grave. She didn't want to be buried in that red dirt. You know she didn't. She always said so." Rob slapped his hand on the counter, and when his father sat up higher on his stool, he finally regarded what he had sitting in front of him. "Get your hand out of my face."

Venancio seemed to be doing the math of what was standing in front of him. Rob thought he was right. He was stepping up and speaking up for his mother, for what he thought she wanted. He wasn't crying or whining. He hadn't fully attacked, but he hadn't backed down either. Had the world made Rob something close to the kind of man he'd hoped he'd have in a son? He sat there, thinking the situation over a beat too long, because Rob spoke louder but in a more even tone, "I said get your fucking hand out of my face."

Venancio kept his hand up, his finger pointed just as hard and angry at Rob, but he pulled his head back a few inches and seemed to approve of the situation that was unfolding in front of him and the man with whom he hadn't butted heads in a couple of decades. It felt like an old glove, fighting with his son, and he might have gotten up and even further in his son's face in order to prompt an actual fistfight, because how much closer can you really get to a man than having his knuckles on your face and putting yours on his? How much closer can you get to someone than bleeding on them and being bled on by them? Conflict was the only real relationship the father and son had made for themselves, and in so charged and angry and hangover-and-hair-of-the-dog-dulled a moment, a fight might have reminded the men, like only mortal violence can, that they were still alive, goddamnit. But not today. Not this morning. Perla was on a cold slab in a hospital, and the casket he was about to buy was going to have to be closed. She would be buried in Greenton. The decision had been made. It hurt and angered the boy, but it's what was going to happen. Venancio pulled his hand down from the conflict zone between himself and his son and picked up his coffee with it. He took a slow, deep drink, put down the mug, and gave his exaggerated, "ahh."

Rob softened his posture, and Maria took this as a cue to step up and try to bring him down further off of his anger. She put her body between Rob and Venancio, putting Rob in a tight hug and giving his father her back. Rob considered pushing her out of the way in order to tap back into the anger that had broken through the numbness he'd felt since hearing the news, but he didn't have it in him. He wrapped his arms lazily around Maria, just to reciprocate her gesture, and when he did, he could feel she was shaking. He'd never made her feel like that. He wanted to believe that the last time he'd been made to feel that way, it was by his father, in this very same house. But if he had the capacity for emotional honesty at that moment, he would remember that it was his mother who'd last made him shake with hopeless, fearful anger—it would most certainly have been in that house, and it most certainly would have been her last desperate reaction to some crime, legal or familial, Rob had committed. He gave Maria a hard squeeze and a reassuring glance into her watering eyes.

"All of my life, I heard the two of you argue. All of my life. She always said she didn't want to be buried out there," Rob said over Maria's shoulder at his father, who had looked away from the kind of love being displayed that had died to him long before a drunk driver sped the wrong way up the JFK Causeway and into his wife's Town Car.

"Yes, we argued about that. It started when your brother died. We didn't want to think of where we wanted to be buried then. We sure didn't want to have to think about where to bury our unborn baby. After that, she said Corpus. We looked at plots, but it didn't feel right. I said Greenton. We argued about this before you could talk."

"Then why bury her in Greenton? Why bury her where she didn't want to be?"

"We settled this years ago. It's in our wills. You'll see. Whoever survived the other would pick where we're buried. In fact, that's wrong. It specifically says that if I died, I'd be buried here, and if she died, she'd be buried in Greenton. We specifically made it that way so that neither of us would get sentimental and insist on something they didn't really want. If we both died together, you'd pick. It's all in there. By the way," Venancio paused and waited for Maria to turn and face him too, "you're getting a pretty big chunk of money. Maybe you guys can move out of that shitty apartment and into a house."

"I like our apartment," Maria said.

"But why, Dad? Who cares what the will says? You know she was terrified of that place. Why the Greenton Cemetery?"

"Well, I'm not going to drill teeth forever. I'm already pretty much part-time as it is. When I'm ready to call it quits, I want to move back over for the quiet."

Rob finished his drink in the silence of considering his father's words. He grabbed the bottle from in front of his father and filled his glass again without looking at it. He took another small sip and thought some more.

The smell of liquor being breathed out and into the room made Maria lightheaded. She could only imagine how much further the evening would devolve if they kept going. She wasn't going to stop them in the middle of their grief—it and the scotch were the only things they'd shared in decades other than acrimony—so she figured she'd try to soften the blow of the booze. "You guys want me to cook something?" When she looked in the fridge, she didn't see anything that could be easily cooked that wouldn't be either labor-intensive or a stark reminder of Perla. "Or pizza? How about pizza?"

"So, what? You'll go see her? You're still here, and so, of course, you won't see her from here. But when you move there, you'll go see her, what, every day? Every week? You'll spend that much time with her? You'll pay that much attention to her now that she's dead when you didn't when she was alive?"

Rob picked up his glass and held it hard in his palm after saying this. Already in their short marriage, Maria had seen Rob do this, zoom all of his attention in a situation to the point that he grabbed onto whatever was at hand wholly. He lived his life in his head, floating above what the rest of the world could see in a cloud of ideas and opinions and notes and melodies that no one else could understand, but when he was pulled back fully into the world, he had a fire in his eyes, and he gripped not with his fingers but his palms. She tried again to pull him out of his rage by holding onto him, but he rolled his shoulder back hard, rebuking her touch, her efforts.

"That cuts both ways, son." Venancio turned to face Rob and let an amused smile pull up the left corner of his lips. "Are you going to come down here? You gonna water her grave if she's buried here in Corpus? How often are you going to have your graveside picnics? Tell me. I'll come along."

"That's beside the point," Rob said.

"Why? Because the bar is set so low for you? All you had to do for her to love you was exactly nothing. You never had to call. You didn't even have to answer when she called you. You just had to be the one that didn't die. You could fuck your life up on drugs and fuck our lives up with your drugs. You're doing pretty well right now. Thank you, Maria." Venancio flashed a sober look at Maria—it was all sincerity and gratitude—before swinging back into the momentum of his previous contempt with a snort. "Why do you care now? She and I made the arrangements. She and I planned for our deaths, planned them so you'd be taken care of. I may not have been perfect. . . . No. Let's not insult the memory of your mom. I was a terrible husband, but she was my wife. She didn't always like me, but she loved me, and when she didn't love me, she liked me enough to stay. She didn't have to. She could have left like you did."

"I hate you so fucking much." Rob's voice raised to a shout by the end of the sentence, but Maria could feel the effort drain him, could feel the whole conversation, the reality of who he was and wasn't for his mom, drain him.

"Andale, hijo. Good to have you home." Venancio took on last deep drink of his coffee, picked up the lowball glass in his left hand and wrapped his right around the neck of the bottle, and walked out of the kitchen without looking back.

"I'll fucking kill him," Rob managed to say with the last gust of anger in him before the sadness washed over him and stopped him dead mid-lunge on his way after his father. His shoulders just fell dead on the rest of his body, and if Maria hadn't been there ready to stop him from killing his father, he might have fallen under the weight of so much sorrow.

"I'm right fucking here, mijo. Right fucking here," Venancio shouted over his shoulder on his way up to his office.

The rosary wasn't as disastrous as Rob had kept telling Maria it would be. Rob spent his time with the body before anyone—because that's all she was, and he was somewhat grateful for the deep trench in her face that had to have been caused either by her cheek being ripped open by the bone underneath or by a part of her car smashing through it, as the orange-brown layer of makeup that was meant to putty it closed, or close to closed, was a stark declaration of the fact that it wasn't his mother there in that box, wasn't her crushed and bleeding dry in all of that mangled steel and broken glass for very long after the impact of the crash—until his father and Maria showed up.

He further comforted himself with the memory of smoking DMT in Berkeley with a poet who taught there and wanted to fuck Penny or Rob or both. The poet had said that our brains produce the drug, that it's released to calm, comfort, and prepare us for the cosmic after realm we journey to. Even in the fog of the booze and pot he'd had that night, along with the walking-catatonia opioid numbness he lived in back then, Rob remembered that the DMT had pulled him up and out of himself. It had shown him a world in a universe of love and compassion he'd always been too cynical to imagine. It had told him that he was worthy of it. The experience shook him, and he tried his hardest in his dick-headed Gen-X way to scoff it off as a byproduct of being in the living room of a poet who wouldn't shut the fuck up about how powerful and paradigm-altering the drug was. Still, it had always hung around in the back of his skeptical mind—the possibility of it all being more than an empty nothing—and he hoped in the empty funeral parlor that she might have felt like he had on the cold morning that dawned on the night that hadn't ended when the poet drove them out to Indian Rock where they looked out at the bay, the sun rising behind them revealing the earth to be nothing more than the rock minerals in their bones; the trees the air they breathed and greens they ate; the water and salt of the bay their blood. Rob didn't realize he was crying until, as it had in the moment, the memory of the poet declaring to Rob and Penny that they hadn't spoken a word in hours killed his high. Rob smiled at the thought that, if his mother had been comforted and enlightened, she certainly would have died before the banality of living would have brought her back down from her own holy high.

No truce had been called, spoken or unspoken, between Rob and Venancio. They'd simply gone back to only existing in the minds and lives of each other as they had for the last two decades for the sake of Perla. They'd each drifted through the house like ghosts—Perla and Maurice had become the living inhabitants—around and near each other, sometimes even crossing paths, but their anger at each other was secondary to the pains each of them was feeling. They'd lost a wife and a mother, respectively, but they were both hurting not over that loss but over their own unique manners in which they'd failed the woman. If either of them was willing to talk about it, they'd realize that their mutual disdain over the years wasn't about one being too harsh and removed a father and the other being too fucked up and disrespectful a son; it was that each of them reminded the other of his own failings, of the fact that, no matter how steadfast they were in their opposition to what the other stood for, they'd worked in efficient tandem at taking all of her love and giving mostly pain in return.

Rob was surprised to see Venancio at the kneeler before the open casket that contained Perla when he arrived that morning. He and Maria left the house quietly that morning, opting to buy coffee at Starbucks to not wake his father with the sounds and smell of grinding and brewing the morning pot. They'd shared a brief peace the night previous when Rob and Maria arrived at the house after a night of her worriedly watching him drink to his sorrows to the unmistaken analog warmth of 180-gram vinyl being played through a tube amp. She worried constantly about his past vices resurfacing because as well as she thought she knew him, there was as much about him that she didn't understand as there was about heroin and a young adulthood in the Bay Area in the early '90s.

In the living room, Venancio, seemingly further into his night than his son, was sitting with a drink in his hand—record crates and a high-end stereo system disturbing the established order of the room. Rob didn't realize until he was too many more drinks and several records into the impromptu musical wake he and his father held that night that his father didn't have to get up to get the glass he filled with scotch and handed to Rob or the one he splashed into and handed to Maria. He'd had them on hand. He was waiting for them to join him.

"Oh my god, Dad," Rob said, the rest of his thought stolen from him by the pull the records had on him. He flipped through them like he was young and almost innocent in Aquarius Records on a lazy but electric day in the Mission District.

"It's yours. All of it. This isn't even all the records."

Rob turned from the records, and his father handed him a glass. "Dad, I can't."

"It's in the will. We planned all of this. She wanted you to have them." Venancio held his glass up, Rob and Maria did the same. They nodded and drank in silent tribute. "She wanted you to play too."

"I didn't bring my guitar," Rob said.

Venancio nodded in the direction of the show guitar that stood behind one of the speakers he had set up. It had been invisible for its permanence in the room, just another bit of background that held stories that would die shortly after Perla because who was left to tell them? Like the urn that Rob took off of the mantle in the foyer, ready for burial with Perla, it was a relic of love and pain that only Perla felt or remembered. Rob wanted to protest, but he knew it had to be that guitar.

They stayed up drinking for so long it hurt Rob to wake up. He assumed his father was sleeping hard when he woke that morning as he had continued on past when Rob left him in the living room, only propped up by his grasp on his glass and his desire to cling to the night in order to avoid the morning. Based on how Rob felt, he was surprised to see his father so well put together, looking a million times better than he had any right to. Rob interrupted him mid-sentence, and he turned to look back over his shoulder at who had intruded on the last of his time with his wife. When he saw Rob, the angry suspicion left his eyes, and he gave a warm nod. He turned and faced Perla and said a few last hurried words. He rose from the kneeler and gestured for Rob to take his turn before walking up to the first pew where he would sit for the rest of the service.

Hands were shaken. Awkward hugs were mostly avoided. Too many tears that Rob didn't deem worthy or necessary were cried for him to do the complex calculus of why he resented them, but it all went by just fine other than a hangover headache and raw stomach (exacerbated by nerves) like Rob hadn't felt in years. Like they had back then, the hangover and the nerves were calmed when he picked up the guitar. The mic stand had been lowered to catch and project the guitar sound, but Rob knew it wouldn't matter much for how haphazardly it was set up. He leaned over the guitar before he started playing and declared a kind of apology to the assembled.

"This guitar's a real piece of shit—" some people laughed, but mostly everyone looked on concerned at the state of Perla's artistic flameout son, "but she loved it. She was always real good about that."

Rob played through harmonics to try to find something as close to slightly sharper than proper tuning to account for how badly he knew the guitar would slip out during his playing. When he found something close enough to exactly the right amount of wrong, he struck the first chord of "How Deep Is Your Love" and didn't look up until he was done with his slowed-down, Spanish-style rendition of the song his mother had gifted to him and his brother so many years ago. He knew he'd played well, that the guitar hadn't thrown off the sound too much—as if anyone in the room would have been able to hear if it did—he just hoped he had done some kind of justice to his mother, to the love she felt for it and to how much it had meant to her. When he opened his eyes, he could see everyone in the room crying. He was used to this. He'd moved whole rooms of people before, but this time he took it as a small bit of validation for his efforts because whether he'd done the service justice or not, done her justice or not, they thought he did. He got up and walked right out of the room. Maria seemed to know that he would because as he approached their pew, she stood up, her purse already on her shoulder, and turned heel to walk in step with him, just half a pace back.

The next day, over the course of the nearly three-hour drive to Greenton, Rob cried while Maria drove. At first, he tried his best between sobs so heavy he thought he might pass out to explain himself to her.

"If only I could . . ." He would start.

"I just wish. . . . That motherfucker and his . . ."

With each successive attempt at wrapping his mind and words around the pain and frustration of the moment, Rob fell apart harder. By the time they reached Kingsville, he'd stopped trying altogether. He didn't realize until they reached Concepcion, when they passed the road that led to the small church on the right side of the road that he always paid mind to drag a dutiful sign of the cross across his chest upon driving by, that he'd cried himself to peaceful sleep. He looked over at Maria, who upon realizing he'd woken, resumed with the caressing of his head that had aided the exhaustion of such draining crying in putting him to sleep.

That day was when they knew. On that day, they became one, creating the real compact that would hold them together in actual, nitty-gritty wedded slog. She stepped up that day. She found herself needed, and she rose to the occasion. Rob needed nothing more in the world than Maria that day. Nothing was going to make the day hurt any less, but she could stand beside him and make the hurt okay. She was the wife he needed, the wife that only she could be. Everything was broken, and he was looking to her to fix it. He didn't know he would need her like that. He had never needed anyone like that, not any of the women he'd been with before, not even his parents. It was strange, opening himself to not only the possibility that Maria might be able to fix him, but the admission that he was broken in any way that he hadn't chosen to smash to bits on his own.

On that day, Rob and Maria found their actual shared future in the car in the middle of nowhere between a hometown Rob would never get over hating and one his father could never get over loving. Maria was ready to be let down, for Rob to reveal himself as being less than she needed, less than he seemed. Sure, she loved him. He impressed her, inspired her in his stubborn self-assuredness and constant need to push back against the norms of polite, passive acceptance of all the ways in which life makes you just accept your fate—your job, your family, your gender. She'd fallen in love with him, and she really knew it was love when he met her mother for the first time. There was a way in which he seemed able to pick up on every bit of passive-aggressive judgment Eunice was throwing out in some way or another. With a flippant remark or even with a look of exaggerated bafflement that he didn't bother hiding from Eunice because her questions, her posture and tone, were revealed in his eyes to be petty and ridiculous. He declawed her. Later, when she found her birth name and adopted it legally—Zarate, a real name, a Mexican name—he blocked all of Eunice's cruel Trojan Horse roundhouses of fake interest and concern and, eventually, naked betrayal with his calm practicality. He scoffed it away like he did all of life's other absurdities.

She fell in love with him then.

And she knew she'd love him forever when his mother died because whereas he had made her stronger by sharing with her his punk comportment, he made her want to be stronger, want to be good for him like she'd never wanted to be for anyone since she was a small girl, for him in his hour of need.

For his part, she was no longer the next in a line of adventures and potential, probable, mistakes to Rob. She was his wife, but that meant nothing. The institution of marriage was fucked up—emotionally immature and transactionally emotionless. It was fairy tales and lawsuits and expectations so simple and basic that they crushed everyone involved when they weren't lived up to. But when he woke up in time to cross himself when passing by the last landmark they'd pass before arriving in Greenton, he looked over at Maria and saw someone worth living for, worth growing up and buying a house and getting serious about studio work for. Sure, marriage was stupid—he'd asked her to marry him on a lark, in half a midlife panic, and God only knows why she'd said yes—but so was everything else. All of it. Society. Love. Family. All flawed and fucked. Existence is chaos. Out in the cosmos. In nature. If you're born in this fucked up world, if you're lucky enough to survive birth without getting strangled to death by your umbilical cord, all that awaits you is death. But in all of that ugly nothing, there's music. There's sex. There's love, and apparently, Rob learned that day, there are loves worth making yourself vulnerable for, loves that make you throw up your hands and give up your nihilistic bullshit and dive into like you believe there's a net to catch your fall, because as cool or tough as that nihilism might convince you into believing you are, it's really just there to protect you from hurt because there's no way trying can hurt you if you refuse to believe any reason for trying exists.

CHAPTER EIGHTEEN—*(2018)*

Maria wasn't who Rob needed her to be, and she hadn't been in a long time. Rob could readily admit to himself he wasn't who she probably needed him to be either, wasn't being a husband worth showing up for, and, even if he was, he didn't know what he needed, either of her or of life. Success? Validation? It had started long before Eunice got sick, before New Year's even, but of course, he was made to feel even worse about this new kind of selfishness he'd found himself capable of. He couldn't ignore the truth of what he was feeling, no matter how wrong he was to be feeling it. She wasn't being the wife who took the wheel and let him cry himself to sleep, who made even the worst day of his life okay.

Rob knew it wasn't fair to begrudge her for not showing up—in that trying time or at any other—particularly when he wasn't willing to either, but Rob didn't know how to play fair. If ever Rob didn't have the upper hand in life, he wasn't up for playing, and if anyone pressed him to try, he would flip over tables in protest. It's what he'd done with catdragbird, with Penny, and now he was doing it with Maria. At the forefront of his mind, Rob wanted to believe that's what he was doing, but somewhere behind all that was the truth that he wasn't fighting as pointless a good fight as he ever did in his stubborn belligerence. He was, instead, using the idea of that fight to justify the petty weaseling out from under a ton of domestic drudgery. It's one thing to rage against your wife and against the idea of marriage and the expectation that the institution is supposed to be enough in and of itself to keep you in line and miserable, but it's another to run out and make noise with the cool kids and feel good about yourself because someone's looking at you through a new pair of lusting eyes and because you're just bored, a tired old cliché.

Bits of all of this had swirled around Rob's head in the two weeks since he'd seen Maria. He didn't give any active thought to it. He avoided it, in fact, but in the quiet moments between songs, even in the rest notes, because what's music if not the silence that toys with the noise we offer up in futile rebellion of it before boring of it and snuffing it out and restoring the order of its very nature which, as sure as entropy, will always win over our need to fill it. He'd have to face it eventually. Of course, he would, or he'd let it drive him crazy, but not tonight. Tonight, he would drown it out by playing an SG that he can't for the life of him remember buying or trading for through an Orange amp that he would otherwise hate but worked perfectly for Penny and the sound they'd been chasing after since she decided to stay in Austin and play some shows around town while recording some tracks with him.

C-Boy's Heart and Soul is a SoCo bar that Rob could finally agree upon as somewhere that felt right for his impromptu dates playing with Penny. Their first couple of shows were played to a bunch of regulars, a couple of neighborhood drunks clearly in to drink but—the shells that remained of old scenesters whose idea of what's hip predated the newest wave of Austin hipsters by decades—were too cool and wealthy to have to drink at cheaper joints or alone at home and some rockabilly purists, with their unironic pompadours and anecdotes from when they'd crossed paths with Stevie Ray or Jimmy Vaughan, or both, back when at Antone's or Hole in the Wall or the Continental Club, sticking around at the joint after a Dale Watson set. Snoop was at the first one, lending stakes to the night for Rob, not because he cared to impress her, but because he had to do the job of multitasking between her attention and following along with Penny's tempo changes in the songs she called off the top of her head.

For her part, Penny was nice enough to Snoop at the living room gig. Snoop was clearly a fan, and Penny always appreciated the admiration of fans in a way that Rob could never allow himself to be vulnerable enough to admit to, but upon seeing her at C-Boy's or, really, seeing how Rob was looking at her, Penny seemed wary of both the young teacher and of Rob's intentions with her.

Snoop hung around after the show when the bar was closing up. At last call, Penny and Rob made no effort to get ready to leave. They were used to bottles left on the bar when the house lights were up, drinking and hanging out past the last of the sad, sloppy hookups and the career drunks calling up their last bits of composure to focus on the task of stepping away from the bar without falling down because if they could make that step, they could certainly stumble or drive home without incident, as goes the logic at the rocky bottom of that barrel.

It was Tuesday, two days after their living room show. Penny spoke directly at Rob when she asked, "You have school tomorrow?"

"No, I don't teach Wednesdays, just Tuesdays, Thursdays, and some Fridays," he said. He was burning off the last of the performance's energy, a kind of energy he hadn't felt in years.

"And you?" Penny asked this at Snoop hard before Rob was even finished answering. "I bet you have class tomorrow."

"Yeah," Snoop answered, already too comfortable in her response to Penny—she'd been invited in for pleasantries, and she took it upon herself to overstay her welcome after their first meeting— "but I don't have a class first period, and I don't sleep much, so—"

"Well, good luck with that," Penny said. She got up from her stool, pulled the leather snap-top cigarette purse from her bag, and stepped out to the patio to join the bartenders and manager for a smoke.

Snoop deflated at this, and Rob didn't know her well enough to know the right kind of lie to tell her that would lift her spirits, so he opted for the truth. "She doesn't like anyone staying after shows. Almost every fight we got into was because there was no one else for her to be shitty to after shows."

"Yeah," Snoop said, trying to hide the tears she still felt uncomfortable enough to cry in front of Rob from the corners of her eyes. "I get it. Totally."

Rob knew she didn't. He nodded and did her the courtesy of looking away from her attempt to get herself together before leaving. Before she walked away, Rob declared to Snoop what he had only been kicking around in his head as a possibility, meaning he was making an offer to her that he wasn't even sure he meant to make, "So, I listened to your songs."

She stopped in her tracks. Rob took a drink from the beer sitting on the bar in front of him. He was thankful for Penny having stormed off when she did because if she were there to watch him play cool or hear what he was about to say, she would give him a righteous slug in the face. Snoop was taken aback, and for the swing from the low of being cast out by a childhood hero she thought she was buddying up to, it didn't seem like she could handle waiting a second longer for what she needed to be positive feedback.

"There's a lot there. It's rough, but I think we can do something with it."

"We?"

"For now, yeah. I have a studio setup at home where we can lay down vocals and guitar and bass tracks. I can see about getting us a few hours here or there in a proper studio for laying down drum tracks. You can make an EP to sell and demo around. If you want to." Rob looked up from his beer, and Snoop wasn't in his line of sight where he expected her. She was two steps closer, a second away from wrapping Rob in a hug that would have knocked down someone smaller.

"Oh my god!" Snoop just grabbed onto him and held him, pressing her body hard against his.

Rob looked down at her. Her eyes were closed hard like she was trying to grab the moment with them. When she opened them and saw him looking at her, she grabbed his face in her hand and planted an exaggerated Bugs Bunny kiss on his lips. He laughed at this and leaned back to catch sight of her joy in front of him. He watched it, the moment that joy turned to desire for him.

Seeming intent to regain a kind of control, Snoops face dimmed. The wild grin slowed, leaving a wry smirk on her face, and her eyes softened and fell heavily on Rob's lips. She put her hand on Rob's face, leaving it there for her own pause that was even heavier than Rob's a moment before. She rested her palm there and rubbed his lips softly with her thumb.

"I got lipstick on you," she said. "Wouldn't want anyone to get the wrong idea."

"I'll text you tomorrow with some ideas, and we can iron out a day that will work for both of us so we can record," Rob told her.

She still had her hand on his face. Rob looked down in the direction of that hand, but she didn't recede from his recognition. She held it there a beat longer before turning to leave, and Rob sat there in appreciation of the power Snoop had, newly aware of the fact that it wasn't just her youth or her beauty or her clever wordplay and dusky voice over better playing than he expected on guitar, but the fact that she clearly knew how to use them. She would be fine with or without him. If she hadn't met him, she would use that power, not just of sexuality and attraction, that electricity, to get what she wanted on her way to where she wanted to be. She didn't need him. She knew it, catching onto it as he just had, which made what was happening feel that much more exciting and valid to Rob.

Penny came back in and sat next to Rob. She put her cigarette purse back in her bag, pulled a small mirror out, and was checking the state of her lipstick when she spoke to Rob without turning to face him.

"What are you doing with her?"

"I'm going to help her with some recording. She has some songs." Rob, in turn, didn't look back over at her.

"Rob, watch it with her. Be careful." Penny stood on the rung of her stool to lean over the bar and grab the bar gun on the other side, squirting soda into the empty cup that sat in front of her.

Rob could have played a defense of himself, his interest in and time spent with Snoop, but there was something about Penny, about what they were after surviving each other and reuniting like this—on this side of the millennium, of addiction, of forty—that robbed him of his bullshit in the moment. All that time had robbed him of his will and intent toward bullshitting, at least.

"I will," he said.

Penny still seemed not to believe him. "Yeah, right," she said.

"Penny." He looked over at her and tried to convey with his eyes that he meant what he was saying. "I'm doing the best I can right now."

"With her, with your wife, or with me?" She chuckled here.

"All of it."

"Well then, God pity us all because if all you've got is your best, we're all fucked."

Rob wanted to leave, but he had nothing to leave for, nothing to go home to. Penny's company—her bouncing ideas off of him and giving him shit and punishing him for having hurt her and loving him for having loved her long ago—was the other noise Rob was using to drown out the silence in his life just then.

"But speaking of songs," she said, slapping him hard on the arm to jolt him out of his moment of self-pity. "I owe my label an album, an EP, at least. And I really like what we've been doing."

"You want to do a catdragbird album?" The artistic possibilities filled Rob with so much energy that he sat up higher than just excited posture. He perked up to the point of almost falling forward off of his stool.

"No way. Fuck them. They don't deserve that. We'll do it under my name. Or, hell, we could do it under both our names, but if we do it under just mine, we can sell a catdragbird album to them or to the highest bidder. There's already demand out there, but if we do something special on this next solo thing, we can really rake the fuckers across the coals. It's been years since I had any kind of leverage on a deal. What do you say?" Penny held her hand out here high between the two of them. "Shake it like you got a pair, *Vuh-nancy-oh.*"

Rob smiled here at their shared history. Saying those words like she always did, Penny revealed herself to be more than an ex-girlfriend, ex-lover, ex-bandmate, and new business partner: she was maybe the only friend, or family, even, that he had in the world.

"You've got yourself a deal, Penelope," he said as he grabbed and shook her hand.

CHAPTER NINETEEN

There were times during the first week Maria was back home in Humble when the devious nature of whatever disease they were dealing with (the doctor had told her that they couldn't necessarily say if it was Alzheimer's, as there were a number of potential causes for Eunice's dementia) revealed itself. There were moments when Eunice was not only lucid, but she seemed more irrepressibly herself than she had in years, but Maria knew this wasn't a good metric of prognosis because she didn't really know how or who Eunice had been in years. After work, Maria called home to let Eunice know she was coming over, and while Eunice seemed pleasantly surprised by the announcement—like it didn't occur to her why her daughter would be driving over to spend a weekend, like she didn't remember the frights of the last couple nights when Danielle had come in to check in on her and she didn't recognize her—she had made up the bed in Maria's room and even had Golden Jade takeout waiting when Maria got in that night, some four hours after she had called to make her announcement.

It was a small relief to Maria that Eunice remembered she was coming. She had set up some small test for Eunice, and she'd passed. Everything became a small kind of test like that. She'd remembered that Maria was coming, even ordered food and had the presence of mind to set up the guest bed. All of this was good. Over dinner, she even asked, "And where is Rob tonight?"

Maria wasn't trying to conceal what she had gone through the night before, that morning, what had become of her marriage since the New Year, how it had been headed that way for too long. She wasn't trying to hide all that from her mother or to ignore or deny it herself. But as soon as she spoke, Eunice could sense in her daughter a pain and exhaustion at the very thought of her husband.

"Oh, he's . . . home, I guess," Maria said.

"Is he busy this weekend? Playing?"

"I don't know. Probably."

Maria trailed off here. It had all exhausted her—work, drinking too much the night before, the drive that day, her worry over her mom and, of course, Rob—but the way she trailed off worried Eunice.

"Dear heart, is everything okay?"

It all caught up to her, the day, the year, her life in her marriage. Eunice, remaining so tuned to her daughter's feelings—and, dementia notwithstanding, all of the time they'd spent apart and all of the coldness that had filled the distance between them made it seem like that connection might no longer exist between the two of them—served as a wrecking ball that toppled over the tottering house of cards. Maria cried. She cried and cried, and Eunice gave her time, let her get her tears and even her start-and-stop blubbering out of the way of her telling the story. She got up from her seat at the dining table and walked over to Maria, who fell onto her standing lap.

"There you go," she said down onto the back of her seated daughter's head. "Let it out, Maria. Let it all out."

And Maria did. She cried herself until she was hoarse. She cried out all of the painful tension that was wringing her muscles and bones and had her slouching a couple of inches shorter than she normally would sit or stand over the last months. After her late arrival and having tiptoed around the house and her mother's entire domestic world in anticipation of a landmine that she didn't find, Maria wasn't sure what time she ended up falling asleep. She just knew that she felt safe and loved, mothered like she hadn't been since childhood, and listened to and accepted like she had maybe never been in that house she had grown up in before.

After the first wave of anger and pain were purged in the dining room, Eunice helped Maria up and over to the living room so that they could sit more comfortably. She went into the kitchen and made a ginger ale and bourbon, which would have been a fine enough drink if she'd ever had any practice drinking it to know how to pour it right.

The overwhelming kick of bourbon sent a shockwave up Maria's chest and back, causing her to cough some of the drink into her nose. She sat up, pulled hard out of her mind and breaking heart by being forced to feel her body. It hurt, and she had to lean forward and take deep breaths to cool her burning chest, but she was awake.

"Did I do it wrong," Eunice asked, an embarrassed look on her face, her hands pulled up to cover her mouth.

"I guess it depends who you made that for," Maria said. "If it was for someone used to drinking a tumbler of booze with a splash of ginger ale, it would be just fine."

"Oh, hush." Eunice went into the kitchen and brought back another can of ginger ale. "You can cut it more with this."

Maria only had a few more sips of the drink, but when they were finally settled on the couch, the pleasant quiet of being there was almost too sweet to disturb, but when Eunice spoke, Maria was relieved because she didn't know how long the moment, their night, or her mother's lucidity would last. Could her mind come and go in the time it took the echoes of contented laughter to die in the carpet and couch?

"I don't drink the stuff," she started.

"But the cupboard doesn't feel right without a bottle of bourbon on the top shelf." Maria smiled at the thought of her dad.

"I miss him every day," Eunice said. "Every single day, I have an incomplete feeling like I've forgotten my jacket when it's cold outside."

"I miss him too, Mom."

"It used to kill me when he would be away for work. I couldn't stand it, but obviously, it's nothing like these last twenty years have been." Eunice grabbed the glass from Maria and took half a sip that she almost spit out before scrunching up her face in shocked displeasure.

"I can't believe it's been that long," Maria said.

"And here you are without your husband," Eunice said. "Of course, you're visiting your mom, and he's a musician, and his work happens on the weekend, but you're here and he's there, and you're crying for some reason other than you missing him."

Maria took one last sip of the drink and put the glass on the end table. Then, she sank into her mother's embrace as she told her about what had been going on, about New Year's Eve and the kind of anger that Rob had been displaying with all of his fights and the dissatisfaction he no longer tried to hide with her, their home, their life. She told Eunice about splitting the couch, about how mad she was, and how they had been sneaking into the bedroom for sex—this was the first and last time she had ever spoken to Eunice about sex—and how she'd needed him the night before—she said she'd needed him because of work stress, which was true enough, but not because of how worried she was about Eunice—and how he'd pushed her away. She told her she didn't know what she could do to save the marriage.

Eunice issued out more than just "I know" and "Oh, baby, I'm sorry" and "Shhh, Dear Heart, just you rest" that night, but Maria wouldn't remember much more than that. The kind wisdom her mother dispensed with that night would be lost, as would be the illusion of a mother who might be well, at least might not be that bad, in the morning when dementia's trickster-like cruelty revealed itself.

The warmth of her mother and the pain of having slept awkwardly on the couch continued Maria's ruse of potential normalcy. The first of her mother's words to her that morning would be the last and most affecting bit of the prank's impact to hit Maria, to catch her unaware.

"Whoops," Eunice said like it was any other morning like they used to have after Thom died, holding on to each other for comfort and consolation. The kind, amused smile on her face was the exact one she used to flash when their nights were more about their love for one another than their pain over their mutual loss. It made Maria feel at home, and it put her at ease over what the next few days were going to be like. She would interview more permanent help. She would take Eunice to a doctor to see exactly what was happening and needed to be done. She could manage this. Her mom got confused. . . . She was old. That happens.

Maria got up from the couch and went to the bathroom. She washed up and brushed her teeth, changing into clothes more comfortable than her Friday work-casuals she hadn't changed from upon leaving the office on her way to Humble. When she came into the kitchen, a single burner glowed hot blue on the stove, but Eunice was nowhere to be found. She was sitting in the dining room eating a bowl of Corn Flakes.

"Mom," Maria said upon entering. "Why is the stove on?"

"Oh, Dear Heart, you surprised me coming in like that!" Eunice smiled big here, delighted at her daughter's presence. "Have some breakfast quick because you'll have to change before you go. It's late already."

"Mom, I'm not going anywhere. I'll be here a while. The stove, why is it—"

Eunice seemed to realize something here, and she spoke past Maria as if trying to outrun suspicion. "That's right. I have you for a few days. Thank God."

"Mom, the stove." Maria walked into the kitchen, and Eunice followed her.

"That's right. I was going to make tea. I was going to heat water for tea, but *I'll be*. I can't find the kettle." Eunice looked around for a second and shrugged her concession.

Maria turned off the burner. She looked around the kitchen.

"You want me to cook you some breakfast?" Eunice asked. "Some bacon and eggs?"

"No, Mom. I'm fine. I'll have some cereal."

Maria dropped some cereal into a bowl and grabbed the milk from the fridge. As she did this, Eunice made her way back to the dining room.

"I just love it when you're home. I know you're so busy up there. I know it's so hard. I just thank God when you can make time to fly down," Eunice called from the other room.

Just some confusion, Maria thought. She's old. It happens. She opened the milk jug and could thankfully smell its fermentation before she tasted it. She ran the sink and emptied the jug into the drain. She stepped on the pedal to open the wastebasket at the end of the counter and would have simply thrown in the jug and gone about the rest of her already declining morning if she hadn't noticed that it wasn't lined with a bag. She grabbed one from the box under the sink, flapped it open in front of her, and made to put it in the basket. When she did this, she could see the shine of a foreign metal object in the bin. She reached in and pulled out a tea kettle, originally red but ringed at its circumference a brownish-black char; the weld that connected its spout to its body had burnt and broken, and its handle had melted. It had been left on the stove too long.

Maria put it in the bag along with the empty milk jug. She went back into the dining room, ready to face what was in front of her. "Mom, the tea kettle, it was in—"

"Oh, Dear Heart, you surprised me coming in like that!" Eunice flashed the same delighted look then glanced at the clock on the wall next to the elegant, bleeding-Christ-less crucifix. "Oh, it's getting late. You grab some toast and dress quick, or you'll be late for school."

Maria sat down at her seat at the table. She buried her face in her hands for just a second before looking over at Eunice, who seemed to be trying to figure out the situation unfolding in front of her. She wanted to grab her mother and take her back to the couch and go back to sleep and stay there forever—each safe and loved in the other's arms, untouched by illness or heartbreak or the resentments and pains of the past, just all they ever needed the other to be, mother and daughter, as simple as that is and can ever be. Eunice couldn't seem to read the situation for what it was, couldn't pick up clues enough to piece together when it was and how her daughter came to be sitting there in front of her. For want of something to do, she pulled the bowl in front of her close and grabbed the spoon. Maria grabbed it from her gently.

"Mom, I think the milk has gone bad. I can get us some breakfast. I've had such a long work week, and I would really love to just relax with some breakfast tacos from La Lupita."

She got up with the bowl and stood steeling herself at the kitchen sink, letting the sound of water rushing drown out her crying. When she got back to the dining room, she could see that Eunice had been concentrating hard.

"I tell you. I haven't had La Lupita in years. I can't wait." They'd had La Lupita the weekend before. "Now, where is Rob again this weekend? Where's he playing?"

Maria realized that Eunice was losing her mind, but that didn't mean she wasn't still smart. How long had she been doing this, tossing out feelers and letting the world around her—just Maria, really, because what else was there of the world now that she hadn't been going to Church, as Maria learned the previous weekend—and tuning herself into whatever frequency the feedback was being broadcast to her on.

"Just there in Austin," Maria said, too tired to lie for her mother's sake and too heartbroken to repeat the previous night's truths.

CHAPTER TWENTY

Thunderbird Studio was all classy-vintage like a Fender Twin Reverb—all knobs and hardware and tweed grille cloth on tan leather. Danny El seemed to keep it this way for the same reason Rob always made sure to have a Tele on hand ready to plug into the actual Twin Reverb amp at the studio because, of course, either of them, as producer or musician or vice versa, could use the newest and fanciest tools to accomplish whatever goal any part-time partner and employer might have in mind. Still, when push came to shove, if either of them needed to show what they could really do, they could just plug that guitar into that amp or set up those mics in that room and run the knobs and show why they were worth their pay, why what they made was art and why they were artists.

As soon as she walked in, Penny blurted out her blessing before even taking her sunglasses off. "Oh, fuck yeah. This will do."

They knocked out cuts of the first two songs on the first day. After rehearsing for a week and performing in a packed C-boy's house once buzz picked up that she was in town and they were doing a few nights of sets at the SoCo bar, they were locked in tight. Danny had a young drummer of his liking, a guy who just went by "Man" (Rob would later learn that his actual last name was Mann, but the guy never explained that himself) who, despite some drummer eccentricities, was a nice enough guy and a hell of a player.

Rob made sure not to bring Snoop around the sessions or to even mention her in front of Penny. After he spent the better part of a week with her every night, Penny asked about Maria.

"The old ball and chain doesn't mind you being out so much?" she'd asked.

Rob now regretted offering up the truth, as he hadn't really expected Snoop's presence to complicate the matter.

"She's been back home. Her mom is sick," he'd told her.

He knew that in a rush to explain away their troubles, and his need to be out of the house in their wake, he'd made Maria out to be a sympathetic figure and that he couldn't easily pivot away from being the opposite of that if Penny were to learn about their estrangement, his end of it. That was a problem to face later, another bit of bleed dirtying the mix of his peace of mind or what he had that could pass for it. This, too, he would try to cover up with noise.

On the second day, they hit a wall after recording an upbeat number. Mann laid down a drum track they asked for. It was a straight-eight surf groove, and the backbeat was as loud and cracking as they'd agreed to try, but still, something wasn't working. They sat, Penny, Rob, Danny, and Mann, trying to brainstorm some way to make it sound like it did, poppy and surfy to contrast Rob's heavy, down-tuned sludge dirge.

"I want to keep the upbeat nature of the drums, just not the sound," Penny said.

Rob nodded, lost in the catalog of sounds in his mind.

"Maybe we could add something on top of it, like castanets or something, or a tambourine," Danny said, mimicking layers on top of layers with his hands.

"You and your castanets," Rob said.

Danny pulled his left hand out to give Rob the middle finger for a second before putting it back to use in illustrating his idea. "Maracas . . . something like that to put on top and then take the bottom out from."

"Handclaps," Rob said.

"There you go," Danny said. "Handclaps."

"And castanets?" Rob said.

"Fuck you," Danny said, shaking his head. "They cut right through a track for the right kind of song."

"Handclaps!" Penny pumped her fists at this. "I fucking love handclaps. You got anyone who might want a girlfriend credit in the liner notes?"

"I know someone," Rob said.

"You have got to be fucking kidding me," Penny said, ready to shout.

"Benji," Rob said, stopping her in her tracks.

Penny smiled big at this, and Danny nodded his head and gave a groovy, "Al-right!"

"Who's Benji?" Mann asked, thinking they might be referring to a session percussionist or someone else he might be expected to know.

The next day, Benji came into Thunderbird, eyes wide with wonder at the world of real, professional recording. They played the track back for Benji in the control room, and he focused on the beat, as simple as it was, going into the handclaps on the second verse.

"Easy, right?" Danny asked.

"Easy," Benji said.

"Alright," Danny said. "I have a mic set up in the bathroom off the main room and some headphones for playback."

"The bathroom?" Benji asked.

"You'll get it when you hear it. It's perfect." Danny gave a reassuring nod. "And it's all ready for you."

"Wait," Rob said. "Let me go in and check the connections and the playback one more time to be sure."

"You sure?" Danny caught on to the joke a second later than Rob would have liked, but he didn't ruin it.

"If it's worth doing, it's worth doing right the first time," Rob said.

Danny held his hands up in acquiescence. Rob could hardly leave the control room without laughing. When he got into the bathroom, he spoke into the microphone, "Start playback, Danny." When the playback started, he turned off the mic, dropped his pants, and took what ended up being a satisfyingly putrid shit, thanks to having spent a week and a half eating and drinking like a twenty-year-old with a forty-year-old's gut. Leaving the bathroom, toilet unflushed, he made sure to turn the mic back on.

"It's all yours," he told Benji upon entering the control room.

As soon as Benji left the room, Rob fell out laughing, and Danny turned the bathroom mic up on the board. Danny shushed him, and Rob could barely contain his giggles as they heard the door to the bathroom open, and Benji let out a disgusted "ugh" and, finally, heard him say, "Goddamn it," when he saw what Rob had left in the toilet.

"You didn't," Penny said. She shook her head at Rob and looked at Danny. "He didn't . . ."

When the sound of the toilet flushing filled the control room, Penny joined them in their laughter. After a moment, Benji entered the room, seeming mad, yet unable to hold back his own laughter at the prank.

"What the fuck?" he started to shout, but by the end of his question, he was laughing too. "That's disgusting. Go to a doctor, asshole."

At this, Rob couldn't take the laughter anymore. In what was mostly a playful move, he slid out of his chair and onto the floor. His sides hurt, and he felt like he might pass out. Even before it brought him to the floor, the laughter that filled Rob's lungs was fuller and truer, more joyous than he could remember issuing out in too long. When was the last time he'd really laughed from joy instead of scoffing out of cynicism?

After falling apart with the room, threatening to kick Rob's ass, and getting a big hug and a kiss on the forehead from Penny, Benji went back into the restroom and laid down his handclaps like he was part of a band, not just someone who was floated a vanity credit. Mann played the straight eights on a huge ride cymbal and the backbeats and rolls with mallets on a huge bass drum set up horizontal to the ground like a floor tom.

When they played the song with the new drum track, it turned out so excitingly well that Rob was inspired to lay down a playful new surf solo— all fuzz and tremolo-turned-to-ten affect—and Penny insisted on recording new "ooh, aah" harmonies to be sung by all of them, Mann included. When the track was almost done, she looked over at Benji, still all grin and bright eyes, and made an ominous proclamation.

"Benji boy, I hope this has all been worth it because right now I'm really gonna hurt you . . ."

She took him into the vocal booth and walked him through the harmonies. She'd been here. Rob had been here; Mann here. Then she sang for him his note. Once she heard him hit it a couple of times, she put her hands on his shoulders.

"Good. Perfect. You have a fabulous voice. Now I want you to shred it the fuck up."

Benji stood taller here. He nodded along with Penny, who was working to fire him up.

"We'll set up playback of that final chorus, and when it comes to that note, both times, I want you to scream as loud and hard as you can. Try to hit that note, but I really want fucking rage to spill out of you. Can you do that?"

"Yeah."

"Yeah?" she yelled.

"Yeah!"

"Fucking rage?" she asked.

"Fucking rage!" he shouted.

Rob became sad hearing them from the control room. If not for Penny's mental illness, for her addictions, if she'd lived a normal life, she might have made a wonderful CEO or field general or high school soccer coach.

Benji did two takes and nailed both of them. When Danny played back the song, it was electric. This is what some crazies, longhairs, and burnouts could make when given the chance. When the final chorus came around, and Benji's screams filled the room, everyone clapped, jumped, and fuck-yeah-ed.

Mann left to smoke a joint on the patio that was pretty much only meant for that purpose right outside the attic behind the studio. Penny asked Benji about his voice, and when he said, "It's fine," he did so through such a crackled rasp that Penny told him to relax, that she'd make him some tea with honey. Benji spun around once in the desk chair he was sitting in and let the momentum of his spin die as Rob sank down into his seat, tired from having worked in the studio until nearly midnight. He was happy to have shared this with Benji.

"You have fun today?" he asked.

"Oh my god. So much." Benji looked up at the ceiling, running the evening through his mind. "It was pretty amazing. Pretty perfect, really."

"What could have made it better?"

Benji thought about the question sincerely. "Nothing."

"Want to fuck with some guitars and my pedalboard?" Rob knew that would make it better.

"Yes!"

It was almost two in the morning when Penny decided it was time to head out. She was renting a small house through Airbnb in North Austin, and she offered to give Benji a ride home. It was working exactly to Rob's plans. Before Mann left, Rob asked him if he wouldn't mind Rob laying down some drum tracks on something he was working on. Mann said of course he could. The drums were mic'd up in the room, and if Rob had access to a studio and ideas worth recording, it would be almost criminal for him not to.

At two-thirty, Blake showed up. He had just played a gig at Dizzy Rooster and was in a good mood. He and Rob made small talk while they waited for Snoop, who had to take her pedicab to the warehouse after her shift. They had some beers and talked over what Rob was looking for in the drumming—swinging, but not jazzy—and their time constraints. By the time Snoop showed up, Rob had played through the five rough cuts they were hoping to record, and Blake was ready to knock them out.

"So, you're really going to go by Snoop," Blake asked after trading handshakes with her. "Like, you'll record under that?"

"No. Not at all. He's the only one who calls me that. My name's Cait—with a 'C.' Cait Hayden."

"See, now that's a good name." Blake turned to Rob as if convincing someone who really believed she should go by Snoop. He was a good drummer and a great mechanic, but Blake wasn't smart. "It has, like, the sound thing, like alliteration or something."

"Assonance," Snoop said. When Blake raised an eyebrow at this, she explained. "The internal vowel sounds being the same like that, it's assonance."

Blake pursed his lips at this new knowledge. Rob pointed a thumb back at her and shrugged.

"She's an English teacher."

"Oh. No wonder your lyrics are so solid. Really good shit," Blake said. "Me? I use sticks to make a boom. You have any other pointers or requests before I go in and do this?"

"No. I trust whatever he said," Snoop pointed to Rob. "Thank you so much for even doing this."

In the control room, Rob was all focused on the recording at hand. He was all over the mixing board, not turning to face Snoop, who wasn't talking for fear of revealing herself to be as overwhelmed as she was.

"Alright," Rob said into the intercom mic. "Track one, take one. Don't fuck this up, Blakey Boy."

On his side of the glass, Blake held up his middle finger, bopping his head to the count of the click track. Then he rolled his shoulders loose and clicked out a four-count in the air in front of him before diving into the song. Rob listened to a couple of bars of the song for one last bit of quality assurance before taking off his headphones and spinning around to face Snoop.

"And that's it. It's happening," he told her.

"That's it? You're just recording him? And when he's done, it's done?"

Snoop was looking at the mixing board in front of Rob, out at Blake playing to the sound of her music.

"Yeah, unless he fucks up. He won't. He's a pro, a prog, and a jazz nerd who makes his money playing country. He won't drop the beat, and he has touch and instinct enough to lay down better tracks than I can direct him to. There's an overhead track recording his playing for an organic R&B feel, and we've got all his drums and cymbals mic'd up, so we can push anything up in the mix when we finalize. This is as good a setup as we'll get in such a short time, and Danny set up the drum mics, so we're getting world-class sound." Rob leaned back in the chair, closing his eyes and feeling the exhaustion of his fifteenth hour in the studio.

"Danny El engineered the drums on my Demo?" She held her hands together, fingers intertwined, and raised them to her mouth like she was praying her thanks for her good fortune.

"About that," Rob said, opening his eyes but not looking at Snoop, just staring up and out past the ceiling in his line of sight. "I'm sure someday we'll all laugh about this, but let's not go around saying that for now. He doesn't know we're doing this, recording an EP worth of drums in here, guerilla-style." He closed his eyes again to focus on the drums and to give them some rest. "Release this. Play shows. Get signed. He'll appreciate you recording an actual album here with a label paying for the time."

Rob was in a kind of freefall for a second. So lost was he in the groove and the comfortable peace of the studio after his plan unhatched as perfectly as it had that he had very nearly fallen asleep, or something close to it, when he was pushed forward hard from his recline in his chair. Between that and the feeling of Snoop's weight on his lap surprising him when she jumped down onto him, he shouted out in a way that would have been embarrassing if anyone heard it, but Blake was busy playing, and Snoop was too intent in her passion at that moment for Rob to know if she had noticed, as she was kissing him hard, gripping the hair behind his ears to pull him hard into her.

That was the first time in days Rob thought of Maria. Before that, he'd been walking on a tightrope in his dealings with Snoop. He was flirting and flexing his musician muscles, sure, but it was before anything as real and immediate as Snoop straddling him on the control room chair, the momentum of her jump onto him sliding them back away from the control board, adrift on the hardwood floor in the dark room, jettisoning away from the illusion of the whole exercise ever having been about helping a musician or fortuitous scheduling with Penny and Snoop both having material to record or some kind of act of rebellion toward Maria who, he could tell himself before, deserved it, but who was alone in Humble with a mother who herself was lost in space.

But before that moment, he was just toying with potentialities. He knew what *could* and *might* happen. He knew he was doing more than he should for Snoop, that he was the one pushing past boundaries. He understood that from the beginning. He knew how this would progress and could anticipate the shifts in tempo and key. He was a pro. But until the real weight of her was on his lap, the taut amplitude of her body pressed up against his, her mouth on his mouth, he had only been playing a game of chess with himself. Now the game was up. He had won, and he had lost. As with almost all of his other major fuckups in life, he had pushed the envelope, gone further and further and further for the sake of the feel of nearing total self-destruction, and now that he'd crossed the line, it was only really the people closest to him, those he loved and never really wanted to hurt, who would have to deal with the consequences.

He put his hands on Snoop's hips and kissed up back at her, trying to keep up, to reciprocate her heat and passion, but knowing he couldn't because the only card he had left to play was to resist the temptation sitting right on top of him. He pulled his head back and pushed her away a bit. In order to be able to preserve the mood and momentum of her passion, he spoke an explanation that was more stuttered and desperate than he would have liked it to sound.

"We can't do this right now. Blake is here to record for a project I believe in, not for some girl I want to . . . do this with."

Snoop got off of Rob, ran her hands through her hair, and shook the energy of the moment out from her shoulders down to her fingertips. She pointed at Rob, shaking her head and issuing a sly smile.

"You're gonna get it. We'll finish this, but when we're done, you're mine."

Rob wanted to make sure Blake felt like this was a professional endeavor. That much was true. But when he looked out the glass at the trance of concentration and rocking the drummer was in, Rob knew he was mostly glad to not have been seen in the middle of his efforts with Snoop paying off because if there were any outsider in the world, Penny included, who Rob didn't want to have seen what was happening in that control room, it was Blake. Blake who had been there that first day, on the evening of Rob and Maria's second first date, who had even been out for drinks at the Driskill six years before in celebration of their having been married by a Justice of the Peace earlier in the day.

"That was perfect," Rob spoke into the monitor. "That's a take we can keep if you're happy."

"Felt good," Blake said, panting a bit. He took a deep drink from the bottle of water he'd taken with him into the studio. "If you're ready, I can do the next song too."

Rob had three more hours and four more songs to fill his mind with, but it didn't help. He tried, in that time, to convince himself by any leap of logic available to him that what he was doing was anything but what it was. There were no mental gymnastics that he could engage in that would allow him to convince himself that what was happening with Snoop was organic or meaningful enough to detonate his life with, or that all of those months of freeze-out with Maria had made what he was about to do right or just, or that any vestiges of punk rock fuck-it-all were rising up in him as if embodying any India-ink-needle-on-the-end-of-a-busted-cassette-player-tattoo aphorism would mean anything about him other than he was either a sucker or a pathetic *Heavy Metal Parking Lot* scene casualty, or both.

There was no other way that Rob could justify to himself what he was about to do than there was a chance he could talk himself out of it like he tried listening to Blake drum, attempting to ignore Snoop's lusty glances or push past her coming up behind him and nibbling his ear, whispering breathy declarations about what she was going to do to him when Blake left. He'd tried, but that was more mental treadmill running—wasting time and exhausting himself with his effort but knowing he'd get nowhere.

"Alright, man. If you need me to fix or recut anything, you'll have to give me a few days' notice. I'm booked solid." Blake shook Rob's hand, looking as exhausted as one might expect but also used to this kind of night of music. "I have some Euridice Ascending tracks I could use your help with, playing and recording."

"Shit, I'll need a few weeks to practice if we're doing that," Rob said.

"Definitely." Blake held his hand out for Snoop to shake. "Snoop Assonance, it's been a pleasure."

Snoop pushed past the hand and gave him a big hug and a kiss on the cheek. When she stepped away, out of sight of Blake, he pointed to his cheek where she had kissed him and mocked agony at being tormented by her beauty. If only he'd known.

Rob locked the back door to the studio after Blake left. Walking back into the lounge behind the control room, Snoop leading the way, looking back at him with those eyes he knew he couldn't deny, Rob gave up the ghost about any of it ever having mattered for anything other than what was about to happen. Even New Year's, the fight and the broken hand from before then, it was all just bucking up against what Rob thought, at the time, was his dissatisfaction with the comfort his life and marriage had afforded him, against a life that wasn't as real or invigorating or exciting or rock 'n' fuckin' roll as the one he'd lived with a needle in his arm and a guitar on his hip and rooms of young fans screaming at him for more. But what became clear to him at that moment, walking behind Snoop as young and vital as she was, tricked as she was into believing him to be vital too, was that he was just shy of his 41st birthday with a wife going through the kind of crisis, one worse even, that she had helped him through years before three hundred miles and a million tears away, and he was about to get exactly what he'd wanted the whole time from a woman very nearly half his age. The thought of his birthday upcoming, along with a wife neglected by a wandering husband out on the prowl to feed an ego his whole life had taught him was above reproach, made him think of his mother and her nights alone and the stories she would tell to anyone who would listen; lord knows her son stopped listening to them as soon as he was old enough to ignore her. He thought of his father out those nights, bedding dental hygienists and young activists and women whose kids needed fillings or crownwork and whose baby daddies were in the wind or too fucked up to object to her being out and paying as she did.

It was all almost too much. It all almost overwhelmed him to realize how chained he was to the mistakes of his father and the cycle of dysfunction and destruction that had broken his family how it did. It almost stopped him in his tracks, made him cut bait and tell Snoop thanks but no thanks. Almost.

There's almost nothing that good sense and self-awareness can do in the face of young beauty, nearly naked and still shedding clothes, revealing the guesswork of Rob's previous fantasizing about the curvature of muscle and tissue, the design of art on the skin that covered it all to have been very nearly dead-on, and his margin of error being thusly corrected, to have almost made the wreck Rob revealed himself to be making of his life, his marriage, and his psyche worth it. Again, almost.

Nothing was worth all of that, not even Cait Hayden, perfect and cool and naked and now taking his clothes off. Nothing. But Rob couldn't think of that or anything else between then and their walk to her car in the early morning sun of a Saturday downtown. His brain gave in to his body, and the final straw was laid upon any claim Rob could make to any reason for it all that wasn't her and how she could serve his ego, his need for her to make him young and cool and sexy and needed.

It was disgusting in how cliched it was; he was the suit who'd tossed around his clout for the pretty girl. But it wasn't disgusting enough to make him stop. And that fact, on top of all the others, was just one more thing Rob would have to hate himself over later. That night, in that early predawn morning in the studio, Rob would make his mistakes worth making.

Chapter Twenty-One

Maria had thought about calling Rob every day, and it was that clinging to the phantom love that had hurt her for what she wanted to believe was the last time. It was her own source of self-loathing, which was a welcome bit of emotional self-care because between working remotely and worrying about and caring for her mother, Maria didn't have much time or energy left for herself, and those moments of anger at wanting to call him were all that she could do to remind herself that she existed as someone who had any feelings left just for her.

The days were a blur of Eunice's confusion and amusement at having Maria around. As soon as they could get in to see a doctor the first Monday after Maria came into town, they went to a nearby medical center. Eunice seemed sporadically able to retain information, but mostly she was just blank. After asking twice for her to get dressed to go, Maria realized that Eunice wasn't getting distracted. She was forgetting that she was in her room to dress at all. She went in and sat at the bed while Eunice went into her closet, happily humming and singing aloud, "What to wear? What to wear? What to wear?"

Eventually, the singing trailed off, and then the humming. Maria thought this was because she was dressing, but when Eunice walked out carrying a box of pictures, Maria realized she'd lost the task at hand and moved on to something else.

"Let's look at pictures!" Eunice said.

In the moment, she seemed to want Maria to believe she had grabbed the box with her in mind, as if it were something she had planned with consideration for her daughter, but she could hear the surprise in her mother's voice.

"When we come back, Mom," Maria said. Upon seeing the confusion in Eunice's eyes, Maria added, "From the doctor. When we come back from the doctor, we'll look at pictures."

At the medical center, Maria sat in the office of Dr. Kurzydlo as he gave an administered Mini-Mental State Exam. She was at various points scared and anxious at being in an unfamiliar setting and childishly excited at being dressed up and out on the town with her daughter. When Dr. K came in, he made small talk enough with Maria and Eunice to set both of them at ease to not have the test results he was going to administer be affected by a tension in the room.

Eunice looked over at Maria's skirt and sandals and correctly surmised that it was spring, even correctly guessed the month to be March, but couldn't come up with the day or year. She stared hard at Dr. K, looking at his desk. Then, she spotted a picture of him posed with a group of young doctors in white coats and realized they were at a doctor's office in Texas. She thought for a second and incorrectly offered Houston as her guess for where they were. Maria thought it was going well, but when Dr. K told her the words, "coffee, fireplace, and telephone," explaining that he would be asking her to remember them, she couldn't get past 'fireplace' even in speaking the words back.

After some back and forth trying to get her to repeat the words, Dr. K assured her that it was okay. He then asked her to spell her name backwards. She laughed at this, said it seemed silly. Dr. K assured her that he understood it was silly, but still part of the test.

"Spell? Backwards?" Eunice asked.

"Yes, ma'am," Dr. K said. "Your name. Backwards."

"Okay," Eunice said. She sat up in her seat, eager to perform a task she knew she could excel at. "Eunice. E-U-N—"

"Mrs. Smithey." Dr. K held up his hand and smiled consolingly. "Backwards. Can you please spell it backwards?"

Eunice giggled and clapped her hands at the fun of the game she was playing. "Right. That's right! I can do this. Eunice. E-U . . . E . . . I'm sorry, what was the question again?"

After asking her one more time, Dr. K moved on. Maria felt like she was watching her mother in a fight, and her mother was losing. Eunice looked over at her and flashed a reassuring, if apologetic, smile. Maria wished there was some way she could step in and fight this fight for her mother, but it only amounted to as much as any of those hopes ever do.

"I'm sorry," Eunice said. "I'm just so nervous."

"Don't worry, Mrs. Smithey. You're doing great. Would you like some water?" When Eunice said no, Dr. K continued. "Earlier, I asked you to remember three words. Do you remember what those were?"

It went on like this for the rest of the appointment. With each new question or task, Maria felt more and more flush with heat. The sound of her breath heavy and oppressive in her ears almost drowned out Eunice correctly naming the clock but failing to name a pen.

"It's a . . . a metal pencil. Why can't I remember the name . . . ? A metal pencil. . . . I'm sorry, what was the question?" she said.

"I'm sorry," Maria declared as she jumped up. She felt that if she had sat there in that seat for one second more, she might pass out. "I just have to step out. Mom, will you be okay?"

"Dear Heart, you don't look so good," Eunice said.

"I just need to . . ." Maria said.

"The bathroom's at the end of the hall, if you need to step out," Dr. K said. "We're almost done in here. We'll be fine."

Maria ran out and into the restroom. She fell to her knees hard on the tile in the bathroom just in time to make the toilet with her vomit. She emptied herself of all of the food in her gut, then all of the bile, then all of the comfort and security of a life that was made comfortable and good by the grace and love of her adoptive parents. Her chest and her ribs behind it ached when she was done. Looking in the mirror washing her hands after, she could see that a blood vessel had popped in her right eye. Indeed, she did look and feel like she had stepped in to fight in place of her mother and had gotten the shit kicked out of her.

Listening to Dr. K give her a rundown of the situation, Maria's arms and chest were trembling from the strain and hurt of being pulled up and out of her mouth. Eunice was severely cognitively impaired; for any patient, but especially for someone with her educational background, she should have scored markedly better; chances were she would need 24/7 supervision, if not care altogether. She and Eunice were consulted by a social worker who could tell almost immediately that Maria was in pain, waylaid by the impact of the day.

"Now, I can go over all of this again with you over the phone," she started, "or you can come back in, whichever works, but you're going to have to consider care for your mother. I see you're with her now, but you live in Austin. This might necessitate securing full-time custodial care."

"Like, a nursing home?" Maria asked.

"That's an option. But an expensive one. Most insurance companies won't cover them. So, there are custodial care services that can be employed, but that's out of pocket too. Do you have any family in the area? Any siblings or anyone else who could stay with your mother? Between a few family members and some hired help, the price can be made manageable."

"No," Maria said. "It's just me."

"And Rob," Eunice said. "Her husband is a very successful musician."

Hearing Eunice say his name made Maria want all over again to call Rob, but this time not for support or consolation. She wanted to call him and curse his name and existence. She was past the point of olive branches and reckonings for the sake of their strength as a unit. It shouldn't have to be just her. She shouldn't have to face it alone. She wanted nothing more than to call him and be able to reach through the phone and slap him across the face, but none of that was going to happen, so she calmed herself with thoughts of the value of their house and how much of its sale she could expect in a divorce. Even in her revenge fantasy, Maria was a lawyer, so she knew she would have to employ as strong an attorney as possible to hope to convince a judge she deserved half of the value of the house since the majority of their down payment had come from money left behind after the death of her mother-in-law. Even as an imaginary punching bag set up for divorcing and wishing hell upon, Rob was proving himself to be a shitty husband.

One gift Rob gave Maria in the wake of their last fight was that, with the fact that she could work from the living room table in the house in Humble, there was no reason for her to leave and nothing in Austin to return to. It was saving money, if nothing else, and dealing with Eunice in her various mental and emotional states felt like a crash course in being a daughter because how much time do you actually spend paying attention to and caring for a parent in your visits home from college and thereafter? All of this intense focus on her mother—any time she entered a room, Maria had to study Eunice's eyes to see how there she was; any time she left the room, Maria had to trail behind and shadow to make sure she wasn't doing anything too dangerous—felt like making up for lost time. Was this her penance for all of those lost days, all of the minutes and, maybe, hours of actual interaction that would have populated those days that they lost to Eunice's lies and Maria's pain and, she could admit to herself now, overreaction to them?

One day, Maria came into the room to take out a tray she'd served Eunice food on. Eunice had fallen asleep, most of the food uneaten on the tray that was on the bed next to her. When she woke, she was startled, but she bounced back as quickly as she could into the day.

"Oh, I'm sorry. I appear to have fallen asleep," she said.

"That's alright—" Maria started before Eunice cut her off.

"Say, have you seen my husband around here?"

"No," Maria said, no longer hurt or even thrown off by her mother's confusion. "I'm sorry."

"Aren't you pretty?" Eunice said. "You're Mexican, right? I hope you don't mind my asking."

"Yes. Yes, I am." Maria smiled at this. The previous day, Eunice hadn't remembered why she was in town and was afraid she'd shown up to deliver bad news. "Mexican, that is."

"I knew it. See, I ask because my daughter—you may have seen her come in to visit—is Mexican too. Well, she's American, but she's from Mexico."

Maria had never heard Eunice say that she was from Mexico. It just wasn't something she talked about. She certainly hadn't heard her call her Mexican.

"And how did you come to have a Mexican daughter?" Maria was only playing along to keep the cordial spirit alive between them. It was only to keep Eunice smiling.

"Well, my husband and I tried and tried, and then we went to the doctor and, what do you know, I can't have babies. Some problem with my ovaries. It was just horrible, but my husband said, 'We'll just adopt. We have all this love to give. I don't need you to bear a child for me to love it with you. And just because we won't conceive doesn't mean we have to stop trying.' You believe that?"

Maria almost fell over, here. She braced herself on the end table and slid into the bedside chair. She had, of course, been told about their decision, the polycystic ovary syndrome, but she had never heard this telling. Maybe it was because of the sex joke at the end of his sentiment, but Eunice had never told her this story.

"In my day, well, in my parents' day, some men would have used that as a reason to run around. I even heard my mother say of a neighbor who got a hysterectomy, 'She's not a whole woman anymore.' But not only did my Thom not run around, he pushed for adoption. We heard adoption could happen faster, especially with newborns, in Mexico. So, we got our Maria. Can you believe that? The worst news I ever got in my life led to the best thing that ever happened to me. She's so smart and sweet. It's hard to recognize it in the moment, but God has a plan for all of us. He blessed me with cruddy ovaries. Blessed me."

Maria sat, crying at the memory of her father and watching her mother drift off to wherever her mind was taking her past her gaze at the ceiling. Happiness, sweet spell of confusion, be damned, she got up and hugged her mother hard and kissed her sweetly on her cheek.

"Oh, dear," Eunice said happily. "Dear Heart, I don't know what I did to deserve that, but thank you. When did you get in?"

Of course, it wasn't all that nice. Eunice grew more and more irritable at her confusion surrounding Maria being present, almost as if her daughter's being around were what was causing her to forget so much instead of just reminding her that she was doing so. Maria had Danielle over for three hours each afternoon for help so that she could shower or leave and get groceries, and that was mostly working out if Maria didn't mind constant exhaustion, which, at the time, she didn't.

There were minor annoyances. Eunice kept asking after Rob when she could remember that he existed. She would ask about Thom and Maria's grades, asking if she was sure to wear a hat on those cold New England days. This was all fine enough. It was dispiriting, but Maria came to expect it. She knew what she was dealing with, but the Rob questions just got under her skin. Maria was trying her best to ignore her mother's prodding, which really made her feel at home, but one day, she wouldn't stop.

"Rob's playing a show tonight in Austin," Eunice said.

"I know, Mom. He plays shows in Austin."

"It's apparently some kind of big deal," Eunice continued.

"Yes, Mom. He's a big deal."

"The crazy singer lady, what's her name? Something dumb sounding. She's there too. People are excited."

Maria didn't immediately know what Eunice was talking about, but she was exhausted and had been feeling dizzy lately. She knew she hadn't been eating enough, hadn't been remembering, but it was really all serving to make her feel so drained and weak, and trying to get aboard Eunice's runaway train of thought was mentally taxing. So, she didn't even try.

"Yeah, Mom. Her."

"People are talking about a reunion. There's buzz. catdragbird, right? That's a dumb name. And why don't they capitalize the darn thing?"

"What?"

"Rob's old band, with the crazy lady. They've been playing in Austin. The article said there's buzz. They're recording. That's good, right?"

Maria wished she'd tried to keep up earlier. She stood dumbfounded, and her mother seemed to be drifting off to other things. "What? Where are you hearing this?"

"Huh?"

"About Rob, catdragbird? Where are you getting this?"

"Oh, my phone. I put his name in the thing a long time ago, and now it emails me whenever he's in the news. It's been a while, huh?"

It had been a while. All thoughts of Rob had receded to the back of her mind along with all others that weren't Sundry Services and Eunice's wellbeing. For a moment, Maria was jealous, but then she was happy, hopeful, even. Mattering like this might just be what Rob needed; it might just have fixed something in him. If she had any more energy to devote to the moment, she would have let that hope blossom, and she might then have stomped down on that hope and kicked herself for wanting it, but she just didn't have it in her.

A week later, Maria was on a call at the dining room table. She was almost wrapped up, and she was genuinely surprised when she heard Eunice cry out. She had scheduled the call to coincide with Eunice's after-lunch nap, and it had all gone mostly to plan. Aside from the fact that her mother was supposed to be asleep, Maria was shocked to the point of dropping her headset without ending the call because Eunice never cried out like that. When she got into the bedroom, Maria didn't initially understand the commotion. Eunice was standing, seeming to have stopped mid-step away from her bed. Before she could say anything, Maria smelled the mishap that had caused her to cry out.

To that point, Eunice had been toileting well enough. The helpless look in her eyes pulled Maria out of herself. She didn't allow herself to recoil at the smell or react in any way whatsoever that wasn't immediate care for her mother. She waved away Eunice's sorrys and helped her into the restroom, straight into the tub.

"Oh, dear. I just missed it. I just, I didn't realize I had to go, but then I did, and I didn't make it." Eunice howled, a howl full of the kind of angry despair that Maria didn't have time to work out words for inside herself, and if she could have, she would have howled with her.

"It's okay, Mom. Let's just get you cleaned up," she said.

"I can clean myself," Eunice said.

"I know but let me help you."

"Goddamnit, Maria. I may have just shit my pants, but I'm not so helpless that I can't clean myself up."

Maria hadn't heard Eunice yell like that in years. That rage filled her with a kind of relief. *Thank you, Mom. Thank you for being as mad at this as me!* Still, she was going to help when she heard the doorbell. It was Danielle there to work her shift. Maria said she would be back and headed for the front door. Upon turning the corner from the hallway outside her mother's room, Maria saw the table, her computer open and the headset lying there like a bike left on a front yard by a careless kid.

"Hello? Melancon? Appleman?"

No one answered when she spoke. The doorbell rang again. She went up and let Danielle in. Danielle could immediately see the state the frantic scene had put Maria in.

"Girl," she said in calm sympathy, "I'm here. I got you."

Maria let some of the tension out of her shoulders and ended up slumping into Danielle's powdery-smelling embrace. She ran down what had happened at the doorstep. The whole thing didn't take any more than thirty seconds.

"She's in the shower now?" Danielle couldn't help but betray her worry at the situation.

They rushed back to the bathroom off Eunice's room. She was standing there, no water running, unsure of why she was cold and sticky, naked from the waist down. The sight and smell were too much for Maria, who stopped outside the bathroom.

"I've got it now, Maria," Danielle told her. "Isn't that right, Miss Eunice? Tell Maria that Danielle's here to help." Before Eunice could speak up, Danielle gave the prompting she knew was needed. "Isn't that right? Tell her Danielle's the best nurse in the world."

It all overwhelmed Eunice, but she held back the tears and spoke through only a minimally cracking voice. "That's right, Dear Heart, Danielle has me. I'm with the nurse now."

Maria left them to do the dirty work of preserving some of Eunice's dignity. That was the first time Maria was glad that her mother had dementia, that if she was on that side of her decline, at least she would be granted the peace of forgetting her stops along the way. She almost made it to the table when it all caught up to her. She had to use the kitchen sink, but at least she could use the side that had the garbage disposal to not have to fish any of her sick chunks out of the other side.

Her chest and arms were now more prepared for the strain of the heaving. In the weeks since the trip to Dr. K's office, it was as if some kind of regulator was taken off of her constitution, and she had vomited three times between that cold linoleum floor and the kitchen sink.

After the strain of the accident and showering and dressing, Eunice went right back to bed. Danielle came back out, and Maria offered her a glass of wine. Danielle scoffed at this, but Maria told her she at least had to take a bottle home at the end of her shift. Danielle agreed. They sat at the table, Maria all but done with her day after calling her colleagues and apologizing for her disappearing act and talked about the implications of what happened.

"She's not really performing her activities of daily living," Danielle said. "She's declining, and she's lost weight."

"I know," Maria said. "I have her eating a little bit healthier, and she doesn't always like what I make. But I get her to have some Ensure with her meals."

"I understand," Danielle said. "But we may have to reevaluate her situation. It might be time for a different kind of care. This is all too much for you."

"It's really not."

"That's not what I mean. You're being great. You're giving her all you have, but it's about to be too much for you to handle. More than you're capable or qualified to deal with. This isn't about what you can offer, what you want to be able to give. It's about what she needs."

"I met with a social worker at the hospital. It was all a blur, but she gave me her card," Maria said. "I can call her and ask if it stays this bad or gets worse. This is really just one incident."

Maria didn't call the hospital that day. When Eunice woke, she seemed okay enough. Everything seemed normal enough. So, she'd had an accident, but that's all it was, an accident. The days continued like that until a week later when Eunice woke one day and wouldn't, couldn't talk.

Maria tried all she could to coax her mother into talking. She could follow simple commands, even point to a glass of water Maria had brought for her to drink, but she just couldn't talk. This was the start of the hardest days, but at least Maria would get more help. When she talked to the hospital social worker, it was determined that she, with Danielle a few hours a day, wasn't enough. And however much she might have disagreed with that, not but two days later, Eunice herself would prove the assessment to be correct.

CHAPTER TWENTY-TWO

Rob's car got a flat tire just south of Tilden, Texas. He pulled over to the side of the road and changed it out himself. The donut spare he had didn't have many miles on it because he had used it once before for longer than he should have. He had a choice to make: he could backtrack up to Pleasanton, where he saw a Walmart, in the hopes they would have a tire to swap out with his, or he could continue south, which he knew he would have to do if he hoped to get to town before the cemetery closed its gates and hope he could find someone to change it out down there.

He continued on south to Greenton.

It was nearly dark out when Rob got to the cemetery. He'd wished he had brought flowers, but he did as best he could to get out of the studio and out of Austin in time to beat traffic both there and in San Antonio. He also could have stood to shower and get a fresh change of clothes on him. By that time, he had let Penny know that Maria was gone, had been for almost a month. When she asked if they were done, he told her that he didn't know. She hadn't reached out, and he wasn't going to be the one calling out to her.

"But her mom's sick, right?" Penny had said.

"She's the one who said she wanted to end it. She said that and left. If she wants it done, it's done. If it can be fixed, she can be the one to reach out to try and fix it," he had told her.

"Real convenient for you, with a twenty-year-old on your dick," Penny said.

"Do you want to fight me over this? Is that what this is? You think I deserve to get kicked around over this, that I deserve to take shit? Because I'm not going to take shit over this." Rob was more tired than angry at the conversation. He only shouted because volume was the only tool he could employ in trying to make his bullshit seem anything even approaching believable.

"Honey, if I wanted a fight, I would have attacked, and you'd have lost already," Penny said. They were in the bar upstairs from C-Boy's, a too-hip joint that she thought was kitschy—"It looks like a scene from fucking Twin Peaks," she said—but Rob didn't care to correct her by telling her, was anything but. It was boutique kitsch, a three-hundred-dollar pair of pre-torn and faded blue jeans in the form of a bar. "It's just that if I know anything, it's your flameout patterns and regret. From the second I saw you at the Marineros show, I knew you were flaming out. Hell, you were punctuating some point you'd just made in your head by slamming a bottle of water onto the ground on a crowded patio. And I know regret. And I don't want you to regret what you're doing. Fuck your little doll. Push your wife away. Divorce her, for all I care. But if you can stop this ride and get off right now, do you think it might save you from some regret later?"

Rob looked over at her bathed in red neon light and was sorry he'd ever hurt her. If he could have traded it all—the tours, the reputation that he lived and gigged and built a career off of—for never having loved and hurt her because he wasn't sure how much of her current life situation he was responsible for, how much of her regret he'd caused, but he knew it was more than none, and what a lasting effect he had made on it had almost all been bad—he certainly would.

"I don't know, Penny," he said, knowing that even if he wanted to lie, she would see through it. "But thanks for not fighting me."

"Yeah, well, maybe I do want to kick you around a little. Maybe some part of me that won't ever go away will always be mad at you."

That, of course, was valid.

Whereas he'd told Penny about his situation with Maria or, really, her situation with her mother, all he told Snoop was that she was gone. She'd asked him to leave, but he refused. He'd paid the down payment on the house with an inheritance he'd gotten from his mother, which he made sure to tell her. But still, while they could record vocals and guitar and bass tracks at his house, he didn't want to be there for any other part of what they were doing.

"It just feels wrong," he'd told her when he stopped her advances one night after recording.

She seemed to think he was being sweet or noble or something like that by exercising restraint. What she didn't know was that it felt wrong because it very clearly was wrong. Rob didn't know what he was doing with her, what would happen with Maria. He didn't even know what he was doing with Penny. Would they tour? Was the band back together? Could he even do that? He didn't know, but he knew for absolute certain that he was wrong in almost every way possible to almost everyone around him.

None of that was to say Rob wasn't fully taking advantage of his new relationship with Snoop, just that he wasn't doing it in the house. This had them sneaking around the studio, which was close enough to her apartment and where she could easily meet up with him after her shifts pedicabbing, but even that came to an end when Penny showed up one morning, ready to work before the sun. They had been on their way out, and she was on his back, letting him walk her out on piggyback, claiming to be too tired after a night of riding.

"Hey," she'd said meekly to Penny, who she saw in front of them before he did.

Penny just laughed and shook her head, walking past them and saying back at them without turning to face them, "Night, guys!"

And so, the night before heading south, Rob had gotten to Snoop's apartment at three and didn't remember falling asleep when she woke to go into school for extra money running Saturday school at seven. From there, he could go home, but that was so far north, and he had a standing meeting set for eleven at the studio with Penny and Danny as they were working on the final mix of the EP. When he got to the studio that morning, Penny was there having a coffee and writing in her notebook.

"Jesus Christ, are you here this early every morning?" Rob asked.

"What do you want me to do? I have insomnia and nowhere else to go.

What am I supposed to do, go walk Town Lake?" she said. "What's your excuse?"

"I was just going to crash before the mixing session."

Penny lifted the reading glasses Rob had finally gotten used to seeing her wear when she was reading lyrics in the booth and studied the state of Rob in front of her. She couldn't hide the playful look of real disapproval on her face. She raised her eyebrows when she pointed a thumb to the back lounge. "By all means."

Rob went back to the lounge, feeling near-passing out tired. He sat on the couch, ready to lie down when the memory of Penny's dumb smirk made him get up and walk back up to the main lounge and push back as hard as he had felt she'd pushed him in encroaching on his mental space with her judgment and her very presence in the space he'd hoped to occupy alone.

"You don't have to," he started upon entering the room, but stopped when she pointed to a steaming cup of coffee she'd poured and had waiting for him when he came back in.

"I know," she said. "I know I don't have to. I didn't mean to, but I did. I knew you wouldn't be able to sleep after that, so I poured you some coffee as an apology."

Mollified as he was by having had his offended sense of righteousness—no matter how wrong he knew it to be—acknowledged, Rob slid into the chair opposite Penny at the round Formica table. He took a sip of the coffee and immediately felt better. He was tired, and he knew it showed. He couldn't keep running this way on this kind of schedule. It was too much.

"So, what do you do all morning?" he asked.

"Just write, really," Penny said, not looking up from her notebook. The sound of her pencil scratching across it was one he remembered hearing in his sleep so many years ago.

"Lyrics?" Rob asked.

"Yeah." Penny put the pencil down and closed the notebook. "That and other stuff. Poetry I'd never sing out loud. Musings. Thoughts."

"Like, for a book, or something?"

"Sweetie, I write to write. But, yeah, there might be a book in my notebooks. A few, really," she said.

"Ooh, am I the bad guy?" Rob said, smiling.

Penny didn't smile back. "Of course not. I mean, I guess you're something of a tragic hero. You're the love of my life, I guess. At least in the older books."

"And now?"

"And now you're something like the love of my life for a life I lived too long ago to remember, but you're back to save me. You're my knight in shining armor if the knight in shining armor broke the princess before coming back to save her." She smiled, and Rob stopped. "I do have some lyrics I'm thinking of specifically for catdrag, for our next thing. You wanna see them?"

"Are you kidding me? I'd love to," Rob said. And with that, he was fully awake and would stay that way through mixing with Danny and for long enough to record rough guitar tracks for two of Penny's songs.

The high of the rest of the recording session, of actually creating and not just playing along, as well as a couple more pots of coffee through the morning and into the afternoon, kept Rob wired and ready to go through San Antonio. But by the time he turned off the interstate and got into Jourdanton, he was feeling the previous night's, the past three weeks', really, misspent hours. He leaned forward, hanging on to the top of the steering wheel to power through the rest of the drive to Greenton in as focused a manner as possible, and if it weren't for the flat in Tilden, he might have had to pull over for rest or to pour more coffee on his already raw gut.

The shock and mild panic of the flat on the middle of the road, coupled with the sweaty exertion of changing the tire on the asphalt made frying-pan hot for the April sun that had forgotten spring's sweet promises—Rob's right palm blistered from when he'd propped himself with it on the ground for all of the two seconds it took his brain to register the pain of the sear—had worked to both wake Rob alert for the last stretch of his drive to Greenton, and to add into the cocktail of his day. That day, in and of itself, was heavy enough to fill his mind with memories of a love so sweet it made his guilt over squandering it that much more bitter. But coming as it did after his night, that morning, that month, and those last three months, an intense distillation of brain chemicals and electricity kicking around the sleep-dependent neurotransmitter-and-inhibiter-deprived cortices lent to that last stretch of road and that sunset drive into the Greenton Cemetery a truly hallucinatory sheen.

Rob almost couldn't register what to do with the locked gate at the front of the cemetery. There were cars inside. Had they been locked in? Were they broken down? No. They had gone in through the side entrance. Instead of turning out onto Fal Highway and driving up a half-mile to turn around and turn down the side street he'd passed to try the main entrance, he drove in reverse through the roadside grass and backed onto Vaello Ave to cut a direct path to the cemetery entrance. Vaello was a street he only ever recalled being a rocky two-lane byway out of Greenton and down to Zapata. When he heard the sharp peels of police sirens behind him, he saw that the road had come to house a roadside trailer home that served as a Border Patrol outpost. There were four Border Patrol trucks and two cars done up in the white and green colors of the law enforcement agency that had always seemed silly to Rob when he drove into town with his father because he had never had cause in his life to know why those same colors were menacing to other people.

One of the cars peeled off of the idling unit and came to an aggressive screeching halt next to Rob's car. An agent got out of the car, his hand on the gun on his hip, and shouted loud enough for Rob to hear in his car.

"What the fuck do you think you're doing?"

Rob rolled down the window slowly. Judging by the look of the car and Rob's easy disregard of the danger in the situation, the agent seemed to know immediately that Rob was an American. Rob held his palms up in what otherwise would have been smartass mock-surrender, but the agent's power trip had been satiated, and he no longer looked ready to kill, just to bully.

"I'm coming to the cemetery," Rob said. "Main entrance is closed for some reason."

"And that gives you the right to drive like a maniac?" The agent pulled his glasses down his nose, seemingly so he could lean his head further down and stare even more intently at Rob from under the brim of his cowboy hat.

"I'll grant that I probably broke a law there, but I didn't drive like a maniac."

"Are you questioning my judgment as an officer of the law?"

"No. I specifically said I wasn't. I might have broken the law. I don't know that. You do. But I wasn't driving like a maniac."

The agent wasn't quick. He was used to locals offering him deference and outsiders mostly being truckers or illegals. Greenton wasn't somewhere people drove *through* anymore, much less somewhere they drove *to*.

"Where you driving in from?"

"Austin," Rob said.

"Well, shit." The agent relaxed a bit, seeming to have thought this was some kind of victory for him. He crossed his arms across his chest. "That might as well count for probable cause for me to search you."

"Listen, man." Rob rubbed his eyes with the backs of his hands. "I've had a long day. I just want to get in here and visit my mom's grave before the cemetery closes. It's her birthday."

The agent took off his sunglasses and put them in the breast pocket of his shirt. He walked around the back of his cruiser, shaking his head, and leaned into Rob's window. "Are you telling me you're from here?"

"No. I'm not. I'm telling you my mom is buried here. My dad's from here. Venancio Vera. He—"

"Dr. Vera?" the agent leaned back out of the window to get a better look at Rob. "The dentist?"

"Yeah," Rob said. "The dentist."

"He helped my boy with a busted tooth a couple months ago. Numbed it, pulled out the pieces, and prescribed something for the pain. He's a good man."

"You could say that," Rob said.

"ID?"

Rob handed his license over. The agent took one look at it, scanning only for the likeness and to check the name.

"Don't drive like that in front of cops, huh? Makes it real hard for us to ignore, you understand?"

"Sorry. Maybe illegal, but I'll agree that I was driving like an asshole."

"There you go. Don't drive like an asshole. At least in front of cops." He turned around and reported to his colleagues up the road on his shoulder radio that it was all good as he walked to his car and drove off.

The work still yields, Rob thought.

The Greenton Cemetery is small but, like the rest of that town that Rob never took seriously, bigger and more complex than it looked. If you don't pay it respect, like Rob didn't, you could easily get lost, like Rob did. He had only ever driven in through the main entrance, and coming in that way, it was just a straight shot up the main drive and a left at the spigot of non-potable water for any family who chose to, like Venancio did now that he lived in town permanently, bring a hose to water the graves of those who preceded you in death. Coming in, as he did, from the side, Rob didn't know which row of graves to drive up to to get to the landmark on the main drive. He got out of his car where the row he chose intersected the main drive and, looking for the spigot, walked up and down the road.

The sun was setting, and while he feared he wouldn't easily find the grave, at least he was in. Even if he had to walk grave to grave, he'd find his mother. He walked down the main drive one last time in an attempt to find the spigot. When he didn't, he walked back to his car and picked the row he'd come in on to head down to begin his search.

"How the hell are you lost in a cemetery that's smaller than a city block, Robin?" a familiar voice called to him three rows of graves back from the one Rob was walking down.

"Because, Ben, I'm used to coming in from the main entrance." Rob walked back to where his father was standing.

"So, you go to the entrance you're used to coming in from and take it like you would any other day." Venancio held his hand out, and Rob shook it. "I was wondering if you'd make it."

"But the spigot isn't where it used to be. I used to see it and know to turn left."

"Some drunk asshole ran over it, and all the PVC in the ground was shattered. When the county replaced it, I asked them to put it in the back. It's easier to reach your mom from there," Venancio said.

"And just like that, they moved it?"

"I paid for some new PEX piping for the irrigation pipe and paid the labor. They put it where I wanted it. Simple."

"South Texas politics. . . . Vote with your wallet, right?"

"It's more than that, but you're close," Venancio said.

They walked over to the Vera family plot. There were three single headstones—Venceslao, Venancio Sr., and Tomasa Vera—and a double above the plot that contained the shared grave of Perla and Maurice Vera and the one awaiting the body of Venancio Jr. The state of the grave was a testament of the care Venancio put into its upkeep, and Rob had previously had the suspicion upon visiting the grave that Venancio might just have taken such good care of the family graves to prove himself right for having wanted Perla buried in Greenton when she died. Even at his most spiteful, Rob could never believe this to actually be the case because for his entire life, Venancio had never gone out of his way to justify himself to his son or to anyone else. That was Rob's personal brand of asshole. Venancio would never go out of his way to prove himself right, just like he would never apologize for being wrong. To do so would be to acknowledge that any opinion outside his own mattered, and to him, none did.

"I'll give you a minute," Venancio said.

For a second, Rob wanted to tell him that that would be unnecessary, but he knew it would be an act of weakness that, sure, his father would likely oblige without too much obvious judgment, but there are some instincts too deeply imprinted to ignore, and one of those prevented him from dropping his guard in the moment. Moments of silent contemplation like this made Rob long for believing in a way like he couldn't really remember. He held his hands together in the manner of someone who'd been taught the posture of belief before he'd had a choice in the matter. He could only really recall ever having faked his way through praying. Still, it would have been nice to believe there was some force that had shepherded his mother to some better place, that he could send his thanks and praise to that force and even talk to the continued and eternal consciousness of his mom in that paradise, but all he could muster was the silent gesture of assuming that position and attempting to convince himself to try.

"Happy birthday, Mom," he said to nothing and couldn't stop the brook of self-disgust that ran in him for even attempting the gesture.

"Rob," Venancio said softly from behind him.

Rob turned to face his father, his frustration at having no greater connection to his mother than the draw of her memory bringing him there to the town she hated welling up in the corner in his eyes. Venancio held out a hand that held two glasses stacked. Rob grabbed them. In his other hand, Venancio held a bottle. It was the same kind of scotch they'd had five years prior in the kitchen in the chaotic shadow of Perla's death. It was a fresh bottle, and Venancio seemed to struggle to get the tin wrapping off of the bottle's top. When he did, he pulled off the cork and took a satisfying whiff. He grabbed a glass from Rob, filled it up halfway, and handed it back before grabbing the second and filling it for himself.

"To Perla," he held his glass out to Rob, who tapped it with his.

"To Mom," Rob said.

They each took a drink, and Venancio poured what remained in the bottle onto the ground before losing himself in thoughts of his wife. Rob could clearly see how his father stared down at the ground and seemed to see something more than six feet of cover between himself and his wife's bones that the man believed. He put his hand on his father's shoulder.

"Do you want a minute alone?"

"No, mijo. I've been here more or less all day," Venancio said.

He turned a tender glance at his son, who he could have hugged for just showing up. The softness left his eyes when he regarded what was standing in front of him. There was at least a week of scruff on Rob's face, and his hair was a matted, greasy mess, and his eyes had clearly not seen sleep in what appeared to be days.

"Say, Rob, where's Maria?" he asked.

Rob didn't have any lies in him, and he was too weak in every way he could be to fight at the moment. All he could lean on was the truth he was willing to share and the extent to which he was willing to lie through omission.

"Humble. Eunice is sick."

"Oh, no. Is she okay?"

"I honestly don't know. It's that she's been forgetting things. Maria's over there trying to figure out exactly what kind of help she'll need. She's been over there almost a month."

"Well, that's just terrible. Give her my best."

"I will." Rob had to lie sooner or later.

"Well, it's getting late," Venancio announced, "and you look like absolute dog shit. You want to stay over for the night?"

"No." Rob realized there was no way to fake laid-back cool to his father because his father had never seen him laid back. "I'm in the middle of mixing an album I've been working on. It was hell getting out of the studio today as it was."

Venancio nodded at this. If there was one thing he knew he and his wife had given their son in equal measure, it was work ethic. He saw it when Rob first started getting paid gigs around Corpus when he was thirteen. It started as a little hobby easy enough to ignore, his playing in warehouses and back yards and ranches around town, but when the boy came to his parents with a proposal to miss three weeks of school to go on a tour through Louisiana up into Arkansas and back, Venancio realized that the boy had taken it upon himself to put his childish things to use and enter the world a young man who, Venancio realized, had never spoken or understood as a child.

"Okay. Makes sense. Do you at least want dinner? How much would your mother love the thought of you and me sitting at a taqueria in Greenton as two men not being forced by her to share a meal?"

"Well, Dad . . ." Rob wasn't trying to let the old man down easy. He really couldn't come up with any kind of convincing objection at the moment.

"No, no. It's okay. I understand if you have to go. Let's go to Bryan's to gas you up, and I can have them brew you some fresh coffee before you go."

Rob nodded at this. If this wasn't a successful trip—getting out of Austin, away from Snoop, if even only for that day and night, and now having a positive interaction with his father at the foot of his mother's grave—Rob had never had one. He walked over to his car and scrolled through his phone before he was startled by the sound of a truck's horn.

Venancio had pulled his car up next to Rob's and was motioning for Rob to roll down his window when he looked up.

"Are you out of your goddamn mind driving on that?"

Rob didn't immediately register what his father was saying. Venancio pointed to the back driver's side tire, and Rob remembered the donut.

"Oh, yeah." Rob's reserves were empty. He felt the urge to attack, to deflect, to fight his way out of the corner. "Happened outside of Tilden. I'll get it fixed in Pleasanton."

"Pleasanton is a hundred twenty miles away!" Venancio seemed to find a mode he was familiar with in his angry bafflement at his son's stupidity. He put an exasperated palm over his eyes and took a deep breath. "Listen. Come with me. I'll call the guy to change it out. We can have dinner, and you can get it changed at a reasonable rate. You're not going to risk trying to make it to Pleasanton on that piece of shit. Follow me."

He didn't give Rob a chance to object. He just pulled away from him and drove out to the cemetery exit and sat there waiting for Rob to five-point turn his car around on the small caliche drive to get on the small path out. Pulling up behind his father's car, Rob saw a familiar sight, his father rolling by someone in town—this time it was the Border Patrol agents—recognize them, and hail them with a sharp whistle blown between his thumb and forefinger. The agents heard, and the one who Rob had dealt with earlier was shouting something to him that prompted Venancio to point his thumb back at Rob. He ended his drive-by bullshit session the same way he always did, with a lazy wave out the window and a slow high nod at his temporary audience. For as much as there was to admire and hate about his father, for as similar as that frustrating moment was to so many he'd experienced with him in the past, and despite the fact that in that moment Rob was happy to have a solution to the problem of his tire and excited at the prospect of actual good Mexican food (his definition of which was actual Rio Grande Plain Tex-Mex), all Rob could think of pulling out of the cemetery in his father's wake was that the man had never taught him to whistle like that.

The last time Rob was in the building that housed the restaurant where he and his father sat down to dinner, it was a gas station. The Pachanga had closed down before Perla died, and it stood abandoned when Maria drove Rob through town in the procession to the cemetery all those years ago. A twenty-pump gas station opened up down the road that had a fully staffed kitchen of people cooking tacos and tortillas and tamales as good as you would expect them to be when cooked by people around these parts. It was part of a chain large enough to sweep in and undercut and sink the local stores all around it. The Pachanga had closed. The Circle-C had closed. Even the Stop-n-Shop and the Maverick Markets had closed. Only Bryan's remained open across Main Street from the behemoth Tiger Mart, and while that interloper took all of the passing-through traffic of eighteen-wheelers and Border Patrol agents and roughnecks and frackers in the area to inject their poisons into the ground in order to pull out its lifeblood, Greentonites had stuck by Bryan's.

The Pachanga was an ideal location for a restaurant, as the store was big enough and even had a drive-through window that people had used to pull up to and ring the bell to get their beer and cigarettes from the comfort of their cars or trucks. Walking in, everyone turned and greeted Venancio, and Rob realized that, no matter how big the audiences or how devoted the fans of his work were, he would never be as big a rock star out there as his father was in Greenton, Texas.

They sat, and Venancio ordered more food than the two of them could be expected to eat together, telling Rob it was all so good he had to try everything and they would box any leftovers for him to take and eat for the week. He was in his element presiding over the room, and Rob was glad that his father had moved back to Greenton. Appetizers and a bucket of beer arrived at the table just as Venancio's phone buzzed.

"Goyo!" he said happily into the phone. "You want to come in and grab something to eat? No? Que bueno. Listen, he's planning on leaving tonight. Can you turn this around? I'll pay you extra. And can you see if you have a full-sized spare for his car? That donut is on its last legs. Okay. Thanks. Open the trunk," he said to Rob after putting his phone down.

Rob used his key fob to open the trunk and looked out the window at a man close to his age pull the flat tire out the back of his car. Seeing he was being watched, Goyo, the mechanic, waved high and gave a slow nod at Rob, who only felt a little fake returning the gesture.

"Alright. Let's eat. He should have that changed in no time," Venancio said, grabbing a tortilla, tearing off a piece, and scooping up some rice and beans to start with like he always did.

Rob dove into the food. His father was right. It was very good, but it was particularly good in that it was exactly what Rob thought it should be. He didn't need to taste an enchilada that was the platonic ideal of enchilada-ness, or carne guisada or mole, for that matter, but seeing his father watch his every bite, hoping to see a deep appreciation, reminded Rob of playing a favorite record for someone. He ate more than he wanted that night.

"So, what are you working on that has you on such a schedule?" Venancio asked.

"Actually," Rob said without looking up from his food. "I'm working on writing new stuff for catdragbird. Penny's up in Austin, and I recorded a solo thing with her. Her contract is up, and we're going to use the name and milk some nostalgia dollars out of the label for our next thing."

Rob had spent so long with the current, medicated, old Penny—safe and boring, turning in early at night and showing up early to the studio Penny—that it didn't immediately occur to him that the name, the woman, might rouse fear and suspicion in his father. When he looked across the table and saw the smile gone from his face, Rob realized that the last Venancio had heard or thought of Penny was when Rob washed up on Corpus dope sick and broke. He could see Venancio looking at the state of him again, unshaved or showered, clearly not having slept fully in days, and he knew he had to say something.

"She's doing a lot better. Therapy and meds and all that. For everything she's been through, she's kind of just a boring old lady now," Rob said. "Well, boring, old, crazy lady."

"Rob, I'm only going to ask this once. Have you been using?"

"No! Using? I'm too old for that shit, and as tired as I am, I don't want to die." Rob put his fork down and stared right at his dad, who had been lied to enough times to know when his son was telling him the truth.

"So, you won't mind if I call Maria and ask her how everything's going?" Venancio grabbed his beer and took a drink, not taking his eyes off of Rob or blinking as he took a long gulp.

"Of course not," Rob said. "Go right ahead. But—" The sight of his father picking his phone up off the table and thumbing through his contacts put a panic in Rob. "Wait. . . . Just, wait."

Venancio stopped tapping on his phone but didn't put it down. He sat, looking hard at Rob. "Fine. I'll wait. Tell me why I need to wait because if I wait until you get in that car and drive off to call her and she tells me you sold the TV and she hasn't seen you in a week, it'll probably be the last time I see you."

"Sold the TV?" Rob was shaking his head in incredulity over his father's melodramatic notions of what rock bottom might look like.

"Fuck you. Like I know what you'd do on drugs. Your mom always handled that." Venancio put his phone down. "What's going on?"

"First of all, this has nothing to do with Penny. She was in town for *South-by*, and we ran into each other. We played a gig, then another, then I recorded for her. It's been productive. Lucrative, even.

"Maria is in Humble. Eunice is sick. But I haven't talked to Maria in almost a month. We've been fighting. It was over nothing. Well, over me being an asshole, but she was wrong too. She was . . . She didn't. . . . It was over me being an asshole. And she left to deal with her mom, and she hasn't been back since."

Rob pushed away the plate from in front of him and took a drink of his beer. Venancio sat studying Rob, working to solve in his head the riddle that sat in front of him. He picked up his phone.

"And I can call her right now, and she'll confirm all of this?" he asked.

"Yeah," Rob said. "If she'll answer. I'm not her favorite person in the world at the moment."

Venancio thumbed through his phone, watching Rob for a reaction. When he just shrugged, Venancio seemed to think twice. He clicked through a few buttons and then typed and sent a text. He put the phone on the table and folded his arms across his chest.

"You can relax," Rob said. "If she texts back, you're just going to be disappointed, in more ways than one."

Venancio's phone buzzed. He looked down at it, arms still crossed. Then it buzzed again. He picked the phone up, and the stern look on his face dissolved to one of concern. He looked at Rob, seeming to have found the exact kind of disappointment he would be filled with over this. Rob sat there as the texts kept buzzing in, and his father fell into the truth of the moment. He typed up a text, then put his phone down.

"Ah, Rob," he said, but before he could continue, his phone buzzed one last time. He picked it up and smiled at the message. He sent a quick one back. "She's a good woman."

"I know."

"And a good wife."

"I know."

"And her mom is sick."

"I know."

Venancio handed Rob his phone. Rob read the conversation and felt smaller than he ever did stealing the last bills in some lady's purse and the last food in her fridge after fucking her and before stealing away into the night on the road to the next gig, next fix, next low.

>*I just talked to Rob. How's your mom?*

<*Fine.*

<I mean, I guess?

<There was a rapid decline

<She's gone nonverbal. Not really eating but taking fluids. We might do a home

<We're waiting for a consult from the hospital social worker

<She was talking last week. Forgetting things, needing help, but talking. I just don't know.

>Maria, I'm so sorry. If I can help, let me know.

<Will do.

>Seriously. Anything.

<Oh, hey. Happy Birthday Perla

>Yes! Happy Birthday!!!

Rob handed his father his phone. "I didn't mean to do this. Not like this. Not now. Not at all, really."

"A month? And you can't just drive over to Humble and fix it?" Venancio asked.

"It didn't occur to me to. I've been busy. Been keeping myself busy."

"Rob, are you fucking Penny?"

"Whoa! No way. That already almost killed her once. Working with her has actually helped me think about some of this stuff."

"How much more thinking do you have to do? Eunice is sick. The kind of sick that doesn't get fixed."

"Everything is just so broken, and Eunice wasn't sick this whole time. This goes back. This isn't happening because of Eunice."

"And you've kept your nose clean? While she's been gone?"

"'Kept my nose clean?' Do you know nothing about drugs?" Rob rolled his eyes involuntarily. He certainly wasn't trying to come off as such a child, but Venancio brought that out in him.

"That's not what I mean," Venancio said, sounding patient, knowing.

"Well, then, what do you mean?"

"Have you kept your dick dry?"

Rob recoiled from the question, from its vulgarity, and from all of the insight behind its asking. Venancio nodded knowingly.

"Every time I left, I had a good reason. No matter how long I was gone, if it was an evening or a week, I always had a good reason to go. I was always right."

Rob didn't like his father's familiarity at the moment. He shook his head and pointed a finger at him, ready to tell him how this wasn't that.

"I'm absolutely serious. She would be nagging and nagging, asking where I'd been when I really had been at the office, or you would be a fucking terror, always arguing, always disrespecting, and she would defend you no matter what. She always chose your side. Every time I was the bad guy, even when you were clearly just trying to piss me off."

"Bullshit," Rob said. "She—"

"Just listen. Every time I left, I was right. I had the moral high ground. Every. Single. Time. I knew it. Sometimes I would sleep at the office. Sometimes I would drive out here and stay with my uncle, but almost every time, I ended up in someone else's bed. Every time I told myself I was right. I was pushed out. What was I going to do? Be wronged and just take it? I was a man! A doctor. I had needs. I had a right to certain things. Every time I told myself I was justified. Every time I actually believed it. I let myself believe that every woman was some kind of coincidence or bi-product. But sitting here, with her mom dying in Humble and you looking like you've been out fucking around, I can be honest. On your mother's birthday," Venancio said, standing up to take the check to the counter, "I can be honest enough to say what I was doing, to say why I thought it was fine to keep doing it."

Goyo got back within an hour of coming by to get the tire and had already changed out the fixed tire with the donut when he came into The Pachanga to tell the Veras he was done. When he got in, a blank check and a plastic bag of food awaited him—Venancio had asked the waitress to add two to-go orders of whatever Goyo's favorite dish was to his ticket. Venancio and Rob had sat nearly silent after his moment of novel honesty. Rob was too occupied reckoning with his own self-deceptions and justifications to think through his father's revelations of his own.

How much had he added to Maria's pain over what she was going through with her mom? For what? He was physically exhausted, but he also itched under his skin to get up and leave. When Goyo got there and asked Rob to pop his trunk so that he could put in his new full-size spare, Rob wasn't sure how long he'd sat there in silence, his father continuing to pick at the food in one of the six Styrofoam containers the waitress had packed their leftovers into.

When they got up, Rob walked his father to his truck in order to share a goodbye that would probably have to be awkward because he honestly didn't know what he was going to do with the tightness in his stomach that had formed upon hearing his father's confession that made him want, now more than ever, to deck him.

When the wind picked up and blew a stack of napkins that sat atop the Styrofoam containers in one of the plastic bags Venancio was carrying on either side of himself, Venancio scrambled to put the bags down on the hood of his truck to try to run after the napkins. Rob saw him as an old man. He was almost seventy-six, and though he was still vibrant and as full of the same irrepressible self-assuredness that had always previously made Rob want to hit him, on that new old man—his hair now fully white where it had been salt and pepper, his always ropy, tone shape now seeming brittle—it just served to make him seem vulnerable, as if, whereas he had previously seemed so willing to stand his ground in his righteousness because he was ready and able to fight anyone offended by being wrong, he now seemed still ready to spit in the world's eye but ignorant of the fact of his own physical decline like a prizefighter past his prime, too punchy to know he's no longer of champion-caliber in anything but memory.

Rob ran out ahead of his father and grabbed the napkins. He stuffed them down the side of one of the plastic bags, picked the bags up, and put them in the back seat of his father's truck.

"Thank you," Venancio said. "The last thing I need is to fall and break my ass outside the damn Pachanga."

"No problem," Rob said. He held his hand out here for his father to shake before their parting.

"I can't convince you to stay? You really do look like shit," Venancio said, not taking his son's hand.

"No. I think I'm better off driving and sleeping in my own bed. Besides, I can use the time to think some things through."

"Fine. But do me a favor. Follow me to the house. I have something to give you. I would have packed it in my truck if I knew you were coming. I hoped you would, but if I had known, I would have put it in my car."

Rob looked at his father, trying to figure out what he was angling towards. Venancio recognized the searching his son was doing.

"Honestly. You won't even have to get out of your car. I'll just run in and bring it out to you."

Rob looked at his phone. It was almost nine. At this rate, he would be home at around one. He made to speak, but his father cut him off.

"What's ten more minutes? Besides, I can call Bryan's from the car. By the time you're done picking the thing up, they can have a fresh pot of coffee waiting for you. Come on."

Rob waited outside his father's house, a kind of ranch-style McMansion he'd had the good fortune of scooping up after a roughneck spent big to have it built after the last big oil boom but hadn't saved enough money to pay off before the bust that followed. It was big and tacky, but dirt cheap, as Venancio always reminded people. While Rob hated staying there because it meant more time spent with his dad, Maria couldn't bear to because it had clearly been designed and built for a family that had fallen apart with the price of crude. Venancio came out carrying a milk crate and walked straight to the passenger door. Without asking, he opened the door and put the crate in the seat.

As he walked around the front of the car to Rob's window, Rob flipped through the contents. When he reached the front, Rob was ready to make him go back around and get the crate.

"Dad, I don't need any more records. All the other ones are just taking up space in the attic above my garage as it is."

"I know, but not these. These were your mom's absolute favorites. She adored them. All the ones you have, they're the ones we kept in storage. This case, she kept in her office at the house. She loved them. They reminded her of growing up, of being young, of me. They reminded her of you and Maurice." Venancio's arms were folded, propping him up in his lean against the frame of Rob's door. He was bent down, his head almost in the car. "I know she would want you to have them. I know it, so . . . Happy Birthday, Mom."

Rob offered his hand again. Venancio took it and gave it a shake.

"Rob, I . . ."

Rob hadn't heard that particular kind of quiver in his father's voice before, and he wondered on the ride back home if it was because his father, in his old age, was crying in some new kind of way or because, and Rob came to think this was more likely the case, he'd never really listened to his father in any way that tried to understand him or how he felt. He'd always just projected his shitty attitude and waited with his asshole-son sonar to see what hit and how it would ping back.

When he got to Bryan's, the cashier had poured him the entire pot of freshly made coffee into a twenty-ounce coffee mug and a forty-four-ounce Styrofoam soda cup and had put handfuls of sugar and creamers in a plastic bag. In the face of such kind hospitality, he took them because he didn't have the heart to tell her that he took it black.

Back in his car, the whitish-blue, fluorescent light that fell on the front seat through the windshield made the image on the outmost facing record leaning back on the rest of the stack in the crate glow in the otherwise dark car. It was the Bee Gees, backlit in white suits, hovering over John Travolta disco-pointing at the sky and standing on the lit dance floor from *Saturday Night Fever*. He flipped through the rest of the records, and they sure were her favorites. There were Chicago, Abba, Simon and Garfunkel, and Beatles records. Behind the last record, Rob found a cylindrical box. It was a bottle of scotch, the brand and label he and his father had shared at the grave. He held the box up to the light and saw that his father had written on it in marker, "Thanks for coming, Son." He smiled and put the records back how they were, the Bee Gees and Travolta staring up at him.

Rob didn't immediately figure why he felt such a strong need to reach out to Maria when he saw the record. He didn't have enough time. Upon seeing it, he took his phone out of his pocket and tapped the Messages icon. Danny was the last person he had texted. When he clicked back to go out to all of his conversations, he could see that he'd texted Danny, Penny, Snoop, Mann, Blake, and even Galindo more recently than he'd texted his wife. He scrolled down to her name and tapped it. With the cursor in the text box blinking at him, Rob could think of nothing to type or say other than two words, which he had hoped would cover everything because they certainly applied to everything.

>*I'm sorry.*

It wasn't much, but it was all he could muster after the day he'd had. There was more to say, more he knew he should say, but he couldn't, and he was apologizing for that too. He was apologizing for being his father's son, for having ever hurt her like his father had hurt his mother. He was apologizing for needing more than was reasonable or fair, for lashing out when he didn't get it. He was confessing to her, to the dark silence that separated them, that he had failed his mother before her death and that he'd probably fucked it up so bad with his father that he'd never get to fix it before he died too. He was apologizing for having broken Penny to whatever degree he'd actually been culpable in breaking whatever part of her he'd been responsible for, for having met and led on and lied to Snoop. He was sorry for all of it and more, and he knew those two words weren't enough to express that just like he knew he wouldn't be able to answer Maria's one-word response when she finally sent it after a solid minute of three dots showing that she was drafting it.

<Why?

He put his phone down on the passenger seat next to the crate of records, turned on the car, and drove north. He hoped Maria, on her end of their conversation which he'd dropped just as abruptly as he'd picked it up, wouldn't take his not answering to mean he wasn't trying because, in fact, he was. He was trying to think the whole way up to Austin of what he could possibly type to her in response. He was driving, trying to come up with anything, ready to pick up the phone and type with his wrists on the steering wheel or pull over to the dark side of a highway or even just pull off and get a room for the night at a roadside motel in order to call her and talk the whole night through about everything he'd done wrong, for how wrong he'd been, but no one thing came to mind, and before he knew it, he was home, exhausted and unable to remember whole stretches of the drive.

In their bed, Rob fell asleep almost right away. He'd brought the crate of records into the house, and it sat on the dresser on the wall in front of the bed. He couldn't really see it in the dark, but he imagined the image of the Bee Gees leaning on one another, arms crossed in their white suits, staring out at him from the crate. He thought of his mother and even of his brother, and the normal guilt that surfaced whenever such thoughts arose reminded him that in the fluorescent buzz of Bryan's gas station in Greenton, he'd reached out. He'd apologized. There was work to do, work he was too tired to even conceive of, but he'd made the first step. He'd said his two words, and he was ready to do the work of coming up with an answer to the one she'd given back.

That night, though he didn't know how to answer her question, he was ready to try to tell her why.

CHAPTER TWENTY-THREE

Maria woke before the alarm she'd set for the next morning. She'd fallen asleep wondering if Rob would text her back, debating over a glass of wine which she could finally keep down now that she seemed to have recovered from her weeks of chronic nausea. She blew past the point of being drunk enough to be mean. She had still not been eating too much, and between her empty stomach and being worn so thin from having to work and care for her mother, she was out cold after only a few sips. She went into the kitchen and started the morning's coffee and had eggs and bacon going by the time Danielle arrived for the morning shift.

"Morning," she told Danielle at the door. "She's still asleep. Coffee's on."

"Thank the lord," Danielle said, throwing her hands up. "I was in such a rush getting over. I thought I was going to be late."

"It would be fine if you were late. You've been such a big help. I don't know what I would have done without you."

"You wouldn't be taking care of yourself. That's for sure," Danielle said. She put a plastic bag on the table. "I made it over to Walgreens. Everything you asked for."

After a couple of quick gulps of coffee, Danielle went in to wake and change Eunice. They'd had to start diapering her after the first incident of her soiling herself had been followed up too often to chalk up to just an accident, and while Maria was up to the task of cleaning her mother, she was always glad to not have to.

When she finished cooking the breakfast, Maria placed it on two plates with a can of Ensure on a tray into the bedroom. She placed it on the overbed table and rolled it over Eunice.

"Good morning, Mom!" She made sure, at this point, to always project positivity in tone and posture. "Breakfast time."

The faintest of smiles pulled back in the corner of Eunice's lips. They were dry from the night, so Maria opened an oral care swab from the pack that Danielle had brought and put it in the glass of water at Eunice's bedside to soak. It was a silly-seeming invention, a kind of sponge lollipop, but this is what had become of Eunice's life, of Maria's relationship with her, a series of products and prescriptions for oral care swabs and nutritional supplements, adult diapers, rented beds and stands on wheels, morphine drops, and words like "palliative" and "dysphagia."

"Your lips are pretty dry, mom. I'm just going to wet them a little."

She took the swab and rubbed it across her mother's lips, prompting an even bigger smile. She put the swab back in the water, swirled it around, and gave Eunice an "ahh" to prompt her to open her mouth. Maria then rubbed the swab on her mother's tongue and cheeks. She put the swab down on the tray and pressed the button on the arm of the bed that lifted the back to a sitting position. She picked up the glass of water and held it in front of Eunice.

"Water?"

Eunice closed her lips tight and shook her head. Maria expected this.

"Hungry?" Maria held the Ensure up, but again Eunice shook her head. Maria was working on validating Eunice in whatever way possible like the social worker had suggested. "No problem, Mom. I'll just have my breakfast. I made some for Danielle here too."

"That smells delicious!" Danielle declared as she walked around the bed, checking Eunice's vitals.

They ate, just talking and performing happy mundanity for Eunice who seemed to enjoy as much of it as she stayed awake for. She was tired, weak really, but Maria kept thoughts of weakness and frailty in the back of her mind. Of course, it dominated her every thought, but kind deception was the name of the game around the house. Validating Eunice's delusions or where they seemed to be taking her in her nonverbal state and sense of normalcy was now of paramount importance.

One of the nurses had come in with breakfast a few days prior, and after having to calm Eunice down a bit from her furious gesturing and frustration, they realized that she was asking for, demanding, some of the food he was eating. Maria looked over at him, unsure. The nurse just smiled.

"Mom, you can't—" Maria started.

"Oh no, Maria. I don't mind sharing. What kind of guest would I be if I didn't share? What kind of nurse wouldn't give such a great patient food?"

Maria was confused, somewhat panicked. The nurse grabbed her hands in his.

"It's comfort care. If food will comfort her, we can give it."

He took his fork and put some of his eggs in her mouth. She chewed on the food, moving it around in her mouth and smiling at savoring something. After a moment of this, a look of panic flashed in Eunice's eyes.

"You can spit it out, Mrs. Smithey. I have a tray here."

He held the kidney-shaped tray to her chin, and she spat out the chew-pureed eggs. She couldn't get all of it, though, and when she swallowed some, she coughed the same kind of cough that had kept her from eating or drinking. Maria came to her mother's side and rubbed her back tenderly.

"That's alright. You're alright," she said.

After, the nurse explained that she wouldn't likely want food very often, but the fact that she wanted anything and was trying so hard to communicate meant she was still there with them, and that was a good thing. Of course, she'd coughed, some food had gone down, and of course, that was painful, but a lot was.

Maria understood.

"She's never asked for any of your food?" he asked after, in the living room.

"I honestly haven't been eating too much," Maria confessed, feeling as close to this man as she did to the whole rest of his team. "I'm sorry. I've forgotten your name."

"Oh, it's alright. It's Jeremy. Listen, you need to make it a point to take care of yourself. After your mom, you're the most important person on this team. You need your strength."

"I know. I've been trying. It's just that I had a while there where I couldn't keep anything down. It was when this all started. A little over a few weeks ago. My god. She was walking and talking and failing cognitive tests at doctors' offices less than a month ago." Maria closed her eyes and sank back into her seat on the couch that she'd nap at when she wasn't working and nurses were there in the room with Eunice. "I kind of lost my appetite after that."

"Well, you at least need your three meals," Jeremy said. "You have to stay even and capable of responding to any situations that might arise."

"Yeah. I'll be honest. I've been feeling it, the not eating. I've been dizzy, weaker than usual. I work long hours and sometimes get so busy I go whole days without eating, and I've never felt like this."

"This is a rough time. These days of not taking care of yourself accumulate. You aren't eating, probably aren't getting good sleep either. You're not in your own bed. It can all catch up to you if you don't stay ahead of it."

"I know. Thanks, Jeremy."

For every meal thereafter, Maria had cooked herself the most delicious-smelling and easy to chew food she could think of. She had gone to the store that evening and couldn't help herself when she saw Eunice's favorite, a strawberry cheesecake, in the bakery section of the story she zombie-walked through. After her dinner roused no appetite or desire to taste in Eunice, Maria had brought in a slice of the cake and talked up its delicious flavor.

Eunice motioned for the cake, but when Maria brought the plate up to her mouth and tried to feed her a small bit, Eunice shook her head profusely. Maria pulled the fork back, and Eunice did a quick sniff, as if to show she only wanted to smell it. Maria brought the whole plate right up to her nose, and Eunice took a slow, deep breath of the cold cake. She smiled. She opened her mouth and gave a slight nod to Maria. She put the small forkful into her mother's mouth, and Eunice closed her eyes in tired ecstasy at the taste. When Maria brought up the spit tray, Eunice slowly shook her head. She wanted to stay bathed in that sensation as long as possible.

The forkful had been small, but Maria still worried. After a while, it seemed like Eunice might have fallen asleep, and Maria really worried that she might aspirate in her sleep. When she got closer to her, Eunice opened her eyes and tipped her head toward the water on the overbed table. Maria poured the smallest sip into her mom's mouth and held up the spit tray. After the milky water dribbled into the tray, Eunice coughed at the small bit of water that snuck back down her throat and entered into her lungs. When the coughing settled, she fell asleep looking more happy than blank, and Maria herself was able to fall into a deep sleep herself after finishing the slice she'd cut for her mom.

That was the last food her mother would ask for or want. Maria would still try like she had that morning with the bacon and eggs, but it would be for naught. Settled as she was that morning, her mother back asleep, the bacon and eggs eaten by Danielle and herself, Maria sat down to go over her work schedule and emails to make a plan for the week. Her computer was fired up; her files all in their stacks on the table, ready for her to browse through and re-order in her Sunday ritual, but she couldn't help herself. She opened her phone and looked at the text Rob had sent her the night before.

That's right, he was sorry. That's right, he couldn't just talk or type or play past his explanation for why, his apologies for all the ways he'd fucked up. He'd been playing and recording with Penny, the rumor had it. He'd been to see his father the night before, had even told him about her, about her mom. She'd honestly thought he'd forgotten about her or he was so dedicated to ignoring her that he'd abandoned her in her time of need. Could it have been he was giving her space? Waiting for her to reach out? She knew she was giving him too much credit, but she also knew how lonely she'd been, how tired she was, and how much she needed him. She tapped the text box under their brief conversation from the night before and put the ball in his court.

>*Can you talk?*

In less than a minute, her phone was ringing.

"Hello?" In the best of times, Maria and Rob didn't call each other much, so when she saw his number and greeted him, she felt the need to address the strangeness of talking on the phone after all that time.

"Well, working backwards, chronologically, I'm sorry my dad has had more contact with you than I have in the last month."

"Well, he only texted me because you were telling him about me, so I guess I can accept that one."

"Come to think of it, I've had more contact with my dad than I have with you over the last month too. Strange days, huh?"

"You with your dad and me with my mom . . . . strange days, indeed."

Each of them was smiling on their end of the conversation: Maria exhausted and weary on hers, Rob relieved and penitent on his. They were as okay on the phone for a moment as they were in their lives at home before when they would pass each other at various points in the day and night, he would be lost in his mind and his music coming down from his recording room for food or drink and would run into her at the dining room table, her files spread out, computer open, headset on in the middle of negotiations with lawyers for businesses on all corners of the world, sometimes exchanging glances, sometimes sharing kisses, sometimes ignoring each other altogether because, in those good days, their love was so secure, and they so secure in it, that they didn't need to express or acknowledge or nurture it.

Talk of parents, of his father and his dead mother having been the reason he went to visit to begin with the day before, brought to mind her mom. Sure, she was judgmental of Rob and controlling of Maria, but once she had accepted him as her son-in-law and he got to know her a bit better, he came to realize that Eunice was only so because she wanted the world to be good enough for the daughter that she tried to make strong enough to face the fact that it never would be.

"How's your mom?" he asked.

"She . . . I just . . . ."

Maria swallowed hard here and took a deep breath. Hearing all that pain, Rob was taken back to his mother's pains—ones caused by a shitty husband, ones by a dead son and his shitty brother, ones by a father who had failed her—and all the ways he could have made them hurt less by just being there. He knew he should speak up, but what words would be adequate?

"Can we just talk about something else? There's time to talk about her.

What have you been doing?" Maria sounded tired like he'd never heard her.

"Oh, well. Just working." Rob didn't feel like he was lying at that moment. She hadn't asked specifically if he'd been faithful. He figured there would be some time in the future, probably, to come clean about Snoop. He'd thought that over since she'd texted him back asking what he was sorry for the night before. He didn't want to be the kind of husband who cheated and lied about it, didn't want to be like Venancio, but he was already failing to be the kind of man and husband he wanted to be in so many ways. What's one more lie on top of the already mounting acts of betrayal when the good of the lie so vastly outweighed the pain of the truth? It was, of course, why he wasn't telling her now. What kind of person would break that kind of news to someone nursing their ailing mother? While Rob, obviously, was the kind of person to have strayed from his marriage in his wife's time of crisis, he had the good sense and compassion to not bring up his wrongdoing at such a time, and at that moment, Rob could test drive the compassionate small lie that might eventually lead to a larger one he could eventually live and, if he were lucky enough, die with.

"But speaking of my mom, a few weeks ago, when she was already in and out of reality, she said you were recording and playing shows in Austin. I said, 'Sure, Mom,' because you're supposed to play along so they don't get frustrated. But she kept getting more and more specific. And she mentioned catdragbird and, what do you know? She had a google alert for you on her phone. Isn't that funny?"

"Yeah." Rob chuckled at the sweetness in the situation and the ease of answering to the line of questioning that would likely arise from this fact. "I ran into her at *South-by* that night when—" He only dropped the conversation for half a beat, but he knew Maria would have caught on to it. 'That night when you came to me and I pushed you away,' he could have said, but he opted for, "that night when I took the kids to shows."

"Small world," Maria said, not sounding suspicious or accusatory.

"Especially for musicians downtown during *South-by*. Anyway, Penny was playing a living room show for some rich asshole, and she asked if I wanted to join on acoustic. It went so well, I joined her for some gigs at this bar on South Congress, and we ended up recording at Thunderbird."

"That's Danny's place, right?"

"Yeah. Just me, her, him, and a drummer. We knocked out nine songs in a few weeks. I was even able to get my kid, Benji—I had told you about him..."

"Yeah, Benji."

"I had him come in and do handclaps and backing vocals. It was all great."

"So," here's where she sounded worried for the first time. "How is Penny?"

"Good, you know? Medicated, handling her stuff. She's been out touring on her solo stuff pretty much since we broke up. Well, when she was able to. She's a real road warrior, a punk all grownup."

"And how are things with you guys?" Maria asked.

"Alright. It's still there. It's like an open wound that will be there forever, but what happened to her wasn't all my fault. Enough of it was, but not all of it. We've both grown. She gets a kick out of me having a wife, a home, and students. If you want to hear something funny, the reason my dad texted you last night was because he was worried about Penny being around, worried I'd be using or messing up otherwise."

"For all I know, you could be," Maria said.

"Maria, we're not. . . . I'm not using. It's like catching up with an estranged sister. And it's been productive. We're going to record another album, but as catdragbird. We're going to shop around to try to get an advance on the record. We might actually get paid to record because of the name. This could be big."

"Does it make you feel . . . better? Could it make you happy?"

Rob thought on this for so long that Maria was about to speak up to ask if he was still there when he said, "Better. Better now. It's creating something real and good. Something close to mine. But I don't know if I'll ever be happy. It can get better and better, and I think I'll find reason enough to not be happy. I'm sorry for that too, by the way."

Now it was Maria's turn to hold onto her silence. If this was going to get fixed, they were going to have to work on that. Work. That's all that seemed left of them, but that's the kind of devotion to them, to anyone, that she wanted. Fixing the wrong and riding out the mundane, and its resultant existential crises were the hard work of making a marriage work. But was that worth feeling like this? Worth crying alone on a couch a wall away from your dying mother while your husband is too many counties away pouting after his self-righteous tantrum?

"Really sorry," Rob said after too long.

"My mom's . . . She's not good."

She told him what she hadn't told his father, that they were working with hospice to make the end comfortable at home.

"It didn't feel right to mention on your mom's birthday," she said, reminding him of how much he loved and didn't deserve her good heart.

She recounted everything—her drive in and the initial hope it filled her with, their trip to the doctor, how miserably she had failed the doctor's tests, the sad, frustrated anger her mother had been feeling the longer she was there, how quickly she'd declined. She described the mother she'd found there trying to power through the fog of confusion, then diminishing in mental and emotional age and going from a woman who forgets to a kid that couldn't be trusted with fire to a toddler unable to reliably toilet to a nonverbal baby bedridden and being all but bottle-fed to what she was now.

She told him Eunice had been NPO because of the dysphagia, how she'd stopped eating and drinking because it hurt due to it all going to her lungs, how they'd been hydrating her via IV. She talked about feeding via peg tube, what that would entail. The doctor mentioned several times how invasive that was, 'aggressive' he'd said, a 'temporary fix.' They'd decided to discontinue, would take her off the fluid that day.

"So . . . you know." She trailed off here, running through in her mind what she'd just said as if she'd just heard it for the first time upon her telling of it to Rob.

"When . . . how long?" Rob asked.

"They say it can take as little as a few days, and she can last as long as a week or more."

"I'll go over today," Rob told her.

"Just . . . wait," she said.

"Listen. I'm sorry. I'm so sorry for what I did, for how I've been. You don't have to be alone right now. I don't want you to be alone right now."

"It's not that. I just have a rhythm here. I have a schedule working with the hospice team, and I have back-to-back work calls tomorrow. And, besides, you don't need to run over now. The nurse said she can tell when it gets closer. There's a way the breathing sounds, a way they hold their hands, and the color of their toes. All this is their business. If you come tomorrow, you could be here a couple weeks with the funeral and all that. Just wait," Maria said. "And you have classes and recording."

"We just finished the album," Rob said. "We're writing for the next one, but she'll understand."

"Good. But just take this slow. This is going to be big. It's going to take time, and God, help me, I'm going to need you, so we'll stay in touch, and you'll be on standby. Tomorrow at work, let Galindo know about the situation, about how you might have to miss days. Keep a bag packed. If your suit's not clean, get it done. Pack your dress shoes."

Maria didn't mean to hearken back to when they did this for his mother, but once she'd said it, she was reminded of that time, of how that time had made them, a solidified and validated them, for her. She couldn't help but smile on her end, and Rob couldn't fight the tears in his eyes on his.

"I love you, Maria," he said, his voice cracked and wet with tears.

"Just be on standby," she said. "I'm going to need you."

CHAPTER TWENTY-FOUR

When they hung up, he was left to think of the unreturned profession of love, and he knew she was as right as she'd ever been to not say it like he did; she was as right as anyone would ever be, for what she didn't know as much as for what she already did, to hate him like he did himself. He checked the state of his black suit. It would work. He took out the box from the back of his closet that contained the dress shoes they'd bought in Corpus all those years ago, his funeral shoes. They were shiny like new. Of course, they were. He'd only worn them once.

He took his phone out of his pocket after getting the clothes ready and tapped on Snoop's name on his Messages app. When their running conversation popped up, he could see the vacuous patter—her stupid emojis and memes and his humoring her to keep their thing going. His hands were dirty. He couldn't deny it then any more than he'd be able to in the future if Maria ever found out, but that was a worry for a different day. Right then, he had to end it, all of it, with Snoop.

> *The project is about done.*

It needs to be done.

I can't keep working with you, doing any of it.

My wife, her mother's dying. It's soon. I need to be there for her. I need to try to.

<I totally understand.

>I can get you drives with the master recordings and a final mix wrapped up.

By later today I can have it done.

<I'm busy all day. You can drop them off to me at my place after work. It should be slow. I can maybe get out by midnight.

>I can't make that. Maybe you can drive up to me to get them when you're done?

<That works.

>Alright. I'll see you around 1.

<K. Thx.

If ever there were an indication that Rob had been out of his mind with Snoop, out of his element and out of his depth, the string of emojis she sent after that text was it. He would have been disgusted with himself if he had time to think of it. As it was, there was work to do. He needed to finalize the mix on her EP so he could get it and all the recordings in her hands and be done with her as cleanly as possible. It was going to be a long day.

Rob had tried to keep Snoop out of his mind since he'd arrived in Greenton in the previous day's haze that lent a feeling of distance—physical, temporal, and existential—from everything that had happened before that and his new now. Sure, he was hardly more than twenty-four hours from waking in Snoop's bed, but that was then. That was him under the spell of a set of justifications and arguments that had been rendered null by having seen past the lies of their magic. Driving out of Greenton, missing his mom, hurting for his wife, Rob kept her outside the walls of his active thought. He was good at doing that. Her in his mind was mostly what got him in this trouble. The other contributor to the clusterfuck Rob had made of his marriage and his life in just over a month (give or take three other months or, really, a lifetime) was the music.

Even working to keep Snoop in the back of his mind, as he was with the reality of her, the riddle of a problem she existed as that needed solving was the music. He'd told her he would produce the tracks. They were almost done, but even over the course of his drive home, Rob could think of a small shopping list of fixes and additions that needed to be made before he could hand it over and part ways peacefully. After getting off the phone with Maria, he set about working to fix and finalize what they'd worked on.

CHAPTER TWENTY-FIVE

Maria spent most of the morning at the dining room table working. She was ready to tackle her negotiations on her end and had even drafted and sent out emails to Joanie and Melancon so they would all be on the same page regarding some changes to the language in each contract and her proposal to their client for implementing them. If she weren't at her dying mother's dining room table in Humble, it might feel like a normal Sunday.

The social worker had suggested home hospice, and Maria had been resistant to it. It had felt like giving up. However, she knew it was the right course of action when she heard out the social worker. Eunice wasn't able to complete her activities of daily living, and she hadn't been for a while. By the time Maria sat down with the social worker, the fact of her status had become clear—with the weight she was losing, her refusal to eat or drink, her inability to meet even the most basic of self-care needs—she was "failing to thrive," as they called it. She could be kept comfortable for this last bit of her life, however long or short it might be, or she could be put in a care facility. Regardless of her misguided revulsion at the idea of home hospice, the choice was an easy one because that house was the setting of every one of her life's biggest joys and pains. They'd taken Maria home there after trying and trying and, according to Eunice, continuing to try, regardless of knowing failure was assured, to conceive a child. Thom had died there on a Thursday morning that Eunice insisted on keeping as normal as possible for Maria, and it was her memory of that, of Eunice so wanting her daughter's life to continue undisturbed that she put off dealing with her dead husband so that her daughter wouldn't have to deal with her dead father, that told Maria this is what Eunice would have wanted.

That afternoon, after Danielle left, Maria fell into a sleep that was as deep and uneasy as all the rest of her exhausted crisis sleep had been. Her mind was racing, amped up from the coffee she had come to live off of after her weeks of nausea had subsided, and that combined with the drained state of her body led to the kind of half-awake, half-dream thoughts that she had come to almost even enjoy, as she was able upon waking to remember large scraps of the flood of thoughts that overcame her.

She had her normal rundown of work thoughts—checklists of to-dos and backburnered items that needed rotating up to make way for new future stricken-through items in her planner—then came the thoughts of Eunice and the routine day she would come to expect, which included the novel addition of discontinuing the IV fluid that evening upon the doctor's arrival, and finally came the appraisal and running down of her situation with Rob.

He had fucked up. Of course, he had. She had held down her side of their argument, of their cohabitating estrangement. She could have ended it by being the bigger person—which she had always been and knew she was expected to continue to be. But Rob had fucked up by doing this when he did. Sure, what was happening with Eunice wasn't his fault. It was a sad, dark coincidence. Maria knew that. She wasn't going to hold that against him. Not really. But in her analytical mind, she had won the upper hand forever in this argument because Rob had fucked up and decided to scorn her while her mother was losing her mind, forgetting who her daughter was, how to talk or to eat or drink without asphyxiating herself. Of course, Maria was mad at having to go through most of it alone, but as blank of a screen to be projected upon by her unfiltered mind as she was, Maria had to admit that with everything having unfolded how it did, she had won.

She didn't want to win, though. Not necessarily. But having won allowed her to go back to Rob, to let him back in after he pushed her out in such a way that meant she could turn to him with abandon. The previous issue had been settled. It was dumb. He was an asshole, and, sure, she could have ended it, but he went and fucked up and did this when he did, so she won. Settled. Now she could melt in him, fall to pieces and expect him to pick them up and put them back together like she had done for him without having to forfeit or concede anything.

She only remembered the highlights of this train of thought upon waking, but she very specifically remembered the feeling of the smile that came across her face involuntarily upon her arriving at her conclusion. She remembered the exact feeling of its pull on the corners of her mouth, and she figured upon measuring the sense that if anyone could have seen her sleeping there on the couch, the smile they would have observed coming over her would have looked cartoonishly devious. She was okay with that.

The ring of the doorbell, the doctor's arrival, woke Maria, and when she got up off the couch to answer the door, the ache of her sleep on the couch and the weakness of her exhaustion overwhelmed her senses and being, but the feeling of that smile remained burned on her face like an image a screen was too slow to forget.

CHAPTER TWENTY-SIX

Fucking around with frills and effects had made the guitar tracks strong on Snoop's demo. Rob had been wasting time showing off, teasing out, and building up Snoop's expectations with all the guitar bullshit he could cook up to lay down. Blake had done good enough work, but if Rob had more time or cared a whit more about the final product, he would have liked to layer more percussion on the songs. But time was up. Two of the tracks had rudimentary basslines laid down on them, ones he figured he could waste more time on replacing and which would buy him more days in the studio with Snoop, playing in front of her, shining in front of her. It was pathetic, but he had to face facts—by putting them off for a later date, Rob had put himself in a bind. He burned a few hours coming up with appropriate, if generic, tones to use and recording the basslines he had integrity enough (musical integrity, the only kind he had left if ever he'd had any other) to not half-ass it.

The heat of the afternoon was Rob's first indication that he'd spent most of the day working on the finally completed tracks. The second was the crawling traffic downtown on Mopac as he made his way down to Thunderbird to catch Penny to hear a track she'd worked out on a keyboard the night before. By the time he got there, he was lost, mentally overrun with the sounds of too many disparate music projects and the possible outcomes with Maria—lies he could keep up, witnesses who were or were not likely to run into Maria, the likelihood that, say, Blake would mention Snoop if they all ran into one another, and who among them all could be asked to lie on his behalf. It was too much. It had gone too far. He had taken it there.

But that was a problem for the future. He could live and die in the anxiety of how that would all fall apart, or he could finish up Snoop's project and tie up all other loose ends in town in preparation of the call he knew would come. One of those loose ends was waiting for him at Thunderbird. Thank God for Penny just then. He could drown it all out with music.

He walked into the main control room right when she had clicked play on the track she had talked to him about. It was perfect timing because whatever she might have said to him, whatever comment or joke she would have made, or bullshit she would have given, they both had respect enough for playback in the studio that they gave all their attention to listening. As the sound of Penny starting with vocal count-in a "one-two-three, one-two-three" set the mood of the track, Rob slid into a chair next to the door.

Each of them retreated into their minds, staring out—down at the floor for Rob, at the drums on the other side of the glass for Penny. It was a slow 6/8 number, rudimentary but rich. When her vocal came in, Rob knew she'd made something as close to perfect as he'd heard in too long. It wasn't until he the chorus came in that Rob heard Penny singing, if not to him, for him.

"And it makes your pain seem noble
Your death, something to see
You lived the tale you loved to tell
And died for irony

And it makes your life feel worthy
Of all the loves who left
To write an end they'll tell again
To end it with your death"

Rob had dealt in other people's art for so long that he had almost forgotten what it felt like to be so close to the words of a real writer. He hadn't felt like that since their second album. Finally, he was back there, back in creation pure and true. By the time the next verse came in, Rob had stopped listening. He had to hear it all again, had to see the entire painting, his only goal being to see a picture and not a technique.

"What do you think?" Penny asked when the song ended.

"It's good. Perfect. Absolutely perfect."

"Oh, shut the fuck up." She took her cigarette purse from on the console in front of her and lit up. "I'm serious. What's it need?"

"Nothing," Rob said, listening to the music again in his head. "Absolutely nothing. Keep it keys and vocal. What keyboard did you use?"

"The 200A Danny has it in the back room, covered and dusty. I have half a mind to steal it."

"It's perfect. As big as we're getting with the rest of this album, keep that one small."

"You're serious?"

"Absolutely. Play it again."

"I had thought about keeping it, but I thought that would go away with time. I thought you'd lay your ears on it and find its bigger form." Penny took a long drag of her cigarette, pressed play on the track, and went back to staring out at the drums.

"See what I mean?" Rob said. "It has to stay. It's a perfect track."

"Then would you do a track?" Penny dropped the remains of her cigarette in the middle of the full ashtray that, for all Rob knew, she might have filled up all on her own that day.

"Me?"

"Yeah. This is catdragbird. If I get a track, you get a track."

"I mean, back then, the instrumental tracks I put on those records were songs I'd had for years, ideas I had to put on record. I haven't composed a song like that in too long."

"So, maybe don't do an instrumental track."

"What, I sing? I do a singer-songwriter thing? No way."

"You write songs for people to sing, for me to sing, all the time. Why not just do that but for you?"

"I write for a voice. Even when I'm getting paid to write with a country singer, I write to their voice, their persona. I don't have a voice. I am persona-less."

"Okay, hear me out. I've had this idea for twenty years, but I never brought it up because it was so un-punk, but that's bullshit. It's the most goddamn punk thing in the world. What about a cover? A golden oldie, maybe even disco."

"Are you off your meds?" Rob sat up here and couldn't hide the annoyance on his face.

"Fuck you, man. I'm serious. Strip it down, the progressions, the composition. Break it down, play it on guitar, and sing. Just you and the studio. As polished or dirty as you want it to be."

"I wouldn't even know where to start. I have no real inspiration for that."

"Now, hear me out. This is why I've been thinking about it for twenty years. What if you did '25 or 6 to 4'?"

Rob smiled. He got it. "Too rock already. Not enough to change."

"Or what about the Bee Gees song? The one you said she played for you."

Hearing the story relayed to him from Penny reminded him of the love they shared because he truly no longer recalled ever having told it to her.

"'How Deep Is Your Love,'" he reminded her.

"Yes. Why not do that. Strip it. Do it acoustic."

"I did that for her funeral. Her rosary, really."

"Even more reason to do the track, then," Penny said.

"Why all this interest in my mom, all of a sudden?"

"I just want you to lay down a track alone. I've thought it would be great forever. I've always had the idea."

"Well, what about your song? About dying, telling stories, making it all matter?"

"That's not about your mom."

"Come on . . ." Rob raised his eyebrow here, but only theatrically. He thought it was sweet what Penny was doing.

"If you're asking, it's about your wife. Her mom. It's about what you're doing with that girl." Penny raised her palms up and shrugged. "I didn't mean to, but that's what came out."

"Penny, you don't—"

"I don't what? I don't know? Don't understand? I'm not doing this to fuck with you. No one else will know. My parents are dead. More of our old friends than I can count are dead. It's an elegy. That's all anyone will know."

"But..." Rob tried to come up with an objection, but for the second time that day, his dedication to music had gotten the better of his bad instincts. "It's a good song."

"It is," Penny said.

"Fuck." Rob got up out of the control room, breathing deeply, holding his hands up over his head to not pass out from the intense panic that washed over him.

Penny was on his heels, concerned but skeptical of his motivation. "Come on, Rob. This can't be too much. It's just a song. I didn't even know it was about that when the words started coming."

"It's not that. The song's great. It stays. It's Maria." Rob realized that he hadn't spoken her name to Penny. She'd just been an abstraction like she had been to Snoop. Rob knew Maria would love Penny if she got to know her. "Her mom. They've got hospice care going to the house. She's stopped eating, drinking. Can't talk. It's almost over. When it happens, I'll have to go over."

"That could be months," Penny said. "Hospice was with us for four months when my dad died. He had cancer, different game, but still. It's not like they're there to kill her. Be patient. Be ready to go and be strong for her."

"But, what do I do? I've fucked it all up."

"Maybe not. Just end the thing with the kid."

"She's not a—"

"How old is she?"

"Fine."

"No. How old?"

"Twenty-four" Rob closed his eyes and cringed at those words.

"And how old are you?"

"I know, Penny. I get it." Eyes still shut hard, trying to keep the light of revelation out and his pounding brain in, Rob buried his face in his hands.

"But really. She's twenty-four. You're forty-one?"

"Almost 42." Rob felt kindness in the hands Penny laid on his shoulders.

"You remember that show at the Red House right before it all got big? Remember that exec guy from L.A. came in and was talking big and got me in his car and pulled his dick out?"

"You ripped the Jaguar off his hood." Rob opened his eyes. He was tired, still not having caught up on his sleep from his night with Snoop and his drive to Greenton. He grabbed onto each of Penny's arms like they were at a middle school dance.

She waited for the reeling in Rob's eyes to subside, for him to center his focus on her. She had his attention, but still she called to him to bring him further into the moment.

"Rob? Rob. I was 25, and he was 41."

"Fuck!"

Rob sank back into his hands. Penny went back to her chair and the pack of cigarettes on the console. She lit another and sat there humming the tune to her new song.

"You just end it with the girl. That's your first job. And whatever you choose to do about telling your wife, make sure that you're choosing it with her in mind. Don't do it to ease your conscience or unburden yourself. Don't do anything to save yourself. Fuck yourself. Every decision you make about telling her or hiding it has to be about her. And then after that, beg for forgiveness." She continued humming to herself and got out her notebook. She opened a new page and wrote the words 'Fuck Yourself' in the top margin. "I'm doing something with that."

"Yeah," Rob told her as he emerged from his. "I guess I will too."

CHAPTER TWENTY-SEVEN

The doctor was a new one, but she was as kind as Dr. Ross, the woman who had been visiting once a week. It was an easy enough process, taking her off the I.V. hydration. Dr. Torres, the new one, simply removed the tape, held gauze on Eunice's arm, and pulled on the tube. The catheter dripped a mixture of hydration and blood onto Eunice's arm, and Maria could tell by the doctor's deftness at wiping it up that she had a lot of practice making the messy insides of death palatable for those who would live on.

"And that's it," she said while taping fresh gauze to the small wound. "I bet she'll be happy to not have to be poked again."

"That was easy," Maria said from the armchair by the bed where she'd sat in the same position almost constantly outside of work hours and nurse visits, vigil beside her mother, holding her hand.

"Really, the nurse could have done it, but with a big change in measures like this, we like to have a doctor on hand to answer any questions families might have. So, Mrs. Zarate, do you have any questions?"

"Well, I guess, what's next? I mean, I know what's next, but . . ."

"Well, at this point we'll continue with your scheduled care visits. Should you notice any major changes or anything alarming, you can call the hotline and they'll get the on-call nurse here as quickly as possible. But other than that, we'll evaluate every day to see when she'll need more constant care. Comfort is key. When we notice she's getting closer and needs more palliative medicine and care, we'll get that to her."

"So, how will I know when to call?" Maria grabbed a notepad she kept by her armchair.

"Well, hopefully, you won't have to. Hopefully, there won't be any episodes, and we'll be able to track her status naturally and up the level of care from there. But if you notice anything major like a seizure or anything where she looks to be in major pain, give us a call," Dr. Torres said. She gently checked Eunice's responses to light and pain and verbal cues and wrote her update in the chart that, yeah, Eunice Smithey was still dying.

"How will I know when it gets closer if the nurses aren't here?" Maria asked.

"You'll notice her go pale. What I always point to is the nails. Look at her fingernails and toenails. If they're going blue, you'll know it's getting closer. If her eyes become jaundiced, it's getting closer. If her breathing becomes louder and she goes for long stretches between breaths, don't get too alarmed. It's getting closer. Of course, call us, but by that time, we'll probably be in constant care time." Having finished her tests and her notes, Dr. Torres grabbed Maria's free hand in hers. "There are a number of paths this can go down. They won't look pretty to you, but they'll be peaceful for her."

Maria had just sautéed some vegetables for dinner. It was just a frozen green bean mix she'd gotten at Whole Foods, plain enough to not upset her stomach. Anything more substantive in either sustenance or taste would be wasted on her, anyway. This was just fuel. She was on "E" and putting in two bucks of unleaded. That's all she had been allowing herself, really. She just needed to keep going. For work. For Eunice. She just needed enough strength to meet their needs. It had transformed her, this trial of pain and vomit and deprivation she'd put herself through.

Her monastic existence of the last five weeks had acquainted her with silence and hunger intimately, just like she had gotten to know the whole-body pain and weakness of heaving herself empty three times a day briefly. She had gotten into them, uncomfortable with them, angry at them, and now they had changed her. She felt smaller in body and ego. Her time with her mother, the shell that remained of her, allowed Maria to mediate on who she was, what they were. She didn't have Eunice's feelings to consider in her evaluation of the mother she had left. She didn't have her own animosities and wounded past selves to honor and revenge. Absent any of what her mother had done or said to her—any of the lies or crossed boundaries or abnegated personhoods, scoreboard ignored and mistakes forgiven or ignored wholesale—Maria knew that all she bore in her heart for her mother was love. That kind of acceptance, the emotional amnesia required of it, made Maria feel like the most real daughter she'd ever been since she posed screaming for a polaroid on the arm of her exhausted biological mother, opposite the brother she'd never know on that forgotten mother's unfamiliar arm, and it disabused her of any notion of strength, anger, or self-respect precluding her from taking Rob back.

As bland as she wanted the food to be, as welcome as something close to nothing would have been, Maria still diced half a fresh onion and pressed a clove of garlic, setting that in the frying pan before adding the vegetables. When she took the food into the bedroom and took her seat next to Eunice, she fanned the heat rising off the food in the direction of the bed. She didn't expect this to wake Eunice up, to make her snap to and say, 'Hi! Thanks for the food. That's exactly what I was waiting for!', but the gesture felt nice, and all she had left to give in the way of love or affection to her mother were gestures, and that was better than nothing.

Maria scrolled mindlessly through her phone while she ate. She hardly opened up social networking sites. Interest in and connection to anything and anyone on them was something else she'd shed in her time at her mother's side like so much lost weight and muscle mass (she'd find out when she finally went to the doctor after). She opened up her mail app and refreshed three times within the time it took to finish eating.

It was early, not even ten, when she turned the bedroom light off, leaving the light of a standup lamp behind the bed to backlight Eunice like a fairytale princess awaiting a kiss. She'd washed the few dishes she'd dirtied over dinner, brushed her teeth, and done her wandering around the house, walking into her childhood bedroom she couldn't remember sleeping in before she slept there with her husband.

She'd stopped talking to Eunice. Not fully. She knew that somewhere in there, Eunice could hear, but she stopped believing that she was being listened to. She would still announce a doctor or nurse or social worker, still talk her through getting pricked or touched with the cold of a stethoscope or her blood pressure taken. But she was done with the novelty of a completely captive audience.

Her initial declarations to her mother were mostly to calm her own nerves.

"Well, isn't this something? You're sick in bed, and I'm here taking care of you."

She'd gone about trying to kickstart her mother's memory with tales of past happiness.

"... and Dad insisted he could do it himself, but when he turned the circuit breaker back on, the bulbs on the fixture all blew, and we lost power to that whole side of the house and had to have an electrician fix it!"

She'd seized on the church silence of the room and filled it with her confessions.

"I just couldn't stay. I couldn't stay one more minute. I had to get away. I just got in the car and drove. And I was driving in the middle of Bumfuck, Arkansas when I realized I was mad at her as much as I was at you, maybe more. I was mad that I could look at that picture and see her, that she was real. Seeing that picture robbed me of whatever bullshit lie I was going to tell myself. I could have been kidnapped. She could still be out there looking for me. But no. She wasn't some faceless victim anymore. She had given me up. And, of course, I understand it, but in the moment, it all just hurt so much that I left. I saw you crying in the driveway, heard you yelling and screaming at me, but I needed to drive. I needed to get away. I think you can understand that."

Now, outside of giving Eunice the courtesy of announcing bodily encroachments, Maria had stopped talking. She felt connected to Eunice, like Eunice could feel when she would enter the room. There were even times when she felt like she was communicating with Eunice without words, like a silent prayer to Jesus or the conversations she used to have with Thom in her mind, convinced that if she could broadcast up to heaven for one holy ghost, certainly she could for others.

But still, she touched her. Through the very end, she touched her. She held her hand almost constantly, brushed her hair every morning, and massaged her feet gently, having to work around the compression therapy wraps that were connected to an air compressor working to keep her blood circulating.

That night she fell asleep holding her hand like she had been for the last week. She'd wish later that she'd been thinking of anything other than two back-to-back negotiations and her status with Rob when she fell asleep, but she was no more in control of those last thoughts that night than she would be when she'd come to regret them thereafter. Like the last words she'd told her mother before, she'd wish she could remember specifically what had her smiling when she fell asleep, but only be able to remember that it was about Rob, and she'd hate herself for making him the bookend start to the nightmare that unfolded after he'd come to make himself its end.

CHAPTER TWENTY-EIGHT

Maria didn't know what time it was when Eunice woke her. Time doesn't exist when you're pulled up from the cold depths of exhausted sleep fast and hard, and the bends of panic fog your senses to the extent that you can't see or hear and don't know where you are. Maria knew she was in Humble, but for a second she thought she was in her room and had to run to her mother. Her hearing came to her before her wits did.

Eunice was doing a kind of wheezing yell and slapping the bed beside her. Her eyes were wide open like Maria hadn't seen since the night she drove in, and they shared in laughter over something she couldn't remember. But there was a fire in them now. She looked scared, terrified. With her left hand, she slapped at the bed, and she clutched her chest with her right.

Something was happening. Maria had to call the hotline. She had to get a nurse over. In her stupefied bolting up from the armchair, she had launched the phone off of her lap and under the bed.

"Mom, I'm right here. It's okay. I'm here."

Eunice paused at the sound of Maria's voice.

"Let me just get my phone. It's going to be okay. I'll just call the doctor."

Eunice slammed her hand on the bed harder now, faster. The light behind the fire in her eyes shifted. The fear had moved over to make way for a desperate pleading. Maria grabbed it, and Eunice stopped her slapping. She was still clutching her chest with the right, and Maria grabbed it.

"Mom, it's fine. I'm here. I just need to grab my phone. It's under the bed. I just need to—" She tried to let go of Eunice's right hand. She could crouch down and grab the phone without letting go of Eunice's left, but the grip Eunice put on it conveyed a deep, true message to her daughter. Please, it asked, don't let me go.

The hard wheeze softened, but the breathing was still ragged. The sound produced by the air fighting its way past Eunice's vocal cords made a moaning sound, now. It sounded like the body, if not the woman herself, was humming a dirge. Maria tried again to slide her hand out of her mother's grip, but when she did, she felt on the backs of both of her hands, Eunice's thumbs begin to rub small, kind circles of reassuring love into them.

Maria didn't have time to wonder, like she would later, if her mother, brain ravaged by disease and dehydration, would still have the presence of mind and strength enough to employ the tips of her thumbs to calm her daughter and make that moment all okay. She would wonder later, and at times she would have to concede that she probably couldn't have, that muscles spasm and contract upon death when a clot has traveled up your leg and into your lung and you're slipping, as peacefully as they'd promised, into the hereafter. But even in those moments of weakness and intellectual curiosity when her lawyer's instinct to see both sides of the chessboard kicked in, Maria would tell herself that it didn't matter. She didn't know. Her wondering couldn't make either outcome true, so she chose to believe Eunice did it to comfort her. And regardless of all of that, of the intent and ability and cognitive function and the physiology dying, she had been comforted. The 'how' or 'why' didn't matter. Her mom had made it all okay.

"Okay, Mom," she said, resigning to the comfort of her mother's caressing her hands. "We're okay. I'm sorry. I just . . . I didn't . . ."

She realized it was happening. This was it. She squeezed Eunice's hands and put her head down on the pillow next to Eunice, blessing her with the sanctity of a daughter's tears for her mother.

"Mom," she whispered into her ear. "Mommy, I'm sorry. I . . . . Mommy, I'm so sorry. I love you, Mommy. Thank you so much, Mom. Thank you so much, Mom."

Eunice was no longer fighting the pain of suffocation, and so she drifted off and away. Her breath was all slow, uneven pulls in. They were coming farther and farther apart. Finally, she let go of Maria's hands, and Maria spilled onto the floor, weak in every muscle she had. Her face was on the carpet, and after a bit of crying, her vision cleared up enough for her to see her phone. She grabbed it and called the hotline.

The social worker who came was kind; they were all kind. Jeremy showed up shortly thereafter, and Maria almost didn't recognize him in the dark of the house. She had turned no lights on, and the social worker had just sat with her in the dark living room awaiting a nurse. Eunice was pronounced dead. Maria sat in the armchair holding Eunice's hand like she would have if she were just sleeping. Jeremy explained everything he was doing. He gathered all the medicines in the house, medicines they'd previously inventoried, and pulverized them in a small porcelain pestle and mortar he had. He grabbed some toilet cleaner from under the bathroom sink, put the remaining medicines in a diaper he had in his bag, and doused it in the blue chemicals. He closed up the diaper like he might have if it were full of a baby's urine, bagged it in plastic, and put it in his bag.

When the man from the funeral home got there, it was the first time Maria thought to check the time. It was almost midnight. The state of the man, hair done up impeccably and wearing a suit and tie made Maria doubt the time of day. Could it be morning? No. He was just that good. He explained what he would be doing and suggested Maria go to the other room unless he absolutely wanted to watch him work. She didn't, and less than five minutes seemed to have passed when he rolled the stretcher that held the bag looked too small to contain a body out of the room and house.

"Wait, is he gone?" Maria broke the silence in the living room by asking. "I didn't get to thank him. He did such a great job."

She had been sitting there feeling faint and focusing on the backs of her hands on the couch. The nurse and social worker were both sitting there waiting with her, each respecting her silence. Jeremy had tried to hold her hand, and, Maria would recall later, she pulled away from him hard. It wasn't about him. She still felt Eunice pressing on them and didn't want to let it go. The nurse didn't seem to mind at all. He and the social worker both knew how to be there for someone so recently bereaved. But, of course, they knew how to be there in that capacity. It was their job, and being alone in that room, the only comfort offered her being the presence of two people being paid to be there, made Maria burn for solitude. When she realized the mortician wasn't coming back in, the social worker spoke up.

"He left a card. It's on the counter. You'll be in contact with him. You can thank him then," the social worker said. "Now, do you have anyone you want to call? Your husband?"

"I . . . Yes. I'll call him. But, it's late. It's late, and I'm so tired. I could fall asleep sitting here," Maria said. Finally, her mother's pain over and done with, Maria remembered that she felt too. "It's late, and I don't want to worry him. I will sleep and call him in the morning. I just need to get some sleep."

"Maria," Jeremy said. He hadn't spoken since they left the bedroom. "Have you been eating anymore?"

"Yes. Three meals a day," she said.

"Have you given any consideration into what we talked about last time?"

"Yeah. I had Danielle, the day nurse, the one I kept on to work with you guys, go to Walgreens for me. She took care of me. I'm on top of it," Maria said. "I had sautéed vegetables and rice for dinner. I just need to sleep."

"Do you still feel weak? Are you faint?" Jeremy asked.

"Just tired. Guys, this isn't done. I'll have to deal with it tomorrow. Danielle will come by. I have to tell her. She can check up on me. Right now, I need to sleep."

Jeremy and the social worker exchanged a look. They each seemed concerned, but they eventually shared a shrug and a head nod and decided that leaving was the right thing to do. They expressed their condolences one last time, and Maria thanked them both profusely.

"Thank you, Jeremy. Thank you for all the help you've given me and my mom. And thank you too," Maria looked at the social worker. "I don't seem to remember your name."

"That's okay," The social worker said. Then she shared her name, but there was no way in the world Maria would remember it.

Maria made her way to her room first, but its emptiness reminded her of everyone who wasn't there. Thom read her stories before bed. Eunice prayed with her right after. Rob listened to her complain there, her whispered shouts hardly any less audible than if she'd spoken them in her normal speaking voice. Always she complained to him, always Eunice would do this or that, press this button or another, to upset Maria within the first twelve hours of her and Rob's visit home.

She considered the living room couch next. Sleeping there was only ever right if she'd fallen asleep next to her mother. She would never do that again, and she fled the thought of it.

In Eunice's bedroom, Maria found even more reason to be thankful to the mortician. He had made the bed back up, straightened out the sheets, and fluffed the pillow like a considerate guest might do after spending the night at your house. All of the medical accoutrements were boxed neatly underneath the head of the bed, and not having seen them upon walking in was a blessing. She didn't have to see the impression her mother's body had left on the bed or the lifesaving instruments that had failed at their only job.

Maria sat in the armchair where she lived outside of her work hours for the last five weeks, thinking. She considered having to email work about her situation, and the effort that would require was so exhausting. She thought she might just phone in for the day's negotiations and only tell Joanie the news when they were done. She leaned back in the chair, trying to sink into the sleep position her body had become familiar with, but when she did, her right hand automatically reached out for Eunice's. When it did, Maria knew what she had to do. She put on house slippers, grabbed her purse, and headed for her car in the garage. Exhausted as she was on the tail end of more than a month of living and caring for her mother, and with all of the work and arrangements that lay in front of her, Maria knew she wouldn't be able to sleep but in her own bed at home. She backed out of the garage, and when she hit the button to close the garage door and drove off, she could have sworn she heard the echoes of Eunice on the driveway calling for her to please come back.

CHAPTER TWENTY-NINE

Rob had been at home for hours and, though it didn't excuse anything, he drank like he was awaiting sentencing. He could have stayed at the studio, but it was booked out for the evening, and Rob didn't feel like being in an atmosphere where he might be called upon to lend his ears or his hands or his thoughts. Just two days prior, he would have loved to stay there, as he had been for most of the previous month, writing and bullshitting with Penny and sitting in on Danny's sessions with various bands and artists who came in to record.

He got home at ten-thirty, early by the standard of hours he'd been keeping the last month. All of the nervous energy that ran through him was too much to deal with. He didn't sneak around when he was sixteen. It felt so stupid to even acknowledge that he should then. So, it felt even absolutely idiotic, highlighting the immature nature of his whole dalliance with Snoop, to be doing it a quarter-century later.

He sat at his desk in his studio and listened to the EP one last time. If one didn't account for taste, which Rob didn't because he could turn his off at will when it came to working on other people's music, it sounded fine, good even. He couldn't hear it one more time, though, and he sat there at his desk in the silence of a padded room in an empty house. He didn't plan on getting drunk, but he looked at the crate in the corner and, for want of noise to pour on the silence, brought it over to the desk. He flipped through the records, not content to let himself off the hook with Beatles or Simon and Garfunkel and picked out an Abba album. *Super Trouper*. Goddamn, these bands in the seventies loved their white suits and spotlight on their album covers.

He didn't often use the turntable on the hi-fi he kept in the closet, wired to the mixer and speakers in the room, but it felt good to hold on to an artifact of real creation. That vinyl was more tactile and meaningful than any note he'd recorded for Snoop. And that's not to discredit what she did for its pop-leaning sound. This was Abba. Abba was the Genghis Khan that spread its seed so far and wide that somehow its bastard great-great-great-great less-than-great great-granddaughter was Snoop and her music. It wasn't until the crackle of the needle on the record brought Rob's focus back into the room that he saw the bottle of scotch his father had put in the crate. What else was he going to do?

The women's voices were sweet in that false way that Abba songs sound sweet like they might intentionally be poisoning you with their sugar. That aside, damn, they could sing. When the music came in, just a bass, a keyboard, and drums, it created a sound as big and bright as a laser light show, and while it was undeniably organic, with guitar flourishes ringing out here and there, it felt proto-robotic, a kind of pre-computer digital, like sci-fi about machines taking over the world, but written before computers had entered homes and offices. It seemed prophetic, and Rob thought, taking his first drink of scotch directly from the bottle, that this could very well have been where it all went wrong. He looked at the record jacket. 1980. Made sense. The artistic hangover of one decade left a mess of all of its worst attributes for the world to deal with. Rob grabbed a coffee mug from his desk, emptied it of the pencils it held, and rinsed it out in the bathroom a door down so as to not have to go downstairs. He poured the mug nearly full of the scotch and listened on.

It was two-thirty when Snoop got to the house. She rang the doorbell several times, but

Rob had closed the door to the upstairs studio and was listening to *Super Trouper* for a third time. He'd listened to it back-to-back but took a break to try to get into *Chicago II*, which was so simultaneously different from and similar to the Abba record that it was muddying up the truths he thought he had unlocked in the Swedish art. He got up from his chair to flip the record over when he heard his phone buzz. It was the fourth text Snoop had sent in the last twelve minutes.

"Sorry," he said when he opened the front door to let her in. "I was upstairs listening to music. Can't hear the bell up there, and I didn't notice my phone."

Standing there tired from a shift of cycling people all over downtown and annoyed at having had to wait on Rob, Cait Hayden showed her implicit bias toward forgiving Rob, her immaturity in matters of relationship partners, and all the ways they can let you down. When she looked Rob in his dilated eyes, she realized he was drunk. She'd never come home to a partner who she depended on for anything more than fun and excitement this far into the night, and so she wasn't disappointed. This was just more fun, just more excitement. The only tool she had was a good time hammer, and he was a good time nail.

She seemed to have believed he'd meant that he was listening to her music. When they got to the room upstairs, she grabbed the coffee cup off the table and belted back a gulp like she'd never had a drink that wasn't terrible. She sat heavily on the couch next to the desk. The crate of records was on the floor in front of her, and she made herself at home, flipping through them like she was shopping at a thrift store.

"Oh, man. I love records. I have some at home, but I don't have a turntable. I even have some I've never listened to. I bought a white vinyl EP at a Red Fang show that I've never even heard because I don't have anything to listen to it on." She looked into the closet and saw the stereo setup in there. "Oh, shit! Can we listen to it?"

"It's pretty late," Rob said. "And we'll want to listen to your EP before you go. We have school tomorrow and all."

"Come on . . . one song?"

She made a pouty face, and Rob had finally been fully awakened to the *Twilight Zone* hell he'd put himself in. At this point, giving her what she wanted seemed to require the least energy of all possible courses of action. He went over to the turntable and used the cueing lever to lay the needle down to play the song he'd been most struck by in his listens.

The lead-in notes had barely reached the descending chords before Snoop had spoken up and already broken the spell of the music.

"This sounds like a song they play at the Olympics. Like, 'triumph of victory' music."

Was it just that he was done with her? Would he have been so inclined to want to kick her out of his house, throwing an external hard drive of her recordings out after her if they had any future ahead of them, even one as shallow as what they'd been sharing for the last month? Hard to tell, but he wouldn't act on it. He still, in a very small capacity as he was only there part-time and her class was clear across campus from the fine arts building, had to work with her. For as cool as she was being about this ending, he could try to be as close to cool as he got.

When the vocal came in, "I don't want to talk about things we've gone through. Though it's hurting me, now it's history," her giggling at what she thought was kitsch cut short. She sat and went into her own listening zone, looking down at the floor. As young and above-it-all as she was, she *was* a musician. She didn't speak until the second chorus came in.

"Jesus Christ, this song. The drums and bassline just hopping like it's a dance number. That major key! It's like music didn't know it was supposed to be sad." Tears were welling in her eyes, and, unashamedly, she let them.

Rob nodded his head. "Or it refuses to be sad. Like someone whose heart is breaking but insists on smiling."

In her seat, Snoop looked up at Rob for a second to nod her head in agreement, then retreated to gaze at the spot on the floor she had established for abandoning to focus on the song. She grabbed her purse near the end of the song, pulled out a notebook, and jotted down a note. She put the notebook back in her bag before the song was over.

"That's really something else," she said.

"It really is," Rob told her.

"Do you just have all kinds of shit like that you've studied and know for inspiration and stuff?"

"You know what, no. I kind of have very narrow taste. I never listen to this or anything like this. This record was—" Rob stopped. That wasn't for her. "It was just in that crate I got recently."

"Well, can I have it?" Snoop was looking at the record jacket.

"No." Rob said this fast and hard, without an ounce of playful flirtation, and Snoop didn't quite know how to be told 'no' by anyone, much less him. He softened a bit. "You don't even have a record player, and I have homework to do."

"Speaking of homework, you ready to turn in yours?" She clapped her hands and rubbed them.

"I sure am."

Rob sat at his desk, switched the input on his receiver, and cued up the final mix of her EP. Thirty-two minutes later, they each just sat there in the silence of the room, her words and his music echoing in their minds. Rob didn't even look over at her for a while. When he did, he could see that she was happy. He'd done his job. This could end clean.

"So, I'll just give you this hard drive. You open here," he showed her the screen on his computer, "and there are files with each of the tracks we recorded in this file if you want to remaster anything, and the final mix is in this folder. You can compress that and send the zip file around to labels or promoters and burn copies to give to people. Any questions?"

"Are you sure about your wife? About fixing the marriage and all that?" she said.

"Yeah. I'm sure."

"Well, fuck. Seeing you here like this is so damn sexy I could just fall in love with you."

So much of this struck Rob as a wrong—equating attraction to a skillset with potential for love, thinking his marriage would be the only impediment to a relationship with him, that love or a relationship with him anyway, he of an already shattered marriage, two decades older than her, and was already treating her coldly even before deciding to go back to being a husband—but he didn't care enough about her to tell her so.

"Lucky you, then. You don't want to love me," he said.

Snoop rose from the couch to a crouch between herself and Rob. She grabbed at his shirt and pulled him back to the couch. She tried to pull him to her, but he opted to sit beside her instead. She put her hands on his face and draped her legs across his lap.

"And so, this is it?" she asked.

"You take your hard drive and ride off into the sunset, Snoop." Rob grabbed her wrists and slid her hands off of his face.

"I hate when you call me that. You know, if I had to go to jail in the morning, I'd break as many laws as possible the night before." She took his act of pulling her hands down from his face as an opportunity to put them on his crotch. "Because what could one more time hurt, right?"

Rob couldn't stop her hands any more than he could prevent her then from climbing up and straddling him. In all of his reasoning around justifying to himself whatever course of action he would take with Maria, he hadn't considered having one last go with Snoop. He honestly hadn't. Before, all of his actions with her had been in what he might consider ethical and logical good faith. Maria had left. She had pushed him away, and then he'd pushed her away; they hadn't been happy in a long time before any of that anyway. But once he even considered that they would work out, he shut the door on Snoop and worked as hard as he could to get the EP to cut ties and move on. All of that was well and good in the abstract—just like the cold war he'd imagined to be worse than it was coming from Maria's end of the silence over the last month—but now there she was on his lap, kissing at his neck and biting his ear and grinding him into submission.

Now he was wrong. Fully wrong. Now it was indefensible. If he were a stronger man, he would have stopped it, but he wasn't. He'd have to deal with the implications of being wrong later, have to think his way through justifying it. But that was another problem for later, and right then, there was no later. There was no after to think about until it was done. No thinking. The whole world could end for him after; it could all burn down around him at that moment in the soundproofed bedroom he called his studio. Could and would, but for just one time, he would give himself up to being one hundred percent wrong.

CHAPTER THIRTY

The biggest problem Rob had with Snoop, the thing she did that got on his nerves the absolute most, was how she acted during sex. He thought that first time in the studio that she might have been joking with her exaggerated moans at any of his movements inside her and her concerning-sounding gagging at any instance of performing fellatio on him, but after a few times, even at four-thirty in the morning at her apartment when there was no one around who might hear them and serve as an audience (he'd thought she'd been playing exhibitionist at the studio because someone might walk in, and in that setting, the only kind of sex she wanted to be having was rock star sex), he realized that she'd affected mind blown for so long that it was now her default, like someone with a cutesy or otherwise idiosyncratic sneeze they'd tried on as a kid and never grown out of. It wasn't until later that Rob realized that, having been born in the mid-90s, she'd been watching porn for longer than she'd been sexually active, right there on her hand-me-down iPad next to the educational games and silly face selfie apps.

It was more annoying that night because the whisky wasn't doing him any favors in the potency department, and her sincere, false enthusiasm felt like a challenge and a sarcastic taunt, like his dick was a fat guy she was calling 'Tiny.' He just wanted it to be done (the whiskey wasn't doing him any favors there, either), and the actual thought popped up in his head that he needed to come up with a reason or way to wrap it up when the light from the hallway fell into the room.

Snoop was too busy on top of him moaning and shouting and nearly pouting, eyes closed, hands tugging on her nipples, to notice that the door had opened and they'd been joined by the other owner of the house. Rob didn't throw her off so much as he sat her down fast and hard on her hip. Even then, she didn't open her eyes, thinking that Rob was just changing positions.

"Maria, wait!" Rob yelled, pulling Snoop out of her pleasure. He was pulling his pants on, running out the door before she realized what was going on.

Maria walked right into the bedroom over to her side of the bed. She picked the duvet off the ground and fished her pillows out of the mass of blankets and pillows on Rob's side of the bed. She lay down on one that wasn't actually hers and pulled the duvet over her head.

"Maria, listen—" Rob started.

"Rob, please stop. I'm very tired. Please just don't talk. Go to her house. Sleep on the couch. Whatever. I don't care. But please just shut up. If you can just do me the favor of shutting the fuck up right now, I can go to sleep, and we can deal with this when I wake up. Can you do that?" She asked all of this from under the cover.

Rob truly had no defense, nothing he could say to make any of this better. If nothing else, this would buy him time to come up with the best spin to put on this, one last Hail Mary of an argument to try and convince her to take him back. "This might just work," he thought in the seconds between when Maria pleaded with him and when Snoop bounded into the room.

"I'm sorry. I'm so, so, so, so sorry. I swear. It's all my fault. Rob told me you guys are going to work it out. You guys are going to give it another go. He didn't want that, upstairs, but I jumped him. I thought one last time wouldn't hurt. I swear, he didn't want this. Please don't hate him right now. It's my fault. I swear. I'm so sorry." She walked nearer the bed, and Rob could have strangled her and every twenty-something ever who thought they might be able to fix something that actual grownups had broken. He wanted to crush every bit of youth and innocence in the world.

"My name's Cait, by the way."

Maria didn't move from under the covers. In fact, her breathing seemed to slow and deepen. This might all actually work.

"Alright, Snoop, you need to go," he said.

"I asked you to shut the fuck up." Maria threw the covers off herself. "Nice to meet you, Cait. I'm Maria. I don't know what you know about me, but my mother just died," she picked her purse off the ground where she'd dropped it and took her phone out, "four hours ago, give or take. It took a while for the nurse to get there and officially declare her dead."

Snoop's hands came up to cover her mouth, and tears filled her eyes faster than any did Rob's. She turned to face him, to look away from Maria. Rob just dropped his head.

"I've only been gone for five weeks. Five weeks to take care of my mom. Think about that when you think about apologizing for him," Maria said, slipping her shoes back on and heading out of the bedroom.

It was only when Snoop walked out after her that made Rob leave the two square feet of ground he was sinking into in the bedroom. In the living room, he tried to speak up and ask Maria not to go, but he couldn't. His head hurt, his bones did too. All of this was happening, the sounds of Maria gathering herself to walk out the door and of Snoop now fully sobbing, walking after her like she was the hostess of a party that had just ended.

"I'm sorry to hear that, Maria. I'm so sorry." She began to cry even harder, but then she turned heel and slapped Rob so hard and flush on his ear that he was certain she'd ruptured his eardrum.

He fought every bit of instinct inside him that was pulling his hand up to cover his ear. The pain was excruciating, and the ring in his ear was an F-sharp, the exact key of that damn Abba song he couldn't stop listening to earlier.

"Well," Maria said. "Thank you so much for your condolences, Cait. You seem very lovely." Here, she looked at Snoop fully for the first time. "Good god, Rob. Is she a fucking student?"

"No," Snoop said. "I'm a teacher."

"Well, at least there's that," Maria said at the front door. Before she slammed it and got back into her car, she weighed the possible implications and consequences of being wrong in what she was about to announce. If she was wrong, it would only hurt and confuse him, and if it gave him any cause to take up some kind of twisted-logic high ground, then so be it. The test was still there in the Walgreen's bag in Humble. She hadn't been avoiding taking it, it's just that everything but her took precedence. Now, it sure would be nice to have pissed on the stick and either seen the line or not. Oh well. They were done with right and wrong. He was wrong, would be forever, but it didn't matter. They weren't taking score anymore. The game was over. They were over, mostly (probably). There was no downside to sharing the possibility as if it were the truth.

"Also," she said. Snoop hung on her every syllable, but she waited for Rob's eyes, for his full attention before she announced, in the slamming shut of the door, "I'm pregnant."

The door slammed, and she shouted in through it, "Don't call me."

Inside, Snoop turned to strike Rob again, but she didn't see him in her eyeline when she did. He was on the ground, holding his ear and sobbing like a baby. It truly had to have been a disgusting sight. She went upstairs and gathered her things, her purse and the hard drive, and left without another word to Rob.

When Rob woke on the living room floor the next morning, there was a voicemail message from Galindo letting him know that it would probably not be a good idea for him to return to the school. He would have slept through when he was supposed to show up for class anyway. Of course, before then, he would have called Maria dozens of times, and each time his call would go to voicemail. He tried the truth in some of the messages he left, but he was really just blubbering, begging.

For her part, Maria called Joanie's direct line at the office as soon as she got into her car at her wrecked home and left a simple message: "My mom died a few hours ago. I haven't slept all night. I can't do the calls. Sorry."

As a professional courtesy, she called Melancon and was annoyed when he answered.

"Yeah," he said, sounding stressed.

"Jesus Christ, why are you answering your fucking phone right now?" she said.

"Well, I'm up, going over the negotiation stuff. I wouldn't have answered for anyone but you. What's up."

"Alright, then. You're the one making this awkward by picking this up.

My mom died. A few hours ago. I haven't slept. You're solo tomorrow." Maria didn't plan a destination when she took off, but occupied thus with calling in for the morning, her instincts kicked in, and she was on 290 East before she realized what she was doing.

"Okay, well, with the Branford addendum—"

"Are you fucking serious right now, Melancon?" Maria truly wanted more to kill Melancon at that moment more than she had with her husband when she saw him balls-deep in someone young enough to be his daughter.

"Right. Sorry. I'm sorry for your loss," he said.

"That's better, you fucking robot. Good luck."

She hit the button to hang up the call on her steering wheel and drove on through the darkness to Humble where she would arrive in town just in time to see the beauty of the sun rising on the booming, polluted Houston metroplex, assuring her that mothers could die, marriages could too, but new days would rise with beauty too stunning to perceive out past and above all the ugly that spread from here to the end of the world.

SECTION FOUR—
TWO TWINS

The girls were in the living room playing in that way that was both cooperative with and independent of one another. Rob used that as an opportunity to go into the dining room, take the plastic covers off the high chairs, and scrub them clean of the food that hadn't made it into or onto the girls. He made sure to do a good job, use soap and hot water, not just push a sponge in circles around them, because Maria had complained about coming home to a half-assed kitchen and had specifically named the high chairs as one of the many ways he'd failed in holding it down while she was at her work thing.

"Alright, girlies. Bath time!" Rob said.

"Uh-uh," came the choral response of his daughters, and Rob thought, as he did every time that in their young lives his daughters refused one of his demands or requests, that this was just divine revenge.

Eleven months in, and they already seemed to be working to collect on the karmic tab Rob had run up with his parents. This thought came in amusement, but when they were asleep and Maria was home, he was left with only quiet and all of the weight of his past sins on the other end of the scale, the one weighed down by his every lie and selfish choice while he was on his own, trying every day to lay down weight on the side of good that seems will never move an inch, much less ever even out with his past. In those lonely moments, Rob would fear reprisal for his past—what if his girls left him and never called, what if they stole from him to buy drugs, what if they got hooked, what if they were ungrateful until it was too late? The truth within him, that he would love, forgive, and then love them even harder no matter what, came to mind clear as day, and some small degree of guilt he had for how he treated his own parents dissipated because he could see now that it hadn't mattered; they'd loved him anyway.

Upstairs, Rob put the girls in the playpen in their room and got the water running and filling the bath. He had become a pro at this after feeling like he could never be alone with them without messing something up for so long. In the time it would take him to wrangle the girls out of their clothes and wipe after their now reliable after-dinner dumps, the water in the tub would be at the perfect height and temperature. They could now be allowed to sit and play without being held onto for every second. One of them might slip while crawling around or playing at the edge of the tub, but it would no longer result in their howling like they'd been waterboarded. Now, they could sit and play with their bath toys, while Rob made sure to try and remember which girl he'd washed first yesterday so he could favor the other today. He could wash them, get them out of the bath, towel and lotion them, and have them in PJs in roughly a half hour. It wasn't easy. Anything could upset either of them, and at this time of night with sleep tugging on their temperaments, it could start a mutually-assured meltdown. Even then, it was fine. It would be hard, but within the hour, they'd be asleep. Tonight wasn't one of those trying nights. Tonight was nice.

After, Rob put the girls down in the living room downstairs and set their bottles in their warmers in the kitchen. By the time the beeps of the warmers sounded, announcing that the nutrients within them were as close to boob-temperature perfect as possible, Rob had laid down blankets on the floor, put Boppies down on them, and placed each of his daughters upon them to wait for their pre-bed bottle.

It had to have been a month before then that the girls started holding their own bottles. That might have changed everything even more than when they were first able to sit in the bath. There they were, his legacy, relaxing safe at home, no worry in the world. These were the moments when he missed his mother the most.

"Alright, girlies. We good?" The girls sucked at their bottles. Rob walked over to the guitar stand in the corner and showed the girls, who began kicking excitedly before he even spoke to them. "Guitar? Daddy play?"

They kicked harder, and right then, nothing Rob had ever done in his life had been wrong, not an ounce of cruelty or gram of smack had been anything but perfect because if anything in the past had been different, he might not have ended up here with them, if even within his limited capacity.

"Okay, girlies. This is a song by a man named Francisco Tarrega. He was alive a hundred and fifty years ago. He wrote my favorite music. I played one of his songs on the night I met your mommy. I told her I didn't do it to impress her that night, but if you'll keep a secret, I was really hoping she would be impressed. Thankfully she was, right?"

Marice kicked her feet, happy. Robin was already drifting off to sleep. Rob played his living room concert for his most important audience and watched proudly as they fell asleep to the sound of real music.

Each girl was in her own world of comfort, completely interdependent with her sister's. Marice was comforted by the mere sound of Robin's breathing, her eyes fighting sleep to keep watching her dad. Robin, though, needed periodically to see her sister. She was drifting off faster and harder, but when her bottle was sucked so full of pressure, the nipple pulled back from her mouth to let some air in, she was startled awake and scared for the second it would take her to look over and see her sister whose presence made the world all okay. She finished her bottle first and was happy lying between sleep and awake.

When Marice finished her bottle, she threw it down, rolled off her cushioned horseshoe perch, and sat up, clapping happily for her dad. Robin followed suit, and by the time Rob hit his last note, the girls were clapping and shouting their contented 'da-da's.

"You know," he said as he put his guitar on the stand, "a guy I used to know in college played that song so well, I never wanted to play it. He was the best guitarist I ever heard. His junior year, he couldn't do it anymore, all the pressure. He took a hammer and smashed his fingers to bits. I never understood that, playing feeling like pressure, but I was never as good as him. After that, I made it a point to learn the song."

Rob looked down at his daughters, full and lulled by his music and the sound of his voice and scooped each girl up to head upstairs for the room that used to be his studio. By simply shutting off the light, Robin was cued that it was time to sleep and sank her head into his chest. He hit the button on the turtle nightlight on the bookshelf that sat where his desk used to be and wound the music box that sat next to it. That's what got Marice down.

He placed each of the girls in their cribs, which were lined up next to one another, each perpendicular to the wall where the couch used to be. They'd tried to put them head-to-head but found the girls every morning balled up at the adjacent head and foot of their respective cribs so that they were as close to each other as possible, so they moved them side-to-side.

"Good night, girlies. I love you," Rob said, closing the door behind him.

Downstairs, Rob washed the bottles and the rest of the dishes in the sink. Before leaving the kitchen, he ground coffee, cleaned out the machine, and programmed it to brew a pot at six-fifteen for it to be ready for when Maria woke for work in the morning. He grabbed the monitor from the bedroom and took it with him into the living room. He turned it as loud as it would go, put it on the end table, and sat eyes closed on the couch next to it. There was no sound more soothing than his daughters' breath as they slept. If he were a real genius, he would score the dynamic profundity of it, but if he was ever that, he wasn't anymore. He couldn't concern himself with any of that anymore—purity or authenticity or transcendent art. He was a working musician, and now he had something to work for. Not that catdragbird was beneath him or his aesthetic pursuits. Well, everything was. It's just that by this point, the futility of even trying to get there would have driven him to destroy it if it weren't for the girls.

The sound of the security system beeping woke Rob, and the swift punching-in of the disarm code let him know it was Maria. Still, he got up and walked to the front door. There she was, his wife taking off her shoes, looking as radiant and alluring as anything you're not allowed to have.

"How were they?" she asked, putting her keys on the credenza she'd bought for the foyer.

"Great. Perfect." Rob said.

"Good. I'll go up and see them."

She went upstairs, and Rob went to the kitchen to get his dinner from the fridge. It only then occurred to him that he hadn't eaten any of it. He'd been too busy feeding the girls their own dinner, then too hungry for the quality time he got about as much of as he would if he lived there, but which he still felt wasn't enough. He folded the blankets and put them and the Boppies on the couch where he had been sitting.

On the monitor, he could hear the creaking of the floorboards upstairs, then the sound of one of the girls getting up from her crib, probably Marice, and saying sleepily, "Mama. Mama." He heard Maria shh the girl quietly back to sleep and made it a point to turn the monitor off before Maria got back downstairs.

"And how was your thing?" he asked, putting on his shoes.

"You know, same old bullshit. But no one got into any drunken brawls, so that's a plus."

Maria mentioned this because at the company Thursday happy hour a month prior, Campbell took a bit of drunken horseplay a bit too far when he decked Appleman at Dave and Buster's. They'd been asked to leave. Campbell gave his resignation the next day. Maria had written him a glowing letter of recommendation at Joanie's request. Already, he'd secured a job in Dallas. Still, she could see the comment landed hard on Rob, who was already in his puppy dog mode of getting ready to go.

"You remember about this weekend?" Rob asked.

"How would I forget?"

"Okay. Will you please send me pictures of the girls?"

"Rob, you'll be in town."

"I'm not used to not seeing them on the weekend."

"Fine." Maria shook her head, but she knew he wasn't asking too much.

"And do you think you guys can do Sunday?" Rob was standing at the door when he asked this.

"I don't know. It seems like a pain," Maria said.

"You have artist entrance passes. You can even do artist parking. VIP everything. It'll be a day at the park, but with a hundred thousand other people. I left two pairs of earmuffs on the table. It'll be fun."

"Rob, I never wanted to go to ACL before I had twins. Why would I go now?"

"So they can see me," Rob said. "So I can see them."

"Fine. We'll go. If not this Sunday, we'll go next Sunday." Maria slapped Rob on the back, and that slight bit of touch pulled each of them out of their goodbye for just a second, reminding each of them of the distance they'd traveled from that love to this.

"If it's nice out, please go. We go on early. You guys can be in and out by sundown."

"Okay. If it's nice out, we'll go." Maria opened the door. "If we don't make it this weekend, break a leg or whatever."

"Break a leg?" Rob scrunched his face and shook his head.

"Fuck you, Rob."

"Night, Maria."

She closed the door, bolted the lock, and armed the security system.

In his car, Rob scrolled through his phone to see if anyone worth heading downtown for was out. Benji had texted, telling of a show he and Penny would be headed to. He had been hired on full-time at Thunderbird and was the go-to guitar tech for catdragbird since he graduated. Of course, there were plenty of events all over Austin. Everyone was in town from Nashville, L.A., New York, London, and even some friends from Mexico, and they were all eating, drinking, and playing secret gigs in advance of the festival. It was enticing, but the thought of getting on MoPac and driving into the heart of the city was exhausting. It could wait. They could wait. Pulling out of the driveway, as it always did, killed Rob just a little.

Upstairs, his girlies were sleeping, and in the master bedroom whose light Rob just saw flip off, his wife whose face they tortured him with—her eyes on Robin and her nose and cheeks on Marice—was sleeping in the room that used to be his. Rob had sentenced himself to two lifetimes of looking at and falling in love with over and over the face of the woman he'd wronged, the woman he was never ready to be a good husband to until she was ready to be done with him.

The girls, their twins, pulled Rob out of himself. They gave him a reason, for the first time in his whole life, to *be* for someone or something other than himself. They awoke him to the reality of how bad he'd been to Maria. Their arrival had finally made him ready to be good enough for her, to be good enough to her, and he was now, but only from the too-big house he'd bought a couple blocks down and only in his capacity as the father of her children.

Inside, Maria had gotten into bed and closed her eyes on an exhausting week of work and family that was just like the one before it and all the ones she would have for the next eighteen years. She was almost asleep when a nagging absence made her sit upright and look around the room. The monitor. Rob had taken it to the living room. She got up and turned it on as soon as she picked it up, waiting the second it took for the machine to pick up the signal to relax. When she heard the girls' breathing, everything was okay. Now she could sleep.

Heading back to the room, she saw the hot pink earmuffs Rob had bought for the girls. Driving downtown during ACL was always a pain in the ass. Aline had come down and insisted they go some years ago. Maria couldn't remember when it was. It was in that strange period of time before the girls came, back when she was married to Rob. Those days were so long ago, so many lives and worlds ago. She felt like she'd lived them underwater, and now she was up and out, and she was older and busier and more tired—God, she was always tired—but at least she was free, the only force weighing her down the gravity of freedom and happiness, finally, with life.

Falling asleep, she remembered that last ACL she went to, how Rob was so cold to her, bitter at pulling strings so that he and Maria and Aline could get backstage and eat free and meet so many artists Maria didn't know. He hated it, swore he'd never go back. And Maria just bore all of his negativity, swallowed all of his anger and frustration until she was to the point of popping and swallowed some more. If she were in a bad mood, she would have brought it up, thrown it in his face, but she was rarely in a mood bad enough to engage Rob in a fight. And besides, by now it had become boring to kick him around. And at least he was trying. Maria could hand it to him; he really was trying.

Maria fell asleep that night happy at having been set free by the girls' arrival. Rob had been too, she hoped he knew. She could overlook that bitter memory of a friend's visit ruined by his mood, and clearly, he could too because not only was he playing the gig, he wanted the girls and her to go too. She was set free and made whole by it. All she ever wanted was to have someone and be had by them in return, to belong to someone and lay claim to them truly, unconditionally.

She'd had parents who didn't want her and parents who'd lied to her as a way to protect themselves from the possibility of her not wanting them back, something she wouldn't have known was even possible if they'd just given her the whole story. In trying to protect themselves from the pain, they'd exposed their weakness by putting extra armor on it.

She'd had a brother somewhere, but she wasn't his sister.

She thought she could get all of that through Rob, by being his wife and having him as her husband. It's why she put up with so much for so long. She was just loving him the way she wished she could have been loved by someone else, warts and all, in the simplest and barest terms. And she would have kept him, kept on keeping him, taking him back after every fight and every tantrum and even forgiven him for what he'd done to their home, in their home, and he would have kept doing it, too, because all he knew was being loved as she loved him, being accepted and forgiven and excused. It's all the world had ever shown him, and nothing was going to make him change how he demanded to be loved or how hard she would have continued to try to meet that demand until the girls.

Even if she had shown up at their home and not found Rob with Cait, if he'd not shared his time and his music with her like he shared their home and his body with her. Even if he'd cleaned the house and had flowers waiting for her and dropped to his knees when she arrived, if he was as sweet as he actually ended up being at Eunice's funeral, sitting there in his suit and his funeral shoes next to his father, she would have pushed for the divorce.

She could weather the storm of his chaotic life, but she refused to do that to their girls. She realized how tenuous and trite her claim to Rob was, how laughably insignificant their marriage was. It was just another contract, and if you have a will and bank big enough, any contract can be broken.

She would always be his wife; she'd just be the one that got away, another love he'd wronged in his selfishness like he had done with Penny, with Perla. But with Maria, Rob could at least work the whole rest of his life to be the best father he knew how to be—which is to say he'd be the opposite of what Venancio was to him, for the most part. He had hurt her, and he would go about the rest of their lives "together"—parallel to one another, forever tied to one another, but evermore apart—trying his damnedest to make up for it through their girls. What he wouldn't realize, though, is that he had made up for everything when he gave Maria the girls.

Because however much he'd always look to Maria as his wife, she no longer looked to him as her husband. She didn't need to. She had the girls now, her Robin and Marice, and they had her as their mother. They needed her. They wanted her. She would always and forever be *theirs*, always and forever live and work to be what they needed in a mother.

Finally, she had found herself. Finally, she had found her true north. She had wandered her whole life trying to find a love to hold up and see herself reflected in, defined by. She had been robbed of who that would have been, of what it would have made her, in Mexico, lied to about what that was in America; she'd tried, really tried to find it in Rob, but the only self Rob had space for in his life was his own. Finally, she had found it, and it made her forgive Eunice because that's all she had been looking for herself back when. It made her forgive her biological mother because, like Perla had told her all those years ago, it must have killed her to know she'd given up one of her twins, to see her in her brother and only be able to hope that she was okay out in the world.

Finally, she was found. Finally, she was saved. Finally, she had a context and a purpose, a story. She was their mother. They were her girls, that beautiful drone of breathing coming in through the monitor she'd placed on the nightstand, those angels asleep directly above her. Finally, she had a self worth knowing and loving, and she'd found it—after abandoning any hope that it could exist in the world, that she was worthy of that kind of good fortune because all of her life had shown her that she wasn't—in her twins.

Acknowledgements

Thank you, Angela, Raziel Gonzalez, Daniel Hinojosa and Aaron Parks for any and all research queries.

Thank you Juan Navarro Early College High School (RIP, Lanier) and anyone who has ever dedicated themselves wholly to the good work that's done there. Thank you, Derek Pope and Abi Perroni, for being great at your jobs and better as people.

Thank you, Macmillan Cancer Centre and all of the nurses who work there (and some of the doctors). Thank you, NHS, for keeping me alive.

Thank you again, Ulyana, for giving our girls the world. I love you.

CPSIA information can be obtained
at www.ICGtesting.com
Printed in the USA
BVHW080959120922
646800BV00018B/601

9 781956 851274